LOVE AND WISDOM

"King Solomon . . . emerges a great and human man."

—Pittsburgh Press

"A considered and imaginative study of the great king in his maturity . . . A good deal better than the average Biblical novel."

—Cleveland Plain Dealer

"Richard Hubler . . . has sifted out the facts and Biblical writings, the legends and customs, to create a living tableaux of Solomon's life."

—Hartford Times

"Carefully researched and written with enthusiasm . . . Well done . . ."

—Publishers' Weekly

LOVE AND WISDOM

A NOVEL

BY RICHARD G. HUBLER

A NATIONAL GENERAL COMPANY

*This low-priced Bantam Book
has been completely reset in a type face
designed for easy reading, and was printed
from new plates. It contains the complete
text of the original hard-cover edition.*
NOT ONE WORD HAS BEEN OMITTED.

LOVE AND WISDOM
*A Bantam Book / published by arrangement with
Crown Publishers*

*PRINTING HISTORY
Crown edition published May 1968
Bantam edition published August 1970*

Published simultaneously in the United States and Canada

Bantam Books are published by Bantam Books, Inc., a National General company. Its trade-mark, consisting of the words "Bantam Books" and the portrayal of a bantam, is registered in the United States Patent Office and in other countries. Marca Registrada. Bantam Books, Inc., 666 Fifth Avenue, New York, N.Y. 10019.

PRINTED IN THE UNITED STATES OF AMERICA

To Jane

LOVE AND WISDOM

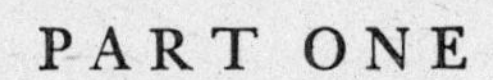

PART ONE

CHAPTER ONE

The Anger of David

However incredible it may seem, what I say is of good report and should be believed. Most of what I write, on this papyrus out of Byblos, I have seen myself. What has not happened before my eyes and ears, I have gotten from the most faithful witnesses, even from Solomon himself. I, Nathan the prophet, have been a man of standing both at court and in the sight of Yahweh in the temple, though not always popular with the people. It has been my task to speak the truth to monarchs and the masses.

I am now retired to my small house in the woods of Ephraim where Absalom was killed by Joab some sixty years ago. I am considered holy by both halves of the nation. I am therefore able to spend much of my time in meditation upon the past. I am very old. I cannot expect any further advantages in this world—even had I been accustomed to lie and flatter.

How long ago it seems since I last saw Absalom, that arrogant son of David with his handsome scowl and his notoriously thick black hair that he used to cut off as love-gifts to maidens! I always admired him. But I knew his overweening would be fatal to him in the end. I was never of his party because he disdained the men of Yahweh (excepting Abiathar, who was ever his groveling creature). It was Bathsheba I clung to in those hazardous days. I trusted—though my faith was hideously misplaced—that her great dark eyes, sculptured face, and milk-white body would keep David safe in the ways of Yahweh. More men than anyone knows have been brought to the knowledge of the right path by the sweet savor of female flesh than by the odor of the sacrificial baked meats.

But I am beforehand with my story. Solomon, king of the Hebrews for forty golden years—the same span his father, David, ruled and that the tribes spent in the Sinai wilderness—

was either the best of rulers or the worst. This according to which foot-stamping chronicler, either of Judah or Israel, that one listens to nowadays.

Certainly he was the most famous. In his own estimation at least, he was the most glorious. That glory is departed since, with the dividing of the nation after his death. But his fame has increased with the passing of years.

Not that I mean to decry David. Our second king (after ill-fated Saul) was by far the greatest man and leader we have had since Moses. David was all things to the Hebrews. The royal line he began, so declare soothsayers such as Iddo, will last longer than any other—though I myself believe it will be difficult to surpass the record of the kings of Ugarit who reigned nearly seven centuries in this tumultuous and ancient land of Syria.

The difference between Solomon and his father was that David spent his days in creating a kingdom for his people. Solomon occupied himself with exploiting it and in other affairs, mostly personal. There are more contrasts, such as the warrior spirit and conciliatory nature of David, compared to the reluctance in battle and pride of Solomon—perhaps due to the fact he was half Hittite—but these, as well as other matters, will become plain as I proceed.

The first time I saw Solomon, he was a red, wrinkled, sucking atom of flesh. He had been born eight days before. I was to name him during the rite of circumcision, binding him in the covenant. I thought Bathsheba had never looked so beautiful as she did then, reposing on her couch and exposing one perfect breast to his blind fumblings. She was only nineteen years old and I was barely twenty-two.

"Is he not a handsome baby?" she said as I entered her chamber and closed the curtain.

"He is the fourth son you have given David," I said. "Will you never stop bearing?"

"It is a sign of Yahweh's grace," she said proudly. Then, in a lowered voice: "Or of Baal and Ashtoreth."

"You must not speak of heathen gods," I said, shocked.

"You believe that Yahweh is the only god," she said with the mocking smile I knew so well, "but are you sure, Nathan? Do you know?"

"He rides the storm. The lightning is His glance and the thunder is His voice."

"Baal rode the storm long before Yahweh," Bathsheba replied. The child at her breast yawned, its mouth closing behind a milky bubble. "This is the last, I think," she said, looking fondly down, "and the loveliest."

"What is his name to be?"

Bathsheba pouted. Shamelessly, she left her bosom exposed to my sight. "I had thought of Jedediah, beloved of Yahweh," she told me.

"Excellent."

"It will please David. He is becoming very religious with his psalm-singing."

"Yes."

"But I like Solomon, man of peace, better. I see no reason why at least one of my sons should not survive these wars with the other tribes. Why should men quarrel so much?"

"I think Jedediah is better."

"Solomon," Bathsheba said, slowly drawing up the red-dyed flax cloth over her bosom.

So it was that the child was named Jedediah privately and came to be known as Solomon to the world. That was what Bathsheba wanted.

I recall such moments very well but others are clouded in my memory. Even as a concubine, Bathsheba was a power in the kingdom. She was a woman who plotted like a man. She knew her beauty and used it, often shamelessly. Above all, she held over David's head the crime he had committed against her first husband, Uriah. He was like wax warmed in her small white hands; and not only he, but many men, myself included.

I may say frankly that if it had not been for his mother's scheming, Solomon would never have come to the throne of the Hebrews. Before him stretched a long queue of earlier sons, each with his ambitious mother. David had scattered his progeny widely: he had spawned six male offspring before he had taken Bathsheba to himself. All these had been born to him in Hebron. He had settled there after his early successes against the various peoples who occupied Canaan. He had already been crowned by Judah (that tribe was always closest to him afterward) but here the other tribes crowded to do him tribute and chose him as their anointed one, saying, "You are bone of our bone and flesh of our flesh" and that was that.

In Jerusalem, which he captured after seven years and six months of reigning in Hebron, Bathsheba bore him four children. Some say secretly that there were actually five and that she induced David to sacrifice their firstborn to Baal in the Valley of Hinnom by night. This I do not believe. Fond as he was of his girlish concubine, David loved his offspring more. At any rate, there were his older sons and three of Bathsheba's before Solomon might have aspired to the throne —to say nothing of nine additional males born to David's other concubines.

It was a difficult situation in those days. I felt it was up to me to straighten it out. David depended to a degree on my advice (even though I was a young man) because the mantle of the late Samuel, my master, had been put on my shoulders. Later, as he got older, David became rather unmanageable, but he remembered very well that Samuel himself had been only a child when he had been called by Yahweh in the house of Eli.

It was the custom of all nations—especially in Egypt, a country which the Hebrews particularly followed—that the crown should come down to the oldest son. In David's case, Samuel had changed all that. Instead of anointing Ish-Baal, Saul's half-idiot child, as he might have done, he had sought out Jesse and hounded him until he had brought David in from the flocks. "This is the one," Samuel said, scrutinizing David from head to foot. David never forgot that penetrating stare. He believed that he had succeeded Saul because of Samuel's decree from Yahweh. Myself, I think Samuel merely loathed the name of Saul's son as sacrilegious and made a choice of a good, sound, thoroughly Hebrew family, taking the youngest as likely to have the longest time on the throne.

As I say, the line of Saul's blood was ended by Samuel's decision. Anyway, Ish-Baal was murdered by the sons of Rimmon who said they had done it for David's sake. I believe it was Joab, David's general, who inspired them—Joab was always one to clear up any situation by direct means—but it never came out. David chopped off the heads, hands, and feet of the assassins and buried Ish-Baal's head properly.

There remained his own embarrassingly numerous flock. David wavered a long time between Amnon, the oldest, and Absalom, the son of a king's daughter. His quandary was solved by Amnon. He turned lustful for his sister, Tamar, and raped her. This might have been overlooked, except by Absalom, who thought it was his duty to revenge her. He waited two years, caught Amnon off guard at a feast, and had his servants cut him down. After that, Absalom imagined his road was clear (but he did not reckon on Joab who had been a secret adherent of Amnon). Absalom came to think it was time he succeeded David. He had curried favor with the people and thought he had enough support to revolt. Reckless as ever, he even went so far as to enter David's seraglio and enjoy some of his private female stock.

David, always prudent, abandoned his palace. He took to his old hiding places in the hills. Joab roused the army, met Absalom and defeated him, on the edge of this very forest in which I write. In his flight, Absalom caught his thick, flying hair in the low branches of an oak. Before he could cut himself down—reconciling himself to the disgrace that the loss of his locks would entail—Joab heard about it. He came back to transfix him neatly with three javelins. Incidentally, the tree still lives and is called Absalom's Oak.

I tell these bits of common history—which everyone knows—only to indicate why I thought it was my duty to disentangle the succession. The sons of the concubines were out of the question, so I conceived, and I sounded out the four remaining elder heirs. To my surprise, only one sought after high place. Daniel was an outright coward. The other two had no taste for ruling; they were content with their women and their allowances as princes. Adonijah, however, declared frankly that he felt the throne was his by right. He added rudely that he did not need me to tell him so.

Thus rejected—I, the successor of the revered Samuel who had made and unmade kings at the crook of a finger!—I sought solitude and prayer. I waited to Yahweh to call me as he had summoned my predecessor. I must say, despite days of fasting and waiting, I heard nothing. What came to break into my lonely meditations was Bathsheba with her son, now a youth of fourteen.

"Greetings, O Nathan," she said. "You remember my son Solomon."

I had, of course, seen Solomon nearly every day for years but there was something in Bathsheba's voice that made me study him anew. He wore a short tunic of linen, kilts of animal skin; he was barefooted and tanned, with long black hair I knew he had not inherited from David. His face was impudent and had, I thought, a hint of slyness. All the same, there was in him both pride and power, a sense of controlled assurance that I had noticed before only in David himself.

"Greetings to you, Bathsheba, and to you, young Solomon," I said.

"Has Yahweh yet come to you?" demanded Solomon, fixing me with his brilliant blue eyes. I could see how this child would be immensely attractive to women. He had that flair of feminine sensitivity which makes vague hackles rise on a male but which is intensely satisfying to the conceit on which women feed.

"No," I said shortly.

"Why should He?" Solomon glanced about my hut with its simple furnishings. "This is no place to welcome the King of the Universe."

"He comes where a humble and contrite heart dwells," I said sharply.

Solomon's full red lips twisted in a sneer. "Then you wait in vain," he said lightly. I clenched my hands. Nearly three times the age of this stripling, and he dared pull me by the beard even as Adonijah had done! But I said nothing. Solomon was, after all, of David's sacred blood.

"Solomon," Bathsheba said quickly, "return to the city."

Her handsome son looked surprised. "I cannot leave you to travel alone," he said.

"Nathan will come back with me. I wish to talk to him."

"Nathan?" demanded Solomon incredulously. He stared at both of us for a moment, then his lips curled again. "I see," he said. "I obey, my mother. But I shall kiss you before I go, shall I not?"

Bathsheba's glance flickered briefly at me but Solomon advanced to her before she could speak. With consummate impudence, he lifted her face to him. Under her fringed half-cloak, her heavy breasts shone white and bare, upheld by the gold embroidery beneath them, nipples touched with cinnabar. Solomon fastened his lips to hers. His eyes became slowly tranquil, half-closed like those of a cat. For a moment Bathsheba allowed him to remain there. Then, with a shrug, she turned away.

Solomon left without a word. He made a mock obeisance to me and went out the door. We heard the quick thudding of his onager's hoofs dying away in the dust. Bathsheba and I stared at each other in the shadows of the afternoon. I was the first to find my voice.

"I see Solomon is not yet a man," I said hoarsely, my tone shaking in spite of myself. "You have not weaned him."

"Not yet," Bathsheba said.

"No more than years ago."

"A little more," Bathsheba said, slipping from her haunches back onto my pallet, her arms behind her head. Her great eyes regarded me strangely. "He must be made a man tonight," she said. "You must help me."

"Why do you think I shall return to Jerusalem with you?" I demanded.

"Because Adonijah gives a feast tonight by the brook Kidron below the walls," Bathsheba said lazily. She stretched out her arms to me. "Come, Nathan," she said in her voice she knew so well how to make seductive, "and I shall explain everything to you quite clearly." She was beautiful. Long plaited black hair lay piled on her head like a heap of onyx. Her placid, perfect face with its delicate features shone in repose. Her figure—full-hipped, narrow-waisted—showed through the saffron-colored drape she wore.

Without wishing to, I stumbled slowly toward her. All the light that remained in the hut seemed to gather around her in an unnatural radiance.

I halted. "No," I said firmly. "No, let us go to the city."

"I don't know," David said querulously. He repeated: "I don't know. I don't like to do things in haste. Maybe when you're young, that's all right, but when you get old, the world is a little confused. I don't know: choosing a king isn't to be done just like that."

He had a surprisingly deep voice for such a short, thin man. His head was large and noble, with its silver thatch atop, dramatized by his long white beard. He sat huddled on his wooden throne with its curved seat and elaborately carved back—a present from his friend, Pharoah Her-Heru, the Egyptian priest-king. He pulled his robes of wool striped with black-purple around him. He was cold, despite the two copper braziers smoking in the room. David always complained it was hard for him to keep warm, even in the days of the hottest summer.

The throne room glowed in rich colors. Against the lime-washed walls, built of mud bricks arranged endwise, red linen tapestries burned in the half-gloom. A wrapped-weave mat of reeds on the earth floor lay deep blue. The pole ceiling was decorated with fantastic figures.

"May David the king live forever," Bathsheba said submissively, snuggling at the foot of the little stone dais.

"You tell me you want me to live forever but you talk about another king."

"I am sure, great David, you will not forget the pledge made by you to me, before almighty Yahweh."

David looked down at her. He cocked his head like a bird inspecting forbidden food. "I know I gave you some pledge or other," he observed, "but what was it about?"

"About Solomon, our son, O king."

"Solomon," said David reflectively. "A good-looking boy,

somewhat too assured and glib for his age. But he has always been a good son and he sings very well to the harp. What about him?"

Bathsheba prostrated herself before him. "O king," came her muffled voice from the depths of an expensive carpet from Tyre, "it was your oath, sworn to Yahweh, that our son Solomon would become king after you on the throne of the Hebrews."

David stroked his beard with a single trembling hand. "Were there witnesses that night?" he inquired.

"No, great king, but Yahweh heard!"

David's eyes, bright as those of a mouse, watched Bathsheba's undulating bottom with impossible desire. He sighed. "Rise," he said mildly. "Rise and sit again by my feet and tell me about it, my dear. I have become old and forgetful."

Bathsheba got up gracefully. As she did, David spoke again fretfully. "Cold, cold," he said. He raised his voice. "Abishag, Abishag!"

Immediately the curtains of the inner room parted. The king's latest favorite, a plump virgin Shunammite with blond bright hair down to her knees, came running into the room. The king gestured her to come to him. He lifted open his ample robe, showing his once-mighty frame shrunken and naked, except for a loincloth.

"Come here, my girl," he said. "Keep me warm, caress me."

Abishag smiled and extracted a single fibula from her shoulder fold. Her thin gown shimmered down to the floor. She mounted the throne to be enwrapped in David's robe next to his body. He gave a gasp of pleasure at her heat.

"There is no need for this woman," Bathsheba said with an irritation she did not conceal. "I would have performed my lord's needs."

"No, no," David said with satisfaction. "Sit by my feet, as I said, and tell me about my kingdom, my dear. Abishag, place your hands so, your legs across my lap."

It was two hours after sunset. There was not a breath of wind in the chamber. The scent of myrrh which always pervaded David's lodgings was strong in my nostrils. The reed lights in the many lamps lifted themselves erect and still. I stood in the shadow of the corner and watched the scene unfold.

Bathsheba obediently sat on the step next to David's feet, sandaled in gilded leather. Her hand strayed to his exposed toes and caressed them. "What is the will of my lord the king that I speak of first?" she murmured.

"Bathsheba," David said calmly, "you are tickling me. When you do that, you want some favor. But you were ever the one to know my affairs of state. Tell me about my descendants, about my kingdom and my throne."

"The kingdom of David is at peace from Dan in the north to Beersheba in the south, from the sea to the great river."

"Except for the Philistines, the Amalekites, the Hittites, and occasionally the Egyptians," said David dryly.

Bathsheba went on as if she had not heard him. "The rule of David is secure forever," she said, "if his son comes to sit upon his throne in his place when David joins his fathers."

David shivered, despite the snuggling movements of Abishag. "The very thing I would have expected Bathsheba to say," he said. "But you have not told me which son." His tone was sardonic. I felt a film of fear start out on my body. The king was playing with Bathsheba and her ambitions; it might be my lot to take more of a part in this drama than I had supposed.

"Illustrious David," Bathsheba went on, "you have had many wives."

"And many sons, as well," David concurred with a trace of sadness.

"That is true. Amnon from that Jezreel woman."

"My firstborn."

"Daniel, of Abigail, the widow of Nabal."

"My first love she was, for whom I showed mercy."

"Absalom, of the daughter of the king of Geshur."

David paled. He whispered unintelligibly.

"Adonijah, son of Haggith," Bathsheba went on.

"Lusty, ambitious fellow that he is," David said slowly.

"And Shephetiah, of Abital; and Ithream, from the womb of Eglah."

"All the seed of my loins," David sighed. "But are there not others?"

Bathsheba bowed her head. "I do not count the children of the concubines," she said softly.

"Not even one other?"

Bathsheba looked up to meet his eye. "One," she said. "My son Solomon that I first called Jedediah."

"I thought so," David said. "You spoke of a pledge."

"An oath," Bathsheba corrected him. "You swore by the Lord to me, your handmaid, in these words: 'Assuredly,

Solomon your son shall reign after me and he shall sit upon my throne.' "

David pursed his lips, drawing his robe closer about him and Abishag. He glanced up vaguely. "There is a draft here," he said. He looked down at Bathsheba again.

"Did I say that?"

"As my soul lives."

"Then I was out of my mind with love," David said sharply. "Solomon is merely a child."

"But he is our child."

"Worse, he is a weakling. Shall such a one sit upon the throne of Israel that must only be held by a brave, strong man?"

"Solomon is clever," Bathsheba whispered, tears standing in her great eyes, breathing the words into David's lap, as Abishag drew him closer resentfully. David thrust Bathsheba up and off, gently, with firm old hands. He looked at her with his bright, incurious eyes. "Now I can breathe," he said, "without being strangled by your Sabean perfumes." David coughed and paused. Abishag also coughed ostentatiously and nuzzled his neck. Bathsheba stood by the throne, scarcely daring to breathe.

"My dear," David said at last, wiping phlegm on his kingly robes, "why do you make Nathan wait? Tell him to speak. You talked to him long enough before you came into this chamber."

Bathsheba sucked in a hissing breath. "You knew that?" she murmured, eyes downcast. David chuckled thinly. "I have eyes and ears beyond my own," he told her. "Benaiah, my captain of the guard, came and told me of your meeting. What plots have you concocted now?"

"No plots," Bathsheba said strongly, her breasts heaving. David licked his lips. "You are no longer king!"

"Am I not?"

"Behold, Adonijah is king! If you do not know it, he has slain oxen and cattle and sheep in abundance. He has called the sons of your body, together with Abiathar, the high priest, and Joab the captain of the hosts—but Solomon, your servant and son, he has not called!"

Deep behind the flickering of David's eyes, a fire began to glow. Abishag stroked his cheek but his face remained impassive. Bathsheba went on passionately, "He has said to many, I will be king! He has prepared chariots and horses. This very day he rode through the streets of the city of David with fifty men running before him!"

"There is no treachery in a feast," David said calmly, "no matter who is uninvited. Nor is there falseness in a parade. If Adonijah is as you say, would he be so foolish as to proclaim it before all my people?"

Bathsheba dropped to her knees beside the throne, careless of the tears and sobs which marred her beauty, careless of what she said. "My lord the king," she cried, "the eyes of all your people are upon you! Do you forget that Absalom, your son, ascended to the roof of the palace at noon and sported among your women!"

"Silence!" shouted David. With an energy I would not have believed him to possess at his age, he stood upright. The surprised Abishag shot out of his lap. She landed sprawling on the floor. No one noticed her as the stunned girl picked herself up and crept off. David stretched his arms up to heaven; his eyes overflowed with tears.

"O Absalom, my son, my son Absalom!" he wept. "Would to Yahweh I had died for you, Absalom my son!"

It was incredible. After so many years, the memory of the slaying of his favorite stood still alive and terrible in his mind. David sank back onto his throne, huddling his robe about him, his grief streaming down his convulsed face. It was time I spoke: Bathsheba was frightened and speechless. Unless I intervened, our cause would go for nothing. I stepped forward.

"O great King David," I said, "I weep with you." As I spoke I ripped my garments judiciously.

David regarded me blankly. "He was not your son," he muttered.

"But he was the hope of all," I told him. "It was Absalom who should have followed his father in his glory."

David nodded, tears beginning to trickle down his face once more. I hastened to speak. "You say the truth as always," I said. "Adonijah may march as he wishes, banquet where he pleases. But not with the enemies of David, with the murderers of your friends and family."

David glared at me. "Who says this?"

"I," I said, "I, Nathan, who said you were the man who had sinned against Yahweh in slaying Uriah the Hittite and taking Bathsheba for your own, I who summoned you to repentance."

David did not reply at once. His eyes roamed gloomily about the dimly lit chamber with its murex-colored tapestries, its carpets and woven furs. At length he cast his eyes on me, and in spite of myself I trembled.

"Reproach me not again for what I have done penance for in the dark hours of the night," he said hoarsely. "Say truly what you have to say and no more."

"I am sworn to truth," I answered boldly. "But what I know you have forgotten, O king. Do you not recall Joab? Do you not remember how he took Amasa by the beard as a friend and thrust him through the belly? How he took Abner aside in the gate to speak to him privately and smote him under the ribs?"

"I have not forgotten."

"And who was it that pierced Absalom with his javelins as he hung helpless?"

David stared straight before him. He looked past me; he did not see even Bathsheba cowering against the wall. His eyes gazed through the small square window into the blue spaces of the night sky.

"Joab is most honored of all by Adonijah," I went on pitilessly, "and with him Abiathar, your high priest, who gives all that Joab does the blessings of Yahweh."

Bathsheba broke in with a quavering voice that she strove in vain to control. "Your people know that the great David is as mortal as other men. They wait for your will, for you to tell them who shall reign after you."

"May you live a thousand years, O David," I said.

"I shan't and you know it," David said sharply. I felt relief. He had regained mastery of his feelings.

"If my lord the king shall sleep with his fathers before his will is known, then Bathsheba and Solomon—and I, his servant—shall be counted as enemies of the kingdom and die the death."

David managed a wry smile. "So this is the reason for your solicitude," he said.

I held up my hand. "O king," I said, "if you will deign to listen." I paused. David cocked his head. At length he spoke. "I hear nothing," he said, "except the cry of a child in the night, the murmur of crickets, the faint laughter and jests of roisterers at a feast."

"Yet there is much in these sounds that Yahweh would have you comprehend," I said gravely. "Though you are old, you shall weep as a child. The crickets will devour your kingdom. And you shall be jeered and joked about at feasts, even as they do now."

David sat upright. A flush dyed his parchment cheeks. "You are very bold," he said slowly.

"It is Yahweh who commands me to speak thus," I said recklessly, "even as he commanded Samuel to speak."

David's wrath faded at the mention of the revered prophet's name. But his anger smoldered. "A king is forever surrounded by plots," he said thickly. "What is your purpose?"

"I am a man of Yahweh," I said, drawing myself up. "I do not plot against his anointed."

"Yet you spoke a great while with Bathsheba before you came in to me, so Benaiah told me." I stiffened. This Benaiah, of whom much must be said later, was a man of sullen mien, of prowess in war and plots in peace. He was chief of David's bodyguard, having won his post chiefly by the daring slaying of a wild lion in a snow-filled pit years before, using nothing more than a sharp stick.

"Benaiah was right," I replied. "I came to give her counsel. I came to tell her she must save her life and that of Solomon. It is your sin, O king."

"Mine?" David jerked out.

"You took her from her husband Uriah. Him you sent back to Joab, ordering his death."

"Have you not reproved me before this for that sin? Must you always throw it up to me like dog's vomit?"

"Yes, great David," I said cunningly, "but Joab has neither repented nor been forgiven."

"It was Joab who reproached me as weak-hearted when I wept for Absalom," David said darkly.

"Yahweh has said that the sword shall not depart from your house," I told him. "Already Amnon and Absalom are dead. You have shown Bathsheba much favor and this has brought jealousy upon her. If you die, your shield between her and the rest of the court is taken away."

"Perhaps, perhaps," David replied grudgingly. "But what would you have now with me?"

I bowed deeply. "My lord, have you said that Adonijah, son of Haggith, shall reign after you?"

"No. I have placed my hands on the head of none."

"Then it seems passing strange that Adonijah has slain meat in abundance, provided wine and leafy bowers, and called in the captains of the hosts and Abiathar. They raise their cups to him and cry: 'Hail, king Adonijah!' "

David's head came upright. His faded blue eyes flashed. Then they became lackluster and he said quietly: "But they did not invite you?"

"No. Nor Zadok the priest nor Benaiah—nor Solomon."

"Are you envious of being excluded from the feast?"

I struck my breast with both fists. "Before Yahweh, it is not true!" I said passionately. "I serve David! I am concerned with the honor of the kingdom of the Ḥebrews!"

David jerked his head at Bathsheba. She knew the signal, and silently went out. As the paneled doors closed behind her with a muffled clash, David looked at me.

"One must struggle against women all one's life," he said. "They are the evil *yezers* of man. But I tell you that Solomon shall never sit upon this throne. If Adonijah wishes to take it when I die, let him. Solomon is a child."

"He is tender of years, perhaps," I responded, "but he is quick to learn."

"He who comes after me will have to learn much quickly," David said. "He is young, young."

"Are you not fond of the boy?"

"Fond, yes. He reminds me of myself when I tended the sheep of Jesse and played the *masroquita.* When I played the lyre and sang before Saul. He has an interesting mind, much curiosity, much love of life. Yes, I am fonder of Solomon than any of my other children—but he is weak. He is not, he can never be a warrior. He cannot fight for the Hebrews as he must."

"What cannot be gained by battles can be gained by cleverness."

David knitted his brows. "Cleverness? Solomon needs wisdom, experience, knowledge. Who will give him that?"

"Perhaps Yahweh will bless him," I said.

"If I could be sure of such a child," David murmured.

"David was young when he was anointed by Samuel," I said, "and David was not even the son of Saul."

"Saul loved me as a son."

"And hated you."

"His mind was not always his own," David murmured. He coughed again, racking his frame. He wiped his mouth with his robe and took a deep breath. "It was Samuel who chose me," he said with difficulty. "Do you choose Solomon?"

"I do."

"Why?"

I hesitated. Just at that moment, from down the hill, the chanting of the feast rose louder. I could not distinguish the words but a frown gathered on David's face. There was a burst of voices outside, almost below the royal window.

"Adoni-jah, King! Adoni-jah, King! Hail to Adoni-jah! Yahweh bless King Adoni-jah!"

I started. Horror-stricken, I saw David stand upright. His face suffused with blood. His eyes glared in the lamplight. He swayed like a tree ready to be felled with a last stroke.

"Do they dare?" he shouted. "Do they dare, before my very palace?"

His words stuck in his throat. He clutched his chest. He fell back over the throne, flailing his arms. I sprang to his side. He stared up at me.

"Summon Bathsheba," David mumbled.

I lifted my head but I had no need to call. Bathsheba was beside me, throwing herself down to embrace David in a tempest of weeping. The old king looked up at the painted poles of the ceiling. He spoke solemnly, his voice gaining resonance.

"As Yahweh lives, who has redeemed me out of all distress," he said, "even as I swore to you, Bathsheba, in his name, saying assuredly Solomon, thy son, shall reign after me and sit upon this throne in my stead: so it shall be tonight."

Bathsheba bent her head to the ground. "Let my lord, King David, live forever," she said in stifled tones.

David grimaced. He looked at me. "Sit me up," he said in his old ring of command. He had made his decision; now, as ever, he planned immediate strategy. I obeyed him, propping him on his throne.

"Call me Zadok, he who is next to the high priest Abiathar, and Benaiah, chief of my bodyguard." I rose. A slight movement of David's hand halted me. He had not finished his instructions.

"When they come," David said, "tell them to cause Solomon to be brought to me for the placing of hands. Then he shall be mounted on my own mule. Take him secretly to Gihon. There let Zadok and yourself anoint him with the horn of holy oil from the tabernacle and proclaim him king over the Hebrews."

"Amen," I said.

"Then," David said, closing his eyes but still speaking, "let him be led through the streets of Jerusalem, a hundred men with torches running before him and shouting, 'Yahweh bless King Solomon!' Let the timbrels be beaten, the *hasoserah* blown, the cymbals clashed. Wake every one of the people of the city of David. Tell them I have appointed Solomon king in my place, to rule over Israel and Judah."

His immense will yielded to the strain. He sank back,

fainting. I rose from my knees. I bowed to him, still majestic though unconscious. As my head lifted, my eyes met those of Bathsheba. I could not endure their depths, burning furiously with emotion. I turned my head away.

Suddenly I realized I had recognized the disguised voices which had shouted together in the narrow, echoing street outside the palace window. They had been the voices of Benaiah, of Zadok—and of Bathsheba herself.

CHAPTER TWO

The Thwarting of Joab

"I came to warn you to flee before it is too late," I said. "I speak out of pity, as a friend."

Joab threw back his head and laughed. The fronds of tamarisk of the cut boughs overhead trembled with his breath. "Friend?" he cried. "When has young Nathan been the friend of Joab?"

He wagged his head and chuckled harshly, the crackling of thorns. "If you think David is going to make Solomon king," Joab said comfortably, "you've lost what little inspiration you ever had as a prophet. I know the king's mind, I tell you; I know it better than he does. He's doting, mumbling to himself. He's next to threescore and ten, the age he is always moaning about in his psalms. He's not the man he once was."

"He is not as feeble as you think," I said.

"He was hard on forty years old a generation ago," Joab said, "when I was a youngster. I took Jerusalem for him and he appointed me general of his armies. I was the one who drove back the Amalekites, the Hittites, the Ammonites, the Jebusites, and I don't know how many others. I've done some sticky jobs for David, ones I don't care to talk about in company. I know him to the soul."

"Perhaps not that well," I said.

Joab drank noisily from his huge copper goblet. He set it before him, licked his lips, and rang the metal approvingly with a finger. "David gave me this," he said. "That's how close we are. Studded with garnet bits by Phoenician craftsmen."

"David is very generous," I said.

"Absalom, Uriah, Amasa, Abner—everybody blames me for deeds like that. I could tell you other things but I won't. Yahweh forgave David and David forgave me and there is no such creature as a ghost."

"Saul saw Samuel's ghost at Endor," I said.

"Pfaugh!" Joab drank deeply again of the purple Tabor wine. "I don't say David wasn't a great man in his time, I don't say that," he added indistinctly. "But that day has gone by." He slammed down his goblet and stared at me defiantly.

General of all the armies of the Hebrews, Joab was still a lean, muscular man. He was deeply tanned and with a scar crossing his right cheek that he caressed now and again. His beak of a nose gave him the appearance of a hawk waiting to pounce. His manner was one of supreme self-confidence, tempered with caution. He lived, as everyone knew, outside Jerusalem in a stone hilltop fortress surrounded by forest and protected by a half dozen picked guards. He had been the strong one of the Hebrews for longer than I cared to think about.

His swagger and sureness daunted me. I commenced to think that perhaps he was right, that perhaps what I had seen and heard had not happened. Perhaps I was wrong to have come to warn him to take refuge from the wrath of Solomon, to prevent bloodshed.

"You're a young fool, Nathan," Joab said. "Stick to prophesying about the things you know." He laughed uproariously at his little joke.

"All the same, David is still king," Abiathar said, patting his beard. He was the oldest of this party, almost as old as David. Sitting next to Joab he looked more stooped than ever, more worried than usual. His high forehead, descending from his baldness, showed wrinkles that centuries seemed to have engraved there.

"What does that mean?" demanded Joab. He filled his goblet again from the pitcher, tempering the wine with a little brook water.

"Yes, what do you mean?" echoed Adonijah, scowling at me but speaking to Abiathar. Abiathar glanced quizzically at the burly young man across the table with his hair like brown wires, his muscles bulging under his light tunic, his face broad and guileless.

"You are the king's son," he returned quietly. "You should know what it means."

"It means that I am the one who has succeeded to the

throne of the Hebrews," Adonijah returned angrily. His face was flushed with drink and he spoke with difficulty.

"Yet Nathan tells us differently," murmured Abiathar, "and he is not known as a liar."

"These prophets have great imaginations," Joab said. "What they want to see come about, they think to be a fact."

"Is that what you mean?" Adonijah demanded of me. "That you are against me?"

"He means," Abiathar said, "that old and weak as he is, David is still the supreme power in the land. He is the great spirit, the magnificent name, the leader of us all. He can choose whoever he sees fit for his successor."

"Wrong," Joab said crisply. Wine, no matter how tasty or strong, never went to his head. He could drink four companions into insensibility at any hour of the day. "Wrong, Abiathar. And I'll tell you why."

"I should be pleased to know."

Joab leaned forward and turned slightly, addressing himself to me. "Who made Saul king, young Nathan?" he demanded.

"Samuel, blessed be his memory," I answered.

"And who made David king?"

"The same holy Samuel."

Joab grinned and turned back to the table. "But Samuel was not a king and he had no children," he said, his voice rising. "The man who makes a king is not the father of a king, though that is something, Adonijah, something more than the brat of a concubine. It is the priest, the one who anoints him in the name of Yahweh. And the one who keeps him a king is Joab."

His hoarse tones dominated the whole long table. He paused, enjoying the moment. He must have seen that assembly as I did—as dark faces, bright headdresses, dangling bracelets and earrings, dyed and embroidered robes and tunics. Joab thumped the table lightly with his knotty fist.

"Abiathar is the priest to anoint you, Adonijah," he said. "So far, good. I am next for your consideration."

Abiathar raised a shaking hand but Joab swept on in a torrent of words.

"Who was he who climbed the walls of Jerusalem first against the stones and arrows of the Jebusites? Joab. Who was he who slew Amasa and Abner when no one else dared? Joab. Who was the man who thrust three javelins through the body of Absalom as he hung from the oak? Joab. And who was the one who saved the kingdom for David when he turned womanish and weeping, wailing for his lost son, wishing he were dead in his place? Who stood up to him, told him that he was a fool? Joab, I tell you!"

He had been speaking directly to Abiathar. The little sapless priest shrank from him. Joab twisted heavily on the bench. He stared at the fascinated Adonijah.

"With the priest and myself on your side," he said, "who will dare stand against you? Yahweh is with us, the army is with us, who will be against us?"

"My father loves me," Adonijah said timidly.

Joab snorted. "He loves Solomon better and Bathsheba most of all," he responded. "But he will not give away the throne for love."

He lunged across the table, seizing a half-eaten bone of lamb. He buried his strong yellow teeth in it. The others cried out in drunken approval of his words.

There was the sound of running feet. A panting, disheveled boy broke into the festal bower. He gulped for air. "Welcome, Jonathan, son of Abiathar," said Joab jovially. "You are a valiant youth, you bring good tidings."

"They have come up rejoicing from Gihon," gasped the newcomer.

"Rejoicing? Who rejoices?" demanded Abiathar sharply.

"Zadok, the priest, and Benaiah," the boy gabbled wildly. "They have set him upon King David's mule, he rides into the city."

"Who?" rapped Joab.

"Solomon! David has made Solomon king!"

An alien sound trickled between the shouts of the feasters and the clang of the goblets. It was the high, faint sound of trumpets, the throbbing of timbrels, drifting down from above. I looked up apprehensively. Indeed, the moment for me to depart had come. I had fulfilled my mission of mercy.

"Quiet!" Joab thundered. The tinkle of voices died away. I stood frozen in my place.

Joab, near the open end of the bower—he always took such seats because of his perpetual wariness—had a clear view of the walls of Jerusalem. He stared upward, his eyes bulging.

On high, the torches of the hundred men David had ordered to precede Solomon capered on the walls of Jerusalem. They danced above us like so many stars in heaven. Their shouts rang faintly, clearly, dropping to us word by word in the formula commanded by David: "Hail to Solomon, king of the Hebrews by the will of David!" Again and again the words sank downward in the midst of the paralyzed festive array. They came to us like sounds under the sea, accompanied by huge resinous sparks from the torches like glowing fish swirling into the depths of the Valley of Kidron.

For a long moment, Joab sat motionless. He seemed caught in some sort of catalepsy. Then he wrenched himself upright. He whirled around. He thrust his arm at me. "You!" he spat. "You, young Nathan! You knew!"

"I came to—"

"You came to betray us!"

On the words, Joab snatched up his sword. It lay, as always, on the bench next to him. He seized the scabbard, rasping the rare iron Hittite blade free. He whirled it over his head with both hands.

"He came in peace!" cried Abiathar, beseeching.

"Out of my way!" screamed Joab.

He made a tremendous slash. But I was tense and agile. Joab had lost some of the sinewy quickness that had made him able to scramble up the walls of Jerusalem like an ape. I sprang aside; I darted out of the arbor.

Behind me, Joab's blade slashed through one of the pillars supporting the leafy arch. It wavered, groaned, and collapsed. Its branches snared the clot of men for the moment, saving my life. It extinguished half the lamps. It flung the feast into darkness. Howls of terror rose. Their fears sent them dashing off into the night in panic.

I leaped from rock to rock, up the steep side of the valley of the Kidron, toward the Sheep Gate and the tower Meah. My garments tucked above my knees for speed, I raced upward. My tongue tasted of copper, and my lungs hurt. I stopped for breath: my pounding heart would not let me go further, not even if I died for it. I sank to a ledge and looked fearfully behind me.

My courage revived. I was far ahead of the others. I could see there was no pursuit. Nothing but distant mad yelling and dispersal of tiny dark forms in the night. They were outlined against the background of the blazing bower that only minutes before had been filled with jubilation; I could smell the sweet odor of the smoke.

Three forms below me toiled doggedly up along the zigzag path toward the walls that loomed over me. Without recognizing them, I had a surge of premonition. I knew who they were in my breast. Mouth wide, I gasped exultantly. I knew, as well, where they were going.

They were Joab, Adonijah, and Abiathar. They were

trying to reach the sole spot which could protect them from the wrath of the newly crowned king. They were attempting to reach the tabernacle, to take hold of the horns of the altar. Only there would they be able to live on the bounty of Yahweh's priests until the vengeance of Solomon was stayed—or they emerged to be slaughtered.

David stood erect, head lifted, by the brazen altar on Araunah's rock. He looked far out over the multitude about him. A sea of brown faces, of brown hoods, all lifted toward him in expectation, cups of wool filled with flesh. He waited a moment until humming silence fell. There were only the sounds of wind moving amidst the sycamores and olive trees on the plain below, the light whine of a cur. He shakily stretched out his arms. As he did, Ahithophel his counselor stepped in from the right, and his companion Hushai came from the left. They supported his withered limbs. In a thin clear voice that carried far in the quieted air, David began to speak.

"Hear me, my brothers and my people! For many years I have had in my heart the thought that I would build a house of rest for the far-wandering ark of the covenant of the Lord. I had planned to make it the footstool of Yahweh, I had made ready for the building. But in a dream Yahweh came and said to me: 'Thou shalt not build a house for My name because thou hast been a man of war and hast shed blood.'

David looked sadly about him. His eyes shone blindly with unaccustomed tears: "But I take comfort in the fact that Yahweh chose me out of all the humble house of my father Jesse to be king over the Hebrews. He has preferred me to choose one of my sons to be king after me. Of all of them, as you know—for the Lord has given me many sons—it is His wish that Solomon sit upon the throne of the kingdom of the Lord!"

He beckoned to Solomon. The boy in a plain wool robe rose and came to stand at a respectful distance beside David. "This is my son Solomon," the old king went on, "who shall build the house and the courts of the Lord. I have chosen him to be my successor. I will be his father. According to the promise of Yahweh, He will establish his kingdom forever, if he is taught to do the commandments and judgments of the Lord. I command you all to follow him in that you may possess this good land and have it for inheritance for your children after you forever!"

With this David turned to address Solomon directly. His words carried out to the fringes of the breathless multitude: "And you, Solomon my son, know the Lord of your father and serve Him with a perfect heart and willing mind. Seek Him out wherever He is. You will find Him. But if you do not seek Him, if you forsake Him, He will cast you and yours off forever."

David turned falteringly back, facing his people again. "I have prepared with all my might for the house of the Lord. Gold for things of gold, silver for things of silver, brass for brass and iron for things of iron, wood for things of wood. Precious stones and glistening stones in all manner, marble in abundance. But more than these I have given of my own substance three thousand talents of the gold of Ophir and seven thousand talents of refined silver."

David outspread his arms in a great gesture. "With what I have given," he cried, "who then is willing to consecrate his services, his goods this day unto the Lord?"

A shout went up instantly from the multitude, rumbling and echoing in the gorges. From the midst of the people there was a rising movement of men, a swirl of arms and chatter, people making their way to give pledges of wealth and assistance.

David, exhausted, was led back to his sheltered seat beside the altar by Hushai and Ahithophel while the long files of Hebrews made their pledges and offerings. He heard them out while they contributed their goods to the keeping of Jehiel, the Gershonite.

All through the rest of the long morning the contributions continued. At last there were five thousand talents and ten thousand drams of gold, ten thousand talents of silver and eighteen thousand talents of brass, and a hundred thousand talents of iron, together with heaps of precious stones. All those who had little or nothing to contribute volunteered the work of their hands.

David had not stirred from his place despite the sun beating down on the little striped-linen pavilion under which he sat. When Jahiel said the count was complete, he rose, again supported by his two courtiers, and addressed the heavens:

"Blessed be the Lord God of Israel forever and ever, for it is Your kingdom, Lord, and You are exalted as head above all. Riches and honor have come to me, and in Your hand is power and might. You will make us great and make us small. You will give us strength or weakness, according to Your will.

All this store that we have prepared is to build a house for that Holy Name which is only Yours. We have only given You back Your own."

David turned his head slightly toward Solomon. "With this, my son Solomon, I have finished the accounting of my kingdom. The Lord has promised that He will increase Israel like the stars in heaven. I have trust in His promise. But He is a jealous god. He would have His people worship Him alone. Take heed therefore that you do not depart from the ways of Yahweh."

David then looked down fondly at his people. He addressed them directly, quietly, in a lower tone: "But who am I and what are we that we should offer these things so willingly? We are strangers before the Lord and sojourners in the land as were our fathers. None of us shall abide. But the holy God and His temple shall abide forever."

He stretched out his hands again. "Now bless the Lord your God," he said loudly. Beneath his withered fingers, as though some tremendous power emanated from them, all the congregation bowed down murmuring. They stood up again as one and shouted together in a single great diapason.

David, exhausted, fell back into his seat. Hurriedly, they brought his litter and lifted him into it. He was carried down and away, followed by the shouts of the people who streamed after Solomon and the court officials.

The old king opened his eyes heavily, as if the lids upon them lay like heavy weights. He looked at those of us at the bedside in the dawn light. He moved his head to and fro on the pillow of his couch.

"Solomon," he moaned, "where is Solomon?"

"Here, my father," Solomon said, slipping down beside the soft coverlets of fur. "I am here."

"Ah!" Miraculously, it seemed, David became alert and responsive. His eyes saw, his ears heard: he looked up at us with understanding, even a slight smile.

"Stand up, my son," he said. "You are king now Never be on your knees again. Benaiah?"

"Here, sire."

"Guard him. Zadok?"

"Here, O king."

"Make his ways right before Yahweh. Nathan?"

"Here, great David," I said.

"Guide and protect him, Nathan Now, send out the women, Solomon, as your first act. Make sure they are gone."

Solomon gave a short, imperious gesture to Benaiah. Strange, I thought, watching: how well he assumes a part, as if he had been a king all his life! Not a word was spoken until the room was cleared of the sobbing women. Even Bathsheba was driven out, weeping and complaining.

"First," David said slowly, "let me speak of the things that are. I had hoped to assemble the princes of the tribes, the captains of the hundreds and thousands, my stewards, and my mighty men that they might witness what I say. But it is too late for that: you here shall testify to my words."

We bowed our heads in assent. David went on: "Yahweh chose Solomon for His son and now Yahweh shall be his Father. Honor Him and He will be fond of you; forsake Him and He will forsake you. Take heed: build the house of the Lord: be strong."

David paused, gathering his strength. "In the days when Abiathar was faithful to me," he said painfully, "I gave him the pattern of the temple—of the porch, the treasuries, the upper chambers and the inner parlors, the place of the mercy seat. All this Yahweh made clear, showing me the plan—written by His own hand—in my dreams. I have treasured up with all my might the gold and silver, brass and iron and wood for the furnishings; precious stones and base building stones; for the service—candlesticks, lamps, tables of shew-bread, fleshhooks and bowls, cups and basins; refined gold for the altar of incense and for the chariot and the cherubim that will spread wings above the ark."

Taken with a fit of coughing, David stopped. We waited, hardly daring to breathe. Solomon stood stiff and attentive at the foot of the couch.

"Get this holy plan from Abiathar in whatsoever manner you must. Call upon the people of the tribes, let them work upon the building of the temple with their own hands. But for those things which are not known to the Hebrews, such as fine work by artificers, you may summon the people of my friend, the king of Phoenicia."

He looked at me. "My son, Solomon, is yet young and the work is great. Be his guide, Nathan, help him in time of need." I bowed my head in assent.

"Be of good courage," he said to Solomon. "Do all, fear not, be not dismayed. Yahweh will not fail you until you have finished all the work for His house. Now let us speak of other things."

We remained silent. David's mind seemed to wander, his hands clutching feebly at his beard. "Who am I and what is my people that we should do this?" he said almost inaudibly. "All things come of Yahweh, we give them back to Him. Our days are as the passing of a shadow." He roused himself with an effort.

"It is my task, Solomon," said David, "to tell you some truths. To speak what I have learned through living, by the visitations of Yahweh, by my mistakes and triumphs. You stand there surrounded by the necessaries of ruling: the priest, the commander, the prophet. Reverence, force, planning: these are the great energies of the world. All else derives from them. Remember that."

"I shall remember, my father."

"Come closer, my son. Remember everything passes, blown out like a flame before the breath of Yahweh. You won't have to live as I did; I've seen to that: you won't have to run and hide, run and hide and starve and drink dirty water, have brave men killed for a drink, the way I did. You'll be safe all your life in the city I captured, in the house I built, with the army I made. I've seen to that, for your sake. Once it was for Absalom, now it's for you.

"But you've a weakness, Solomon, the same weakness I had. Oh, I've seen you looking at my concubines out of the side of your eyes, wanting to go in to them like Absalom on the roof but not having courage to do it. You're wild about women, what's between their legs and on their minds, just as I was when I was young. I remember the thrill I had when I lifted Abigail out of the dust and comforted her in my tent. When I saw Bathsheba naked in the courtyard. Oh, you'll have plenty of women and never understand one of them."

"I can take care of myself," Solomon muttered.

"You think you can, and there's your first mistake—because the women will take care of you, and you'll think all the time you're doing it."

"King-father, I shall heed your words."

"I remember my own grandfather, father of the father of Jesse, sitting by the fire and spitting and telling us of what he saw when he first came as a boy to this land: the Hittites, those funny little men with the peaked caps and boots, from the mountains in the north, that were like ants on the hills—that's another thing, Solomon. You must not forget to have many, many children."

"I shall remember."

"If you could have them without women, it would be best but Yahweh has seen it differently, Yahweh knows why."

"I accept His will."

"Well, the Hittites are gone now, most of them—not many left such as Uriah used to be or Ammiel, the father of Bathsheba—but she's left. The Hittites and their kingdoms, all gone. So are their big-breasted Amazons, most of their Greek allies, and their gods, Teshub and Ishtar, bearing their thunderbolts like Yahweh. Sometimes you may think the gods related, cousins in some way, but never tell these things to a priest. He would be scandalized and you would have to do penance and no good would come of it."

"No good at all, sir."

"Keep your thoughts from priests and women, Solomon. I've seen a good deal of wrangling in my time and I've made it easy for you; telling them what you really think only makes trouble. About the Egyptians, now."

"Yes."

"Ah, the Egyptians! You'll learn about them soon enough. They are of our race and they go on and on along the banks of their Nile. Nothing seems to upset them: they have one empire and it is crushed by Yahweh and another one rises. It is better not to fight them at all, Solomon."

"What is one to do?"

"Marry, marry them. When you have the daughter of a father underneath you in bed, helpless and shivering and sighing, conquered—remember you have her loving father conquered as well. You have your best weapon between your thighs, Solomon: use it well!"

"Yes."

"Vulgar? Well, perhaps it is. When you are as old as I am—and cold, all the time—you have a right to be vulgar. And when it comes down to dying, all your mind can recall are the vulgar acts of your life. Believe me, you don't give a curse for the delicate ones. But you'll learn, you'll learn. What else do I want to say?"

"I don't know."

"Women: kill them every night with your blunt circumcised tool. Watch them resurrect refreshed in the morning."

"And Bathsheba?"

"Your mother. I thought I had slain her that way, Solomon. But she rose again from the underworld like Tammuz—I don't know what to do with your mother. You'll have to take on some of your own problems. I can't do everything for you."

"No."

"Priests." David's voice dropped. "Don't trust them at all. They're what's ruining Egypt right now, from what I hear, setting themselves up as kings. Samuel died in time or else I should have had a rival—but he did in poor Saul. I always liked Saul but he got in Samuel's way and so, of course, he had to go. And Abiathar—he was perfectly willing to set up Adonijah in your place—remember Abiathar but don't be too hard on the poor fellow who abided with me in the wilderness."

"I'll remember."

"Treat the army right and you'll be safe; don't be soft with them. Benaiah there is a good man. Keep him happy with a few baubles and promotions and he'll go through fire and flood for you."

David's voice fell off further, murmuring; Solomon bent his ear closer. "My father, I cannot hear you," he whispered frantically.

David's eyes flew open. For an instant they seemed to have once again the fiery deep blue which had enchanted women and mesmerized men. "My son Solomon," he said clearly. "Keep the statutes of Yahweh, walk in his ways, follow the laws of Moses."

"Yes."

"All your heart, all your soul. If you do, Solomon, the Lord has promised me that your children will inherit the throne of Israel."

"I understand."

David's eyes filmed. His head sank back upon the hard bolster. "Show kindness to the sons of Barzillai the Gileadite," he said brokenly. "They came to my help when I fled because of the revolt of Absalom, your brother."

"I will remember Barzillai."

"Shimei, son of Gera," David muttered.

"Yes?"

"He cursed me in the day I went to Mahanaim at the Jordan. I swore I would not kill him but you, Solomon, you have no oath to the Lord to spare him."

"No," said Solomon. "And Joab?"

"And Joab?"

"Yes."

"I have feared him," David said slowly. "He was ever fierce, without mercy, daring and cruel."

"Shall he escape unscathed?" Solomon said into the very porch of David's withered ear.

David's eyes rolled toward him, uncomprehending. "What can you do against Joab?" he quavered.

"Trust me."

A succession of pale smiles flickered about David's lips. At last he was able to speak again, the soft loose flesh of his cheeks pulsing. "You know what he did to Absalom, to Abner and Amasa. He has held your house in contempt. He has shed the blood of war in peace, he has put blood upon his girdle and upon his sandals."

"What do you command, my father?"

David sighed. "Do according to your own wisdom," he said. A spasm of hatred shook him. "Hold him not guiltless!" he cried shrilly. "Bring his hoar head down to the grave in blood!"

He closed his eyes. His mouth worked a moment more. Solomon rose. We stood watching, awed at the almost visible approach of Azrael, the angel of death. But the life-stuff of David was not yet gone. His features ceased to twitch, his mouth assumed a firm line. His eyes opened, staring up into those of Solomon.

"Solomon," he said in a firm resonant voice that startled us, so much did it resemble that of a young man, "I go the way of all the earth. Be you strong, therefore, when I am gone—and show yourself a man."

It was the last flicker of strength left in the old king. His eyes wavered sightlessly. He heaved a final breath. His whole body seemed to shrivel on the couch.

"Bathsheba! Bathsheba!" screamed Solomon. He drew back in horror at the livid tints spreading across the face of his dead father.

Almost instantly Bathsheba was in the room. She knelt at David's side and took the lolling head in her hands. Her thumbs pushed back his eyelids for a long stare into the sightless pupils. She rose and nodded to Solomon. He sank slowly to his knees on the floor, beginning to sob and tear at his garments.

"You are king, my son," Bathsheba said. She looked down at Solomon's bowed head with compassion and, I thought, disdain.

So died King David. He was buried in his own city, in a chamber of rock supported by marble pillars with a table of gold and his scepter and crown upon it. The cavern was sealed forever, the records of its whereabouts destroyed.

After the customary period of mourning by the people and the court, one of the Levite priests of the tabernacle came to Solomon. He said the king's half-brother Adonijah in the tabernacle desired to implore his mercy. "He says, unless the king swears to him that he will not slay his servant by the sword, he will not quit the altar," he declared.

"If he shows himself a man worthy of my trust," Solomon said, "not a hair of his head shall fall to earth. But if wickedness is found in him, he shall die."

By which he meant, of course, that Adonijah should give up all pretensions to the throne. The Levite humbly persisted and asked for the forgiveness of Abiathar because, he added, of the brotherly love between the members of their profession and besides, the provisions of the priests were alarmingly low from feeding the three refugees.

"Tell him," Solomon said severely, "that he is worthy of death. But I will not touch him now because he bore the ark of Yahweh before David, my father, and suffered his sufferings with him. Let him get back to his farm at Anathoth and stay there."

"And Joab?" asked the priest.

"I will consider my answer," said Solomon.

I marveled at the wisdom of the youth. I thought how surely he had risen to the duties of his high office. I respected him even more when he came to me a few weeks later and commanded that a gathering of all the tribes be called. He wished to be crowned a second time in the sight of all the people.

"That is expedient," I said. I made all the arrangements.

On the day set, thousands of Hebrews assembled in Jerusalem and paid honor to Solomon. Publicly, he went through the ceremony performed in secret at Gihon under the hands of Zadok. The crowd shouted hosannahs, the yellow curs roaming the fringes barked. The rams, lambs, and bullocks brought up for the burnt offerings added their bleats and bellowings. After that, all of us blessed Yahweh in unison, bowed down to Him, and presented Him with the blood and entrails of the herds and flocks. The people feasted on what remained (after the priests had their allotted share) and joined in drink-offerings and dancing.

It was a highly successful coronation. Everyone went away satisfied except one: that was Joab, peeping out of the curtains of the tabernacle with haggard face, licking his lips longingly. I noted him well. The next day I approached Solomon in the throne room and as I suspected, Solomon had not missed Joab's face.

"He will be a danger as long as he is alive," he said.

"You have forgiven Abiathar and Adonijah," I pointed out.

"On conditions," Solomon said. "But Joab is not to be trusted with his freedom. Even now he tries to subvert the priests."

"What can be done?" I asked. "He is in sanctuary."

"Perhaps he is not as safe as he thinks," Solomon said thoughtfully. "Send Benaiah to me."

Late that afternoon Solomon summoned me again. "I wish you to go with us," he said, "to the tabernacle. You shall be a witness that I have fulfilled my promise to my father."

We ascended the mountain on which the sun still shone—a peak of gold in the midst of the blue-shadowed plains round about us. We filed solemnly into the courtyard of the sacred enclosure and halted before the triple curtain of the tabernacle. Solomon himself raised the curtains and exposed the holy place. Joab lay stretched out beside the brazen altar, apparently asleep. But he was as alert as an animal. He roused at our appearance and leaped to his feet, neglecting the sword which lay on the ground beside him. His face seemed to melt with terror. He sprang at the altar—reminiscent of the golden calf Aaron had once mistakenly created for our people—and embraced its horns. He twisted his head about, straining backward to see our intentions.

Solomon dropped the curtains. He turned quietly to Benaiah. "Tell Joab to come out," he said.

Benaiah advanced and held the curtains ajar. We saw dimly the form of Joab standing by the altar. "The king commands you to come forth," he said in a loud voice.

"No," Joab said hoarsely. "If I am to die, I shall die here."

Benaiah let the thick curtain fall. He turned questioningly to the king.

"Do not drag him out," I said impulsively.

"No," Solomon said. "He shall remain where he is." He motioned to Benaiah.

"No!" I cried.

Solomon nodded, his young face rigid with his final decision. "Do as Joab wishes," he murmured. "Go in. Fall upon him. Kill him. Bury his carcass next to his house in the wilderness."

Benaiah hesitated, fear glimmering in his eyes. Solomon waved him on. "No sin shall be yours," he said. "The Lord shall return the blood upon Joab himself. He killed Abner and Amasa, two men better and more righteous than he. And you shall inherit his sword of iron."

Benaiah's face brightened. He unsheathed his weapon. We lifted the curtain once more and stepped into the holy place.

None paid attention to my stutterings of horror. Benaiah took Joab by his long, graying back hair. He lifted his blade. It glittered in the long rays of the sun through the door.

"Thus," Benaiah said loudly, "did you thrust Absalom through the back as he hung from the oak."

His arm went downward. Joab uttered a cry. He stiffened, lost his grip on the altar, as the iron vanished into his back. But Benaiah did not let him drop. He twisted the half-conscious man about.

The doomed one-time commander of the Hebrew armies slumped. A stifled moan came from him. His muscles relaxed their insensate hold on life. He had realized that not even the sanctuary of Yahweh was protection against the vengeance of the king. Benaiah withdrew his blade, tinged red. The eyes of Joab, once so terrifying in battle, stared up at him, their light dimming.

"Thus," said Benaiah, louder than before, "did you take Abner and Amasa by the beard and thrust them through."

The sword plunged into the belly of Joab. Joab fell forward. Benaiah twisted the blade and flung the body aside, letting it sprawl face downward. I was speechless with fear of Yahweh.

"Will you have his head, O king?" asked Benaiah.

Solomon made a gesture of repugnance. "When we are gone," he said, his face pale, "cut it off. Throw it into the Valley of Hinnom to burn forever with the rest of the refuse."

He turned and strode out. I almost ran after him. "You have fouled the sanctuary of Yahweh with blood!" I cried.

Solomon smiled thinly. "No," he said. "With justice. But it does not matter. You forget I promised my father David to build a new temple to Yahweh."

CHAPTER THREE

The Reward of Adonijah

I should explain why King Solomon went with Benaiah and myself to witness the execution of Joab. Many may not understand the mystic power of the king, especially among the Hebrews, in those times.

It is enough to say that he was chosen of Yahweh. After generations of wandering and persecution, to find ourselves in a green and pleasant land—united against our enemies instead of bickering and slaughtering among ourselves—was paradise. Under Saul and David, the king had become a symbol of this unity. The people had demanded such a one, even over the objections of Samuel, to lead them in war and peace. He was on earth what Yahweh's might was in the sky. He was beneficent rain and fruitful sun. He was holy because he had been anointed by the servants of Yahweh.

Only his own will or a decree of Yahweh could take the crown from his sacred head. All belonged to the king—people and land; he could give and take back again at his pleasure. He was held in unspeakable awe by everyone—except, I suppose, by prophets and women.

Such respect was soaked into the fabric of the soul of Joab. Solomon knew his very presence would slack the sinews and turn the bowels of the redoubtable general. He might otherwise have resisted Benaiah—but with the king in person, Joab was a sheep under the knife.

It may be well, too, if I explain that my own position as one of the *nahiim* was unique. I was not a priest nor anyone like a priest. As a matter of fact, I regarded them then—as I do now—as far below me, even the high priest. Priests were the slaves of Yahweh. I was His voice, as was Samuel before me, as is Elijah today. I was the teller of fate. I had the gift from Yahweh of peering into the future. It was my duty to warn and chastise, to rebuke or praise the highest and the lowest. I refused my services to none, even as Samuel had consented to find the asses of Kish, Saul's father.

Though the king might slay me—Yahweh did not forbid this—he could not silence me. I owed my office and duty to the Lord. I performed it as inspiration seized me—even, as in the case of Adonijah's feast, to warn evildoers. My charge was to speak of what was to be.

But from the first with Solomon I felt my mission was not as it had been with his father. There was less respect, less heed, if no less honor. Solomon always listened to me. But as the years passed, more and more he went his own way. I rebuked him for this many times. Once, I recall, I said to him: "You must have more knowledge of the Lord."

"All increase of knowledge," he told me wearily, "is increase of sorrow."

I sit here gnawing the end of my *et*—reed pen—wondering where to begin the story of his reign. The shaved lattice of the papyrus—*gillayon*—lies blank before me. I am a scribe myself: I do not have to dictate what I wish inscribed, which cannot be said of many kings. But the words will not come; my thoughts are awry. Yet before the *deyo*—ink—settles, let me put down some facts.

Solomon came to be king of a nation that his father had carefully prepared for the future. During the thirty-three years of his rule in Jerusalem, David had deeply considered the problems of the Hebrews. He abandoned to the cruel sword of Joab most of his military campaigns.

The garment he prepared for his people folded into three like a ritual robe.

His first concern was the ark with its red-leather tent containing the holy tablets of Moses. He desired above all that it should, like the Hebrews, have an end to wanderings and exile. Therefore David decided to build the first true temple of the Hebrews to hold the ark on the crest of Mount Zion, the highest peak of Jerusalem. He called together the forty-eight families of the priests and Levites. He admonished them to assume the keeping of the ark (one family each week, chosen by lot), as well as the charge of the royal treasury. He advised the priests to decide all disputed questions by lot. At the same time, he urged them to pay particular attention to the desires of the people as the surest way to Yahweh's favor. As for myself, he confirmed my position as chief adviser to Solomon. This came as no surprise. I had been consulted by David on many problems, especially that of building the permanent shelter for the ark. I had not been in favor of this. I spoke strongly against it. I pointed out that the old-fashioned way, the portable shrine to Yahweh, seemed to me more acceptable, sanctified by centuries.

"Has Yahweh spoken to you of this?" inquired David anxiously.

I admitted I had received no revelation. David heaved a sigh of relief. "I have had a dream," he told me, "and Yahweh has commanded it."

That settled the matter. As it turned out, it was a vast improvement over the old ways. I myself had a later vision rebuking me for my intransigence—which is one reason I have supported Solomon in his grandiose plans for his own temple. At any rate, David was pleased with my support. "I need someone about the throne who will speak honestly," he said. "I have too many who say yea, yea—and never nay." He elevated me above all priests to be, as he called it, "the inquirer after the will of Yahweh."

I was appointed to be recorder of the kingdom—one entrusted with its history and archives—but I also regulated the ceremonies of state and took Solomon's words to the lesser officials. All palace documents were sealed with Solomon's six-pointed-star seal by my direction. I had an assistant, of course: at first he was David's Egyptian scribe, Shisha. He was expert but getting old. I utilized his small crippled son, Elihaph, to help him as secretary of state.

The second fold of the garment of monarchy was the arrangement of the military. David divided the army into thousands, hundreds, and tens, each group with its own captain. He also created a corps of cavalry after the model of the Egyptians, ordering a hundred chariots to be built and horses procured.

Among the twelve army divisions, he included strong contingents from Judah, his favorite tribe, as well as mercenaries from the Hittites, Phoenicians, and even Philistines (with whom he had soldiered at one time). He was not sure of the loyalty of the northern tribes. He remembered Shimei's venom and the cry of some: "We have no part in David! Every man to his tents!" It was a slogan which was to plague Solomon afterward.

The third fold was, naturally, the government of the Hebrews themselves. Although our nation had risen to be the greatest of the small kingdoms of the world, it was still subject to unexpected raids from almost every direction, even including the seacoast (which had spawned the iron-bearing Sea Peoples). Therefore David decreed that each hilltop should have a fortress of stone wherein his people might retire in time of danger. Built of enormous stones, they often had walls twenty-five feet thick. They invariably included a tower from which fire-and-smoke signals might be made to the towers of neighboring villages.

David was proud that Yahweh had directed him to such ends. "See!" he said to me one day as we stood upon a promontory not far from Jerusalem. "Our people till their fields down the sides of the hill slopes to the course of the streams, terracing where the fall is too great. They hew cisterns to hold rainwater in drought times, cut of the solid rock, with canals to carry the flow from one to the other. They sink jars of grain into the ground in case of siege. Each village has an armory. The inhabitants are trained in arms and assigned to watch duty."

"Excellent, O king," I said, my bosom swelling with emotion.

"I have also seen to it that each citadel is always occupied by a small body of armed men paid out of my own treasury. I have installed governors whose duties are to see that laws are kept, the ordinances of religion observed, taxes collected, and the region defended from all incursions. For the lessening of blood feuds, I have allotted the whole of the land—except Jerusalem, which is, of course, a neutral meeting ground—to the twelve tribes. I have marked the boundaries plainly with stone cairns."

Beyond the boundaries of our country, in the lands he had conquered, David set up other governors. They had much the same responsibilities as our own officials—except that David allowed them to condone local religious practices. One of the most hazardous and desolate of these areas was to the south in the desert of the Negeb. It was also one of the most profitable. Though we might sell produce and woven cloth and similar articles, such merchandise brought no great prices. But in the Valley of Arabah, after he had conquered the Edomites, David found copper and iron. He used the subject peoples as slaves to mine the ore. As the holy writings had predicted, we had inherited a land "whose stones are iron and out of whose hills you shall dig copper."

David set up smelting furnaces of brick, taking advantage of the strong north desert winds to blow up the fires. Ingots of these metals could be traded easily at high prices, though it was a dangerous enterprise. There was always the possibility of revolt. Hadad, one of the princes of Edom who had escaped into Egypt, kept up inceasing guerrilla warfare in the region. Joab had waged war there for six months until he had cut off every male in the land, but Hadad—then no older than Solomon—had escaped. He had married the young sister of Tahpenes, wife of the pharaoh.

Most important of all, news of David's victories had spread throughout all lands. The king of Phoenicia in Tyre heard of them. He offered gifts which David—understanding that the Phoenicians, being seafarers, had no ambitions for conquest on land—gratefully accepted. It was a friendship that was to prove of great benefit to Solomon.

All of these conquests and pacifications, of course, gave David control of the chief trade routes to Mesopotamia and Arabia. Of importance in this regard were the people of Sheba, far down on the eastern shore of the Red Sea. David himself, who had as canny an eye for the trading health of his kingdom as for the wealth and security of his people, descanted to me upon this topic. "The men of Sheba," he said pensively, "surpass all others in wealth and extravagance. They have never suffered an invasion—because of their seclusion—and are the cleverest traders in the world. They have goblets of silver and gold, couches with silver feet, halls with gilded columns, and even chests made of gold set with precious stones. Silver is esteemed there almost as a base metal. Ivory and ebony are used everywhere in carving and decoration, I hear, inlaid with the most sparkling gems."

Despite the injunction of his father on his deathbed, Solomon did not begin to build his new temple for nearly four years after David's death. I did not cast this up to him. There were, as I knew, sufficient reasons for his delay.

The Hebrews at that time were not skilled craftsmen, except in pottery, dyeing, and weaving. These skills might be useful in ornamenting the house of Yahweh but we had no knowledge whatsoever of how to design a building, how to erect it with dressed stones or, above all, how to execute the cunning workmanship of metals. Solomon realized that only in Phoenicia did such workers in stone and metal and wood exist.

David had carefully cultivated their friendship. He admired their arts. He had paid the old king of Tyre nearly a talent for the plans which had been inspired by the Lord. He had negotiated for workmen but the monarch of Tyre had been reluctant to allow his people to come into such an unruly war-torn land as that of the Hebrews. So Solomon was forced to wait for three long years, until the old king died to be succeeded by his son Hiram.

Moreover, there was much to be done within our kingdom itself. As might be expected, there was the settling-in period after the pomp and splendor and national mourning upon David's death. Not all the northern tribes approved of the throne going to Solomon. Some refused to march in the funeral procession. Solomon bade me blanket my ass and make several trips into their territories to placate them and, to a degree at least, I succeeded in my mission for peace.

There were many accounts to be reviewed, many reports to be received by the new king. During his long reign David had organized a complex administrative and secretarial staff. He used it not only to transact government business but also to dictate and record his psalms. Such tablets were particularly valuable to young Solomon—who had an excellent head both for poetry and business—especially as it related to love or foreign trade.

I made no secret to Solomon of my conviction that his rule would be as long and illustrious as that of his father. It pleased him so much that he made no objection to my continuing and enlarging the school that David had created for training scribes. I had two rooms in the palace filled with benches, pottery writing desks which held moist clay to be stylized, small shells to facilitate counting and numbering, and numerous shelves on which to store the clay tablets.

Most of this, of course, was routine. What was more subtle and important was that, despite the machinations of Bathsheba, the crown did not yet sit firmly upon the brow of Solomon. He had to deal with the rivals who had aspired to his power. The son of Jonathan, son of Saul—Merib-baal—had survived by the kindness of David. He offered no threat as the last of his line. Abiathar, the old priest-companion of David, had been utterly broken in his old age by his disgrace. When allowed by Solomon to come into Jerusalem, he spent his time mumbling in a corner of the tabernacle yard or staring sightlessly at the horizon from a housetop.

There were still Shimei and Adonijah. The more dangerous of the two was the big-boned, brawny, outspoken Shimei from the north. He was fearless and had a great many followers. I reported this to Solomon. He summoned Shimei to his presence.

"I know very well your grievance," Solomon told him. "You bitterly cursed my father, the king of the Hebrews. You were of Saul's household and enraged because David ordered two of Saul's sons and five grandsons hanged to placate the Gibeonites whom Saul had ravaged. You are wrong to feel so. If I willed it, I might have you executed by Benaiah this instant."

Shimei raised his bowed head and stared at Solomon defiantly. My young master went on: "But I am merciful. I shall spare you on the condition that you raise no more threats against me. And that you build a house in Jerusalem, never to leave the city without my permission."

"The king is wise and merciful," said Shimei huskily. "I take oath before Yahweh."

Solomon leaned toward him. "In the day that you pass over the brook Kidron," he said slowly, "your blood shall be on your own head, even as his was on Joab's."

Shimei bowed and retired. Solomon glanced at me. I nodded in approbation. I truly believed that Shimei would reconcile himself to the interests of the kingdom. As it turned out, I was wrong. Two years later, a pair of the slaves of Shimei ran away to serve the king of Gath. I suppose he was so blinded with rage that he forgot his oath. He went to Gath, captured his property, and brought the slaves back to Jerusalem for punishment. Solomon heard of it. He sent for him.

"Why have you not kept your oath to the Lord and the commandment I charged you with?" Solomon demanded without preliminary. "You yourself know your secret wickedness. The Lord shall give you back your sins on your own head."

He made a gesture of dismissal. Shimei, without a word, shambled out. Solomon gave Benaiah a nod. His captain rasped out his sword and plunged through the doors after the condemned man. I heard Shimei grunt in a fading sigh as he fell outside.

"Have I done well?" Solomon asked me softly.

I shrugged. "The tribes in the north will nurse revenge," I said.

"I shall deal with them in other ways," Solomon said musingly. "The building of the house of Yahweh will need many laborers."

The affair of Adonijah was now uppermost in Solomon's mind. The supports of the throne appeared rotten as long as Adonijah was alive. The other sons of David, even those of his concubines, had long ago made their submissions and grown fat and peaceful. Only Adonijah still stalked the streets and secretly recruited adherents. Solomon feared him more than any other man in the kingdom. Yet it was Bathsheba, by no mere chance of fate, who was clever enough to become the instrument for his downfall.

The firmness of Solomon with Shimei had been applauded in Judah and received with sullen silence by the north. But in Jerusalem, all was peace. I found time, in my favorite spot on the roof of the king's palace, for meditation and communion with my spirit in the glorious afternoons of late summer. I drank in the air like wine. My thoughts seemed to ride across the heavens.

The palace of David, which Solomon had inherited, was the largest building in Jerusalem. When the city was captured from the Jebusites (who actually held only the southern ridge and thus gave our people a commanding strategic advantage from the higher north), David had marked this eyrie for his own. On it he had erected a handsome two-story house built of mud-brick held together by mats and cables of reed interworked in the courses. It had a central court paved with multicolored tiles from Mesopotamia. Gilded cedar posts from Lebanon upheld the wooden balconies around the court. There were, of course, such regal decorations as mats and carpets and ornate imported jars, with trinket caskets of ivory and gold, of silver and ebony; chests of cedarwood, acacia, and sycamore with grain knots hidden under paint or gold leaf, as well as linen and manuscript cabinets of cypress, juniper, and pine veneered with strange woods from Egypt. There were a few stools, a table or two, but no chairs except the throne itself. David also had a palanquin of cedar for his elder days, decorated with palm-leaf carvings, and a bed of stretched linen with a curved headrest.

The palace was in the midst of a cluster of three buildings separated by alleys of no more than two or three feet. To the east was the tabernacle, connected by a special door so that David might enter alone to meditate and pray. On the other side was the house formerly owned by the doomed Uriah, where David had first seen Bathsheba naked, bathing in the courtyard.

Now Uriah's house was used for Solomon's wives. The tabernacle, except on high holy days, was his private chapel. The unusual height of David's palace allowed anyone on the roof—made of bitumen from the Dead Sea and baked earth-bricks for coolness—to overlook not only the neighboring houses but the whole panorama of the land. It was here I climbed most often, using the steps molded to the outside of the building.

Though it was an ideal place for spying, I had no thought of this. I was surprised when I heard a woman's voice, that of Bathsheba, speaking in the king's court below. I had thought there was none else but myself in the palace that day. Solomon and his attendants and guards had gone to Gibeon, five miles to the west, a favorite resort of the king's to think upon his decisions when problems arose.

I heard Bathsheba's slow seductive tones that I knew so well, that she reserved for men only. A spasm of strange emotion gripped me. Almost without volition, I set myself to listen.

"I sent for you," she said, her words drifting up to me, "because your welfare has been in my thoughts night and day since Solomon assumed the throne."

"You know," said a surly voice that I recognized with astonishment as that of Adonijah, "that the kingdom was mine. All Israel had set their faces toward me, that I should reign. But the world is turned about. Now it is Solomon's, from the Lord. I am content."

"Yes," Bathsheba said calmly. "Solomon, my son, is king. But it is not right that the son of Haggith, David's wife, should be without comfort. I am sure Solomon in his grace would say as much."

Adonijah cleared his throat with a kind of defiance.

"May I speak without fear?" he demanded.

"Did you come in peace?" Bathsheba asked tranquilly.

"In peace."

"Say on."

"Do you speak as the king?"

"I speak as the mother of the king."

"Why do you wish to talk to me thus?"

"I offer you a gift."

"What gift?" asked Adonijah skeptically.

"I have seen with my own eyes," said Bathsheba, "how many times your glance has dwelt on Abishag, the concubine of David and of Solomon. I have seen her smile, lower her eyes; I have seen her blush under your gaze. Would you have her as your wife?"

"My wife!" exclaimed Adonijah. Bathsheba made a sharp hissing sound, warning him to lower his voice.

"But she belongs to Solomon," Adonijah went on. "No one dares ask such a favor!"

"She is not his wife," Bathsheba said. "David was too old, he never knew her. And I am Solomon's mother. I know that he has not had intercourse with her. She is a virgin."

"It makes no difference."

"If you asked yourself, perhaps it would anger Solomon."

"No one else would dare ask."

"I would," Bathsheba responded. "Solomon would not refuse me. The blame, if there was blame, would not be yours."

I heard Adonijah move restlessly. Neither of them spoke for a moment. Adonijah said in a changed tone: "You are right, mother of Solomon. I covet the girl. I am lonely and forsaken. She would comfort me."

"Then trust me," Bathsheba said. "I will speak to my son on your behalf. He was better off without the girl. I shall be glad to see her go to your house."

"But say that I had no part in it," Adonijah muttered. "It is your thought and deed. I wash my hands of it."

"It is a small petition. Solomon will not say me nay. I shall demand his permission before I speak your name. Now go. Let no one know we have spoken to each other lest blame fall upon you."

"Do you swear it?" stammered Adonijah.

"I swear before Yahweh."

"To say no more than that?"

"No more than that. Come early for an audience with the king tomorrow."

With an ejaculation between jubilation and wonder, I heard Adonijah back out from Bathsheba's presence without another word. I sat still above them, scarcely believing what I had heard.

What puzzled me beyond measure was Bathsheba's plea to Adonijah that he consent to allow her to ask for Abishag as his wife from Solomon. Perhaps she did not know—but assuredly Adonijah did—the meaning of such a request. Women belonging to a king were his most prized possessions. For some, he might have a passion of lust (such as David for Bathsheba herself) and with others he might have commerce in order to breed many sons. But all were reckoned as part of his treasury: signs of his virility, of his conquests. David's harem held females of Amorite, Amalekite, Hittite, Aramite, and Jebusite blood, showing he had captured women from the leaders of many tribes.

Adonijah had told Bathsheba that she would ask of Solomon not only one of his choice possessions but she would be questioning his right to rule—as Absalom had known when he went among David's wives. It was a clear challenge to Solomon and the throne.

Moreover, I could not imagine how Adonijah had got access to the guarded palace of Solomon. I thought of traitors, of bribery, of stealth—of a dozen ways—but none of them seemed to fit the circumstances of such a private interview. It would have been impossible, I thought, without the connivance and command of someone in the palace itself. Adonijah, already weighted by suspicion, had been encouraged by someone in a high place. As if an inexorable finger had pointed, I knew the reasons of the person who had prompted him, who had got him entrance, who had put the idea into Adonijah's stupid head. My heart filled with darkness; I ground my teeth until they hurt. I hurried to the outer stairs to descend.

Bathsheba had remained in the courtyard of the palace. Her guard announced me; he was bade by her to let me enter. I pushed through the doorway and saw her sitting silently in the sun in one corner. She sat upon her favorite stool—one of brass, its legs cast into twining serpents which were symbols of the house of David and of Moses.

"You have been absent from the court a long while," she greeted me. "Have you had a vision from Yahweh?"

I frowned at her light tone. "No," I said stiffly, goaded into reply. "The future is hidden from me. But I have been able to look into what-has-been."

Like all women, such a prospect enchanted Bathsheba. She looked up at me expectantly, her rich lips apart. "Tell me, Nathan!" she commanded.

"I know," I said deliberately, "that you have had this day a visit from Adonijah, son of David."

Her eyes took on a strange light, almost that of fear. Her lips became prim, her features hardened.

"He has asked you a great favor," I continued.

"Has he?"

"And you have granted it."

Bathsheba stared at me. "What else do you see in your backward look?" she asked. "You stand there, prophet, lean and tall, arms folded, knowing what you have no business to know! What else?"

"Nothing else," I said, baffled by her self-control.

I watched her. Bathsheba sat still a long while. A rhomb of yellow sunlight moved imperceptibly down her fringed shawl, down her form. It rested upon her lap, upon her clasped hands. Her gold snake rings gleamed. Tiny beads of perspiration formed on her flesh, drying as the breeze sprang up out of evening. I stood before her motionless, waiting. But she did not speak again. At last I went out.

Two hours after dawn the next day, Solomon returned from Gibeon. Clad in my special white robe of office, I waited in the courtyard. He greeted me and went directly to the throne room to prepare for the day's business. I joined his entourage and followed: I wished to see the end of this deadly game that Bathsheba played.

Not to my surprise, she was there before her son. He bowed to her and, sitting upon the throne, ordered that her stool should be brought and placed next to him, a little lower than himself—an extraordinary honor to his mother.

In my post of He-Who-Is-Over-the-House—as Solomon's

first minister—I was first to approach the king. I presented myself formally, gave him a report on what had happened while he was away, offered him the daily account of the treasury and the sealed documents which had been brought in or were about to be sent out and—finally—opened the doors of the palace to further business.

Hardly to my surprise, Adonijah craved admittance among the first. He pushed past me—the big handsome son of David, his fingers pulling uncertainly at his short blond beard. He paused and looked at me suspiciously.

"Enter, O Adonijah," said Solomon. "You have nothing to fear from Nathan. He knows all secrets." Beside the king, Bathsheba sat white and silent.

Adonijah articulated something, hesitated again, then took courage. He advanced to the foot of the throne. He fell to his knees awkwardly—and, indeed, rarely had he done obeisance before.

"What does my brother seek?" inquired Solomon.

From his right hand, Bathsheba suddenly broke in. "O my son Solomon," she said, "I desire one small thing of you. I pray you, do not refuse me."

Solomon, his young face dignified by the glossy black of his growing beard—cut square in the latest fashion from Assyria—smiled and extended his hand to hers.

"Ask on, my mother," he said. "Be sure I will not say you nay."

Adonijah's head came up in a glow of expectancy. Bathsheba darted a look at him and went on. "Solomon my son," she said, almost whispering, "let you give Abishag, the Shunamite girl, to Adonijah, to be his wife."

Solomon snatched back his hand as if he had touched a viper. His form stiffened on the throne. His eyes blazed as he bent his look first upon the shrinking Bathsheba, then upon Adonijah. He seemed at first to be stricken speechless but his wrath was regal.

"And why," he asked thickly, "do you ask me to give Abishag alone to Adonijah? Why do you not ask me to give him the kingdom of the Hebrews also? Why do you not ask me to surrender all that I have to my elder brother?"

Suddenly he stood upright, in the old gesture of David, stretching out his hands to heaven, his gold-encrusted robes glaring in the morning light.

"Yahweh do so to me and more," he shouted loudly, "if Adonijah has not been condemned out of your own mouth!"

He looked down at the shaking form of Adonijah with

scorn. "Now, therefore, as the Lord lives," he said in utter contempt, "and as He set me on the throne of David and created my house, Adonijah shall be put to death."

Adonijah sprang to his feet. He was without weapons—for none came into the king's presence armed—but he leaped with his hands crooked for a throat. Not at Solomon's but at Bathsheba's fair neck.

Assuredly she would have died on the spot under those clutching fingers of the maddened man but for Benaiah. The head of the king's soldiers was ware and ready. He did to Adonijah as he had done to the lion in the pit: he rammed the butt of his spear upward into his belly. Adonijah collapsed gasping on the floor, writhing and moaning.

"Take him out," Solomon said disdainfully.

After Adonijah had been dragged unceremoniously outside the gates, Solomon sank back onto the throne. He turned his face toward us with a genial, even cheerful, expression. "Well," said Solomon, leaning back, "that affair is over. I shall be able to proceed with the building of my temple."

I was silent. Solomon looked curiously at me. "Do you not think it was well done?" he asked. "Or do you wish to reprove me, as you reproved my father?"

I licked my lips. I found no words to say. David had been a simple man with simple sins. It had been easy for him to offend Yahweh but it was equally easy for him to offer genuine repentance and to be forgiven. Against the subtlety of this young king I felt helpless.

"Well?" persisted Solomon. "What else could I have done? What else would you have advised me to have done, if the throne of the Hebrews is to be secure?"

"Nothing else," I said hollowly. "You have done what you have done, O Solomon."

"Then let us continue with the business of the kingdom before us," Solomon said. Beside her son, as I turned away with a heavy heart, Bathsheba smiled triumphantly.

Adonijah was executed by Benaiah the following day. For four days, his body hung by the heels at the pool of Siloam for all to see. When his corpse commenced to stink, it was cut down and tossed into the valley of Hinnom for the jackals to feast upon.

What truly amazed me was that Solomon did not lift a finger against the women. Bathsheba became more honored than before. As for Abishag, she was promoted to the favorite among Solomon's wives.

Solomon had indeed been weaned—with vengeance.

CHAPTER FOUR

The Plots of Michal

It will seem strange to those who do not know the circumstances, but the one of David's women who hated him most was Michal—who had saved his life. And her hatred extended over the years, even to David's son Solomon.

The reasons for this are not far to find. Michal had been the youngest daughter of Saul. She had fallen in love with David's fresh, blooming face when she had first seen him from a high window of Saul's towered palace. Saul gave her to David in treachery, hoping he might be killed by the awesome Philistines. He demanded of David as Michal's price a hundred Philistine foreskins, a gift which David duly delivered. Then Saul tried to trap David with Michal as bait, but she enabled her husband to escape. After that Saul gave her to another man. David, when he became powerful, recovered her as a matter of pride, I believe, more than love.

It might seem that the bond between Michal and David should have been very close, one of life and death—but there was always that which lay between them like a sword in the bed. It was apparently forbidden by Yahweh that Michal should bear any children; and David, to this proud king's daughter—despite his excellent nature and comeliness—was always no more than a country yokel. Her love turned into contempt, as David neglected her when it became clear she was barren. She despised David for dancing and singing before the ark. For this he put her away from his bed—though he did her no further dishonor.

If events had stayed balanced so, Michal might have been no more than a sour, dried-up hag. But she conceived a desperate longing for children. When her sister, Merab (who had married a Meholathite named Adriel) died, Michal brought up her five sons in the palace as if they were her own. David did not particularly care for this. Such offspring might conceivably make a claim for his throne—but he offered no objection at the time. Later, however, when there was a three-year famine in the land, the Lord spoke to David and made it plain that this was in reprisal for Saul having slain so many of the Gibeonites. David inquired what the penance was. It was declared to him that he should surrender seven of Saul's "bloody house," all males, to be sacrificed.

I never inquired into David's dreams. A dream is a sacred thing. It would be a rash man who would set his own imagination against a true message from Yahweh. But it was curious that David gave up the five sons of Adriel and Merab and two others—while he spared Meribbaal, the son of his old friend Jonathan—so readily to the vengeance of the Gibeonites. At least Michal thought so. She never forgave David nor the seed of his loins. Her curses followed Solomon like birds of prey, hovering over his house.

Not many paid attention to her black prophesies of doom. Michal had been four years younger than David. She had survived him and was by now without influence, merely a wisp of a women—though still with her fine face and straight carriage. Moreover, she had to reckon with one much younger and still beautiful in Bathsheba.

The first hint I had of Michal's scheming against Solomon came from Benaiah. He approached me one morning in my chambers as I was at work on the tallies of tribute from Israel. "Do I interrupt?" he inquired in his hoarse half-sneering soldier's voice.

"Not if it is business of state," I said, setting the notched sticks aside. Benaiah nodded and mopped his face: he sweated much. His clothes always held this pungence. He looked about him and addressed me in a lower tone.

"You should know, Nathan," Benaiah said, "that Michal plots against the king."

I felt a tingle of surprise. "That fantastic old woman?" I inquired.

"Fantastic or not, she would see him dead rather than on the throne."

"Why?" I was suspicious of such volunteered information.

"Solomon is the son of Bathsheba and David—not of Michal and David."

"At her age, she still holds such madness?" I asked incredulously.

Benaiah shrugged. "She should be watched," he said.

"Have you proof?"

"My spies say so," Benaiah returned, "and I believe them."

"You have spies?" I asked, frowning.

"Everyone at court has them," Benaiah grinned, "even the prophet."

My face grew hot. "I know nothing against Michal," I said curtly. "Someone must be king. Who else does she count worthy? Surely not Meribbaal?" I said. This I thought shrewd because the idea had been in my mind before, though I knew Meribbaal was elderly and cautious, dwelling in the country outside the city, careful of his friends, and watched by Solomon's informants.

"No," Benaiah said. He hesitated a beat. "Myself," he said.

I could not help myself. I burst out in laughter, rocking in my place. "You!" I cried. "You, a king?"

Benaiah stared coldly at me, his face impassive. "Soldiers have been kings before," he reminded me.

"A king needs more than courage," I said contemptuously. "He needs wisdom and faith and—" I broke off and held up the sheet on which I was ciphering. "Read me this," I said.

Benaiah did not glance at it. "Kings may hire others to do such things," he said. "But I laughed as you do at such a proposal."

"Why do you come to tell me of it?" I demanded.

"Because she herself may come to you and accuse me of plots," Benaiah responded. "I have no wish to see my head impaled over the Dung Gate."

I nodded. "That was wise of you," I said. Benaiah nodded abruptly. "Bear me witness that I have done my duty," he said. He wheeled about; his stocky figure shadowed the sunlight in the doorway and vanished.

I gazed after him in irritation. My fingers rolled the pen between them as I pondered. Plainly it was time to determine what Michal had been doing—but to say the truth, I somehow suspected Benaiah more. I decided to see Bathsheba for advice.

Unfortunately, I was handicapped by lack of time. My duties had increased enormously under Solomon. He had placed upon my shoulders overmuch of the duties of state. Zadok had gained his son, Azariah, to help him in the priestly functions. I had my own twenty-four-year-old son, also named Azariah, and a second son, Zabud (whose mother of Judah had died giving him birth). Solomon, at my request, made Azariah chief of the court officers but he favored seventeen-year-old Zabud—as being his own age and his companion in love with all that was gorgeous and luxurious—so far as to place him at his side and call him the king's friend.

I had requested of Solomon that Ahiah, second son of Shisha, be added to Elihaph, and the pair be ranked as herald and recorder, even as Ahishar was over the household and Adoniram was responsible for the collecting of tribute and the treasury. Such an arrangement left me more occasion to be the king's counselor. I could also devote time to meditation and prayer, even though the king would not allow me to assign to another the duty of preparing the official history of his reign, the Acts of Solomon. I did not complain: such a post left me in a position to know all that was going on as a matter of royal command.

The household of Solomon and his court had swelled enormously. David before him had lived simply, unostentatiously. His son made his estate nearly as magnificent as that of a king of Egypt. It is only necessary to point out that the royal entourage devoured each day thirty measures of fine flour and double that of meal; ten fattened oxen, twenty more lean from the pastures and a hundred sheep, besides numerous deer and fat fowl.

Despite this rich palace living, however, none of the Hebrews complained. The land was at peace from Tiphsah to Azzah, from Dan to Beersheba (and even south of that city). All of both Judah and Israel lived every man under his vine and fig tree and their children multiplied, as Yahweh had promised, like the sands of the sea. It was not until three months after Benaiah's visit that the crisis about Michal came about. It was Bathsheba this time, emboldened by her successes, the most powerful influence in the court—if the most shadowy—whose spies brought it to a head.

The occasion came with shocking suddenness. The governor of Edom reported by swift courier that his domain had been raided out of the west by a band of unknown brigands out of Egypt. They had killed a dozen Hebrew overseers. They had set free more than a hundred Edomite slaves. Benaiah immediately sent five hundred men into the south but they came back hangdog without as much as a skirmish with the raiders.

Bathsheba called me into her presence. I entered her private room at the palace, hung with tapestries and well-enough furnished as to be next only to the king's apartments. Even in the dim light from the high square windows the colors blinded the eye: bright yellows, crimsons, purples were everywhere. Prominent among all the rest was a splendid Egyptian jar of transparent alabaster—Bathsheba's favorite possession. It was cunningly wrought, carved with heathen figures, a water clock that dripped out the hours according to the days from sundown to sundown. Bathsheba regulated her whole life by this device.

"I have sent for you, Nathan," she said without preliminary, "because the king's power has been challenged in Edom."

I spread my hands. "This is not my affair," I said. "Its responsibility is that of the governor, of Benaiah."

"But whence does it come?"

"Who knows?"

"I know," Bathsheba said severely from her brazen stool. "I have information"—she never identified her sources further than that—"of the return of Hadad, the prince of Edom, from Egypt. He has prospered there. His son Genubath lives in the pharaoh's household, among the royal children."

My interest quickened. "Did he send the marauders?" I inquired. Perhaps he was sponsored by Michal, I thought.

"He led them," Bathsheba replied. "When he heard that David and Joab were dead, he besought the pharaoh, 'Let me depart that I may go into my own country again.' "

"The king of Egypt permitted him?" I asked, surprised.

"He said: 'What have you lacked here, Hadad, that you want to go back to Edom?' To which Hadad returned: 'Nothing, O great pharaoh, but my heart is sick for my own and I wish to depart.' "

"How do you know what they said?" I demanded.

Bathsheba shrugged daintily. "I know what I know," she said evasively. "What I guess is more important. The death of David, of course, was known to all the world. But how did Hadad hear of Joab meeting his end?"

I stroked my beard reflectively. "I cannot tell," I said. "His head was buried in Hinnom, his body in the wilderness, both by night. Solomon ordered Benaiah that all be done secretly in order that the name of Joab might still strike terror into our enemies."

"There must be someone in the palace," Bathsheba said decisively, "who is an agent of Egypt."

"Perhaps Benaiah unwittingly said something," I murmured. I was surprised at the slight flush which rose to Bathsheba's face. "No," she told me, "Benaiah is loyal."

"Then I do not know where such a person might be found."

"If you have no suspicions," Bathsheba said, "I do. That is why I have ordered you here."

"Myself?" I was aghast.

Bathsheba looked lazily up—she seemed to be always looking up at men. She smiled like a cat. "Sometimes, Nathan," she said, "I think that the priest who circumcized you must have cut off a bit too much."

"You have no shame to say that," I mumbled. "You do not understand me."

Bathsheba laughed in her light, silvery way. "Yes, good Nathan," she said. "You are always predictable, always on the side of peace and good will, always faithful. Sometimes one might wish you were otherwise but that is impossible. No, I mean another. I have asked you here to be a witness."

"What need have you of that?" I asked.

"My son does not entirely trust women," Bathsheba said. "He believes his prophet Nathan more." She paused as the guard came in and whispered to her. She nodded and dismissed him. "Behind that screen," she said authoritatively, pointing to a corner alcove covered by wool curtains. "Wait. You shall hear."

I repressed my irritation at being used in this fashion—perhaps because of my own curiosity—and obeyed. Behind the curtains, sitting on my haunches and clasping my knees, I waited. For minutes, only the drip-drop of the water clock sounded in the room. Finally I heard someone enter.

"Welcome, Michal," Bathsheba said loudly.

"You have wished me to come here but I do not know the reason," responded the high-pitched voice of the old woman. I sat still, frozen by speculation and wonder. I dared not interfere. Bathsheba might be head of the women of Solomon as queen mother but Michal still held great respect as the first wife of David.

"Between us," Bathsheba said comfortably, "we have managed to confuse poor Solomon."

"I have not spoken to the king."

"It is not necessary. Your presence reminds him of the wisdom of David."

"I agree," Michal said dryly, "that our king does not yet know his head from his feet. Is that why you have summoned me?"

"I wish to take advantage of your knowledge. We women know truths and hear news that men cannot know."

"More than that," Michal said. "Their honor, the honor of the Hebrew people, is in the hands of women, is it not?"

"Yes," Bathsheba said. "We are the ones who guard it, who avenge it. We will nurse it, pass it along with our children's milk, wait for the moment and spy and report—we will even kill for it. Where most men draw back, we are merciless."

"We have no thought for ourselves," Michal said composedly. "We will even go fearlessly to death—or triumph like Jael driving the nail through the head of sleeping Sisera."

"Even so. I have counseled Solomon on many things but a wiser, older head is needed. I thought of you, Michal."

Michal gave a grunt of surprise. "We should quarrel over many things," she said.

"That is the way of men, not women. We can never really quarrel among ourselves about a man unless it is a question of love."

"And we are both past the age for love, are we not, Bathsheba?" asked Michal maliciously.

Bathsheba gave a nervous laugh. "Certainly," she said.

"Do you seriously propose me to advise your son?"

"To help me."

"Why?"

"The people remember David," Bathsheba said, "and you are the daughter of Saul."

"Who pays attention to the common herd and what they wish?" said Michal haughtily.

"As to that, when the wives of kings place themselves too far above the herd, the herd tears them to pieces." Bathsheba's voice turned sharper. "Shall we tell each other all, Michal, swearing by the ark of Moses?"

"By all means."

"All?"

"Is that not enough?" asked Michal mordantly.

I heard the scrape of Bathsheba's stool being drawn nearer to Michal. "Then I can say that I never loved David, Solomon's father," she murmured, to my bewilderment. "The man I loved was not a foolish singer of songs and maker of verse. He was a man of war, strong and tall and great. He was Uriah the Hittite."

"Yet David was a mighty man of war," said Michal.

"Who fled from Absalom and let Joab fight his battles."

"Then why did you come to his chamber?"

"One was a king, the other a captain."

"How could you betray your lawful lord?"

"After all," Bathsheba said, "I was Hittite, not Hebrew. The Tables of the Law did not bind me."

"But they bound David!" cried Michal, the rasp of passion in her voice.

Evidently Bathsheba found herself in a position she did not

relish. I grinned to myself. When she spoke next it was in an altered businesslike tone.

"I summoned you," she said coldly, "because I have heard that Hadad, prince of Edom, recently raided the southern part of my son's kingdom."

Michal hesitated almost imperceptibly. "I did not hear of it," she said.

"You must have known that Solomon sent Benaiah and his men south," said Bathsheba in exasperation.

"Everyone knows that but not the reason. Raiders, yes; I am surprised at their leader." Michal spoke carefully, choosing her words. I became alert to her change of tone.

"Somehow Hadad heard that Joab was dead. It prompted him to dare this thing." Bathsheba was persistent.

"Do you think so?"

"It is the only thought possible. But how did he know of Joab's death unless someone in the palace told him?"

"I cannot tell you," Michal returned coldly. At that moment I knew her for a traitress and forgot my suspicions of Benaiah.

There was a noise I could not identify in the room; then I heard the exultant voice of Solomon. "Mother, mother Bathsheba!" he cried. His tone changed. "Greetings, wife of David," he said formally.

"Greetings, O king," Michal's voice said with perfect dignity. "Have I permission to retire?"

"If you wish," Solomon said slowly. There was an interval and heavy breathings, the sound of shuffling. As they died away, I heard Solomon speak to Bathsheba in tight accents.

"What was Michal doing here?" he demanded.

"Be not angry, my son," Bathsheba said calmly. "Two women together, having a chat about woman things."

"What do you conceal from me?"

"Nothing, my son."

"You know she hates me."

"I know. I shall not forget your welfare. But from where have you returned?"

The jubilant note crept into Solomon's voice again. "I have been again to Gibeon," he said rapturously, "to the high place. I spent the night there alone. Yahweh sent me a dream." There was no mistaking the ecstasy of his words.

"What did He say?" Bathsheba's tones were unmistakably skeptical.

"He asked me that which I desired of Him as a gift."

"Did He, indeed? That was good of Him."

"Do you know what I asked for, my mother?"

"No. Riches, honor, wives, land? No, I cannot imagine."

"None of these things," Solomon responded. "I said that the Lord had showed David, my father, great mercy. He had walked before the Most High in truth and righteousness and Yahweh had blessed him by allowing the throne to come to me."

"You did not answer the question."

"Patience. I said to the Lord in my dream that He had made me His servant as king but that I was still a little child, not knowing even how to go in or come out in the midst of the multitude of my people."

"You were unnecessarily modest, my son."

"Give me, therefore, I said to Him," Solomon said, his voice assuming an unwonted dignity, "an understanding heart to rule my people so that I may judge between good and evil."

"I see," Bathsheba said. "What was the response?"

"Yahweh was pleased that I had not asked for riches or long life or revenge on my enemies. He told me that He would bestow upon me wisdom so that there shall be none like me before or to come."

"Is that all?" demanded Bathsheba.

"No, my mother. Because of my prayer, the Lord promised me both riches and honor above all other kings. He said that if I kept His commandments my days should be long."

Bathsheba was silent. Solomon addressed her anxiously: "I rejoice; do you rejoice as well?"

"I rejoice," Bathsheba said in a strange tone.

"Very well," Solomon said. "I shall go before the ark of the covenant of the Lord and offer up burnt offerings and peace offerings and make a feast to all my household."

"Wait," Bathsheba said. "What did Yahweh look like?"

"Hands," Solomon said vaguely. "Hands and a beard. A white robe, a voice that sounded in the depths of my ear."

"His face?"

"I never saw it."

"His voice?"

"A thousand harps murmuring."

"And the rest?"

"His robe and His beard were like those of my father David. But his hands—"

"Yes?"

"His hands were like yours, my mother."

I heard him go. There was silence for a long moment. I stepped cautiously from behind the screen. To my surprise, I found Bathsheba still on her stool, bent over and heaving with emotion. I placed my hand on her shoulder in sympathy. She straightened and looked me in the face.

To my amazement, she was not sobbing. She was laughing.

There are three things too wonderful for me to understand; yes, four that are full of mystery. They are the way of an eagle in the air, a ship in the sea, a serpent on the rock, and a man with a woman. But more wonderful than all these is the way of a son with his mother. I say this for the reason that no more than a week later, Solomon desired me to attend him in private. I had no sooner got past Benaiah, who always slept across the door to the king's apartments, than Solomon began.

"I must have faithful men about me," he said.

I bowed. "None is more faithful than your servant Nathan," I replied.

"But is he loyal to the king—or to his mother?" demanded Solomon.

The question caught me so much unaware that I came near stammering. But I found what I hoped was a sufficient escape. "I am loyal to the will of Yahweh," I said.

Solomon—who had sprung up surprisingly from a stripling these past four years—tall, well-bearded, with much dignity in his demeanor—swirled his scarlet robe around him impatiently. "What does that mean?" he wanted to know. "My will on earth is the will of the Lord in heaven!"

I drew a deep breath. Here was a monarch bursting into the full knowledge of his power! "So it is," I said humbly, "unless it is revealed otherwise to me."

Solomon smiled. It was one of his characteristically winning changes of mood, a quick, frank expression. "As long as it is not Ashtoreth in the person of Bathsheba," he said.

"What do you know of Ashtoreth?" I cried, scandalized.

"I have studied many gods," Solomon said carelessly. "Before us there were many in this land; after us, there will be many more."

"You speak too much like your mother. There is One, and His name, blessed be it, is Yahweh!"

"Is that the name which Zadok whispers once a year in secret in the most holy place?" inquired Solomon. He laughed. "You are a comely prophet," he said approvingly, "and my mother has a taste for men with a spiritual face and a handsome figure."

I did not know what to say. Solomon went on, disregarding my silence. "She is inclined to interfere with my affairs," he said, "and this cannot be permitted. You shall be my man or hers. Speak, O Nathan!"

"I am your servant," I muttered. "Yours."

"Very well. Then do not in future eavesdrop behind the curtains in her rooms—especially when I can see your sandals beneath them. But enough: I take you at your word. I wish to speak of something else. The time is come to build the temple that I promised my father David. I know that you were against the building of the tabernacle in his day. Are you against my temple, too?"

"It is the command of the Lord," I said, my head giddy with the overknowledge revealed by Solomon. "As He said, so it must be done."

"Good," Solomon said briskly. From beside his throne he took up two rolls of papyrus. "As you know, I sent a message to Hiram of Tyre when he succeeded his father on the throne."

"Yes."

"What you do not know—for I commanded Elihaph, on the pain of death to keep it secret—was that he responded. That the correspondence has continued. Here are the last two messages. I know their content but I wish them read aloud to me again to be sure."

I spread the papyrus wide between my trembling hands. I read aloud, striving to keep any tremor out of my voice:

" 'To Hiram, lord of the kingdom of Tyre, thus from his friend, Solomon, king of the Hebrews. You know how David, my father, could not build a house for Yahweh because of the wars which compassed him about. Now the wars are over. There is peace, his enemies are under the soles of my feet. The Lord has given me rest on every side, there is neither adversary nor evil. Behold, I now propose to build such a house. Therefore command that cedars be cut upon Lebanon. You know that among my people there is none with skill to hew such timber. My servants shall work with your servants, and I will give hire for your people as you shall request. Let the lord Hiram not turn his face from me.' "

Solomon nodded as I finished reading. I opened the second scroll. I was able to decipher the Phoenician writing easily:

" 'To Solomon, lord of the kingdom of Hebrews, thus from his friend Hiram. May your kingdom endure as long as heaven and earth. I have considered what you have asked of me. I will do your desire, not only in cedar but fir also. My servants shall bring them down from Lebanon to the sea and my ships shall take them to the place on the coast that you shall appoint to receive them. In return, fulfill my desire for food for my household and add to my servants those of your own. Let the lord Solomon desire no other friend but myself.' "

I looked at Solomon in surprise. "This is a mighty agreement," I said. "What must be done to fulfill it?"

"That is why I have summoned you," Solomon told me. "We shall give to Hiram twenty thousand measures of wheat and twenty measures of oil a year for his sustenance."

"Our land flourishes," I admitted. "All this may be done."

Solomon came closer to me; I could smell faint incense upon his robes. "The rest is more hazardous," he said in a lower tone. "I shall need many workers from our people."

"To be sent to the mountains of Phoenicia?"

"Yes."

"That will be difficult," I said uneasily. "Our people are satisfied with the land of their fathers, and each has enough to supply his needs."

"Yet you know what I have agreed with Hiram," Solomon replied, throwing back his head haughtily.

"Perhaps a thousand," I said dubiously.

"A thousand! I shall require thirty thousand to go to Lebanon alone!"

I was thunderstruck. "So many will never consent," I told the young king.

"I am Solomon," he said coldly. "I shall not ask, I shall command." He looked at me calculatingly. "Besides," he said, "the work is not for me but for the Lord."

"Perhaps it may be done," I answered, reluctant.

"And I shall require thousands more to bear burdens and to cut stone in our mountains."

"Who will be in charge of this?" I asked in a low tone. "Surely he will be the most hated of the Hebrews."

"It is tribute," Solomon said. "For such a task, Adoniram is fit. First, however, he shall find three thousand and more overseers among our people. You must help him. All of the palace staff—except perhaps Zabud—shall join in the work. We shall begin this spring, in the month of Zif."

"Let the lord, my king, then warn Benaiah to increase his troops before that time," I said. "For there will be murmurings and cursings and perhaps impious hands raised against the crown."

Solomon again smiled in his boyish way. He was getting what he desired. He believed he had foreseen all obstacles. "That is a clever suggestion," he replied, "and I have already spoken to Benaiah. I have commanded him to fortify the strongholds and to fence the cities with stone. He will put his best captains in them and store of victuals with oil and wine; every city shall have its armory of slings, swords, and shields."

"But in whom shall the king put the trust of his arms?"

Solomon nodded. "Your mind accords with mine own," he agreed. "Those who labor shall be those who are left of the Amorites, Hittites, Perizzites, Hivites, Jebusites, and other subject tribes. On those we have conquered shall be put a tribute of bond servants. And the rest shall come from the northern tribes of Israel, to work for Solomon and Yahweh."

"Your own people?" I asked, incredulous.

"They mutter and talk of revolt," Solomon said. "I shall give their idle hands work to do for years."

"And the soldiers?"

"They shall be herded like sheep by the children of Judah who shall be my men of war, my princes and servants and captains and charioteers. We shall see who is most powerful!"

I bowed myself humbly before him. I did not dare express my thoughts: Yahweh had given me no revelation upon this matter. Until such a time my lips were sealed. Yet I seemed to see the Hebrews divided and quarreling, the old wounds which David had partially healed rent wide open again.

Solomon assumed my silence to be consent. "Of course," he added, "the men of Hiram shall come into our country and do the trimming of stone and the building and the casting and fine work of the metals. It is all arranged. Hiram has even offered to contribute of his substance. He is a neighbor with whom we need not quarrel. He and I are of an age and like mind."

"I assume Hiram sent gifts with his message," I said.

Solomon made an impatient gesture. "Some gold, some curious trifles that I commanded Adoniram to convey to the treasury," he replied. Then his face lighted up. "He sent something even better," he added.

"Better than fine gold?"

"Listen, Nathan. If I had a statue for which I gave half the gold, you gave one eighth, Zadok one tenth, and, shall we say, Bathsheba gave one twentieth. But the rest, nine talents, was the gift of the craftsman in metal. How many talents would be in the statue?"

"Did Hiram send such a statue?" I exclaimed. "Magnificent!"

Solomon flung his arms in the air. "No, no!" he cried in disgust. "This is a riddle!"

"It has no other meaning?"

"A riddle is the speech of gods from the ancient days," said Solomon severely.

"Then I do not care to understand it," I replied.

Solomon spoke carefully, as if dictating to a child. "It is not meant for sacrilege," he said. "It is to create quickness of thought, to exercise the brain, to consider a problem from every point of view. Riddles delight the thoughtful, such as myself."

I said nothing. "How many talents in the statue?" persisted Solomon. I shook my head.

"I have already sent the answer to Hiram," responded Solomon, as pleased as if he had solved a problem of state. "It is forty. Twenty and five and four and two and nine. Do you see?"

"I see you have been taught your numbers well," I answered.

"I wish sometimes I had learned to read," Solomon said pensively, "but numbering things is more important. Do you know the riddle I sent back to Hiram?"

"No," I said.

"It is a riddle from Egypt. I have wagered ten minae that Hiram cannot answer it. It goes thus: If I say 'I lie' and so tell the truth, I lie. If I say 'I lie' and so tell a lie, I tell the truth. How do you answer that, Nathan?"

"I don't know," I said.

"You see? Hiram will not know that answer either."

"What is the answer?" I asked.

Solomon furrowed his brow. "I don't know," he confessed. "It will be worth ten minae to find out."

In one of those instant changes of thought which always marked him, Solomon did not wait for me to respond. Instead, he said severely: "You, Nathan, heard my dream from Yahweh that I told Bathsheba, did you not?"

"Yes, O king," I said.

"Do you think it true?"

"Time must tell," I said evasively.

Solomon glanced sharply at me. "Did you hear what my mother and Michal spoke about?"

I bowed my head in assent.

"What was it?"

I could not help myself. I was under the yoke of the king and had no choice but to respond to the goad. Thereupon I recited all that Bathsheba had said and how Michal had replied. A slight growing frown settled on Solomon's forehead.

"Do you believe Michal is a spy for the Edomites?" he demanded.

"I have no knowledge of it," I said honestly.

"My mother meddles too much," Solomon said slowly. "We shall have to mend that."

Then, abruptly, he said: "Find old Abiathar. Secure the plans for the temple which my father entrusted to his keeping."

"I hear and I obey," I said.

But I did not go directly to seek out Abiathar. I knew he had permission to come into Jerusalem from Anathoth, that he would be somewhere in his usual haunts. Instead, I went first to visit Elihaph. I went directly to where I knew he must be, since he spent most of his time scribbling in his cubicle just inside the palace gates. He was, as I expected, crouched over his papyrus, tongue protruding, carefully writing the characters from right to left, wig over his shaved head awry, his hunched back more prominent than ever. He was so concentrated on his work that I had to nudge him with my foot to gain attention.

He sprang to his feet and made obeisance. I motioned to him to sit. He sank down, his face frightened. "I can see you are angry," he said propitiatingly, "but I do not know why."

"You are paid by the palace," I said, "but you are also paid by me to let me know what happens here. Not for my own pleasure, you understand, but for the Acts of Solomon."

"I have told you all."

"All? Of the correspondence between Hiram and our king?"

Elihaph shrank from me, full of fear. "I could not," he whispered. "Solomon commanded me to carry it in my bosom only."

"This post you hold," I said crisply, "is by my will and my recommendation. I am the mouth of the king, his tongue, his head; I speak as the king. If I speak to Solomon, I can destroy your living. Your father Shisha shall suffer as well, old as he is. Do you understand?"

"I understand."

"I wish to know everything. Everything!"

"Yes." Elihaph genuflected profoundly.

"Else how may I protect Solomon from his youth?" I asked in an altered tone.

"Of course."

I made a motion of dismissal. "That is all," I said, "except for one thing. What is this madness of the king's for riddles?"

"He is very fond of them. He likes to think upon them and devise his answers. He says it passes his time so quickly that he never thinks upon the throne and, besides, they make Zabud laugh."

I bent my head. "Between us," I said, "what is this riddle he sent to Hiram about lies and the truth?"

An impish grin split the thick lips of Elihaph. "I gave him that myself," he said proudly. "And I have others. In Egypt, so my father tells me, the sphinx itself does not consider riddles below its dignity—it is famous for them."

I repeated the riddle slowly, Elihaph nodding. "The king has an excellent memory," he said.

"What is the answer?" I demanded.

Elihaph shrugged. "It is nonsense, a play upon words," he said. "The meaning of the same words changes as it is used differently."

"Then there is no answer?"

"None except that which satisfies the most subtle minds."

I nodded and left him. In spite of his reassurances, I was not sure that Elihaph had told me the truth. Still, I was not sure he had lied. The strange similarities between truths and lies bothered me from that time forth—all the more because it seemed that there was no answer to the twisting of the mind.

After throwing the fear of Yahweh into Elihaph, I visited the enclosure of the tabernacle. Again I made no mistake: there, huddled in the morning sunlight, I found the wretched Abiathar.

I approached this filthy, ordure-stinking old man—who had once been one of the most powerful in the kingdom—with some vestiges of respect. Certainly with caution, from the windward side.

"Abiathar," I said tentatively.

From his squatting position, he turned his bleared eyes toward me. For a moment, he did not recognize who it was.

Then he climbed to his feet, swaying as he stood. "Yes, noble Nathan?" he whispered.

"I come to the command of King Solomon," I said, wishing to make my visit as brief as possible. "He wishes you to surrender the plans of the temple which his father David entrusted to you."

"The plans?"

"You are ordered to give them to me—on pain of death if you refuse."

"The plans of the temple?" asked Abiathar vacantly. Slowly his face began to brighten. "Solomon wants them?" he asked, increasingly animated. "He wants them at last?"

"Yes."

"You may have them, of course." His expression changed on the words, to one of sorrow.

"Where are they?"

To my mystification, he did not respond. Instead, he commenced to twirl slowly like one of the mad pretended prophets of the flocks who feed in the desert. As he turned, he sang a little wordless tune to himself, a mournful chant. He opened his ragged garments one by one until his scrawny body stood exposed to the sunlight.

"You see," he said simply, "I have always had the sacred plans of the temple with me."

I blinked. I saw that around his body from neck to thigh was a double thickness of split sheepskin: dirty, sweat-spotted, louse-ridden but still soft and flexible.

"These?" I asked incredulously. Abiathar nodded. Slowly he untied the thong that bound the sheepskins. With shaking hands, he rolled them up and gave them to me, a pitiable, unclad figure in the sunlight. I could not take my eyes away from this little man who stood so alone.

"I have taken good care of them," he said. "You will take good care of them?"

"The king will take care of them," I said falling unconsciously into his idiot rhythms.

Abiathar nodded. His eyes dimmed. Without warning, as if his bones had loosened one from the other, he collapsed in a heap. He lay like a pile of old rags, his head twisted, staring sightlessly at the sun.

I bent over him, then drew back. Abiathar was dead. He had handed over his trust, the only thing which had kept him alive for so long. Now he lay before me like an old dog that, faithful to the last, dies because it has no longer any reason to live.

CHAPTER FIVE

The Cleverness of Solomon

One afternoon, months later, walking down one of the dusty hot streets by the old palace of David, now Solomon's residence, my thought was interrupted. A choked hail, I half turned: a fat old man, limping on a twisted foot, came struggling up to me. He was clad in a knee-length tunic of violent blue, a tasseled girdle of yellow; a cloak with red fringes flapped from his shoulders. Except for a sweatband, his white head was bare to the sun. His inflamed face appeared about to burst.

"Nathan!" he burbled. He clasped me about the shoulders. He hopped up and down. "Nathan! You know me, of course!"

Offended, I thrust him back, holding him at arm's length. But his cackling voice aroused memories. I recognized him. Older, chapfallen, but still the same Merib-baal, son of Jonathan, the same one who had tried and schemed so many times to snatch the throne from David. David had forgiven his treacheries on innumerable occasions. He had even restored to Merib-baal the lands of his grandfather, on account of the love he had borne Jonathan.

"I have not seen you for years," I said stiffly. Seeing him in the city instantly roused my dormant suspicions of a plot against Solomon and the throne.

"You were a youngster then, now you are grown. You will understand many things hidden to you before," responded the panting old man. "I saw you passing, I decided to confess to you."

"What can I do for you?"

"Much," gasped Merib-baal. He took my arm again, looking pleadingly up into my face, fondling my robe with both hands. "You know I have always thought of you, spoken of you to others as one of the great prophets of the Lord."

"Much thanks," I murmured.

"I have never raised my voice, as you know, Nathan,

despite the fact that I am of the stock and bloodline of Saul, when Solomon was lifted to the throne."

"I know that. It was excellent judgment on your part."

Merib-baal glanced fearfully around him, then sprang on me again, his fleshy arms folding me tightly. "We must find a place to talk!" he whispered in my ear. "I must tell you that I will have nothing to do with it!"

"With what?" I demanded, struggling to free myself from his insensate grip. "What do you mean?"

He gave me no answer at all. His body quivered; I heard whistling, sucking sounds. Merib-baal slumped down to his knees, his arms slackening. I stepped back. He slid lower, softly thudding onto his face in the dust.

To my horror, I saw his back had flowered three arrows. They stood half buried in his gay cloak. I dropped to all fours beside him to see if aid was possible: there was none to be given. Merib-baal gurgled blood, his distended eyes already fixed in death.

I heard running footsteps padding quickly toward us. I jerked myself erect. To my bewilderment, I saw it was the stocky, bowlegged form of Benaiah, chief of Solomon's armies and his personal guard. He carried his drawn sword.

Benaiah stopped beside the prone-sprawled figure of Merib-baal. He observed it with a cold, professional eye, prodding it lightly with his sword point. "Dead," he said flatly, an expert opinion.

"Yes," I said, still numb.

"I'm glad I was in time," Benaiah said.

I recovered myself a little. "These arrows bear the serpent device of the palace guard," I said shakily.

Benaiah grinned and nodded. "I saw him running after you," he said. "I saw him try to kill you. So I gave the order."

"What!"

"My gate-watchers warned me Merib-baal had come in. I had him followed. I saw him from the palace wall. He followed you, peering from side to side. I saw him spring on you; I saw you repulse him, I saw him spring on you again. So I signaled the archers."

"He was the grandson of Saul, the king," I said. "You were quite mistaken. He was not attacking me. He had a petition to make."

Benaiah whistled and grunted. He turned the arrow-propped body over with his sandal. A bronze arrowhead shoved through. Benaiah grimaced. "As you say," he agreed carelessly. "His children will be glad of his inheritance. These mistakes happen but it is my duty to protect the palace household in these times." He looked at me, his black eyes boring into mine. "What did Merib-baal tell you?"

"Nothing," I said. "He died before he had a chance to finish speaking."

"Too bad," Benaiah said. He beckoned a couple of his men to take up the body.

"Merib-baal was always unlucky," Benaiah said. He grinned at me again and sheathed his sword. "As for you, prophet Nathan," he added, "you are always lucky. I shall report this immediately to the king."

"You might have killed me as well," I said.

Benaiah shrugged and turned away. "Possibly," he said, "but my men are better marksmen that that."

Without another word, I watched them depart with what remained of Merib-baal sagging between them. I wished to say no more, though my bosom was burning. I sensed a warning in Benaiah's words—one that was hostile to myself. I could not tell the reason. I did not believe that this death had been an accident. Suddenly I wanted desperately for the ghost of Merib-baal to appear before me, to say what he had been forced to leave unsaid.

More than that, I felt an assurance and swagger in Benaiah that I had not noted before in the stalwart little commander. I wondered what his cryptic replies meant—and what Merib-baal had wanted to disown.

My suspicions grew as I paced on down the street. The nerves in my back prickled in the expectation of an attempt on my own life. That night I formed a plan of inquiry, and the next day I set out without telling anyone my purpose or destination.

What I discovered was confirmation of my fears. All the other sons of David had suffered strange fates. Daniel had died of a fall from the rocks by the Water Gate; Ithream had expired in agonies after devouring a pottage of herbs into which someone, apparently by mistake, had slipped some beans of the purple-spotted poison plant which grows by the inland streams and kills many sheep each year. Shephetiah had fled from Jerusalem and vanished into the north, first into Dan and then probably into the teeming city of Sidon in Phoenicia.

Most curious of all, though Benaiah must have told Solomon of the death of Merib-baal, it was not mentioned to me ever after. I went to Bathsheba with the tale—knowing her to be the mistress of all intrigues about the court. To my perplexity, I found she seemed genuinely ignorant of what had happened to David's sons yet was openly cool about the death of Merib-baal.

"He deserved to die many times before this," she said.

"Vengeance is mine, says Yahweh," I told her.

Her lip curled. "That was a saying of David," she said, "but you must have realized he did not practice what he sang."

"Shall Benaiah escape unscathed, having shed royal blood?" I demanded.

"He did it to save your life," Bathsheba responded. "Will you accuse him before the king?"

Her question silenced me. I did not believe it but there was nothing else for me to say. I began to perceive dimly that there were not one but many webs of intrigue spinning within Solomon's court. If Michal plotted, so did Bathsheba; so, too, perhaps did Benaiah. Above all, possibly Solomon himself, who might be taking all into his own hands. There might even be others of whom I knew nothing. I determined to see Elihaph immediately. I would order him to redouble his efforts to seek out hidden motives and acts—and promise an increase in my payments to his purse.

Bathsheba had regarded me during the interval with what seemed to be an expression of amused pity.

"When, dear Nathan," she asked, "will you remember what my son has said: 'When will the simpletons forsake their simplicity?' "

Her tone to me was altogether different than I had ever heard it before. My eyes filled with tears of rage. Luckily I held my tongue tightly between my teeth. I bowed. I hurried away. It was to be years before I stumbled on the real meaning of the death of Merib-baal.

All men know a king is buttressed about with the holiness of Yahweh. The dangers, which also encompass him, come from the desire of other men to achieve his power and sanctity. But few men have the ultimate secret—which is that the will of heaven is most truly embodied in the love of the people. Ignorant and unschooled, nevertheless their adoration of a sovereign rises instinctively from their hearts. Like incense, it embalms the acts of those such as David who rule over them.

It was David who first saw the righteousness of doing away with the tabernacle and erecting the temple. But it was

Solomon who reaped the benefits of this in the eyes of the Hebrew people—and in the teeth of their hatred of slavery and unrequited labor. It was Solomon (with my help and that of Zadok, I am proud to say) who imbued them with pride, with the idea that they offered themselves as living sacrifices to the Most High, with the joy of giving a monument to the future.

Excitement swept the whole country. It centered on Jerusalem. People too poor to contribute any of their substance gave themselves and their children into thralldom for the duration of building. Those of wealth brought in a total of five thousand talents and ten thousand drams of gold, ten thousand talents of silver, eighteen thousand talents of brass, and a hundred thousand talents of iron—plus, of course, countless jewels.

Negotiations with Hiram were concluded. Work commenced in the great forests of Lebanon, felling age-old cedars to be dragged to the shore and hauled—three huge trunks at a time—behind Phoenician biremes to one of our ports. Thence they were carted inland by oxen and by wain ropes manned by our people, to the foot of Mount Zion. At this spot, they were shaped and carved and finally hauled upward to be put into place.

The site had been selected by David, next to the famous rock of Araunah, exposed continuously to sun and rain, weather and wind. Here Solomon set about making a flat spot of nearly twenty acres—atop the sharp-spined ridge. He used cut stones which were sometimes as large as twenty feet long, ten feet wide, and seven feet thick. These took incredible effort to put into place—after they had been rubbed endlessly atop each other with oil, sand, and water between, smoothing them to make them fit tightly. They were laid in solidly, sited deep in the earth. They would grow to the soil and resist the wear of time.

The grand court of the Israelites was paved entirely with split slabs of limestone. This in turn was enclosed by a wall of three layers of hewn stones more than ten feet thick. To this was added a palisade of split cedar logs, planted upright to exclude not only the presence but even the cynosure of anyone except the chosen people of Yahweh.

During this preliminary work, naturally, the craftsmen of Hiram had arrived. Their head was an elderly, strong-faced and opinionated artist called Hiram-abi. He immediately set about planning the metalwork and decoration of the temple in concert with Solomon. His next step, odd as it seemed, was to find a plain of fine sand in the desert—but his reasons were good, as I soon comprehended. He expected to cast the works of molten metal in sand forms, then scrape and polish them down to their final form. How he was to do this was unknown to anyone at the time. His methods (which we later adopted) finally became clear to us as we watched him work with his crew of metal artificers.

The point of all this preparation, as Solomon explained to me, was to prepare the way to the Lord in quietness. "His house," he said impressively, "shall be a house of peace. Every stone shall be made ready before it is brought here. The wood shall be carved and the metal fashioned elsewhere. Neither the sound of hammer nor axe nor any tool shall be heard while it is building."

Materials poured in. Not only from Phoenicia (as we sent them their price of grain and oil) but from all over Solomon's kingdom. One district officer I may mention as especially commendable in his zeal. He was Ben-Deker, one of the tribe of Dan, in the north, overseer of that area at Both-shemesh. I should add that he was a cousin of David's son, Shephatiah, which might have had something to do with his energy to serve Solomon—and remove suspicion of kingly ambition from himself.

Enough of the preliminaries of the temple building. During this period, when his popularity was still in question and the wisdom promised him by Yahweh was still to appear, Solomon created his real reputation. He had ordered several somewhat reprehensible things (at the urging of Zabud, my son, I suspect), such as banning the use of purple murex cloth and employment of gold for any purpose except to ornament the throne or royal perquisites. Now he endeavored to overcome the feeling of his people that he was merely a luxury-loving wastrel. He devoted himself to quite another kind of pleasure.

Solomon was eighteen when the work on the temple began. He was twenty-five when it ended. During this interval of intriguing and building, he won himself the praise of all the Hebrews. Not only that: when the king was not watching or advising on the work—or consulting on the plans of his own palace-to-be—he paid assiduous attention to the demands of the tribes. He began to acquire his reputation for wisdom.

This fame of Solomon was justified, I say. But it was not the wisdom of which I approved; it was not the knowledge of

Yahweh without which all is dust and chaff. It was of the world. Solomon showed to all that he would not have wished it any other way. He reveled in his reputation. One could pay him no greater flattery (as many did) than to hail him as the "wisest man in the universe." It was true that it became him as a king; but not as the will of Yahweh.

In fine, I am sure that Solomon misinterpreted the mandate given him in his dream by Yahweh. It was all the more important to him because his cleverness delighted Bathsheba.

The penetration of Solomon in the many problems that came before him was wonderful. Never had a king so young proved so expert at unraveling the skein of human nature. Yet his decisions were, after all, no more than to satisfy the excitement of his mind which had been so heedless before. His problems with his people gave him a focus, an energy that was incredibly acute. Soon he had the reputation of being wiser than all men, his understanding exceeding that of all others, his largeness of heart being even as the sand that is on the edge of the sea. Among some sages, the name of Solomon for this quality exceeded the names of all in the past country—even the fabled wisdom of Egypt.

Here I may offer examples of his wisdom which raised him to such a pinnacle that Solomon became a byword for subtle and extraordinary intelligence. During the seven years of waiting for the temple to be finished—seven years stretching out as long as the weary time Jacob had labored for Rachel's hand—Solomon sat in the gold-and-crimson-hung hall of David, on his father's Egyptian throne. He was easy of access. Anyone with a complaint was sure to have a hearing from him. Not only because such was the tradition of David (in contrast to the gloomy seclusion and suspicion of Saul) but also because of Solomon's omnivorous curiosity. He was fascinated by people, particularly women. He could never hear enough of their strange wit, of their obscure processes of thought, of how and why they acted as they did. I confess all such feminine antics are still puzzles to me; but it was precisely because they were human riddles that they interested Solomon so much.

Take the famous case of the two widows. I grant that the incident is know now throughout the world—but at the time it was a study of merit. The women—widows of the lowest class—lived together in the same house. They had become pregnant at the same time, just before their soldier husbands were killed in the sally of Benaiah against the raid of Hadad in Edom. More than this I never learned of their past history.

The complaining one said she had been first delivered of her child, a son. Then, three days later, her companion had been delivered, also of a son. (If it had been a pair of girls, no such fuss would have been made about it.) The baby of the first woman had thrived but on the fourth day she found it dead beside her on her bed matting. But the child of the second woman was alive and healthy.

Thereupon both claimed the living child. The charge from the complainant alleged that the second woman had stolen her healthy offspring during the night while she slept and they were alone in their hut, substituting her own dead infant.

Solomon rightly divined that the key to the mother of the child was undoubtedly the test of true mother-love. The story generally given about by the common people is that the king ordered a sword, then commanded Benaiah to divide the living child between the two mothers. Upon this, one of them offered to surrender the child to the other if its life might be spared. The second woman was indifferent to the threat of slaughter. Therefore popular sentiment believed the first to be the true mother.

The real virtue of Solomon's wisdom here was that he was not satisfied with such appearances. He interviewed each woman separately and alone. I attended his questionings.

"Did you love your husband?" he asked the first.

"He was everything to me! Yes, O king!"

"Did he love you?"

"I was his food and drink, sun and shade."

"You were happy when you had his child?"

"I was overjoyed because it was his picture, because if he died it would be company for me."

Solomon dismissed the first woman and I ushered in the second. "Tell me," said the king, "did you love your husband?"

"He is dead now."

"But did you love him?"

"He was a Hebrew, I was an Ammonite. He ravished me—no, great Solomon, I did not love him."

"Were you happy with him?"

"Forgive me, O king, but I speak the truth. Never for a moment. I hated him."

"Then you hated his child?"

"No, why should I hate an innocent child? I loved it."

"Why?"

The second woman considered. "Because it was a child. Because it came from my womb."

Solomon dismissed her. With me in attendance, he returned to the throne room. There he announced his decision: the second woman should have the child to keep and cherish. The first should be given the choice of a husband, to be freed from among the captive Jebusites. Both, on pain of death, were to keep silent about the proceedings.

"How, wise Solomon," I inquired afterward, "did you arrive at the knowledge of which was the true mother?"

"No one will ever know that," Solomon replied. "None except the one who made the exchange—if such there was—and her lips will be forever locked. The problem is the child. Not the mother's possession. Which will make a better man of him—she who dotes on him as the image of her dead husband or she who loves the child for itself?"

I felt impelled to ask one more question. "Tell me," I said humbly, "would you have actually cut the child in two if neither—or both—had desired it?"

Solomon thought a moment. "Why not?" he asked me at last. "Did not Yahweh demand Abraham sacrifice his own son before He would come to a decision?"

This, of course, was wisdom. But it could never be told in such a way, if it was to be acceptable to the minds of the simple people. They understood it differently—and it was probably just as well.

There were other, no less subtle decisions of Solomon during these years. Some that he handed down were merely clever, some were outright flattery. I recall when he was faced with a dispute between two women, twin sisters, who had raised a mighty ado over which was the fairer. Solomon smiled winningly and told them: "Each of you is more beautiful than the other." It was no answer at all but in some mysterious way it satisfied both. Another was the case of the pair of sons who quarreled over the division of their dead father's estate. Said Solomon to one: "You shall divide the estate as equally as possible—and your brother shall have his choice of either portion." He disposed of the complaint between two good friends—who had somehow become deadly enemies, as often happens—by forcing both to work on opposite sides of a wall. This continued for a month, each seeing the other all day and, in much less than the time of their sentence, they were friends again. Solomon explained it to me: "They both resented my decree. This common hostility gave them a common basis to renew their ties."

There were also occasions when Solomon displayed a less superficial knowledge of his subjects. Ezekiel, one of the leading men of the tribe of Benjamin, came to Jerusalem to complain that he was being systematically robbed. He had no idea of who the culprit might be—but his own observations had satisfied him that it must be one of his household. Solomon ordered him to bring all his servants into his presence. At the same time, he commanded five measures of finely ground corn to be sanctified for three days in the holy place.

On the appointed day, Solomon lined up Ezekiel's slaves in the throne room. It was at an hour when the sun slanted sharply along the kneeling line of frightened men and women. He told them sternly that the grain had been blessed. He gave each a double handful to stuff into their mouths simultaneously, to chew and swallow. While this was going on, Solomon descended in a leisurely fashion from the throne and examined the line closely. After a few moments, he stopped before one fellow who was chewing frantically and pointed. "You are the man," he said flatly. To my astonishment, the slave fell on his face and confessed.

"Yahweh has decreed a conscience for each man," Solomon told me afterward. "The knowledge of guilt makes the mouth dry and the skin wet. The slave who had stolen Ezekiel's goods could not swallow the meal; his forehead shone with sweat."

Sometimes he borrowed (as he admitted to me) the lore of nations east of the great river. In one instance, he applied this to several fathers. They had complained to him that their daughters could not fulfill the edict of Yahweh—to multiply and fill the land with our people—for the simple reason that their daughters were so ugly that no young man made them an offer of marriage.

Solomon meditated on this plea for nearly a week. Then he issued a call for every marriageable girl to be assembled in the central square of Jerusalem. When all was ready, he proclaimed by his herald his solution to the problem. The men ready for marriage were required to attend. They were allowed to see the faces and figures of the women, even to talk to them, to ascertain their tempers. After a reasonable time, Solomon commanded that the most comely should—after a manner of speaking—be sold to the highest bidder. The money was placed in a large chest. All of the more appealing maidens were "sold" in this manner. The prices paid were kept together in the common treasury.

When there were no more bids, the less beautiful were called up and offered to view. The herald asked which man would agree to take the ugliest for the smallest sum from the fund collected for the privilege of marrying the others. This was continued until all were disposed of properly. Strangely enough, there was some money left over, which was confiscated by Adoniram as tribute.

"In this way," Solomon said to me with satisfaction, "the beautiful may boast of what their husbands paid for them and the ugly may boast of what their husbands received for them." There was a proviso, of course, that they were all true wives but that if the husband was not satisfied he might separate from his choice. I may add that there were many more beauties put aside later than there were of the less comely. Solomon refused to return any of the bids paid down.

Another of the king's excellent devices dealt with the healing of the sick. There were always, among the elders and experienced, some who had the knowledge of simples and herbs, as well as the manipulations of muscles and bones and the curing of wounds. Solomon himself condescended to touch many of the ill. He achieved (with the help of Yahweh) some amazing restorations. I myself have always believed that there is an inexplicable connection between faith and the body; that if a person has a strong enough belief, in many cases, he will be rescued from ill health. But it is only when there is a deliberate blessing by a person possessed of the powers given by Yahweh that this is possible.

As for those sad cases for whom nothing seemed to work, Solomon decreed that they should be stationed at the gates of Jerusalem. Each passerby was required to stop, to examine and question the invalid, and—if he had endured something similar—to suggest a method of healing. The sick man was given his freedom to follow or discard such advice. Very often, the gratuitous prescriptions worked quite well.

In other ways, Solomon demonstrated a practical insight into the motives of the ordinary person. "If we examine a riddle closely," he said, "and put aside what is impossible, then somewhere in what remains—no matter how incredible it may seem—lies the solution. The puzzle, naturally, comes in the perception of what is truly impossible, not in imagining it."

"Yahweh always will answer the prayers of the distressed," I told him.

Solomon gave me a queer look. "True, O Nathan," he said softly, "but very often Yahweh says no."

In point of this penetration, there was the well-known case of the robbing of the tabernacle treasury. Shortly before his death, David had built a small lodge of stone near his palace. It contained all the gold and silver and precious stones and stuffs belonging to the throne. Every precaution was taken to guard it—but, soon after Solomon assumed the throne, Adoniram reported thefts from this small fortress. It was impossible to suspect the weekly reports of the upright tribute-taker—though Solomon had him under surveillance for a month to be sure. The king tried every expedient: doubling the guard, removing the guard, secret watches, open proclamations. Nothing happened—except that the thieving of treasure continued. Solomon secretly had ashes spread before and within the lodge, hoping to find the tracks of the thief. It failed: in the morning the powdery ash was virgin.

"It is clear," Solomon said to me, "that since this is a human affair, it must be worked by human means."

"It might be demons," I said.

"Nonsense! It is a man. Since he does not come in by the door, he must come down from above."

"But you have guards on the roof."

"Then he passes through the walls."

"But you have guards all about!"

"Then," said Solomon, "he comes up from beneath."

"A demon," I said with satisfaction.

"Perhaps a gopher," Solomon said meaningfully.

He secretly posted men within—after ostentatiously removing the outside guards—and captured the thief. He was the very man who had built the treasure-house—at the same time building himself a trapdoor of stone within that led to a tunnel broaching upon a nearby ravine.

At least one decision during these days of youthful justice recoiled upon Solomon. It was an occasion when a baker of meats complained that a beggar had spent three days loitering outside his shop. The beggar had voluptuously inhaled the savory odors—but bought nothing. "Therefore," said the vendor, a bold fellow of wit, "I demand payment of the beggar for the magnificently delicious odors which he has stolen from me."

Solomon, well aware that the sole reason for the man coming before him was to rid himself of the presence of the beggar, replied without delay. "Here," he said. He produced a gold coin and allowed it to drop on the stone dias of his throne. "This is a case where like should pay like. Inasmuch as he has taken your fragrance of baked meats, do you likewise take the tinkle of this coin."

The petitioner was not abashed. "Great king," he said with his obeisance, "you treat me unjustly."

"How so?"

"The coin belongs to you and the tinkle thereof. The beggar has paid nothing."

Solomon threw back his head and laughed. He tossed the coin to the beggar, another to the petitioner. "This shall be for your ready reply," he said. "But beware of pertness another time, lest you be hewed in two."

Another instance of his shrewd judgment came when Solomon passed his verdict upon a strange dinner. Two Hebrews had sat down by the roadside to eat. One had five loaves, the other three. A stranger—who was not a party to the case—came by and desired to eat with them. They agreed. He ate and, upon rising, left behind him as payment eight pieces of money.

The five-loaf owner took five pieces and left three for the other. The latter promptly complained. The whole dispute finally arrived before Solomon.

"We must think of eight loaves shared by three people," Solomon decreed. "Therefore, they had twenty-four parts. He who had five, provided fifteen; he who had three, gave nine. All ate alike and eight shares went to each man. Therefore the stranger ate seven parts of the first's property and only one of the second's. In justice, the money must be divided accordingly."

Everyone knows about a few of his less practical judgments. One happened when a merchant from Egypt held up two flowers before the throne. One was real, the other an imitation—but so perfectly colored and fashioned, perfumed, even with tiny drops of dew on its leaves, that no one could tell the difference at the distance of a few feet. The merchant humbly challenged Solomon—who merely waved him to a window of the audience chamber. There, in due time, a bee wandered in. It lighted on the true bloom, solving the question.

A second occurred when some roaming jugglers from across the Euphrates—later condemned as spies for the Assyrians and executed—came to amuse the court. They were very ingenious and highly talented. Perhaps the most amazing bit of their art was when they brandished two serpents: one was alive, the other a stuffed facsimile wrought so that none could tell them apart—so skillfully did the dancers keep them in motion. But they did not baffle Solomon. He ordered one of his gifts from Hiram brought in, a small trained ape. Instantly, the pretended serpent was exposed. The ape paid no attention to the counterfeit. It shrank away from the real one, gabbling in hysteria.

"Thus," said Solomon, taking advantage of the moment to impress his hearers, "shall the enemies of the Hebrews be affrighted." He referred, naturally, to the fact that the serpent was the sacred totem of Moses, David, and himself.

I myself brought him a riddle. Elihaph had assured me that it was a famous puzzler offered by the sphinx of Egypt. I begged the attention of the throne and recited it: "There is a thing on earth two-footed and four-footed and three-footed, whose name is one, and it changes its nature alone of all creatures that move creeping on earth or in the air and sea. But when it moves supported on most feet, the swiftness of its legs is at its weakest. What can such a creature be, O Solomon?"

To my discomfiture, the young king replied almost immediately: "Yourself, Nathan. A man who crawls on all fours, and is weakest then; who goes on two, then supports himself with a staff in his old age."

"You have said it," I admitted, prostrating myself before the throne.

"You might have made it better by adding that such a creature goes fastest when lying on its back," Solomon added.

"How so?" I asked.

"When man is dead, his spirit flies to Yahweh," Solomon said briefly.

That afternoon I ordered Elihaph beaten for having embarrassed me before the king.

But as the months and years went on, these things became of less and less interest to Solomon and the Hebrews. Even the machinations of Michal and Bathsheba, the mysterious death of Merib-baal, and the intrigues of court took second place for the time.

Why? I shall tell you with all my mind and heart.

The walls of the temple, the most splendid building of its age, were rising atop Mount Zion. The sight of what they had sacrificed and striven for was before the people. White as a virgin, sparkling as the sea, the glorious approach to Yahweh and His kingdom in the heavens lay open before them.

It was enough for all the tribes to put aside their quarrels, for all hatred to cease in acknowledgment of this symbol of universal love. The Hebrews forgot their sacrifices of substance and treasure, of labor and sweat of which they had complained so bitterly before. They joined—for the first time, perhaps the last—in raising themselves in ecstasy toward the Highest.

CHAPTER SIX

The Dedication of the Temple

"I was glad," sang the high voices, "when they said unto me, Let us go into the house of the Lord."

"Our feet," responded the deep voices, "shall stand within thy gates, O Jerusalem."

Dust rose in a faint golden mist around their feet. The harps and horns sounded softly.

"Jerusalem is builded as a city that is compact together," they sang.

"Whither the tribes go up, the tribes of the Lord," came the antiphonal reply, "unto the testimony of Israel, to give thanks unto the name of our Lord."

"For there are set thrones of judgment," answered the others, "the thrones of the house of David."

"Pray for the peace of Jerusalem: they shall prosper that love thee."

"Peace be within thy walls, and prosperity within thy palaces."

The voices lifted higher and stronger, the music was louder: "For my brethren and companions' sakes, I will now say, Peace be within thee."

The triumphant response: "Because of the house of the Lord our God, I will seek your good."

The noble chant rolled out in a shout of echoes. It shook the walls of the city, bursting from thousands of throats, amplified by the tinkle of cymbals, blasts of trumpets, booming of drums.

"The Lord shall preserve thee from all evil; He shall preserve thy soul."

"The Lord shall preserve thy going out and thy coming in from this time forth, even for evermore."

A deafening roar of hosannas poured forth like a flood too long held back, one of thanksgiving and faith. The solid mass of white robes and filleted heads shimmered in the sinking sunlight. Each man dropped to his knees. He raised his hands in adoration in the great Court of the Hebrews.

It was the finest moment of my life, one of purest beatitude. Standing atop the south pylon of the temple, overlooking the limitless green-pocked land, gazing into the crystal-amber sky, my heart filled to overflowing with rapture. I wept for joy. The tears dimmed my eyes so that I could no longer see.

But even as the rejoicing of the Hebrews rose from below like incense, even as the wind from the sea ruffled my hair like the invisible fingers of seraphim, I still could visualize the scene, stark in the eye of my mind.

The vast stone-paved precincts of the temple unfolded like the petals of a white-and-gold blossom of stone. Around the whole squared-off area below me rose a triple wall of stone blocks, higher than a man's head, a tower at each corner. Just within it, perhaps fifty feet wide and encompassing the whole, was the court of the Gentiles.

The next enclosure was a wall of cedar uprights, a palisade of sweet-smelling Lebanon wood. It surrounded the court of the Hebrews, set around the temple proper like our letter *beth*. Here Yahweh's chosen—except for women and children—might assemble to worship.

Within this, separated by a low wall of carved stone, was another, more sacred place, the court of the priests. Its slabs were polished underfoot, arranged in zigzagged patterns. It was to be trod by the sandals of the priests and Levites only. This square was set directly before the temple, the very bud of buds, the heart of the flower sprung from the hearts of his people to be uplifted to the Lord Himself.

The temple, on the highest point of which I stood, was an oblong building a hundred feet in length, thirty-three feet wide, fifty feet high. It was shaped like one of the famed ziggurats of Babylon—but turned upside down. Each of the three stories which stretched upward from the base broadened out above the lower by nearly two feet. This was not only symbolic (had not Yahweh overturned all other gods?) but also needful. It kept the rafters of acacia—from the reverently dismantled tabernacle—and the beams of cedar, from piercing the temple walls. From top to bottom, except for the wide bronze doors and the brass-latticed windows directly under each ceiling, the temple presented an unbroken façade.

The long building rose on a nine-foot-high stone platform. Ten wide steps led up to the main entrance from the west, the direction from whence came the storms of our Lord riding in His visits to our people. On either side of this broad gate—with its massive threshold and lintel of solid, curiously wrought rock—were the most awe-inspiring objects of all. They were the twin hollow-bronze pillars of Jachin and Boaz.

Each was six feet in diameter and thirty feet high, with eight-foot capitals elaborately worked with intricate nets of checker and chainwork, with lotus lilies and four hundred pomegranates. Jachin on the south meant "He shall establish"; Boaz, to the north, meant "In it is strength." Our saying was that "Boaz is to Jachin as blessing is to the cursing; and both are needed for the world."

These huge free-standing guardians stood watch on the seventeen-foot-wide *ulam*, the porch which stretched across this greater recreation of the tabernacle by Solomon. From here only the priests were allowed access into the *hekel,* the holy place. The entrance lay between two enormous square pylons, eighty feet high, with their interior staircases.

The eight-foot doors were of cypress, hung upon olivewood posts. They were decorated with figures of cherubim, with chiselings of palm trees and fruit buds and open flowers. Within, all was floored with cypress and paneled with cedar. All was intricately carved, inlaid with gold so that the eye could scarcely see for dazzlement.

The *hekal* stretched for nearly seventy feet to the east. Every day the sun threw bars of its own gold through the high windows to lay them as tribute on the floor of the sanctuary. The walls of stone were ten feet thick, hung with the finest tapestries broidered in the sacred colors of purple, blue, and crimson. About the room was placed the furniture dedicated to the Lord. There were lavers, braziers, candlestands, the massive gold *menorah,* the seven-stemmed candelabra, the chests of raiment, the golden shewbread table, the small gold-covered incense altar that stood directly before the flight of three steps which led upward into the innermost holy of holies.

Here was the entrance to the *debir*, the most holy place. It had doors of ornately carved olivewood in the same motifs as the *hekal*, a pair of portals a fifth as wide as the wall. These were never closed. Instead, a rich purple curtain embroidered in gold and silver with pomegranates and the figures of cherubim and seraphim filled the aperture. Protruding through were the polished staves of gold-covered acaciawood which were used to transport the ark of the covenant.

For, truly, this was the abiding place of the ark. The room was a perfect cube of thirty-three feet, windowless and noiseless. There was no light within except the perfect light of the Lord, the *shekinah*. Menacing in the shadows (as Zadok described it to me) were two gigantic cherubim made of olivewood and covered with gold. These winged lions with human heads symbolized the carriers and messengers of Yahweh—over which He stood invisible when we worshipped Him, He that is enthroned on the cherubim. Even as His angels had guarded the garden of Eden, so did His cherubim keep His shrine from unlawful intruders.

The pair of cherubim faced the curtained entrance. One of their great wings stretched out so as almost to touch the richly worked, fantastically carved walls of the sanctuary of sanctuaries. The other wing of each was spread in baldachin over the holiest of all our possessions—the gold-covered ark of the covenant, which Moses had left to us in trust.

As I meditated, a hot fit of pride swept over me—pride in my race, in my discovered Lord. It dried my eyes. I looked down and saw the original brazen altar of Moses. It stood stained dark from the weather and a thousand sacrifices, just before the temple entrance. A hundred feet away from it to the south, gleaming in the sun like polished metal mirrors, were eleven circles of light. They represented the ten 300-gallon lavers of bronze on wheels and the greatest miracle in metal which Hiram-abi of Phoenicia had wrought—the fantastic sea of brass.

It must be remembered that water was a severe problem when Solomon decided to locate the temple where he did. It was essential to the temple ceremonies of purification. But there was no spring at such a spot. The Kidron was far below; Gihon and the pool of Siloam were far off. It was a dilemma which Hiram-abi himself offered to solve.

"You know, of course," he said to Solomon at one of their somewhat informal conferences, "that this temple which has been designed for you by my king is much like that I built only a few years ago for the king of Hattina at Tainat."

"As long as it is not a copy of the Egyptian temple at Karnak, I am pleased," Solomon replied. "Yahweh has conquered the other gods. Like kings on earth, He takes what they have for His own."

"Very well, O king," Hiram said, chewing his short gray beard, "then you will not complain when I suggest that you adapt a device of the Babylonians. They have what they call an *apsu*, a sea, a great bowl of metal which supplies their purification needs."

"We, too, know the sea, the lair of Leviathan," Solomon said. "As long as ours is not an inferior sea."

So it was settled. Hiram went down into the clay beds of the river Jordan near the Jabbok. There he built his model and his smelter. He cast thirty tons of metal into the incredible bowl, eight feet high and fifteen feet across, three inches thick, ornamented with lilies. As a support, it had a dozen great oxen, each three facing into the four directions of heaven. It could hold 16,000 gallons of water. Such capacity took three days for a line of Levites extending almost across the city to the cut-rock channels of the spring of Gihon to fill it thereafter, bucket by bucket.

What caught my eye and held it longest was the sullen bulk of the altar on the rock of Araunah. Solomon had commanded three massive rock layers to be built on the base of the ancient threshing floor. Each succeeding level lay about two feet less than the one below. Atop the third, he had mounted a new, gargantuan brass altar—created by Hiram-abi exactly after the horned one made by Moses—that reared itself almost as high as the top of the temple itself. It was here, we knew, that Yahweh would descend to accept our sacrifices.

That shining day in the seventh month of Ethanim must remain forever in the memories of ourselves and our children. For it was then that we turned our faces to what would be, to the fulfillment of our covenant with Yahweh. In the past weeks, all the Hebrew people had been assembling in and about Jerusalem. The city was crammed. Every room, every corner was taken. Not a coin was charged. The bounty of the king fed all. During that time there were no crimes and no malfeasances; the loving kindness of the people and their brotherhood animated everything. Even the animals seemed to know the beneficence of the season. They stood about, docile and contented, big-eyed and wondering.

Not all the Hebrews who came to Jerusalem were attracted by the ceremonies at the temple. I should not be truthful if I said all our people worshipped Yahweh: a few of them still secretly adored the gods of the Canaanites or the Egyptians, Melkarth of the Phoenicians. I knew that even such a highly placed person as Bathsheba had her chapel in the hills devoted to Baal and Ashtoreth.

But there were other attractions that drew the multitudes, the glittering spectacle: the parade, the costumes, the singing. It was a time of total celebration. Taxes were canceled, tributes forgotten. In every open space in and around Jerusalem the brown and black tents of the visitors appeared. Never had I seen so many Hebrews in one spot—a people that generally loved their solitude and fiercely protected their privacy. But feuds were forgotten and quarrels forgiven: all was charity and open hands. It was plain that we had gone well about the injunction of Yahweh to multiply. Children were more numerous in the streets than frogs in the rainy season.

Barley cakes, oozing their succulent odors, were baked everywhere. Jars of new wine were unsealed and mixed with clear seawater for drinking. There were wild dances with flaring torches until dawn. Feasts were held in even the lowliest houses, old friendships were renewed, new ones made. Girls and boys lingered in the corners of the streets, in the doorways, on the rooftops. Many of them lay locked in the embrace of first love as their elders poured libations and grew ecstatic in the atmosphere that warmed and changed the very air of Jerusalem, charging it with the worship of human and divine.

Evil days had not come upon the land, the years of grace had only begun. The sun shone, the moon and the stars were not darkened by night, rains were plentiful, up to the lips of the cisterns. Processions wound slowly through the narrow, noisome streets of the two cities that were united in Jerusalem, watched by naked children sucking their fingers, mothers with babies at their breasts, beggars that had stopped their whining and cajoling. The keepers of the houses stood watching, strong men bowed themselves, even the incessant sound of grinding ceased. Ceaselessly the fans moved over the marchers, brushing away the crowds of flies whose buzzing was heard whenever the music stopped, so lulled were the cries and chants of everyday life.

Above all loomed the beauty of the temple and the stolid mass of the Araunah altar. But the first drew the hearts of the people as nothing else. Had they not built it? Were not their own representatives of the crown and of Yahweh about to dedicate it to the service of all the Hebrews as one?

As it has always been with every monument that the tribes clasp to their bosoms in songs, wreathed with the inventions of tale-tellers, the temple began to acquire legends almost from the beginning. I listened to some of them with amusement. After a time, I shut my ears. A few verged on blasphemy; most were the imaginings of simple folk. I remember three of them: one, that when the massive bronze gates of the temple were made in Egypt, they were shipped to our shores. On the way, the vessel encountered a storm. The terrified sailors threw the gates overboard. Instead of sinking, the bronze portals floated ashore safely. Such a story might appeal to someone who, unlike myself, knew that the gates had been designed by Phoenicians and cast on the shores of the Jordan. A second story had it that one of the Lebanon cedar beams of the temple was six feet shorter than needed. Solomon prayed for it to be lengthened and lo! it was done. I know the instance: Solomon merely ordered another beam. A third tale of miracle was that the workmen lacked food and that the prayers of Solomon created hot bread in a cold oven. Nonsense: Solomon merely commanded that bread be brought from the ovens of nearby houses for their supply.

But such recountings are useful to provide an air of mystery and miracle. This, in turn, produces reverence and faith, the most powerful forces in the world. I do not disapprove of the miracle-mongering of the people; I encourage it. Of such stuff are eventually woven the true miracles of our people—because the fabulous gives them the courage and persistence to do what seems impossible.

The last and greatest procession, that of final dedication, began its winding way toward the temple at dawn. All assembled outside the Valley Gate, waiting for the first rays of the sun. I was the first who cried out at the discovery; I watched for the very first strike of brightness on the hilltops.

We rejoiced—for it meant that now we could enter into our inheritance. For three days everyone (except perhaps Solomon) had fasted, eating nothing but unleavened cakes and water. We had lit no fires and none had slept with his wife. In the swale between the two cities, the priests appointed to help in the sacrificing had made ready the bullocks, sheep, and lambs. The women had prepared the dough for the festival (though only virgins saw to the baking) and opened the jars of new wine.

Our procession, according to specified order, made its solemn way through the gate. Like some gigantic uncoiling serpent scaled with men, it made its way through most of the streets of the old and new cities in preparation for ascending to the courts of the temple. Caught up in it were all the princes of the Hebrews and the chiefs of the tribes, as well as the king and his court. All the males of our nation followed. Women and children trailed after—they were tolerated as far as the court of the Gentiles but no farther.

Some in the procession wore plates of gold or silver, others the furs of wild beasts or the feathers of birds; still others carried weapons—slings, bows, clubs, spears, swords—but there were no beasts and no wheeled carts or chariots. Singers, dancers, and players of musical instruments surrounded the way of our progress immediately. Following the example of David, who had played and sung and danced from sheer joy before the ark, they were allowed to do what they pleased.

Leading us all came the timbrels, flutes, and drums. Then the ark of the covenant itself, the golden box hung by golden rings from the gold-inlaid acacia poles carried shoulder-high by two white-robed Levites of the most respected families. After them walked the pompous thickset figure of Zadok, the high priest, in the costume prescribed by Moses. He wore the blue linen ephod down to his knees, his head appearing through a hole in the middle. The garment was bound to him by a fringed sash of twined linen. The cloth was embroidered with gold, crimson, and purple figures; there were shoulder plates of gold on each side, set with jewels. Woven pomegranates rose along the hem. Bells of pure gold between each one tinkled at every step. Upon his chest, tight against the ephod—held by rings and chains of gold—was the eight-inch-square breastplate of judgment. This was the sacred Urim and Thummim, composed of a dozen different jewels engraved with the names of the twelve tribes, set into finely worked gold. Above this bobbed the set red face of Zadok, topped with a headdress of blue lace with a gold plate engraved with the words *Holiness to the Lord*.

Behind Zadok, marching with the others, came the figure of Solomon. He was clad in a purple robe ornamented and figured with gold. He wore a white turban with the six-pointed star of David picked out with gems on the front. On his left hand, sober for once, walked his companion and my son, Zabud; I was on his right. Behind us came the dignitaries and officers of the court and after them the white-robed Levites and priests—then, the elders of the tribes. Following all these came the Hebrews themselves, casting aside their thick striped abas as the warmth of the morning increased until—as if the serpent shed its skin—we were clad all in white except for Zadok and Solomon.

The din of our entrance into Jerusalem was indescribable. But it fell off as we advanced, not so much from reverence as exhaustion. During this relatively quiet period, as we trudged upward on the last stage of our journey to the temple, Solomon beckoned me to come closer to his side. Puffing a little—though the young king himself betrayed no distress—I obeyed his gesture. Looking straight ahead, Solomon commenced to speak.

"You, of all people, Nathan, will be pleased to know," Solomon said to me, "that Yahweh has already approved of the temple."

"Praised be His name!" I exclaimed. "But how do you know this?" I struck my hands together in joy.

Solomon lifted his heavy black brows delicately. "As you know, I have just returned from another sojourn at Gibeon," he told me. "There the Lord speaks to me much more clearly than He does in Jerusalem. I had a dream."

"What was it?" I asked eagerly. My throat felt parched; my heart pounded.

Solomon considered. "It seemed to me," he said, as we leisurely mounted the slope, "that I stood upon the roof of a palace far fairer than that of my father. I looked down upon the gardens and orchards, full of rills of water. The colors of the flowers between were so bright that they hurt my dreaming eyes. Beyond was a strange sea, bright with billows.

"I advanced through the air, and my feet came to a house built of bricks of gold and silver. I entered into a room paved with all manner of precious stones—ruby, emerald, balas, filled with vines and trees that bore fruit like unto the jewels. At the rear of this house was a spacious window and, looking out, I saw a flight of winding stairs built of shining black onyx that went up to heaven and vanished into the clouds.

"Then, in my dream, I was afraid. I sat upon a bench of carved crystal and hid my face. I heard a voice, sweet as honey and smooth as women's flesh, speaking to me from without: 'Solomon, I have heard your prayers, I have hallowed My house that you have built. My eyes and My heart will be there forever. If you walk in My ways in uprightness and integrity, I will establish the throne of the Hebrews in your line. There shall not fail you men-children to follow after.' "

"Marvelous!" I murmured devoutly.

Solomon gnawed his lip as he walked on, looking straight

ahead. "I seemed to ask questions from the depths of my heart," he said slowly. "I heard the voice of Yahweh become stern: 'If you turn from Me, or do not keep My statutes and commandments, serving and worshipping other gods, I shall cut off your people. I shall cast My house out of My sight. I shall make the Hebrews a byword of derision in all the world. All that pass by My house shall say, "Why has the Lord done this to His people?" To them I shall say, "Because the king has forsaken his Lord for strange gods." Heed and take care.' "

"These are true words of Yahweh," I said, bowing my head.

"There were no more," Solomon said. "But I wished you to be informed."

We entered the area of the temple. Dancers and singers and musicians fell off and became silent. We slowed our pace. The procession crossed the court of the Gentiles. The Egyptian bronze gates of the court of the Hebrews clanged back, shuddering, resonant. The procession went on, followed now by a silent multitude, across the paving of the court of the Hebrews and into the court of the priests. For an instant, the bearers of the ark, which swayed on its sagging, thirty-five-foot acacia poles, hesitated before the steps that led into the holy place. Then, in cadence, they commenced to mount with the pudgy sweating figure of Zadok doggedly following.

Only Solomon and I came after. The rest waited without, in their respective courts, scarcely daring to breathe. As we entered the holy place with its solemn furniture and high windows that gilded the gold again with the light of early afternoon, I felt the silence behind as smothering as a giant invisible cloak flung over us. I actually breathed more freely as we crossed the porch between the pillars and the pylons.

We entered the sanctuary, blinking from the bright sunlight outside. The semidarkness—that culminated in the absolute blackness of the most holy place—was responsible for a long pause before we entered. We adjusted our sight to the high illumination and the flickering of the *menorah* candles and the tapers of the five golden stands on each side of the curtained entrance to the most holy place.

As the bearers of the ark approached the doors of the most holy place, bearing their gold-ringed golden chest by its golden rings, walking stiff-legged with slow short steps, a thing of dreadful omen happened. The group had advanced no more than half the length of the holy place when the huge cypress doors on either side of the curtained inner sanctum began to move. The motion became more noticeable as we drew closer. The doors began to close in the very face of the ark!

Terrorstricken, we halted at the foot of the stairs. We did not know what to do. Zadok turned about to face Solomon. His lips moved soundlessly, his face was ashen. His form shook under all the ornate gear of the high priest. I stood transfixed.

As I did, I heard Solomon suck in his breath. Just before me, I saw him lift his arms in a regal gesture, throwing back his head in appeal. He began to speak, intoning loudly from one of the psalms of his father David.

"Lift up your heads, O ye gates," he said clearly, chanting the words slowly, "and be ye lift up, ye everlasting doors! And the King of glory shall come in!"

That was all. His voice ceased reverberating in the chamber. We waited in strained silence, the tiny golden bells on the costume of Zadok tinkling as he shivered. To my amazement—as if answering a summons—the great cypress panels swung back again, slowly, very slowly, as if a *yezer* resisted their opening, but nonetheless surely. At last they stood wide. The little procession mounted the stairs into the most holy place.

Only Zadok went in with the Levite bearers. Solomon and I remained at the foot of the stairs. Solomon glanced back at me; I returned his gaze. He shrugged slightly and looked forward again. To this day—for I never inquired—I do not know the meaning of that enigmatic gesture of his.

The ends of the too-long poles made a pair of bumps in the curtain before us, indicating that the ark was in position under the wings of the great carved cherubim inside. The two Levites, pale-faced, came out of the darkness, backing down the steps and going quickly behind us. Zadok alone was within the most holy place, adoring, mumbling almost incoherently.

Over his muffled voice, I heard a humming sound. Raising my bowed head, to my stupefaction, I saw the curtain of the most holy place swaying as if in a wind. Behind it, shining even through the thick weave and figures of the curtain, shining underneath, was the pale luminous light of the *shekinah,* the glory of the Lord. Truly, Yahweh had come to dwell in His house!

There was a cry, a moan, within. The curtain parted. Out of it, staggering as if intoxicated on some divine vision, came Zadok. His eyes were tight-shut, his fists against them. He stumbled at the top of the stairs. We gasped. He fell full length, in all his gorgeous costume, rolling to our feet, whimpering. We set him erect fearfully. He seemed blind, even when he took his fluttering hands from his eyes. His sight roamed aimlessly, whites drowning the dark pupils.

"I have seen the light of the Lord!" he muttered again and again. "The glory of He who sits enthroned upon the cherubim!"

Apprehensively, we drew back from the most holy place. The humming noise increased. The light seemed to become brighter. We had to conquer a feeling of panic, a desire to rush out of the temple to save our lives. Zadok collapsed again. The two Levite bearers uttered choked, hysterical cries. They shuffled backward, bent toward the floor, tumbling out of the entrance to the temple. I quaked where I stood.

Solomon calmly bent over. He held the jerking form of Zadok tightly for a moment. He whispered soothingly in his ear, lifted him up, and slowly turned him about like a doll. He headed him toward the entrance with a slight push.

"Yahweh has come to dwell here, in His house," I heard him intone, "and you must go and make ready the sacrifices that welcome Him to His place."

Zadok went, still staggering like a drunken man but managing to keep his feet. He vanished outside. We heard the cries of the crowded court of the priests, the shouts from the court of Hebrews that welcomed him. In the dusk of the holy place, Solomon and I faced each other. I looked over his shoulder fearfully: the most holy shrine was dark again. The humming had ceased. I saw Solomon frowning.

"What is it, O king?" I managed to whisper.

"I understand the light," Solomon said, "but what was the humming noise?"

"They were the signs of the Lord!"

"Yes, truly," Solomon said. He gave me a look I could not interpret. One that I could not feel was other than something between pity and contempt.

Solomon moved past me. I hastened to keep step with him. "Mount the pylon," he flung over his shoulder. "Zadok should be at the altar by this time."

Outside, as if from nowhere, Zabud appeared at our side. Together the three of us entered the inner stairway of the south pylon and mounted the flights of steps, around and around. We emerged at the top, Solomon forgetting his dignity, hoisting his robe, and leaping to the top level of the pylon over the last three steps. About us spread the wide lands given us by the Lord, over us was His heaven, beneath us were His waiting and adoring people.

A tremendous blast of sound from below arose around us. I felt a nudge next to me. I looked around. I saw the beaded faces of Azariah and Adoniram. The pair of them had come panting up the inner staircase of the pylon only moments after, bearing a heavy white wool treasury-sealed sack between them. We opened it with reverence. We took from it a spiked circlet of heavy red gold.

It was the crown of the Ammonite god Milcom. When David had captured Ammon and the royal city of Rabbah, he had also taken this crown and dedicated it anew to Yahweh. It was the visible sign of his conquest in the name of the Lord. The same Lord who, through the line of David, had become Adonis, chief of the city, Baal, the master, and Melech, the king, worthy of renewed tribute of men and women, flocks and herds, fields and vineyards.

The difficulty, of course, was that the crown weighed sixty pounds. It was worth a full talent of pure metal. Solomon, knowing what was coming, braced himself, neck and back stiff, legs wide. I carefully doffed his turban of linen. Azariah and Adoniram gently lowered the crown upon his sleek black head. Zabud smiled and nodded, his arms pertly akimbo.

Below us a hiss of appreciation came from the multitude. For a long minute Solomon stood unmoving, the great sign of his sovereignty sparkling on his head in the sunshine. Then we lifted it off—leaving a deep red weal about his forehead. I replaced his turban.

Again the long roar of acclamation. Solomon smiled, waiting as he had before. But the hoarse cries did not die down; as he stood unmoving in his place, I looked about me. I heard the mighty antiphonal chant begin. My eyes filled with tears.

Solomon raised his hands. He stretched his arms out over the crowd below. He held them there, suspended, blessing and silencing the host of Hebrews. The voices died away. There was no sound except the hiss of the wind about our perch: the very sun, setting in the west, seemed to wait his words.

"Lord God of the Hebrews," Solomon said, lifting his eyes aloft, "there is no god like You in heaven above or in earth below, who keeps His pledge with the weak men who walk before You, who fulfills His word even to the uttermost." He paused. Below him, the voices of the responsors loudly repeated what he had said. Solomon swayed slightly in the wind. He hesitated, as if unsure what he might say next. His form appeared to grow, to dominate the whole scene, even the rigid form of Zadok atop the altar of Araunah over the way.

"I have built Your house," Solomon said clearly, "therefore O Yahweh, let Your promise to my father David of blessed memory and to myself be hereafter fulfilled—that there shall not fail a man of the line of David to sit upon this throne as long as we walk before You in obedience." Again the responsors lifted up their white draped arms, repeating in shouts the words of Solomon. The crowd swayed and sobbed in unison.

"But will Yahweh indeed dwell here in the temple?" cried Solomon more loudly. "Behold the heaven and the heaven of heavens cannot contain Him! How much less this temple which I have built! Yet He will listen to my cry, to my prayer which I pray today: that His eyes may be open toward His house night and day, the house of which He has said that 'My Name shall be there!' "

He waited until his words had been redelivered below. Then he went on: "I ask of you that when Your people pray, You shall hear them. That when You hear them, You will forgive their sins. That if a man sin or break his oath, You will judge and condemn him but that You will justify the righteous. That if Your people sin against You and are smitten by their enemies, that You forgive them, if they repent, and restore them to their land. That if they sin and You shut up the heavens, that if they repent and turn to You, give them rain again. That if there be famine, or pestilence, or blasting or mildew or locust or caterpillars; that if their enemies besiege them in their cities; or if that sickness comes—and if any of these be due to sin—if Your people repent and supplicate You, be You merciful and hear in heaven. That You give every man according to his deserts. For You and only You know the innermost hearts of the children of men!"

It was a long speech. Solomon waited for his aides below to render it again to the hearing of the people. The ceremonies had now taken up the whole day. The sun squattered low. It burned like the opening of a fiery furnace in the southwest. Its light threw around Solomon a mantle of unearthly color. As the responsors finished their words, I heard a gasp of awe go up from the multitude below, a sound of reverence that made my hair stand on end. I half turned. To my amazement, the setting sun flung its low rays seemingly from below Solomon upward into the zenith, against the bank of clouds behind, to the east, the mass which had lurked there all day.

I saw, against the crimson of the bloody clouds, the gigantic figure of Solomon in shadow, his very form up to the folds of his turban, his slim celestial figure. My knees weakened at this mysterious phantom of the air, this visible sign of Yahweh bestowing upon the king His final benison of approval. The ululations of the people became louder. Solomon stretched up his arms. The eidolon of black against the red cloudbank did the same to their terror. He seemed to be the very symbol of *ayin* with its mystic meaning of seventy, perfect token of the immortal and infinite.

"Let our enemies know You, Your strong hand, Your stretched-out arm! Let them know You to fear You! If we sin against You (and all men sin) and in Your wrath we are defeated and made captive, give us assurances that if we turn again to You, our voices will be heard in Your dwelling place of heaven, that we shall be returned to our own land."

Slowly Solomon lowered his arms. As he did, the growing specter of the clouds elongated enormously over the whole heaven, fading mistily at its height. The crowd below cowered. Solomon remained oblivious. He spoke again: "Blessed be the Lord that has given rest to His people! He has not failed one word of His good promise! Yahweh will be with us as He has been with Moses and our fathers! As long as we walk His ways and keep His commandments, His statutes, and His judgments, He will maintain the cause of His people! All the people of the earth shall know that the Lord is our god and that there is none else!"

Solomon stretched out his arms again. "Let the sacrifices be made," he said in his ordinary voice.

As he did, his shadow behind him, stretching (as it seemed) across all the land, commenced to fade and dislimn rapidly. So quickly did it pass that within a few minutes the sun had vanished. Shadows gathered in a black sea around the torchlit summit of Mount Zion. The crowd sent up massive shouts, cries, and shrieks of awe and approval. But I could see eddies and drifts in the mass of people below which indicated that their attention had already turned to the sacrifices and the meat-feasting that was to follow on for fourteen days and nights.

"How did it seem to you, O Nathan?" Solomon's voice said in my ear.

I whirled. "O king," I said, bowing humbly, "it was sublime."

"They seemed to like it," he said reflectively.

His gaze went past me, toward the darkening summit of the altar of Araunah with its monolithic menace. Torches swarmed about its base. Atop, a lonely fire burned. By its light we could descry the last of the priests and Levites piling entrails and dumping buckets of blood upon them. The form of Zadok, distinguished by the glints of his golden ornaments, waited to one side.

At last came a part of the rite I had never seen before in all the sacrifices before the tabernacle. Squads of priests ran about the altar like shadows, throwing buckets of some liquid upon the offerings.

"What is this ceremonial?" I asked of Solomon. I squinted into the darkness.

"Water of holiness," Solomon said briefly. "I have commanded it in the hope that Yahweh will respond."

Next moment, the operation was ended. Zadok, a tiny figure against the purple horizon, picked up a burning brand. He tossed it onto the heap of offerings atop the altar.

Instantly a great gust of flame burst forth. It appeared as if indeed it had come down from the heavens. There was the sound of a great *whoom!* in the air. Immediately the pile commenced to burn furiously. For a moment, I stood blinded. As I gradually recovered my sight, I noted Zadok had fallen back, into the arms of the priests behind him.

"The Lord has indeed accepted the sacrifice," I said in fear. I pointed to the flames and on upward to where the black smoke rose in a pillar. It broke abruptly in a streaming angle, west to east over our heads, in the direction that Yahweh's messengers always took.

Solomon did not seem to pay attention. He scowled at the sight of Zadok, scorched and seared, being assisted down from his high place. He shook his head and turned, followed by the ever-present Zabud, to go down the pylon stairs.

"I told that fool Zadok not to stand too close to the altar," he said, almost to himself. "It is the same as that 'strange fire' which holy writ tells us that Nadab and Abihu placed before the altar of Yahweh—which they, like Zadok, did not know how to control and 'there went out fire from the Lord and devoured them and they died.' "

Zabud rolled his eyes and shrugged. Solomon caught him familiarly about the shoulders. Together they went down the stairs before me.

As we descended, I could smell the odors of broiling fat and roast meat. The hubbub of the people around the fires served notice that they were already lining the pits with spits full of raw meat—after having surrendered the best parts of the proffered beasts to the priesthood. It was a good smell, a good ending to the day. I licked my lips: I was entitled to choice bits.

All the same, I wondered uneasily what had happened to Zadok at the altar.

CHAPTER SEVEN

The Sin of Bathsheba

A little more than a month after the first temple ceremonies, I left my house at dawn. I drew a deep cleansing breath as I surveyed the city of Jerusalem. It delighted my heart. As I went slowly down its steep narrow streets—I preferred to walk—already filled with bustling crowds in the first rays of the sun, I felt happy. In the air, it seemed, the rich odors of the two-week festival of baked meats after the temple ceremonies still lingered. I could see countless small black pocks of ashes that marked the places where the families had camped; hordes of ants still devoured grease spots in the dust.

But the faithful had long since gone home: to their tents and villages, to their little walled towns. Now there were in the city a vast number of those who poured through the gates every day. Jerusalem had become as much a city of the world as it was the great city of the Hebrews. Surely David's dream was being fulfilled.

I came slowly down from the high place, my spirits reviving. My eyes roved over the unruly crowds and the plodding beasts of burden. Some of the passersby I knew but most were foreign to me. Men and women from a score of nations walked our narrow streets and haggled in our markets. Strange animals bore their goods. Colors that smote the eye were everywhere; odd costumes were so common as to be unremarked. The dust was thick with the imprints of sandals of cleated leather, woven papyrus, or carved wood, overlaid with the callus-marks of multitudes of footprints. Most of the people wore the short shirts that reached to the knees (to the ankles for those of high rank, to whom it gave dignity), with tasseled girdles and shoulder capes with metal or jeweled clasps.

Wigs of flax, wool, and palm fiber were everywhere—black, yellow, blue, red, even the faded awry felt ones of the poor. Those who kept their own hair—instead of wig-shaving their heads to keep off lice—wore it long and oiled and perfumed. Every man had a beard, elaborately curled and often interwoven with gold and silver wires.

These strangers had come, some to spy, some to trade, some merely to travel and to admire the temple. Assyrians with their hooked noses, frizzed beards, and fringed bright shawls; sullen dark-skinned Phoenicians with their sudden white smiles and cunning eyes; Canaanites, who looked aside and moved out of one's way in their dainty linens; Egyptians in their transparent gauzes and wigs of wool, mincing along; Hittites, small and sturdy, with their copper-studded boots and strong jaws always chewing some reddish substance; bare-footed slaves in their loincloths, roped each to each; soldiers in file with their spears held erect and usually a little drunk, fresh from the beer shops; palanquins and carts and even, occasionally, a shining chariot from the palace, careless in its rush through the crowds.

Cries of wares to sell and endless conversations at the street corners, chatter impeded by the flow-between of passersby: "I have just come back, my friend, this moment, I swear!"

"I understand your sorrows in being away. Traveling is the worst curse of all."

"Aye and aye again! When you halt in the evening, the day's ride has shattered your body, pulverized your bones. Your slave-groom is an idler, and you must tie up your horse and feed him by yourself."

"How well I know! Your camp is invaded by night while you sleep and then you find not only your groom is lazy, he has vanished—and your horse and goods, even your clothes, are gone!"

"You are lucky to be alive. What did you do in such a case?"

"The usual: tug at my ear madly and utter curses!"

Laughter and caresses and the passing-on of two friends. Two onagers moved leisurely side by side and one rider sympathized with the other:

"I quite share your feelings in this strange land where everything goes up and down. Nothing lies flat as in your beloved Nile-land. I know how you feel, for I have visited Egypt."

"How can you know the shudder when I find that the chasm is on one side, the mountain on the other? You are used to it but I shiver, my hair stands on end! I get out of my chair and tell the bearers—who shake like myself—to go on ahead; I walk behind, fearful that the mountain will fall on my head!"

"But we have such solid mountains here!"

"Don't joke at it! My heart thumps like a drum. The sky seems vast and threatening. I imagine that an enemy with arrow strung or sword drawn creeps close behind me."

"But you are safe."

"Thanks be to Isis!"

"Shush! You are in the city of Yahweh!"

Two fat merchants in wine-stained clothes with their pot-shaped hats and deerskin boots—with heavily decorated tunics in gold and silver embroidery, all the same—confided in each other. They sat under an arbor decorated with greens and flowers, close by the coolness of the pool of Siloam that runs chuckling through its aqueducts carved out of rock to the cisterns below:

"These people are the most hospitable in the world, eh?"

"As long as one has money."

"That is so anywhere in the world and here, at least, one is not robbed."

"Never think so! Or, at least, they make one pay for favors. As I came into the land from the sea, I approached an unwalled vineyard and, naturally, I stopped to pluck a few grapes."

"But there were no guards?"

"Only a very pretty girl, and she granted me innumerable favors in the furrows under the vine leaves. Then, suddenly, I was aroused from my bliss."

"I thought so."

"Her threatening relatives surrounded me, and for a moment I thought I was doomed to marry the girl. But they were very proud and demanded only confession of my sins."

"Is that all?"

"And my money and my apron woven of fine Egyptian cotton and my bow, my quiver, and my dagger. But they left me my beast, even though they took its blanket. I went on and he became lame. I left him and proceeded on foot. I crossed the hot sands and came to an inn but when I asked for wine and food, they pretended not to hear—for I seemed a beggar."

"So you died there?"

"Not at all, no. On the contrary, I always have some gold bits hidden in my garments, sewed in, you understand, and the language of gold is understood everywhere, my friend."

I smiled tolerantly and turned past one of Benaiah's guards into the side door that led to Solomon's rooms. To my surprise, the king was already on his throne, head bent, conferring with an older man who squatted beside him. I recognized Hiram-abi, the architect and builder of the temple, with some disquiet; I had thought he had returned to Phoenicia long since.

Solomon raised his head and recognized me. He beckoned to me to rise from my prostration and approach him. He indicated Hiram-abi beside him with a gesture of satisfaction.

"Hiram-abi has consented to build me a new palace," Solomon said. The gray-headed Phoenician squatting next to the throne in his brilliant yellow-and-red costume nodded and muttered something in his guttural version of our tongue.

"Praise be," I said, "to Yahweh."

"He is not altogether of the Phoenicians. He tells me that his mother was of our tribe of Naphtali."

"Yes," Hiram-abi said, nodding.

"All the better," I said, somewhat less stiffly.

"Nor is his talent limited to building," Solomon said carefully. "He is a man I should wish to keep always beside me to learn his secrets—if he were not pledged to serve King Hiram."

"There are many curious things in the world, if one knows how to use them," Hiram-abi said slowly. "Use, that is the important thing."

Solomon looked at me. "Do you recall the flame and blast of the sacrifice at the dedication that burned Zadok?" he inquired.

"I shall never forget the fire sent from heaven by Yahweh," I said reverently. A sting of concern pricked my mind despite my dislike of the high priest. "Is Zadok recovering?" I asked in a different tone. "He will not die?"

"No," Solomon said. "He is swathed in bandages and olive oil from head to foot at this moment, like a mummy out of Egypt."

"I told him to stand well back," Hiram-abi grunted.

"It was the doing of the Lord," I replied resignedly.

Solomon frowned. Beside him, the wizened frog-face of Hiram-abi grinned. "It was not altogether the doing of the Lord," Solomon said. "Have you ever seen blood and entrails consumed so completely before?"

"Never," I confessed. I surveyed him with new interest. "You knew what would happen?" I asked. "Do you have the gift of prophecy?"

Hiram-abi made an impatient gesture. "It has always happened," he said. "It will always happen."

"But this is against the nature of water," I said earnestly. "Water does not create fire, it extinguishes it."

Hiram-abi gave a hoarse croak of amusement. Solomon said: "This man does not believe in any gods. He believes only in what he sees and knows."

"I call this Naphtali water," Hiram-abi said. "There is much of it, oozing from rocks where your cities of Sodom and Gomorrah used to be. Perhaps your god Yahweh destroyed them by means of it."

"I have reserved it for future ceremonies," Solomon said. "It has a smell that irritates the nose. A man can get drunk on the smell. But it is impossible to drink."

"Possibly this water is of Yahweh," I agreed, "since He has created all things, blessed be His name. But tell me, Phoenician man of arts, how do you explain a greater miracle, that of the *shekinah* at the dedication of the temple? I myself saw it, the king saw it."

Hiram-abi gave another snort. Solomon intervened smoothly, enjoying the moment. "There is a trapdoor in the roof of the most holy place," he explained. "It was necessary because of the curse that lies on anyone except the high priest who enters through the curtain—yet the priests would be unwilling and unskilled in any of the work of repair that might have to be done."

"I sat on the roof during the ceremony," Hiram-abi said. "At the proper moment, I lifted the trapdoor. I let the sunlight in, reflected by a silver mirror. As you must know, O Nathan, the interior of the most holy place is entirely plated with burnished gold and such illumination would have blinded anyone, as it did Zadok."

"I know nothing of what is within," I said with dignity.

"I do," Hiram-abi said rudely. "I built it."

The hair of my head prickled with anger. "Was it you, as well, that caused the tremendous humming in the air?" I demanded. "If so, by what magic?"

Hiram's face became serious. Solomon's expression was

unreadable. "No," he confessed. "I had nothing to do with that. I do not know where it came from."

"Perhaps that was the true sign of Yahweh," suggested Solomon in a low tone.

"And the swinging-to of the doors of cypress?" I persisted. Hiram-abi again shook his head while the king nodded his sleek black locks. I caught the odor of perfume. "Perhaps that, too," Solomon murmured. "But Yahweh instructs them who gain wisdom by themselves. We shall learn."

"It is holy to do that which helps holiness," I said, not knowing what else to say.

"There is much that the people would not understand in religious ceremonies," Solomon agreed instantly. "It would only confuse them if it were explained. We tell you these things rather than Zadok. You have the means to comprehend. He is like the worshippers themselves who would rather believe than understand. Mystery is the heart of all belief."

"I would rather have faith than knowledge," I muttered.

"The fear of the Lord is the beginning of knowledge, certainly," Solomon said, withdrawing the warmth of his tone. "But only the fool despises wisdom and instruction. A wise man will hear and will increase learning; a man of understanding, and only he, attains to wise counsels."

I could find no words to reply. I bowed my head deeply and began to retreat. "Wait," Solomon commanded. He turned to Hiram-abi. "Leave us for a time," he said. The Phoenician rose silently, made his obeisance, and vanished. The king turned back to me, lounging on his throne, and observing me speculatively.

"You have heard of the great goddess Ashtoreth?" he inquired abruptly.

"My lord and king," I said, "I have heard all sorts of idle tales of other gods."

"Do you think she exists?"

"There is no god but Yahweh," I said with emphasis.

"But can there be a god without a goddess?" inquired Solomon. "Is this not something unnatural? Do not the women have a right to complain?"

I could not tell if he were in earnest or not. "The women in your harem have no right to complain," I said.

"But they exist, O Nathan," he replied.

"Yahweh is known by what He does, as Moses said, blessed be his name," I said loudly. Solomon considered, stroking his beard.

"Yahweh, of course," he said, "is God over all gods. But is it entirely impossible that another, a goddess, exists as well?"

"Even to speak of such a thing is hateful," I said. "We are chosen."

Solomon nodded his head slightly, but as if he could not believe what I had said. I felt the cold fist of growing shock grip my stomach.

"You know that all of our people do not worship Yahweh," he said softly. "Goddess of the sea, goddess of love, goddess of fertility, goddess of sex, does not Ashtoreth appeal to you, Nathan?"

"My lord the king," I said with difficulty, "I must warn you against blasphemy. You hold the Hebrews only under the hand of Yahweh. He has promised you many things but He has also told you they shall be taken away if you depart from His statutes."

Solomon widened his sleepy eyes. "I do not depart," he said. "My mother departs. She is Hittite and worships as she believes."

I was silent. Solomon went on: "I obey Yahweh in all things. I follow the advice of Zadok and yourself to the letter. I guard the holy ark, I attend the temple services, and I have commanded that they shall be held three times a year."

"Then how can you speak of this Ashtoreth in the same breath, this goddess of the moon and the cow, as the mate of Yahweh who created the sun and the moon?"

"Yet our own altar," Solomon said, "has the horns of her worship still clinging to it. Did not Yahweh once deign to ride on the golden calf created by His own priest, Aaron?"

I forebore to tell him what he knew, what Moses had done to the golden image. Solomon closed his eyes. "All gods need worshippers," he mused. "They draw their life from them as we do from the gods."

"It is true that Yahweh must be worshipped," I said stiffly.

"The *asherim*, the poles for which the women weave garments in the courtyard of the temple, what do they mean, Nathan?"

"They are very old—the meaning has been lost."

"What does it mean when we name our children Adoni-jah or Adoni-ram—or use the name of Baal?"

"We are crushing the power of the false gods!" I cried.

Solomon opened his piercing blue eyes and stared at me. "I think it may be because all gods are the same," he said. "They gather each other into each other."

"Yahweh is all gods and is God," I said, glad to agree.
"And all gods are Yahweh?" laughed Solomon.
"Never!" I sputtered.
"It needs much thought," Solomon said.
Approaching closer to him and greatly daring, I inquired: "Who, O king, has been saying these things to you?"
Solomon shook his head. "No, good Nathan," he responded. "You would hunt them down like wild animals for the sake of Yahweh—and I should be forced to hand you over to Benaiah in justice."
"These are false and dangerous doctrines," I replied. "No man can believe them and live."
"No man, perhaps," Solomon said. He chuckled. "No, no man."
It was a slender clue, words and tone, but it was all I had to enable me to discover what I had to know. As soon as I could, I opened the doors of the palace, completed my task in the audiences of the king, and begged my freedom from Solomon for the rest of the day. I hurried directly to the one who would know.

Elihaph gave me a grin, as twisted as his body. "I have no definite information," he said cautiously.
"Ten silver shekels," I said fiercely, "if you tell me those with whom Solomon consorts and what they have talked about."
"There is yourself, of course," Elihaph said slyly.
"Fool!" I exclaimed. I raised my hand. He cowered but with a peculiar insolence. "If what I think is true," he said rapidly, "I should not be the one to tell you."
"Why not?"
"I may accuse an innocent person."
"We must find out the source of these sacrilegious speculations!"
"Then," said Elihaph deliberately, "there is only one who is as close to the king as yourself."
"Who?"
"Your own son, Zabud."
I took a step backward, as if I had been struck. My sight swam, my thoughts whirled. I turned away from the leering face of Elihaph and began to walk away with a faltering step. "My shekels!" he shouted after me. "My ten silver shekels!"
I paid no attention to his cries. My thoughts settled in my brain, sediment in murky water that formed dark patterns. I

had no choice but to believe what Elihaph had told me. The missing pieces of the puzzle, like one of the intricate carvings from the hands of the Phoenicians, fell into place. By whom else, I asked myself, could Solomon share all the errors of creation? With whom did he spend more time, than with his constant companion Zabud, my son?

A startling thought struck me. If Elihaph was right, where had Zabud himself become infected and damned with all these fantastic notions? But I tucked such a problem away for a future time; my duties depended upon one goal, that of weaning Solomon back, to speak the truth for all to know, to see that our king's feet did not stray from the paths of the Lord.

A second idea came to me: I was convinced that Bathsheba was at the bottom of all this, somehow: that she would be found somewhere near my son.

Zabud's chambers, of course, were in the palace, not far from those of Solomon himself. I gained access easily enough, swept the curtain aside—and stood amazed at the richness of the habitation of Zabud. Polished braziers against the cold of the nights, silver and ivory furnishings, carved gilt of the pillars, rich hangings with not an inch of white on their elaborate surfaces of color, scarlet shadows in the corners—and the rich raiment of Zabud himself waiting uneasily for me, as I was announced by the guard.

It was evening. I had waited this long, impatiently enough, to interview my son because all afternoon following my official duties, Zabud had been at Solomon's side. Now, I knew, there were matters of state for the king and Azariah to discuss. I had guessed correctly that Zabud would be in his apartments. I moved slowly into the middle of the room. "You live well, my son," I said.

"This is part of the palace of the king," he replied. I did not answer: I stared hard at a moving shadow in the corner. "Come forth, Bathsheba," I said.

The figure unhooded itself. It came slowly forward. I felt a sense of bewilderment, of having been deceived. The person in the chambers of Zabud was Michal.

"Your guess was in error, my father," Zabud said with a tinge of malice.

"I knew it would be a woman," I said coldly.

"Greetings, Nathan," said the old woman proudly. "Do you wish to speak to me or to Zabud?"

"What is your business here?" I demanded, a flush of anger

rising in me. I felt bilked of her I had expected to see, annoyed that my expectation had gone so far wrong.

"I have invited her," Zabud said. He was defiant. "It is my right to invite whom I please."

"More company is always welcome," Michal said in her hoarse accents.

I bit my lip. I faced her directly, speaking to her but with the intent of intimidating Zabud.

"I wish to speak to my son, Zabud," I said, "alone."

"Michal will go," Zabud said hastily.

But Michal gave no sign of leaving. "Why?" she croaked. "Zabud wished me to stay. He is afraid you will use the arts of your mind against him."

"Is this true, my son?" I asked sternly.

"No, no," he said.

"Whatever you say," Michal said. "But I know your father and his nature, I know your nature. You are not the same. He is a man fitted to live alone, dreaming. But you, Zabud, shall have many wives and many concubines. The stars foretell it."

"Moses has forbidden such foretelling," I said.

Michal snapped her bony fingers. "He has forbidden many things," she said, "and all of them make life wonderful. I do not have to listen to such things."

"You are the wife of David," I reminded her.

"And you are the father of Zabud," she responded.

I tightened my lips. "What I have to say to you," I said, addressing Zabud, "does not need privacy perhaps. I am distressed at the reports of your life with Solomon: drunkenness, women, feasting, chariot racing, amusements of all sorts. This is not the proper occupation for my son."

"Is not the choice of the king good enough for Zabud?" murmured Michal.

"Yes," Zabud said defiantly. "I do no more than Solomon."

"Silence!" I said. "Do you resist the will of your father?"

"Zabud will not be your comfort in the days when the years grow short and the way darkens," Michal said. "But still you yearn for him. He will not be a prophet but he will yet be a great man in the kingdom of the Hebrews."

"You deceive yourself, wife of David," I said. "I no longer expect my son to come back to my house. I have other sons, like Azariah, who serve the king and Yahweh soberly and in justice—not in revels and dissipation."

"There is nothing wrong in being the boon companion of Solomon," Zabud muttered. "I have learned many things."

"I know," I said. "How sweet are the wines of Egypt, how sonorous the ring of gold, how exhilarating the gallop of a horse, how velvet the loins of women."

"Lies, lies!"

I bent my look upon him. "Do you say your father lies?"

"He says that there is much more he has learned and he is right," Michal retorted sharply. "I have talked much to him. I am his foster mother. Do you expect the woolly lamb to turn into the whiskered lion of Judah in a day?"

"No," Zabud said before I could reply. "I must have practice in clawing and roaring—and in devouring my prey."

My heart turned heavy. Looking around the garish room, I could see how far Zabud had departed from my precepts. "I came as a father," I said, "to renew between us our love."

"I know what lies behind that word," Michal said promptly. "We women know love. Do you threaten Zabud your son?"

"No," I said. "I cannot. My heart will not allow it."

"You are as subtle as the serpent."

"I am not made for love only," Zabud announced. "I shall have great power and glory. Solomon has promised it to me."

My bosom froze. I could not believe my ears. "Zabud," I told him with difficulty, "all things come from the Lord, and we must give account to Him. All that Solomon has is from Yahweh."

Zabud's weak, rosy face became contorted as if he were about to cry. "Perhaps I am not worthy," he mumbled.

"Stop this nonsense!" Michal cried. "You are not one to follow Nathan! You are better than your father!"

"I am afraid," Zabud whimpered.

"What do you fear?" I pressed him.

Zabud's face twisted in indecision. "I feel nothing except cold, as if I were dying," he whispered, staring at the floor.

"You shall not bully the boy," Michal said.

"I am his father," I told her. "To me only does he owe obedience."

"What have you given him as a father? Solomon you have treated as your son but when have you given Zabud love and comfort? You have been a courtier of the court altogether."

Her attack took me by ambush. "Not I, but he," I said. "He has never seen fit to come to his father as is his bounden duty."

"What he is you have forced him into," Michal told me, "you and the king."

"He shall be what I say he shall be."

"Do not be sure," Michal said. "I have taken him as another of my children that David murdered. I am mother and nurse to him. You cannot speak to him this way. I, Michal, say so!"

"Does the honored wife of David and the foster mother of Zabud threaten the father of Zabud?" I asked ironically.

Michal flung down her hands and turned away. Zabud shook his head. "I am sick of quarrels, sick of love," he said.

"Come with me, Zabud," I urged with the fervor of a father's heart, "away from the court. I shall beg the king to set us free. We shall live together in the forest, father and son, with the blessing of Yahweh."

"Why should I leave the court?" muttered Zabud sullenly. "I am happy here. I should be bored to death in the woods. Your life is not mine, my father."

"He is young, he is frightened," Michal flung out sardonically. "He wants to go with you but he lies about what he wants." There was a slow rictus of confidence on her face. It set my teeth on edge, this sort of mocking.

"But you," I bit off, "you, Michal, tell the truth?"

She stood before me, straightening up, proud and defiant. I felt again an inexplicable flicker of respect for her. "For those who have the heart to hear it, yes," she said.

For a moment there was silence except for Zabud's sniffling. The room was black, unrelieved except for the blue glimmer from the small square windows. I began to feel like a phantom in space. I heard Michal's low, grating voice. "Zabud," she said deliberately, "light the lamp, Zabud."

Silence again, estrangement in darkness, except for the shuffle of Zabud in obedience. There was fumbling, a muffled *pop*. A bit of glowing tinder tumbled onto the table. Zabud licked his fingers, snatched it up and applied it to the rush wick of the fine-snouted oil lamp. He blew upon it. Almost instantly the light oil in the rush wick flared up into blue-yellow flame.

Zabud looked up at Michal and myself. He must have found almost identical expressions of astonishment upon our faces. He smiled for the first time, holding up a slender jointed tube of some polished wood.

"What happened?" I demanded, shrinking from him. "Where were the sparks of the firestones? What device of the evil spirit is that?"

"If it is evil, the king is responsible," responded Zabud. "He knows how I love to receive presents from afar. This is from Egypt, what they call a fire tube. See! It is hollow. You place dried pith in the bottom, replace the rod and wadding and strike it sharply—and fire is made!" He was animated for the first time.

"Magic," I murmured.

"Perhaps," Zabud said easily, "but if it is, it is good and convenient magic."

Suddenly my belly sagged with the heaviness of despair. My eyes filled with tears. A wail escaped my lips. I turned and stumbled toward the door. I heard Michal speak behind me: "There is nothing here for you, Nathan."

She was right. My son was beyond me, lost to me. What was left was only the true God and my devotion to Him. Half-blinded by my grief, I made my way out of the palace, into the cold shimmers of the light made by the rising full moon. I dashed the tears out of my eyes and slowly set out, head bowed, for the gate. As I did, I felt an excited jog at my elbow.

"Good Nathan," said Elihaph in a whisper, looking up at me from around his shoulder, "I have just heard news."

"Do not bother me with it now," I said mechanically.

"It concerns Bathsheba."

"That succuba in human form! That Lilith from the pit!"

Elihaph nodded, wrenching his head. "She is highly honored by the king," he said to me. "Do you know what Hiram-abi has been doing, at Solomon's command, these past few weeks?"

"No," I said wearily, "nor do I care."

"He has built her a shrine to Ashtoreth."

My brain caught fire. I seized the little misshapen man by the arms. "Is this true?"

He struggled free and pointed to the hill to the west of Jerusalem. The groves of olives in the moonlight showed their silver-turned leaves in the breeze. "There," he said, "atop that hill. She will be there tonight."

"She! Bathsheba? How do you know?"

Elihaph giggled. "Ashtoreth is the goddess of the moon. She is to be worshipped on nights like these."

I shivered like a man with fever. "Are you sure?" I asked tensely. Elihaph shrugged. In that moment, my mind became clear, fixed in the knowledge of what I must do. I flung him aside. I hastened for the nearest gate, my skirts tucked up about me.

The top of the hill of olives was covered with boulders of all sizes. Working feverishly, I scrabbled among them to select the largest I could carry, an almost round chunk of flint. I clasped it up before my chest and commenced to follow the winding path that led to the platform at the very peak.

The path had been used many times before but it was steep and rugged. Yet I knew, sweating and groaning despite the cool night, that I was approaching the place of Ashtoreth. I made my way slowly, slowly upward. At last I came to a rude flight of slab stairs. I put down the boulder and crept up on hands and knees to view what was above.

It was a flat, paved place. In the very center was an enormous man-high, snow-white cone of strange stone. Fire flickered in blue flame at its very tip. Behind it, impassive and lovely, seeming almost to be alive in the moonlight shadows, sat the statue of Ashtoreth. She was flanked by two carved sphinxes and held a large bowl under her breasts. I knew that this was only her simulacrum. The cone was the real object of worship, the sacred mystic symbol of her powers. I crawled back in cold fury, unafraid, willing to dare the wrath of any unknown deity to do my duty for Yahweh.

I struggled up the steps with the boulder in my hands, the weight sagging my body. I gained the platform, inlaid with innumerable tiles all with the secret sign of Astarte—the skirted woman with upraised hands—engraved upon them. In the middle by the moonlight, erect and aloof, I faced the rounded cone. I felt a shudder of awe come over me; my arms seemed nerveless. I dropped the stone. I stood erect, trying to control my feelings. In a moment, I knew, I should be able to destroy the symbol of Ashtoreth, the witness to wickedness.

"You must be very tired, Nathan," said the voice of Bathsheba. I leaped to one side, crouching in terror. Her tone went up in a trill of laughter. "Lifting all those stones, choosing this one, being unable to do what you wished with it," she said in amusement. She sauntered out into the moonlight from the side of the platform. She regarded me from the lovely shadows of her face. "You are too old to destroy a shrine built of stone," she said critically. "Are you so afraid of Ashtoreth?"

I panted where I was, not yet recovered. Bathsheba moved leisurely away from me. "She loves and does not hate but she is capable of revenge," she said. "Remember, when her brother Anat was murdered by Mot of the underworld, she sought Mot out with her scythe. She cut him into a thousand bits to strew around the world. And her kisses brought Anat back to life."

"I do not believe in your legends," I said, breathing hard.

"Nor do I believe in your legends about Yahweh," said Bathsheba. "But I am sensible enough to pretend that I do. As my son is fond of saying, seek such subtlety and all other things shall come after it."

"What are you doing here?" I asked in spite of myself, to hear her condemned out of her own mouth.

"Why should I not be here? This is the night of the full moon. It is the proper night to worship the goddess of the moon."

My nails dug into my palms. I stared up at the moon sailing toward a rack of black clouds in the west. Silently, I cursed it. Bathsheba gurgled again with laughter.

"I can imagine, Nathan," she said, "what terrible things you are saying about Ashtoreth. But she is a woman and it does not matter. She forgives all manner of curses if her worshippers love her."

"I do not worship her, I do not love her," I said between my teeth.

"But you may," Bathsheba responded. Without warning, she stretched herself out along the floor of the shrine. On her back, eyes wide, she stretched her arms up to the moon. "O Ashtoreth!" she said loudly. "Tonight I sacrifice to you—either a lover or my cherished hair!"

"What do you say?" I demanded, horrified.

"What ought to be said. Nathan, come to me."

"No!" I cried. In that moment, I ought to have fled but my feet refused to obey the commands of my confused brain.

Bathsheba at full length turned leisurely toward me, leaning on arm and hip. "Then why," she asked innocently, "did you come to the shrine of Ashtoreth on such a night?"

"I abhor your goddess!" I cried. "I loathe you! I care about others, about my son!"

"What about Zabud?" said Bathsheba softly.

"Will you swear by Yahweh that you have never spoken of Ashtoreth to my son?"

Bathsheba put out her hands in a graceful gesture, her gold armlets flickering like cold flames in the moonlight. She said simply: "Michal and I have often talked to him of the goddess."

"Are all women liars?" I gasped. "Is all the world no more than the shriek of madness? Michal is a Hebrew of the

Hebrews! She is the daughter of Saul, of the tribe of Benjamin!"

"She is a wise woman," Bathsheba said. "As a woman, she and I have come to understand each other. She is the daughter and wife of kings, I am the wife and mother of kings. We are above the rabble and what they believe. What I do openly in worshipping Ashtoreth, Michal does secretly."

"You lie again!" I panted.

"I tell you a bitter truth," Bathsheba returned. "And I shall tell you more. You are no free man, but a slave! Can you think of an instant in all your years that you have been free of this burden of Yahweh, when you have been a man? Has there been a single hour when you have thought your own thoughts? Who calls your soul to rise in the morning, who calls it in at evening like a greathound on the leash—who but Yahweh?"

"Stop, stop!" I cried in terror.

Wordlessly, without warning, Bathsheba sprang up. She snatched at the little jewel-hilted knife in my girdle. She held it above her head with both hands as if it were an oblation. Then, shaking down her long hair in a frenzied series of movements, she offered it back to me—glittering in the light of the moon. I shrank from her insanity.

"Take it!" she commanded.

"No!"

"Take it, Nathan, and free yourself—either of me or Yahweh!"

A slow congealing ran in my veins. "You mean that I—that I—should—" I could not finish for stammering.

"Do you truly want to be a man? Take the knife—or take me here, before the altar of Ashtoreth!"

I shook my head from side to side, trying to rid myself of what had become a nightmare. My shadow wagged freakishly along with me, across the tiles inscribed with the seals of Ashtoreth. Bathsheba watched me with contempt.

"It is not hard," she said. "See!"

Before I knew what she was about, she held out her left hand. She cut herself across the palm in two swift slashes. She held up the bloody *X* unflinchingly.

"See how easily it flows," she murmured. "The knife was meant to have its drink of blood!"

"A witch shall not be suffered to live," I muttered, drawing back.

"See!" cried Bathsheba. Before I could avoid her she had

smeared her bloody left hand across my face. I staggered back. Bathsheba looked at me with approval.

"Now you show the world a badge of honor," she declared. "This is the mask a real prophet must wear."

Numbly I shook my head, trying to wipe my face free of her clinging blood. She challenged me, leaning past the cone, her breath making the flames flutter.

"Are you the coward that I think you? Is this not the way to prove me wrong?"

"Never, never!" I mumbled, frantically wiping my face, clawing at it with both hands.

Bathsheba's features convulsed with rage. Her lips parted, the knife went forward: she sprang upon me: "Die, then, you bleating sucking calf!"

Almost before I knew it, I found myself clinging to her wrist, locked in embrace, wrestling the perfumed figure of the woman. We swayed together for a moment. Her strength was no match for mine. I bore her back, bending her body to the floor at an impossible angle. She moaned with pain. The knife dropped from her fingers. She crumpled to the stones. I knelt gasping above her, still disbelieving her fierceness.

"You said once to me that you had foregone revenge," I ejaculated.

Bathsheba struggled. I held her wrists down; only her bosom jerked itself upward at me. Then her body went limp and flaccid. "Take your foolish knife," she said. "You are no lover, you are not a man but a eunuch, as I have told you before. Let me rise."

Wordless, I released her. We stood together, Bathsheba smoothing her dress, putting her long hair back. She turned away a step or two, then came back to me. She smiled.

"Look," Bathsheba said, in an almost playful tone, "I shall show you a miracle worthy of Yahweh, Nathan."

From the flickering of the flame that issued from the top of the sacred cone, she selected a burning stick. She approached the image of Ashtoreth. While she chanted under her breath to an unknown tune, she waved the sacrificial flame before the bare stone teats of the goddess. Back and forth, back and forth in a slow, caressing motion. Abruptly, before my astonished eyes, I saw streams of milk burst forth from the carved bosom, arching into the bowl. Bathsheba dropped her little torch.

"Well?" she asked. "Do you believe in the powers of Ashtoreth now, dear Nathan?"

I uttered a choked yell. Before the surprised Bathsheba

could make a sound or move to prevent me, I had snatched up the boulder again. With the superhuman strength given me, I dashed it against the statue of Ashtoreth. It shattered before the blow. Bathsheba gave a cry of pain. The broken head rolled to my feet—and I understood what had happened. It was spilling milk—it had been hollow! The nipples of the breasts must have been stopped with wax, melted by Bathsheba's flame!

The knowledge that I had been deceived so easily by her sent my madness even higher. I sprang once more upon the boulder and heaved it up for a second time, whirling about even as Bathsheba ran to prevent what I intended. I flung it over her head. Yahweh guided my arm. The stone crashed fair against the cone. The symbol of Ashtoreth tottered, fell apart. It rolled helplessly on the mystic tiles. I gave a shout of triumph.

Bathsheba screamed. I staggered back from her onrush. She flung herself past me, at full length, onto the ruins of the round white cone that still rolled mindlessly on the pavement. She fondled the bits to her, moaning in pure agony. Her black hair bathed the pieces of shattered symbol. I watched her, a rising flood of dread in my breast. I stood there with my teeth chattering, not knowing what to do.

Suddenly the sky darkened. I looked up. The swiftly moving rack of dark clouds had obscured the moon. As I watched, terrified, I heard the low angry growl of thunder. From the clouds there came the flicker of lightning. Again and again, as the flickering of a gigantic asp's tongue.

I looked down just in time. Bathsheba had snatched up my knife. On her knees, she drove herself forward. I leaped backward. The stroke of the blade struck sparks from the stone under our feet. The thunder-roll sounded louder overhead. Bathsheba and I stood as shadows in the deadly darkness. I recoiled. She jerked to her feet, her hair spun out into a second ghastly shadow. Her white face glimmered in utter madness. She shrieked again, this time in rage and launched herself at me once more.

I delayed no longer. I jumped from the platform of Ashtoreth in panic, tumbling head over heels among the rocks below. I picked myself up, and half reeling, half running, I careered headlong down the mountainside—expecting at any moment to have my own blade driven into my back.

I was wrong. Bathsheba, still moaning like a demented spirit of the night, had turned back to the shattered symbol of her goddess. But still I fled downward as if demons pursued me. I was driven by my own fears and faithlessness. In my heart, I doubted that Yahweh would—or could—protect me from the wrath of a heathen goddess and the woman that worshipped her.

CHAPTER EIGHT

The Theft of the Ark

In these days of footless tale-telling, where no one knows the truth—when riot and rebellion ride across the once-fair land of the Hebrews—where Rehoboam and Jeroboam, north and south, Israel and Judah, contend for mastery—the mystery of the ark of the covenant is lightly explained. It is said that it was seized after the death of Solomon by the pharaoh Shishak who came out of Egypt in his paralyzing raid on the temple only last summer, the fifth year of the reign of Rehoboam, Solomon's son.

That is not true. Shishak did, to be sure, capture David's city of Jerusalem. He did invade the temple precincts. He did seize the treasures of the temple and rape the king's treasury, stealing the shields of gold that Solomon had fashioned.

But the ark of the covenant he did not capture. Nor does any reliable history—save those of the wandering reciters who deal in witless nonsense—say such a thing.

What truly happened to the ark I now relate for those who are wise enough to read. The reason that Shishak did not pounce upon it and carry it away from under the sheltering wings of the twin cherubim is simple. This is the real story of that precious object, the symbol of all Hebrew hopes.

For those who do not know about it, the ark of the covenant was a sacred chest. It was the most ancient and holy relic of our people. Hewed out of desert acacia wood, it stood forty-five inches long, twenty-seven inches wide, and twenty-seven inches deep. It was covered without (and, some said, within) with sheets of beaten gold. Atop lay another sheet of gold, with two gilt cherubim of olivewood—the mercy seat where the presence of Yahweh descended in moments of stress or danger. Two men, always of the tribe of the Levites, carried it during the long journeyings of the Hebrews from place to place, thrusting long staves of acacia wood through four golden rings. When it rested in the midst of our people, it was covered night and day by a tent of red leather and curtains of finest linen.

What lay within the ark, I never knew. I was never a high priest. Only he was accounted worthy to open the ark. Others—such as the Philistines and some of our more daring people—who had peeped within had been stricken down by plague or apoplexy, like old stout Eli. It was rumored, however, that the ark contained the original covenant tablets of Moses from Sinai, as well as the sacred brazen serpents.

The ark had been long lost—for more than twenty years—in Kirjath-jearim in the house of Abinadab before David had rescued it from obscurity. He brought it back to the tabernacle. Solomon, on the building of the temple, had enshrined it—as we know—in the most holy place. There it remained until one day two years and seven months after the dedication of the temple itself, a day so infamous that even now it must remain unknown lest it become the blackest in the calendar of our people.

My first hint of sacrilege came as I toiled over government papers. I sat in the chamber that Solomon had assigned to me until more spacious quarters would be available in the new palace which Hiram-abi was building for him to the east of the temple area. I was not sure how long it would take. Hiram-abi had promised to finish within five years. But Solomon had made so many changes in the original plans, he had added so much ornamentation that now the completion date seemed more than double that estimate.

However, I was content as I toiled. Occasionally my eyes troubled me—both the fitful light of reed lamps and bright sunlight bothered me—but other than that, I had no complaint. My history of Solomon's reign was well up to date. The king had generously increased my emolument. And Elihaph and others kept me well informed about events in the Hebrew nation.

One sorrow twisted my heart. My older son, Azariah, performed his duties faithfully. I gave praises to Yahweh for his dutiful works. But Zabud—ah, younger and dearer to me!—never came to his father. I heard more reports of his follies with Solomon and more than once tried to seek him out again for remonstrance. As the king's friend he was no longer my child. It weighed on my life; I discovered a father suffers more for the sins of his children than the children themselves.

Thus it was a stunning surprise when, shortly after the dawn, Zabud appeared in my room. I hid my gladness under a mask of stern rebuke. My eyes traveled over his rich costume, stained and muddied as it was by debauch, over his face that was wan, his eyes bloodshot and wandering, his lips pale and slack.

"I am happy to see you once more," I said sardonically. "A good son should visit his parent at least once a year."

"I have not been a good son," Zabud said listlessly. He ran his hand through his long yellow hair.

"But you drive chariots well, judge horses expertly, and play and sing and drink to the king's content," I said bitingly.

"No longer," Zabud said.

"What do you say?"

"Give me a drink of water," Zabud said suddenly. "I die of thirst."

"There," I said, pointing to the baked-clay jar of cooled water in the corner. Zabud made his way over to it, sucking in double handfuls of water until he bloated. At last he turned away, his robe drenched.

"I have come to you," he said, "because there was no one else to come to."

"I am grateful," I said stiffly.

"My father, I was drunk last night with the king."

"I had not thought otherwise," I said. "And the night before and the night before that."

"I do not deny it," Zabud said simply. "But last night was a different night."

"How is that?"

"Afterward—I had a dream."

"What of it? Everyone has dreams."

"This was a strange one."

"I can imagine it was," I said ironically. "Since you ceased to be my son and became the king's companion, you must have had many such dreams."

Zabud remained withdrawn. "I have resigned from the king's service," he said.

"Impossible."

"Yet true."

"When was this sacrifice made?" I demanded.

"Now," Zabud said calmly.

I widened my eyes in spite of myself. "Why?" I asked.

"Even if you plead with Solomon, he will not let you go from his side."

"He will not have the chance to refuse me. Not after my dream."

His tone took me by the throat. This youngster was, after all, my son. Even though he had erred far from the proper way, the statutes of Yahweh and of my family, yet he was to be pitied. My old affection for him came back with a rush.

"Did this dream come from Yahweh?" I inquired in a gentler tone, much more kindly than I intended.

Zabud looked at me. His eyes flashed, then became dull again. "I do not know," he said, "but I believe it came from the Adversary."

"What was it? Perhaps I can interpret it for you."

"No. But, all the same, I shall tell you. I dreamed I was carrying a burden, a box of gold."

"A box of gold?" I said, smiling. "That is an excellent dream. It needs no interpretation."

Zabud made an impatient gesture. "No," he said. "It was not that." He started to speak again, then thought better of it. Ah, if I had shown him sympathy, how many things would have been different afterward! But I was hard and inexorable; I said nothing of pity and my eyes held condemnation.

Zabud sighed and rose. He tried to smile. "Do you know, my father," he asked me, "I must make a decision? It will be one of the first and certainly the greatest decision I have ever made by myself."

"It is time," I said coldly.

"It is useless to ask you to help me," he said, half-questioningly.

I nodded. Zabud's face tightened. Without a word of farewell, he turned to the door and went out. I sat for moments, fighting the urge to call him back, to embrace him and offer forgiveness, no matter what. But I did not: instead, I returned to my papers, mechanically reading and scribing and sealing.

It was late the same morning that I experienced my second surprise. Michal asked to see me. I had not seen the old hag for a longer time than I had my son. I was hesitant about seeing her now but my mind gnawed at me since I had sent Zabud away without a word.

I ordered her admitted and allowed her to sit. She startled me by her appearance. I had not realized that Michal had changed so much during the past few months. Her figure had become stooped, her face had lost its dignity and become wizened and malicious. I had no idea what was working within her flesh but truly she was the very figure of a witch with her grotesque face under her hood, the same face that had once charmed David long years before. Involuntarily I made the secret sign that averted evil. I waited. Michal leered at me with her toothless mouth and cavernous eyes.

"What is it, wife of David?" I asked.

"I come to tell you that the good fortune of Solomon is gone, vanished like smoke into the air," she croaked.

I put the tips of my fingers together and regarded them closely. "You have never loved Solomon," I said.

"He is king of the Hebrews."

"You bow your head but your heart is unbowed," I said severely. "You never wished Solomon good fortune."

"I have never wished him ill," she muttered.

"There was that business of Edom."

"I had nothing to do with it. Hadad has long since retired once more into Egypt."

"Do you know so much?" I asked.

She bobbed her head. "So much is known on every street corner," she replied defiantly.

"There was the death years ago of Merib-baal," I said coolly, staring at her in hopes of making this ancient woman betray herself.

"What has that to do with me?" she demanded.

I sighed. It was impossible to read any expression in those wrinkled features. "What is this information you bring me?" I asked her.

Michal cackled. "I bring you warning only," she said. "Zadok will soon be here. He visited the temple, as was his duty, this morning. Listen well to what he says."

My fingers suddenly felt cold. I thrust my hands into my girdle. "What are you talking about?" I wanted to know.

Michal got waveringly to her feet, hunched over her cane. "I wanted to be the first," she said. "I am nearly dead now but I wanted to be the very first to tell you."

Turning, she hobbled out. I let her go, frowning and blinking after her. I did not know what to say. I returned to my papers but again and again my mind was troubled by her croakings like those of a raven feeding upon the dead.

The unknown news that I dreaded in my soul came less than an hour later. It came from Zadok himself. He staggered into my chamber, his face fixed in a look of horror—the face that was still seamed and tight-shiny-red from the scars he had endured during that first sacrifice at the dedication.

"Nathan!" he gasped. He sank unbidden to a chair before me. He spread his shaking fingers over his face.

"What is it?" I asked him sharply.

He shook his head from side to side, beginning to wail softly. He seemed incapable of controlling himself. "What is it?" I asked again in alarm.

Again Zadok refused to answer. I sprang up, tore his hands from his face and forced up his chin. I glared at him, my bowels working with fear and rage. "Tell me!" I half-shouted.

"The ark!" whimpered Zadok, his mouth dribbling.

"What about the ark?"

"The most holy place!"

I seized him by the shoulders. "Tell me, Zadok!" I hissed at him.

He looked up at me with stricken eyes. His body was as limp as beaten cloth in my fingers, as if all strength had left him. "It is gone," he whispered, "it is gone, it is gone."

"What!"

Zadok put his trembling fingers to his mouth as if he had uttered sacrilege. He nodded and rose. He tottered forward so that I was forced to catch him, though my own limbs had begun to quake. I shook him as hard as I could.

"What do you say?" I demanded again and again. Zadok responded limply, a puppet on invisible strings. His eyes rolled upward. He collapsed in a faint.

I let him fall and sprang to the jar of water in the corner. Dipping up with both hands, I splashed his face again and again. His color gradually returned. His eyes fluttered open. Almost as soon as his short quick breathing slowed, as he regained consciousness, he began rolling his head from side to side. The high priest was almost out of his mind. I feared that he had been afflicted of Yahweh.

I picked up his slight body and carried it to my couch. I squatted down beside him. "Zadok," I said in a low tone, "tell me what happened. Tell me everything, keep nothing back. What has happened in the temple?"

The high priest took a deep shuddering breath. He stared upward and began to speak in hoarse tones, as if he were reciting an event burned into his brain. His story was the most dreadful I had ever heard—even today my pen falters in writing about it.

What he had to say was clear. He had gone into the holy

place as usual that morning to replenish the candles of the *menorah.* As he made his obeisance to the holy of holies, he noticed to his horror that the acacia staves used to carry the ark no longer protruded from the inner chamber. Gripped by cold fear, he did nothing for long moments. Finally getting up courage, he uttered an agonized prayer to Yahweh for forgiveness and slowly approached the most holy place. With black foreboding, he had lifted the sacred curtain and peered inside.

"Could you see?" I urged him.

He nodded. "Yes, yes," he moaned.

"What did you see?"

"Nothing at all, nothing."

"Nothing? Speak, Zadok!"

"Only the great golden wings of the cherubim over an empty space," he gasped. "Only that. Nothing else was there, nothing at all."

"Are you sure?"

He nodded once more, momentarily speechless in his torture of body and mind. "I am sure," he said at last.

"And the *shekinah,* the light of the Lord that beams in the most holy place?" I asked in awe. There was no possibility of another of Hiram-abi's tricks here.

Zadok shook his head. "It was not there," he said, "only the flickering light of the *menorah* from behind me."

"I must see for myself," I said.

Zadok roused, coming to a sitting posture, his disfigured face slimed with sweat and tears. "No," he whispered, "no, it is forbidden, forbidden!"

I beat my hands together helplessly. He was right. I could not look into the sanctuary. I could hardly believe what he had told me but I knew that Zadok would not lie about such a terrible event.

"Perhaps Yahweh has taken it to Himself," I suggested, not believing it for a moment.

A wild light of hope sprang into Zadok's eyes. He gripped my sleeve feverishly. "Do you think that is true?" he asked me.

I shook my head. "No," I said.

"Then—"

"How can I tell?" I cried roughly. I shook myself free of him and stood up.

Zadok fell back, again making strangled sounds of wretchedness. I snatched at my hair in a sudden access of pain, tearing at it by the roots.

"Gone!" I said aloud. "Gone! The ark of the covenant!" I could not help my grief and horror, despite my efforts to remain calm.

"Now that His mercy-seat has vanished," Zadok whined, "the grace of Yahweh is taken from our people. He will not descend to us again."

"He will have mercy," I muttered. "He will not desert us in the hour of tribulation." I forced myself to think; my legs would no longer support me. I sank onto a bench, my head whirling. I had not imagined such desecration possible.

"If Yahweh has not taken the ark," I mumbled, "then it has been taken by an enemy, as it was captured by the Philistines in my youth."

"Enemies? But we have no enemies in Jerusalem!"

It was true. We sat in silence, gazing into nothingness for a long time. The sun waned in the chamber as the golden square clambered imperceptibly up the opposite wall. We strove to subdue our spirits so that we might talk without the stammer of black hopelessness. At last I managed to get to my feet.

"Have you told the king?" I demanded.

Zadok shook his head, fear coming alive in his eyes. "I dare not, I dare not," he muttered. He again took his head in his hands and began to sway back and forth, keening to himself in a monotone. I paced the chamber from end to end, trying not to connect the terrible suspicions in my mind. But at last I knew my duty.

"We must see King Solomon," I said.

In his audience room Solomon listened without a word to what Zadok had to say. I said nothing. When Zadok had finished, Solomon—whose face had hardened into grim lines—asked him to repeat the story again. As Zadok finished for the second time, Solomon held up his hand. He looked at me.

"Do you believe this thing?" he asked.

I swallowed hard. "Zadok would not lie about it," I said. "His life and soul hang upon it."

Solomon nodded jerkily. I could see he was undecided what to do. He pondered a moment while Zadok gulped back his sobs, then commanded me to pass into the next building to bring Bathsheba. "We shall have need of her counsel," he said. "But take care this is not known to anyone else."

Biting my lips to keep from weeping, I did as I was bid. Bathsheba tried to command me into telling her what the occasion of her son's summoning was but I said nothing. She pouted grimly and would not speak to me again. We entered silently into Solomon's chambers and Benaiah closed the doors behind us.

Solomon and Zadok waited in much the same positions as when I had left them. Bathsheba looked at her son. She interrogated him with a lift of her eyebrows. I saw with a queer pang how well she looked, even with her glorious black hair cut short as that of a boy. The king beckoned her closer.

"My mother," Solomon said tersely, "I have asked you to come here because of calamity to our kingdom. We must not speak of it outside this chamber—but I need your advice."

"What is this calamity?" Bathsheba said softly. "You have not sought my advice for so long that I am overwhelmed by the honor."

Solomon leaned toward her. "The ark of the covenant has vanished from the most holy place," he whispered.

Zadok wailed aloud. I could not help imitating his expression of grief. Benaiah at the door seemed unmoved, though Solomon's voice shook with awe and grief. Of us all, Bathsheba seemed untouched by the news: her beautiful mouth even lifted in a slight smile. Her reply to Solomon stunned us.

"I know," she said.

Before we could recover our breath, there was a sharp, insistent hammering at the door. Solomon jerked himself erect. He gestured toward Benaiah who turned to the entrance. We heard the portals creak, an excited colloquy, the curt refusal of Benaiah and the slamming and barring of the doors. There was a wail of anguish from outside, then the sound of running feet that faded down the corridor.

"Who was it?" demanded Solomon tensely. "Is—is what we know already known?"

Benaiah shook his head stolidly. "I do not think so, O king," he replied in his harsh tones. "It was Zabud, demanding to see you."

"Zabud! At this hour? Was he drunk?"

"Perhaps, sire."

"He has no business here," Solomon said. He dismissed the irritation. He bent his fulminating gaze again upon Bathsheba.

"You said you already knew," he said. "Who was it that told you? He must die."

"No one told me," Bathsheba returned serenely.

For a moment, there was silence in the room. We looked at each other, a vast dark premonition seizing our hearts, burning our flesh. I felt my muscles sag, my mouth open. My head swam, and I could no longer think clearly.

"No one?" muttered Solomon hoarsely. "No one? How could you have known otherwise?"

"It was I who took the ark," Bathsheba said clearly.

"You lie!"

"No."

"By the holy name of Yahweh, you lie!"

"I do not lie, my son," Bathsheba said with amazing dignity.

Solomon slumped back in his throne. Benaiah stood rigid. Zadok and I held our breaths, not daring to speak, not knowing what to say or expect, not conscious of anything in this world except that the king's mother had confessed to the most awful sacrilege.

"My mother," Solomon said in a bare whisper, "I wish you, I command you, to say what you said once more so that I can believe my ears."

"I took the ark from the most holy place," Bathsheba said. In spite of her calm, her voice shook.

The air seethed and lowered about her with the incredulity and rage of all of us who heard her. Solomon stared at her, his dark eyes unnaturally wide. I saw that the hair upon his sleek head had risen. I felt the same horripilation down my own back. I shrank from the woman I had once thought the most desirable in the world.

"You!" shouted Solomon, half rising. "What monstrous jest is this? What do you say? My mother is mad!"

"What babble is this, my son?" said Bathsheba, her voice shaking, rising.

"Babble?" Solomon said slowly, vacantly. He flung down his wand of power and ran both hands wildly through his long hair. I could see him groping for his will, seeking control. Bit by bit, he gained it. I waited, every muscle in my body tight, my flesh distended.

Solomon sat very still. His shivering passed. His face became set, gray and expressionless. His eyes bored mercilessly into those of Bathsheba but his hands, clasped before him, worked constantly, the fingers like shuttles of flesh.

"I say I do not believe you, Bathsheba," he enunciated formally. He had ceased to call her mother. "I shall tell you why. The ark of the covenant is heavy with gold. Two men have all they can do to carry it."

"Perhaps I was not alone," Bathsheba murmured. I was

amazed at her tone: she could still take on light, condescending airs, even at such a moment.

"Let us pretend that you committed this crime that is a crime not only against me, not only against the Hebrew people but a crime against Yahweh Himself. Let us agree with you. Let us say you had help." Solomon's voice grew terrible. "Who?" he spat at his mother.

Bathsheba commenced to lose her assurance. The flush in her cheeks faded. Her eyes glimmered with the beginnings of an unheralded fear. "He was drunk," she said. "He was witless. He did not know what he did other than that it was a prank. But he, too, believed it was no crime."

"Then, a man," Solomon said grimly. "Who?"

Bathsheba shook her head. "I shall never tell you," she replied stubbornly.

Solomon paused. "Do you know, Bathsheba," he said with deadly intensity, "what it is to be tortured, bit by bit? Do you not believe that we can tear that lovely flesh of yours, that my father adored, from your bones, piece by piece? Do you know what boiling waters can do, the sear of hot irons? Do you think your tongue will not wag if I say one word only?"

Again I was astonished. Bathsheba intrepidly gave back her son stare for stare. "I shall not betray him, if it is a crime as you pretend," she said in a small voice.

"As I pretend!" cried Solomon. "Do you tell me that the removal of the ark is anything but the greatest crime?"

"I do not worship Yahweh." Bathsheba said. "You know that. I am not a Hebrew, I am Hittite. My gods are not your god. You built me a chapel in the hills. I have sacrificed to Baal there many a time and you have not forbidden it."

Sweat sprang out on Solomon's forehead. "Why?" he demanded thickly. "Why did you steal the ark?"

It was a question Bathsheba had been waiting for. Her face blazed with quick passion. The blood returned to the roots of her hair. She beat her tiny fist on the floor. "Because of Zadok, because of Nathan, because of the priests!" she said vehemently. "Because you were not king any longer! They would consult Yahweh or the ark or the Urim and Thummim—and you would yield! Your voice was lost! Solomon was not king! I knew the reasons!" She half turned and threw her scorn like spittle at us. "There are the men who are responsible! Nathan, who made you a lamb to follow him about and gambol at his bidding—pretending that he had visions or instructions from Yahweh! Zadok, the fool!"

I could find no words. I shook my head from side to side

like a man in agony. Solomon did not notice. His flashing blue eyes were fixed still upon his mother.

"You lie again," he said quietly. "I am king, I sit in judgment upon all that passes. I give my word as I see fit and I am obeyed."

"No, no! I did what I did so that you would be alone upon the throne of David! Your will alone—not with the pretense of this so called Lord at your side!"

For a moment more, Solomon said nothing. The chamber was filled with tension, so much so that I actually feared the walls might burst asunder. The very air smoked with the force of the will that the king in this moment directed against Bathsheba.

"Who was the man?" he said.

Bathsheba, pale as paper now, his gaze bent upon her, yet had her dauntless courage. "I shall not tell you," she answered. "I shall not tear your heart in two."

"*My* heart!" exclaimed Solomon, taken aback. "You have done this by your own confession and you wish to spare me?"

Bathsheba nodded, her head jerking on her shoulders with their clear mountings of perfect skin. "I shall not tell," she said.

Solomon became icy cold. "Then," he said with an air of finality, "we shall have to find out."

Bathsheba leaped to her feet. She tore apart her shawl and exposed her bosom. "Here are my breasts," she said in an unnatural tone. "You sucked at them often enough, long enough. Tear them from my body first. I shall not betray you."

"Betray *me!*"

"All I have done, I have done for your good!"

"You foul witch!" cried Solomon, shuddering, his calm destroyed. "Do you know what this means? When the loss of the ark is known? Do you think the kingdom is safe? The very throne heaves under me at the thought!"

"You can silence all mouths," Bathsheba said.

Solomon rose, shaking. He flung his hands upward. "Curse you, my mother!" he ejaculated. "I appoint terror to you, consumption, the burning ague, consuming your eyes and heart! I shall break the pride of you, I shall chastise you seven times seven, you shall eat your own flesh, suck your own blood!" Breathless, he collapsed.

"What demon prompts you to speak like this?" Bathsheba whispered.

"Demons of honor, of blood, of justice, of truth," Solomon said. "Demons of hatred of lies, of your past and future madness."

"Solomon," Bathsheba said piteously, "you must not speak like this. I did it only for you."

"For me! You desecrate the sanctuary of Yahweh for me!"

"Yes."

"Where does one go to flee from the wrath of the Lord? From love or hate?" Solomon sank back onto the throne, covering his face with his working hands. "I feel nothing except terror and shame and cold—as if I were dying."

"You cannot die," Bathsheba whispered, "for if you die, I die."

Solomon uncovered his face. His haggard features began to move. They fixed themselves like rock under pressure. Bathsheba could not look away; her face reflected the terror she felt. The small cries which escaped her heaving bosom indicated that she knew his thought.

"No!" she cried, cowering back.

Solomon pointed his finger like an avenging angel.

"Kill her," he said, the two words like stones from a sling.

I had not noticed before but Benaiah stood directly behind Bathsheba. As Solomon spoke, quick as lightning, Benaiah's huge hands encircled her lovely neck.

"Wait!" Bathsheba shrieked. Her panic rose to a scream. "Zabud, he will—"

Before she could finish, Benaiah's hands closed their grip. Her voice died in a gurgle.

"Stop!" cried Solomon, springing erect.

"No!" I shouted, flinging myself at Benaiah across the paralyzed Zadok.

We were both too late. Benaiah's muscular thumbs had closed on the back of Bathsheba's neck. Before we could interfere, they bore down upon the nape. Loud in the chamber, we heard the snap of bone. Bathsheba's beautiful head suddenly tilted sideways, loose, without control. Her eyes glazed. Her hands at Benaiah's wrists fell away. She was dead.

Benaiah released her. She slumped lifeless to the floor, a mass of flesh that had been once the love of David and the adoration of Solomon—whom I had truly worshipped but had never been able to touch. I stared at her body, not believing what I saw.

"I have obeyed, O king," Benaiah said.

Together Solomon and I flung ourselves on Bathsheba's corpse in a storm of weeping. Zadok slithered down beside us with a sigh and fainted. Benaiah alone stood erect, motionless.

Bathsheba had spoken the name of Zabud. It was our only hope of finding out what had happened to the sacred ark. As soon as our tempest of sorrow was over, Solomon commanded his general to seek out my son. He was ordered to bring him to the throne room as soon as might be. Again Benaiah obeyed. The news he brought back was a fresh source of grief to Solomon and myself and answered no questions.

Zabud's body was found broken and mangled at the bottom of the Hinnom. He had evidently cast himself from the highest point of the wall of Jerusalem that overlooked that noisome gulf. With him went all hope of discovering the truth about the ark of the covenant. Nor was it ever discovered again. Solomon ordered the most secret and thorough searches carried out in every direction in and around the city, investigating every cranny where such a sacred object might be hidden but without success. So many caves existed, so many places of possible hiding that the finding of the ark proved to be an impossibility. I still dream of it in nightmare, squatting in a rock cleft filled with horsehair and the bones and feathers of strange birds, looking down to see its square golden splendor far in a bottomless gulf, supported by the acacia poles—and find myself unable to move or do anything, except wake in tears and lamentations.

It was true that Zabud and Solomon had indulged in an orgy the night before and that the youngster had vanished, where none knew. We could only guess Bathsheba had inveigled him into such a monstrous prank, that he had come to confess first to me and then to Solomon—and we had both turned him away. As a result, he had hurled himself to destruction in despair and regret. Nor could discreet questioning among the inhabitants of Jerusalem elicit more. The temple, up to this time, had always been unguarded. It was believed to be so holy that guards were unnecessary. Now Solomon appointed seven Levites to be on duty by day in patrolling the grounds, seven more by night.

The only suspicion that remained alive in my brain was that the deed could not have been done by Bathsheba and Zabud alone—the ark was simply too heavy. I believed that three or more were involved, but this was useless guessing. As to the final fact of the disappearance of this holy relic, I recall the day after, when Solomon commanded us into his presence—Benaiah, Zadok, and myself. I had never before seen the young king so worn, so transparent in the flesh with grief—and so worthy for the first time of his high destiny of rule.

He cast round him a long look, as pointed and weighty as tempered iron. He was no longer a frivolous king; he was a monarch weighed down by cares. At one stroke of Yahweh, both his closest and best-loved companion and his most honored mother had been taken from him. Now indeed he was lonely on the highest place. He had assumed a majestic melancholy that never afterward left him. I felt the keenest pangs of sorrow in my own spirit, yearning to cry out and rend my garments for my youngest son and for the woman I loved—but I dared not. And somehow the identity of our grief brought the king and me closer together for all the remaining days of his reign.

Solomon looked at each of us in turn, a piercing, terrible glance. He spoke slowly, as if to allow each word to sink of its own import deep into our memories.

"No one else shall know of this," he said. "Only you, Nathan; you, Benaiah and Zadok; and I have charge of this secret from Yahweh. May all the curses of heaven and earth, in this life and the life to come descend upon that one of us who allows it to be known beyond this room."

"I take oath upon Yahweh," I said.

"I swear by His secret name," Zadok added quaveringly. Benaiah raised his hands and swore the oath.

Solomon nodded but he did not swear. He gestured. We left, hurriedly enough, glad to escape that place of misery.

All this I have written down was a long time ago. Solomon sleeps with David in the tomb, and Zadok and Benaiah have long been dust. The kingdom has been riven by Rehoboam and Jeroboam, harassed and ravaged by Rezon and Shishak. But what happened then should be told. I am absolved by years and events from my oath.

Judah and Israel now should know what became of the ark. They must realize the impossibility of its return. For it dwells neither in Egypt nor Babylon but in the knowledge of the Most High alone. Sometimes I speculated as to what Bathsheba—the only one who knew on earth—might have said when she faced Yahweh before His mercy seat in heaven. That is idle, idle. Still, knowing her, I am sure that she had some feminine excuse for what she did—and that He, in all His masculine majesty, was pleased to forgive her.

CHAPTER NINE

The Duel of Benaiah

Solomon, in the twenty-seventh year of his age and the thirteenth of his reign, after the splendid burial of Bathsheba, discovered that all that had been so simple before now began to turn twisted and intricate. Michal had been right. The good fortune of Solomon had commenced to go out of him. As if the old crone had been the most inspired of prophets, we found that the peace and happiness of our kingdom of the Hebrews—and of Solomon himself—had started to decline with the vanishing of the ark. Michal had disappeared. We were never to see her again in the kingdom of the Hebrews. Years later I heard of her in the domain of the Assyrians, even in her dotage attempting to stir up that warlike nation against Solomon but nothing so far has come of it.

Not that misfortune descended immediately upon the king and his reign. His father David had built the foundation of a strong rule both wisely and soundly. So secure were his works that only gradually did it become apparent that his son, Solomon, stood under the growing wrath of Yahweh. From that time forth, nothing was altogether right though many things had a fair appearance.

Outwardly, all was well. Splendidly, one by one, as in a stately procession, came the designated Feast of Unleavened Bread, the Feast of Weeks, and the Feast of Tabernacles in all their glory before Yahweh. Yet the savor was not as sweet as it had been. The incense from the altar was not as pungent. Nor was the chorus of thanksgiving and praise as golden and crystal as it had been. It is curious how much can change so quickly under the scourge of time, flayed beyond recognition by no more than a few years. "What profit," Solomon once asked me, "has a man of all the labor that he takes under the sun?"

Little enough, to be sure. Those things which have been old and precious become fragile and cannot endure vulgarity and rough handling—but this was always the way of the young. What was, perishes; but what comes is what has already been. I, Nathan, hope that the wheel that Yahweh turns will again bring to pass the same delights we have known but my old eyes cannot see that far into the future. But I do know that much vanished in my own time.

Once the brilliant colors of the temple, for example, did not only excite the eye. They caused vibrations of awe and veneration in the spirit long afterward. They produced chords of sanctity. It was no accident that Solomon chose purple for himself, as Moses had chosen it for the sanctuary. Like crimson and blue—the other holy colors which, of course, combine to make purple—it had a deep trembling effect upon the heart. Now I saw the same colors faded, the edge of feeling dulled, the old ecstasy brought low.

The same was true of the odors of the sanctified oil with myrrh, cinnamon, calamus, and cassia that perfumed the king's head. So, too, the incense burned at the altar with its stacte, onycha, galbanum, and sweet frankincense. Such fragrances were once so delightful that they made some faint and others reel, as if their emotions were too much to endure.

But above all, I must declare the loss of the mystical power of speech. In the days of Samuel, words had tremendous force, far beyond their meaning. They might heal, excite fury or tame passions, even perform miracles at the intonation of certain phrases. Force sprang out of the syllables describing an object with almost the power within the object itself. Cursing, you may imagine, was a fatal talent; just as blessing was a high and joyful one. The ear and the tongue were fearful weapons together. Now they were edgeless and rusty, no more than the gabble of geese or the gruntings of animals.

Above all, our people once remembered. They had passed through mighty experiences as a group. Even though this was hundreds of years before, still they had held it together in remembrance—so thoroughly and sharply had it descended to the present race of Hebrews that any one of us could, at any moment, close his eyes and recall—as if he had been present with his ancestors—the tribulations and triumphs of Moses and Joshua. This racial recollection, more than any single thing given us by the Lord, held us together as one. Quarreling and contentious as we have always been by nature, it took only the old words of enchantment to take us back to the past and bring peace to our minds, minds and bodies that once had to act as one in order to survive.

But in these latter days, this great pool of the past into

which we might plunge for renewal and refreshment has begun to ebb, to shallow. There are no longer the depths that once existed. New usages, new thought, new seekings have made a parched desert of our memories. Our senses are dulled by too much noise, too much activity, too many sights. Now all these are toys to be tossed about, to serve us in our pleasures. Words of doubt have torn down the sacred embroidered veil that once stood between what is holy and what is merely common.

Such things come to me as I write because of what happened so to Solomon after the loss of the ark and the death of Bathsheba. His life commenced to take on shadings of the cynical and sophisticated. He paid less and less attention to the warnings of Yahweh, more and more to worldly things. Part of this was due to the fact that he knew the Hebrews worshipped at a temple from whence the soul of the ark had been taken. Part was due to the fact that Bathsheba was dead and my son, Zabud, with her. Solomon turned less to me for advice and more to Benaiah, who represented the triumph of power, and his own impulses. Never again did Solomon go to the high place at Gibeon where he had been accustomed to wait for the word of the Lord.

Strangely enough, however, Solomon's aptitude for wisdom increased. Though he kept his love for riddles, the king also studied esoteric doctrines. He loved to probe into the secrets of nature. But such knowledge was of the mind, not the spirit; he suffered accordingly. He viewed women especially more as the opponents of man, who had forced him to eat the Sodom's apple of knowledge in the garden of Eden, less as the playthings of a boy. Abishag, who had grown fat and arrogant, he allowed to keep her post as queen of the harem. But he took many other women to comfort him.

In order to gain the king's attention, I was thrown more and more into contact with Benaiah. This squat, powerful man, with his rugged, ugly face and tight-curled black hair, radiated immense physical magnetism—but he cared not an iota about anything but what he could grasp with his senses. He had served both David as a youth and Solomon as a man—willingly and well. Yet I began to suspect him more than ever of depths beyond those that he exhibited.

He had been relieved of his duties as personal guard to the palace and to the person of Solomon. He had been elevated to the king's counselor, on a level near to my own. His philosophy was directly opposed to what I believed. To a degree, it was counter to what Yahweh Himself favored. But

Solomon ever enjoyed pitting Benaiah's brutal philosophy against my more reasoned advice.

I recall the occasion when Benaiah best summed up his thinking. I had visited him in his quarters. I found him polishing his iron sword, the same one that had once belonged to Joab—he was always polishing it—with the usual sand and olive oil. I vividly remember the questions involved in our discussion, and his remarks remain etched in my memory.

"Force is the last act of wisdom," Benaiah said in his precise, rasping voice. He scoured his sword blade harder.

"I cannot think so," I replied. "Reasonable men can sit down together, discuss their differences, and agree."

Benaiah pursed his lips. "If there are such things as reasonable men when their vital interests are threatened," he said politely, "but I have never seen such."

"I am one," I said.

"If we have a discussion and I kill you, I have won."

"Not in the sight of Yahweh."

"It was so in the time of Joshua and in the time of Joab," Benaiah said tonelessly, "and it will be so again."

"If you are correct," I said, "what if someone else uses your argument first?"

"The same prevails."

"If someone kills you?" I asked incredulously.

"Don't you see?" demanded Benaiah impatiently. "Someone else wins but the wisdom of force is still the same."

I was aghast. "But right and wrong," I argued. "Do not these have great importance?"

Benaiah exposed his large yellow teeth mirthlessly. "He who survives is right and he who does not survive is wrong," he said.

"That is wholly in error," I said emphatically.

"Forgive me, O Nathan," Benaiah said, "but you mean that you have not heard what you wanted to hear from me. Therefore, it is irritating. Nothing, I admit, is so annoying as to face the naked facts of our miserable existence."

I felt surprised. "Our existence is miserable?" I asked. Benaiah did not answer and I pressed him: "What about the knowledge of goodness that is in every heart, put there by Yahweh?"

"Once we admit the existence of right and wrong," Benaiah said, "we must, of course, examine our nature. This instinct of Yahweh that you speak of—it is only a discomfort, like an aching muscle, easily conquered."

"What do you mean?"

"If we live, we are entitled to live comfortably—that is, free of the threat of our aches or our enemies. Most of what you believe to be the whisper of Yahweh within us is merely a memory of an act which we may consider evil."

"You are somewhat of a philosopher for a fighting man," I said defensively.

"I must think of everything," Benaiah said. "All that is needed to wipe out this feeling is some act which we think is good. It can easily be done in most cases."

"I don't understand."

Benaiah made a short chopping gesture over his sword across his lap. "Let us take the case of destroying a city, slaughtering men, women, and children," he said. "It has been done many times, by us as well as by our foes. We believe it to be good because we have dedicated their lives and the razing of their stronghold to Yahweh."

"That is different," I said feebly.

"No. The same are the methods of the Egyptians and the Assyrians, for example. But if you desire to stifle your whisper from Yahweh, to kill a certain number of people in a case other than war, it is equally easy."

The debate was carrying me far into a black region that I abhorred but I could not stop the swift flow of the argument. I heard Benaiah go on:

"You simply select from these people the most brutal and degenerate, play upon the most primitive emotions such as greed and lust, appoint them to do the murders. Then you summon their leader—who will become apparent in the process—and increase his appetites. That is, you point out to him how much more secure in his position he will be if all the others are eliminated."

"I don't understand," I said dazedly.

"Once he stands alone as the master killer, you send for the people of law and have him arrested, accused, tried, and executed. At this point the whisper of Yahweh should be very faint indeed. But if it requires a further step, it is easy enough to take the process further—to have the executioner himself condemned to a dungeon for life—not executed, mind you—for having exceeded his instructions."

"I see," I murmered.

"Do you?" Benaiah said in a bored tone. "Have I shown a new way of thought to the great Nathan?"

I roused myself. "If I understand the way you think," I said bitingly, "it does not mean that I agree."

Benaiah nodded, as if my answer were what he had expected. "It is simply a question of convincing yourself that either you had nothing to do with the act or that it was done in justice," he said. "That is all."

"It is not enough!"

"Allow me to say that I, at least, have found it enough. And you must admit that it is so well founded in the nature of men—as it is, I may say, in animals—that it is as infallible as day following night. Yahweh Himself permits it. In fact, He has often demanded it."

This, I felt, was intolerable but it was hard to deny. I stood up to try to conclude the discussion. "Yahweh has often been misunderstood by His ministers," I said severely.

Benaiah's eyes gleamed. "As you say, O Nathan," he agreed. "You are naturally the best judge of that."

Stung, I turned on him. "Your master does not share your view," I said. "Solomon has brought peace to both Israel and Judah. No man need fear attack."

"He inherits what David won for him with the sword—even against his own children," Benaiah responded. "I agree that our king is not a man of war. It is not his business as it is mine."

"Do you mean Solomon is a coward?" I asked.

Benaiah was not to be trapped. "Not at all," he said easily. "He is very wise. He knows it is his business to rule—just as it is my business to fight and your business to prophesy."

"But most kings are warriors," I pressed him. "Would not Solomon be a better king if he were a leader in battles?"

Benaiah's eyes gleamed, then became veiled. "Perhaps," he replied, "but that is your idea, not mine, O Nathan."

"I do not say so," I said quickly, defensively. "All this is mere talk."

"Let it remain between us then," grunted Benaiah. He had effectively silenced me.

"You will find little work for your profession in his reign."

"Hadad still lives in Egypt."

"He will not dare to return."

Not for a moment had Benaiah ceased to rub and polish the dull-gleaming gray of his sword blade. Now he took it and slowly drew a left-curving line on the sand before him.

"What is that?" I asked.

"That is the coast of the sea," he said shortly. Near the bottom of the curve he drew a line toward himself. "That is the river of Egypt," he announced cryptically. "And here"—

he jabbed the point of his sword to the right of the river-mark—"here is Kadesh-barnea, on the tableland."

"What does all this mean?" I wondered.

"It means that we must expect an attack from Egypt. We must prepare for it. Cities for stores, cities for chariots, cities for horsemen and soldiers."

"But we are at peace with Egypt," I protested, "and she is torn to bits with revolt."

"We shall not have to wait long for an invasion," Benaiah said. "Our spies report that a strong man has already risen in middle Egypt."

"Who?"

"His name is Shishak. He is a Libyan general, used to wars, ambitious to extend his rule. He has recently conquered the pharaoh of the delta and has set up his capital at Bubastis. More than that, he is a diplomat. He has married into the Tanite priest dynasty of the land."

"But why should he covet our country?" I demanded.

Benaiah shrugged. "Because he is what he is," he replied. "To the west lies only desert, to the north the sea and the strong sea peoples, to the south the jungles. He can come only to the east, to our land—where Egyptians formerly ruled for a thousand years."

"But why would they invade?"

"Have you forgotten the revenge of Hadad and his people, the raid across the border years ago?"

"But even were this so," I argued, "and I cannot believe it, there is no necessity to fight. We are able to sit down and discuss their claims and ours like wise men."

"As did Joshua?" sneered Benaiah. I said nothing. "This land was promised to us, as you have said so many times, by Yahweh, but the Egyptians do not believe in His promises. They believe in arms."

"Yahweh will protect His own," I said severely.

"Perhaps, perhaps," Benaiah said, "but I am not Yahweh, I am not privy to His thoughts as you are." Again his impudence struck me silent.

"We must fight," Benaiah said, "but in the end we will be conquered."

"How so?" I demanded.

"Egypt is too large, too populous, too wealthy, too powerful."

"Why must we fight at all, then, if we cannot win?"

Benaiah cocked his head at me. "Because the better we fight and the longer we fight, the more we shall be able to live as we please. A man may kill a lion but he is chary of lions afterward—and if he has only wounded the beast, he is likely to avoid it. I know." I recalled Benaiah's single-handed duel with a lion in a snowy pit.

"Does that answer your questions, O Nathan?" inquired Benaiah.

"You have forgotten the Lord of hosts," I said stubbornly. "He will fight on our side. He will give us victory."

Benaiah sucked in his cheeks. "If it pleases Him, He will," he replied obliquely. "But a general cannot depend on His favor. He will do better to see to his troops and weapons."

"Yet if we are defeated," I said in despair, "what shall we do?"

"I think we shall win these first battles," Benaiah said calmly. "Shishak thinks us weak. But he will come again, in more strength."

"What shall such a victory profit us?"

Benaiah grinned. "They will leave us alone for a time," he said with conviction. "And I suspect that Shishak will promote his ambitions in another way."

"How?"

"He has a daughter. He will offer Solomon a wife."

"But that is to conquer by another means," I said.

"Solomon has his own ways of sapping the strength of such a conquest."

"What if Solomon refuses his daughter?"

"You do not know our king," said Benaiah deliberately, "if you believe that."

Watching Benaiah's ceaseless rubbing of his long sword blade, I became half-mesmerized. Unbidden thoughts rolled about in my head. To my alarm, they began to take shape as words.

"You are very close to Solomon," I said. Benaiah looked up without expression and bent to his work again.

"You know his heart and mind," I said, "better than myself who am called his chief counselor."

Benaiah grunted. I went on: "You were among those responsible for convincing David to throne him over Adonijah."

"How?" Benaiah growled.

I did not heed him, rambling on: "I have often thought of how you might have been close to Michal as well," I said. Benaiah's rubbing became slower.

"And Bathsheba, you were close to her."

"You give me much credit with women," Benaiah said. He lifted the blade and glanced along it.

"And the death of Merib-baal," I said, daring everything upon one final thrust of my own. "When he wanted to confess whatever it was, it seemed so opportune."

"What do you mean?" Benaiah said softly.

"I mean," I told him recklessly, "that a little push here or there, in bed or out of it—might have seen Saul's descendant rather than David's on the throne of the Hebrews."

Benaiah gently raised his sword and put its point against my breast. "A little push here might rid the kingdom of a nuisance," he said without inflection. I stared down at the glinting iron and was aware of a dryness in my throat, an emptiness in my stomach. I had gone too far: I had no idea what Benaiah would do next.

Unexpectedly, Benaiah dropped his point. He resumed polishing. He gave a short, husky laugh. "All prophets should have a sense of humor such as yours," he said.

"I have very little humor," I assured him.

"You are mistaken."

"No, I speak truth."

Benaiah stared straight into my eyes, burning my brain. "I say that you are being ridiculous," he asserted. I lowered my eyes. "Yes," I said with difficulty.

"If I helped place Solomon on the throne as you claim," he said, "why should I attempt to replace him with Merib-baal?"

"I don't know," I said.

"Again, your sense of humor. And how might I be close to Bathsheba and Michal at the same time, those two who hated each other?"

"They had become friends," I said thoughtlessly.

Benaiah widened his stare. "Who can say that?" he wondered. "One is dead, the other fled."

"No one," I murmured.

"I do my duties," rejoined Benaiah. He finished polishing his sword, reached for its sheath, and snicked it home. He stood up, rugged and bandy-legged, buckling the belt about him. "I do what the king commands," he said loudly. "If you have complaints, O Nathan, take them to Solomon himself. He will judge wisely, I am sure." He strode out of the room, jangling in his accouterments, leaving me to wonder if his final words were a challenge or a sneer.

The rise of Benaiah as Solomon's right hand dates from this period in our nation's history. It is important here to describe these certain traits of the man which seemed to make him indispensable to the king. If I had objections to his elevation—which, of course, I did not, under the circumstances—they would have been based on the fact that Benaiah was a man of war, whereas I was always of the opinion that peace would win our greatest victories. But I must admit that Solomon used what talents Benaiah and I possessed—sometimes to play us off one against the other—sometimes to combine into a single force—but most often for what he deemed the good of the Hebrews.

Yet there was a single element in Solomon's feelings for Benaiah that did not exist in his relationships with me. He said as much on one occasion when I was alone with him in the throne room.

"What do you think of Benaiah?" said Solomon abruptly.

His question took me by surprise. "Think?" I repeated.

"Does he serve his king or himself, Nathan?"

"He has served you well and faithfully," I said.

"Do you trust him?"

"He has done much service," I replied evasively.

"I cannot help remembering that he slew Bathsheba," Solomon said darkly. Startled, I refrained from reminding the king that it was at his own command.

"I know it was my passion that prompted it," Solomon said, as if he read my thoughts. "Yet—I am like David toward Joab. Like David, I say that this man is too hard for me, too inhuman."

"I, too, have known that," I said. "I have no love for this man. But he has demonstrated his loyalty to the king."

"I must find another for his place," Solomon murmured. "I cannot rule with him by my side. I am stifled by his presence. But I must not be hasty. I still need Benaiah's sword."

I said no more and it ended there. Solomon's suspicions reinforced my own in a fashion but I realized they were guided by his memory of his mother. I might have acted with less caution and wisdom—for Benaiah still had much to do for his master—but I have always thought that Solomon, like David with Joab, despite his power and knowledge, was more than a little intimidated by Benaiah. It was rarely that the king roused himself to show mercy to a foe of the general. The most memorable case of this sort was the time when Benaiah fought Ananias, the elder son of Nebat, and brother of Jeroboam—a duel whose outcome was to prove fateful for the future of our kingdom.

It must not be thought that this meeting was anything on the grand scale of a state duel. It was nothing of the kind. It was simply an encounter between Benaiah and a couple of up-country boys who had come into Jerusalem for the first time. They were determined to make trouble, it seemed. Reports had reached us, even at the palace, of riots incited against the king himself by two black-browed youths accompanied by a gangling, doom-crying fellow named Ahijah who called himself a prophet. This interested me, as a matter of course. Just as there are guilds of dyers and jewel cutters, dedicated to excluding the unskillful, so there is a bond in my own profession compounded of suspicion and brotherhood. I told my scribe, Elihaph, to check closely on what he heard.

What I did not know at the time was that Ananias, the elder, was the real troublemaker. His brother, Jeroboam, was the one of whom we were to hear so much later, who still sways the dubious destiny of our people. At that time he was a tall, handsome, taciturn youth with long shaggy brown hair and a muscular body, without the fire of revenge in his eyes which later possessed him. Ananias, the elder, was as tall but had a stoop to his shoulders and was disfigured by a long red scar from his scalp across his cheek to his chin. His awareness of his ugliness—caused by a slide of shale near his home—made him pugnacious and bitter. He made a fetish out of his desire to quarrel. He taught himself how to fight with sword and dagger and was famous for picking duels with passersby on the road which crossed before the house of his widowed mothers, Zeruah, an Ephrathite of Zereda. I never met the woman but I understand she was a peaceable sort. She deplored this meddlesome mania, begging Jeroboam to dissuade his brother. Her efforts, however, were thwarted by the bizarre prophecies of Ahijah. This groaning, eye-rolling, hands-lifting, self-called "prophet of Yahweh" made it his business to incite both youths at every possible opportunity. He even dared to predict that they were to rise as high as the kingship of the Hebrews.

Naturally, they came to Jerusalem. Equally naturally, the weird shoutings of Ahijah and the love of our people for something new (remarked upon often, as far back as Moses) gave them an attendant crowd. They came before the half-finished palace to denounce Solomon for some obscure misdeed or other that had offended the hill people. The king, who happened to be there inspecting the work with myself and Hiram-abi, simply gestured to Benaiah to do his duty.

"What do you want of the king?" asked Benaiah.

"Justice, justice!" howled Ahijah, capering before him in his spectacular rags.

"The king holds court tomorrow to hear all complaints," Benaiah said civilly enough. "Come to David's old palace. He will hear you as well."

"No," Ananias growled, stepping forward. "We'll see him now, here!"

"At least speak to Nathan, his prophet," said Benaiah with more than his wonted patience.

"Don't bring me into this," I called hastily.

"Now!" shouted Ananias. "Here!"

Benaiah sighed. "Then you will have to deal with me," he said, "and I deal roughly with such as you."

Without more words, Ananias yanked his sword free of its belt and struck it point down in the ground. It was a heavy round bar of bronze, flared at the tip and pointed—unlike the iron weapon of Benaiah which was flat and double-edged along its whole length, as well as pointed. I knew what the response of Solomon's general would be, having heard his philosophy so well detailed before. I drew my robes about me and sat on a block of stone to observe.

Benaiah struck his sword down beside the other. Next moment, they had begun their furious encounter.

Benaiah fought coldly, like a *shaduf*, a machine dipping water up and down from a canal. His sword, the battered redoubtable blade of Joab, captured long ago from the Philistines, went up and down, up and down, working toward its kill. As he advanced, Benaiah planted both his feet firmly, his heavy muscular torso rippling with effort. Sweat sprang out over him, he dripped, his figure shone. He shook his head again and again to rid his eyes of the salt drops that stung his sight in spite of his heavy blue forehead band of wool. Swinging with both hands, cutting short his strokes in powerful arcs lest he leave an opening in his defense, he approached a short step at a time toward his opponent.

I could see where he was backing Ananias. Toward a small rocky gully behind, where his foe would inevitably fall and be at his mercy. I watched, fascinated, as Benaiah kept up his whirling blade at speed like a boy whipping a top. The swords clashed with a musical ring. The smoky smell of iron against bronze thickened in the air, vying with the animal odors of the fighters. Benaiah broke wind once as he stepped forward but his face showed no amusement—nothing but an unnatural intensity for blood.

Ananias leaped and cavorted, ducking and dodging like a man gone mad. He realized that his sword was not of the metal of his Hebrew opponent's (just as Benaiah had realized such an advantage). The other man knew his only chance lay in speed and adroitness, in making the most of his monkeyish agility. The tempo of the fight increased. It reached a height I had not thought possible.

Suddenly Ananias ducked under a flat swing of Benaiah. But Benaiah, as if he expected it, twisted the blade in the air. It curved downward. It was the flat of the weapon—not the edge—that whacked Ananias' head. He tumbled heels high, almost to the edge of the fatal gully.

Benaiah, at once eager to kill, rushed at him. He lifted his sword for the stroke which would be mighty enough to shear the other's body in two. But he lost his chance to deliver it.

Still stunned, Ananias gained his hands and knees. He saw the dreadful menace above him. He did not hesitate. He seized a double handful of sand and flung it up at random. It flew directly into Benaiah's face. His blow faltered. It went awry, the sword striking the earth, spraying clods. Benaiah clawed at his face with one hand. Aimlessly, he swung his sword about him at the same time.

Ananias regained his wits. He saw his opportunity. He flung his sword full into Benaiah's face. The commander of the Hebrews dropped his own weapon. He staggered backward. Next moment, drawing the dagger from his belt, his foe leaped upon him like a lion. He landed full on Benaiah in the midst of the leap. He drove him back and down, flat on his back, by sheer surprise rather than weight or force.

There bloomed a quick burst of unholy joy in my breast. I feared Benaiah. I longed to see his end. Yet the sight, I knew, would sicken me. I turned my eyes away. I did not wish to see the finish of such a redoubtable warrior. I forced myself to think of whom I could recommend to Solomon as his successor.

Thus I did not see the fatal thrust into the throat. But I heard an anguished, unrecognizable yell of pain. It died in a horrible gurgle. All was still. The rest watched what had happened with a horrid fascination. I heard legs thump the ground twice in quick succession. That was all.

Slowly, I turned my head. To my stupefaction, Benaiah was climbing to his feet—covered with blood and dust but unharmed. Ananias, his reckless opponent, lay supine before him as he spurned the body. A pool of blood aureoled the head of the dead man, blackened the sand; already the inevitable flies were gathering. Benaiah picked up the other's sword. He inspected it sourly, shaking his had to indicate his opinion of its inferiority. He flung it down again.

Benaiah had simply fallen on his back as a ruse, his legs drawn up. His double kick had knocked the breath out of his foe. He even had time to wipe his eyes free of sand before he advanced to pick up the dagger and put an end to the affair.

Benaiah struck himself against the chest. "I am Benaiah," he panted loudly, "son of the valiant Jehoida of Kabzeel, who has slain two of Moab dressed in lion skins and a lion itself, in single combat! Last of the mighty four of David, Jashobeam, Eleazar, and Abishai, brother of Joab! Shall I be vanquished by a mere boy?"

Ahijah uttered a hoarse cry. As if it were a signal, Jeroboam sprang forward to pick up his brother's sword. Benaiah, quicker than he, stepped forward. He trod it under his sandal. At the same time he raised his bloody blade above his head, about to cleave the other to his heels. Ahijah clasped his hands and gave a shout of agony. Suddenly he turned and fled like a fallow deer among the rocks.

"Hold!" cried Solomon behind us. "Take him! Do not kill him!"

As the king spoke, a half dozen workmen—brave enough now that the fighting was over—rushed up and surrounded Jeroboam. He offered no resistance, standing still and proud. Benaiah slowly lowered his sword and wiped his brow free of sweat with deliberation. He turned to confront his master.

"Mercy is a mistake with this kind," Benaiah said crisply. "I say this for your own good, king and lord."

Solomon viewed him with tolerance. "Even so, perhaps," he said, "but if you really had your way, Benaiah, you would eliminate all others—even Nathan here—and leave only thee and me."

"The kingdom is better off with such swine as these dead," Benaiah said coldly. "They cause nothing but dissension. They breed maggots of hatred for yourself."

Unruffled, Solomon went on as if he had not heard. "And once it happened that there was only thee and me," he said musingly, "I might suspect you—or you might suspect me, eh?"

Before the direct gaze of the king, Benaiah's eyes fell. He muttered something, completely out of countenance. He turned away. I moved up beside the king, full of excitement.

"I can tell you many things about Benaiah," I said in a low tone.

"To his benefit?" asked Solomon.

"Very little," I replied.

"Then let us remember that he is a faithful servant. We owe him much until that time when he shall be proved otherwise," Solomon said. His manner indicated that he dismissed the subject. I was disappointed.

Solomon raised his voice again to the impassive Benaiah. "Let this one be taken under guard and set to work extending and building the walls of the city," he said.

"I shall see to it personally," Benaiah said.

Solomon smiled. "See to it that at least he stays alive," he said.

I thought then that it was the last we would hear of Jeroboam. But I was in error.

Even yet, as I say in my old age, we have not seen the last of the abominations of Jeroboam.

As one may have observed from the visit of the two sons of the widow Zeruah and the fight of Ananias with Benaiah, all was not well in our nation. The early enthusiasm engendered by the completion of the temple had died down. Its ceremonies, as I have indicated, had become a splendid routine. They would have been even less had the celebrants known that the ark, heart of their adoration, was missing, buried or destroyed. But Zadok had built a cunning scaffolding of acacia to imitate the staves of the ark and continued as usual, puffed up by his pride. Fasting, cleansed, robed, wafted onward by song and chant, he entered the holy place at each sundown to trim the seven candles of the *menorah,* to fill the sacred bowls with blessed oil properly mixed. He emerged to sprinkle incense upon the coals of the altar outside, to pray and preen himself before Yahweh, as the evening lamb was sacrificed above.

In those days temples, even bereft of Yahweh, did very well. Solomon had refused to destroy (to Zadok's baffled disappointment and my secret joy) the platform dedicated to Ashtoreth by Bathsheba. He had removed the remains of the image and the sacrilegious emblem but that was all. Many a night thereafter—but not at the time of the full moon—I went there to pray to the true God for Bathsheba's spirit.

Most of the king's time was now devoted to the building of his palace. Only the first of the underpinnings was laid, of course, but much planning and extra work was in progress.

Sledges and rollers aided by a new device called a pulley (out of old Sumer), aided the men in hauling into position rocks as great as thirty feet long and ten feet thick, lashed to palm-fiber ropes three inches in diameter. The foundation blocks—since the palace, like the temple, was to last forever—were not set in rubble, as some had been in Egypt, but were bonded to bedrock. Atop them were others slid into position on viscid mortar, ground to fit on rollers and on each other. The floors were to be of baked bricks studded with patterns of terracotta cones thrust deep, with their heads enameled in gay colors. The doors were to be set into wooden posts, wide so as to be ample for six abreast. But there were to be few windows—the light to come from an inner court.

Retaining walls of undressed stone were erected, fining off into stepped ashlar courses for the first story. Columns of cedar and cypress were being overlaid with gold (not with copper as was the case in Egypt or Phoenicia). There were to be floor and wall mosaics of gems set in bitumen or fastened with copper wire. What astounded me most was Solomon's plan for washrooms and closets with basins of gold upon baked brick, seats of bitumen (one of carved ivory, for his use alone). They even boasted running water that discharged into a covered sewer outside, without odor or fuss.

The greatest claim upon his attention as monarch came near the end of the year. It arrived in the form of a courier from the south, always the harbinger of bad news. It was to me a corroboration of the prescience of Benaiah in matters military: Shishak I with his army had crossed the borders of Egypt to the east. He had already broken through the weak resistance of our forts in that sector. It appeared clear that this was inspired by the bandit Hadad—that it was a direct threat to the recovery of Edom by the rebel—that more, it was an instant danger to the southern caravan trails and, above all, to the copper and iron mines of Eziongeber in the Arabah.

"I ask permission to attack the Egyptians," Benaiah said. His face twisted in one of his rare grimaces of humor. "And spoil them," he said, referring to the well-known commandment of centuries before by Moses that such was lawful.

"Can we resist?" Solomon asked in surprise.

"If you will come with me to Kadesh-barnea," Benaiah replied, "your majesty shall see how well we are prepared for the occasion."

CHAPTER TEN

The Wedding of Theke

Solomon rapped the brass cuirass of Benaiah with his gold lion-headed wand. The leatherbacked plates sounded flat. He prodded Benaiah in the arm. "Why," he demanded pointedly, "am I here?"

Benaiah saluted. "Your presence will encourage the troops, sire," he replied.

Solomon glanced at me opposite. I pretended to be engrossed in the wide brown valley below, watching the tiny forms of men and toy chariots advancing in a weaving, uncertain line. I had thought military maneuvers were much more precise.

"I should be leading my army into the heart of the battle," Solomon said grandiloquently.

Benaiah sighed. He made a sign of obeisance. "If you so command me, O king," he answered, "I will obey. We shall go down together—Nathan too may come if he wishes—and we shall both certainly be killed together."

"Killed?" Solomon's voice rose slightly. He wrapped his purple robe about him closely. "But that would be a glorious death," he said at last.

Benaiah shrugged. "Glorious or not, it is death," he said.

"My father David, blessed be his memory, led his men into battle."

"That was quite different, O Solomon," I told him.

Benaiah nodded. "He was a man skilled in war," he said, "and foremost when he was yet young. But when he became king, he led no battles. A king, sire, is more important than a general."

"The Assyrians believe such a death is noble," Solomon returned uncertainly.

"Each people to its own customs," Benaiah said. "I merely know that my king dying thus would have died uselessly. In the old times, of course, which the Assyrians revere, such kings very often enjoyed magnificent funerals afterward. But the king of the Hebrews is more valuable to his people if he remains alive."

"You may be right," Solomon said reluctantly.

"Sire, I shall bow to your wishes."

"I have no wishes in time of war," Solomon said quickly. "I have no knowledge of the cruel art. I wish none."

Benaiah half-bowed with a clash of metal. "Then," he said deferentially, "may I ask your majesty to remain here. You will notice that I stand with you and Nathan here on this hilltop yet I do not consider myself a coward—and woe to him who names me that!"

"Nor am I without courage," I put in.

Benaiah flicked a contemptuous look at me. Solomon spoke again. "But will not the king of the Egyptians consider it otherwise?" he demanded.

Benaiah lifted his arm, pointing to the hill on the far side of the valley. Solomon and I shaded our eyes, squinting against the sun. I could see shimmers of color, dim plumes waving and weapons shining, in the midst of what appeared to be a small confused clot of men. "What is that?" I asked.

"That," Benaiah informed us, "is the post of Shishak, the king of the Egyptians. He is wise in battle; he does as we do." He looked aside. "Here come the armies," he added with quickened tempo.

I gazed down into the hot flats beneath us that danced with mirage. I saw Benaiah had spoken truth. His omnivorous curiosity aroused, Solomon leaned forward beside me, his hand quivering on my shoulder.

What we saw appeared to be two great yellow cloaks undulating forward in massive folds. They were pulled toward each other, it seemed, by a horde of innumerable ants. But I knew the ants to be men and that the apparent cloaks were no more than clouds of dust. In the still air of approaching evening, the battle was about to begin.

I felt my gorge fattening on my fears, choking me. Solomon must have had the same reaction. "There must be twice as many of the Egyptians as there are of our men," he whispered aside to Benaiah.

"At least," said the unperturbed soldier, "but they shall not triumph. The blessing of Yahweh and the good right arms of our soldiers shall win the day."

"Yahweh does not help fools!" Solomon exclaimed. "They go to certain defeat! Why have you so many slingers and archers hiding behind the bushes and the rocks below us?"

He flung out his arm. Benaiah, greatly daring, checked the gesture.

"Do not make such motions, O king," he said warningly. "Such may give away my plan of battle. Remember the Egyptian king and his staff, from the eminence across the way, watch us as closely as we watch them. And since they are desert people, their eyes see farther than ours."

"I have not deigned to set my eyes on them," said Solomon disdainfully.

Benaiah grinned. "You should," he said, through his crooked yellow teeth. "There is no better way to discover the enemy intentions."

"What is it you are going to do?" I demanded.

"It is all arranged," Benaiah said. "The wind will decide the day."

"The wind?" Solomon was incredulous. "There is none."

"Notice how it is beginning to blow, however, as evening comes on."

Again Solomon and I peered over the valley. It had been an unusually hot, dry summer. I knew the earth below us lay covered with a layer of at least six inches of fine pulverized dust. It could sting the eyes like flung vinegar, burn the feet, even through sandals, like hot coals. I observed that the Egyptians advanced into the rising wind, that the ragged cloak of dust streamed backward from the front ranks. On the other hand, the Hebrews marched with the wind at their backs, their dust beginning to envelop even the front ranks.

"This is madness!" Solomon exclaimed agitatedly. "By the time our men advance to battle, they will be blinded with dust, unable even to resist the weakest foe!"

"Not so, your majesty," said Benaiah calmly. "Forgive me if I point out that our men are already halting. They wait the charge of the Egyptians and their chariots. They will have time to clear their eyes, to brace themselves. Meanwhile, the dust they have raised and the swirling dust of the leaders of the Egyptian hosts will do for them exactly what you feared for our men."

Solomon shook his head. He was full of doubts and I shared them. My stomach felt empty and my mouth dry. I had little faith in Benaiah. But the issue was set, the battle was about to be joined. There was nothing anyone could do. I sucked my lip: I wondered how fast the horses on Solomon's chariot were, how fast he could flee, where he could go for refuge in case of defeat. Only Jerusalem's walls could protect him. But I had little time to calculate his chances. Forgetful of his rank, Benaiah grasped him by the arm and pointed down into the valley.

Solomon and I saw the hosts of the Egyptians advancing at a rapid pace. In front were forty or fifty single-horsed chariots, each with two men: one to drive, one to brandish a spear or draw a bow. The chariot bodies were of strong wickerwork, shielded in front by plates of brass. Their wheels were guarded with short, sharp scythes that stuck out two feet or more, whirling whirring menaces to anyone who approached too close. Behind the chariots, half-hidden in the dust, were ranks of running spearmen sweating profusely even in their lighter armor. Behind these came a rank of swordsmen, flourishing their weapons. Behind even these and almost completely enveloped in the dust loped long lines of sneezing archers, rank on rank.

I could see no more but I knew that, far in the rear, there would be the carts of supplies. Between these and the fighting men would be the burden-bearing groups of slaves, with women and slaves driving the carts.

The whole of the Egyptian army rushed along at a headlong reckless pace with wild piercing cries, choked by the dust. There was shouting, indistinguishable for the most part, but I could distinguish the names of gods, repeated over and over. Three or four of the chariots put up poles with battle pennants of dusty-bright colors; they crackled angrily in the rising wind.

Returning my gaze to our own army, I saw little to comfort us. As Benaiah had said to Solomon, they had halted. They seemed to be disorganized and fearful.

The Hebrew formation seemed peculiar; before it skirmished a couple of dozen men, each with two spears, each cavorting agilely to dodge any possible enemy lances or arrows. The main body of the Hebrew army remained behind, testing bows, hefting spears, rubbing their swords in the sand to make them bright. From their midst rose no cries—only a low angry ululation. I knew they were due to break forth shortly into the shouted appeals to Yahweh which we had found so greatly inspirited our warriors.

Suddenly I saw our advance spearmen break into a dead run toward the onrushing chariots. Solomon clutched at Benaiah's arm.

"What are they doing?" he said in a strained voice. "What can they possibly hope to do?"

"Wait!" answered Benaiah. "In a moment, you shall see."

Solomon saw and I watched apprehensively. The Hebrew

spearmen broke up into scattered groups of two. Carefully they gauged the speed of the Egyptian chariots. They easily ducked the erratic throws of spears or firing of arrows from the chariots themselves. I noted with rising exultation that by this time the enemy chariots were so far ahead of the main army of the Egyptians that these picked spearmen of the Hebrews could operate with comparative ease.

They waited until the galloping, wide-nostriled horses were almost upon them. They ducked to one side. As the chariots went by, they flung their spears—not at the occupants but at the flashing wheels of the chariots. These heavy staves, sheathed with bronze, were in some cases repelled by the scythes. But almost every chariot snared one or two. These penetrated the spokes of the wheels, snagging under the chariot itself.

Solomon and I suddenly saw a fierce, dashing battle advance transformed into disastrous chaos. As the spear shafts cogged the wheels of the chariots, it forced them to swerve. The unstable chariots teetered on one wheel, lost their balance. They crashed to one side, throwing their occupants into the dust. In some instances, the horses were overthrown as well. They lay kicking, poor beasts, red-eyed and struggling, neighing with fright. Now our men raced behind the chariots only to wheel and make easy work of dispatching their opponents, stunned on the ground, with dagger or sword.

Meantime, the second rank of Hebrews launched a rain of arrows up into the air, down into the dust cloud behind. It milled about uncertainly opposite them. With a shout our spearmen and swordsmen raised their thrilling cries to Yahweh. They rushed forward as fast as their feet would carry them, disregarding the dust, ignoring everything except getting their foes into hand-to-hand combat.

In the murk of yellow that swirled above them still, the Egyptian warriors eddied back and forth, not knowing in which direction the enemy was. Many of these, brave men no doubt, fell by swords they never saw or an arrow invisible before they could come to grips with any opponent.

In a moment, the battle had become an inextricable, murky melee, shot with streaks of light as the dying sun glanced off the swords and spears, a tumult filled with cries of dying and surrender and the fierce war shouts of both sides, a boiling mass in the caldron of the valley.

"Now, now!" Benaiah cried.

He lifted up his sword and shook it in the air three times, swinging it, humming around his head.

As he did, the remaining group of the Hebrew army—stationed in ambush just below the slope—broke free. It tumbled pell-mell down the slope, thirsting for the fray, taking the Egyptians from the flank with a tremendous noise of shouting and spear-and-shield clashing, amplified by the clanging of cymbals borne by the rear rank.

Solomon glanced across the valley to the other side. Benaiah beside him nodded approval. "That's the right way to look," he said. "You can tell the progress of the battle by the progress of the general and his officers."

True enough, the king and generals of the Egyptians had already decamped. Shishak and his household were streaming back over to the other side of the hill, away from the unexpectedly victorious Hebrew army.

Nothing could now be seen in the valley below. The dust was so thick that it surged over both hosts. Gigantic ocher breakers of a sea beating upon both sides of the hills, lapped nearly up to our feet. But much could still be heard. Above all rose the savage cry of "Yahweh! Yahweh! Yahweh gives the victory!" Nothing but confused sounds of dismay came from the Egyptians.

Without warning there rose a resounding clash below. The shrieks and cries grew louder.

"The last effort of the Egyptians," Benaiah said calmly.

It was easy to see and hear how it had failed: one by one, the gay banners of the Egyptians—that had been for minutes the only things to be seen above the dust—drooped, faded, and dipped, finally disappearing altogether.

The cries of our army, hoarser now, took on a lighter but more savage tone. It was drowned out almost instantly by loud wailings of grief, cries of surrender, pleas for mercy from the enemy. From the tail of the Egyptian dust cloud, I could see fugitives streaming back, the carts wheeling about in confusion. It was the beginnings of a rout that would send the invaders back across their border with death at their heels.

"The battle is over," Benaiah said slowly. "But Shishak, being a Libyan general of renown, will have prepared his retreat. We must beware of ambushes. Will it please your majesty and you, prophet Nathan, to go down to the field and see the captives kneeling and the dead around them? Such things inspirit a man!"

I said nothing. Solomon drew himself up. "Not I," he replied, his voice quivering. "Such things may inspirit you, Benaiah. They disgust me."

Thus it came about that this was the first and last battle that Solomon ever saw. Though he was punctiliously invited to every major affray after that by his commander-in-chief—almost maliciously, I thought—he always refused the invitation. Not that he lost his interest in military matters. To the contrary: during any campaign, especially those against the tribes that still remained in the territory which we Hebrews claimed as our own—Hadad renewed his raids subsequently and a new general, Rezon, rose in the east against us—our king would spend long hours poring over maps drawn on skins and sketched in the fine sand of the palace yard.

Sometimes Benaiah himself would come to make his curt but colorful summary of an action. At such times Solomon would sit him down before him on the softest cushions and question him in detail as to the strategy by which he had conquered. He never ceased to wonder at Benaiah's imagination in military affairs, at his fertile inventions of strategy. More than once, in my presence, he congratulated himself for his perspicacity in elevating such a man from head of his bodyguards to the post of commander-in-chief.

Whether it was Benaiah's genius or the new iron of the swords and spears replacing the softer bronze—we had captured the secrets of mining, smelting, and tempering this metal from the Philistines years before—the head of our forces convinced Solomon of his talents. He did not offer many pitched battles, such as the one the king had observed against the Egyptians, unless the conditions were exactly right and his plans almost certain of success. Benaiah confined himself largely to ambush and guerrilla actions, swooping down and chopping marching columns into befuddled bits that could be captured for work on Solomon's projects or destroyed at leisure. He especially liked to attack in the early afternoon under a broiling sun—when it was customary for most armies to take a nap in whatever shade they could find. He cut off food and reinforcements, appropriating or burning the enemy supplies, killing the women and slaves. In such cases, since our forces generally had larger armies within our borders, there was little for the enemy to do except throw themselves on our mercy. Occasionally Benaiah sent out small forces to meet a larger enemy group. He used his men as scavengers on the flanks, harassing from caves and mountaintops. It was a maneuver at which our men became as agile as goats, striking and slipping away and returning to strike again. Only Hadad and Rezon—one supported by Egyptian irregulars, the other sponsored by

Assyria—resisted our power until the last years of Solomon's reign.

Benaiah proved that he was as good a prophet in matters material as he was military. Indeed, as good as I in spiritual things. His cynical predictions came true. The battle in the green valley below and to the west of Kadesh-barnea had proved victorious for the Hebrews. But we had suffered heavy losses, some thousands of men (Benaiah, as usual, would never admit the true count). Shishak's trained mercenaries—most of them veterans from Libya—had fought well. They left over four thousand dead on the field, most with their wounds in front. Perhaps they would not have retreated except for Benaiah's special stratagem at the end, his flank attack which had cut off and captured their supporting caravan. As it was, to Benaiah's chagrin, Shishak and the remnants of his troops regrouped and—in desperate need of food and water for the route home—managed to capture the city of Gezer.

Such a success almost negated the victory in the valley (had it not been for Solomon's later diplomacy, urged by myself). Gezer had been a strategic point on the border, near the old Philistine frontier, from time immemorial. It had been established by the Canaanites, fortified by walls and towers. Captured originally by Joshua, it had been given over wholly to the Levites for defense—standing as it did on its isolated hill which made it a strong point overlooking the western road to Jerusalem. But the Levites were priestly, rather than military. Benaiah acted too late to reinforce them, even to bring their morale up to the pitch necessary for resistance. Shishak had encircled it in siege on his advance (thus appreciably weakening his own army) and had seized it by sapping and assault on his retreat, while Benaiah's forces still licked their wounds after their costly victory.

However accurate his forecasts, Benaiah's timetable of events proved to be in error. Shishak had captured the throne of Egypt when Solomon was twenty-six but he had not invaded our land until two years later. And it was nearly a year after that when we received the message which Benaiah had warned me to expect. I read it aloud to Solomon in private audience:

"To the king of the Hebrews, Solomon, my friend, say: I have commanded that my diviner gather the omens to see if I might come in force to regain the land of my fathers which you now hold—but the omens are unfavorable for a long while to come. Let my lord therefore slay the ass of covenant between us under the oaths of our gods and have peace. If this is agreeable to Solomon, I shall send him my only daughter Thekecritis to be his bride, together with many presents. As to her *mohar,* as you call it, I shall give the city of Gezer."

It was signed with the cartouche of the pharaoh Shishak. With the message came bearers of gold and ivory and jewels, and—most acceptable of all to Solomon, whose own pet had died—a half dozen chattering trained apes.

Besides myself, only Benaiah was with the king in the audience chamber. Solomon stirred. He looked toward his commander-in-chief.

"What do you advise, Benaiah?" he asked.

Benaiah shrugged. "If they come again, they shall be sent home again," he said. "Blood on their heels, blood on their heads."

"Still, a city is a great gift."

"The pharaoh gives you only what is yours by right. We shall retake Gezer soon."

"But it will cost men, many men," mused Solomon. He turned to me. "What do you think, O Nathan?" he asked.

"Is it lawful to take an Egyptian wife?" I asked doubtfully.

"I do no more than has been done," Solomon pointed out. "Did not Joseph take an Egyptian woman? Did not Moses marry outside the tribes, yes, Zipporah, a dark woman at that?"

I could think of no proper answer. "But with all this ceremony?" I questioned weakly.

"Does the king take a woman like a tribesman with a spear and a tent for dowry? I am given a city!"

Benaiah shrugged. "If your desire is toward her, take her," he said. I nodded agreement.

But Solomon turned perverse. "Why," he demanded, "should I obey the king of Egypt? Have we not defeated him?"

I glanced at Benaiah who stared at the floor and said nothing. "Perhaps," I advised diplomatically, "it might be well to agree with him. Peace is preferable to war, though victory is sure."

"Why should I listen to an old man and an alien?"

"Shishak was born the year after you, O great Solomon. He was one of the royal family of Libya. He seized the throne of Egypt when he was twenty-seven. He turned twenty-nine, full of ambition, willing to show his prowess to his people, in this year, when he invaded our land. He underestimated Benaiah and our preparations. He was routed by our troops, but not in confusion. On his way back to Egypt, as you know, he stormed and seized the city of Gezer. He holds it as his own. Now he offers it to you with his daughter. She is, I have heard, a ripe girl of fourteen, the same age at which he married."

"I have no desire to take a daughter of Egypt into my harem." Solomon showed a rare trace of that sulky air which had distinguished him as a youth.

"Shishak is wiser than that," I responded. "He has already married his son, Osorchon, to a daughter of one of the rulers of the Tanite priest dynasty which rules the rest of Egypt."

"It is thus that he intends to expand his lust and his ambition at the same time," Solomon said, "by marrying this girl—is Theke her name?—to me."

I grimaced. "What else is there for such a heathen king as Shishak?" I asked. "For you there is the love and guidance of Yahweh. As for those outside our nation, they walk in darkness."

"At least I should see this girl before I marry her," said Solomon.

"It would be an insult to her father and a challenge to good taste," I responded, "to ask for a likeness to be sent."

Solomon looked at me, his eyes burning. "What choice does a king have?" he demanded bitterly. "Must my whole life be public for every gawking barbarian to see?"

I sighed in sympathy. "Has not my lord the king yet realized that his days must be as an open book?" I asked. "You do not belong to yourself, O Solomon. You belong to the Hebrew people, to Yahweh, whose instrument you are."

"I will not be a fool!" cried Solomon. "I will not be used by anyone—including Yahweh!"

I refused to be disturbed by his blasphemous reference. "Time and fate are the tools of Yahweh," I said calmly. "You and I and everyone else lie under their edges."

"Trouble me no more," Solomon said dully.

Benaiah and I glanced at each other. It was clear that our monarch had again reversed his thought. He had made his decision: he would accept. Perhaps the offer of a princess would not have been enough (as Benaiah had said) but with the offer of a city it was too much in policy to resist.

Two more months of negotiations served to settle the matter. It was agreed that Gezer should be evacuated by the Egyptian soldiers and occupied by our own troops. There would be peace between our nations. Theke—as we already familiarly called her—should be first among the wives of the king's harem, much to the distaste of Abishag, who had ruled her peers for so long.

I carried on the affair as was my duty. I wrote an excellently high styled message for the final agreement:

"To the Lord of Kingdoms, Pharaoh Shishak, your friend King Solomon of the Hebrews. May Yahweh, god of heaven and earth, make your throne as everlasting as the days of the sun. I write to you to say that your daughter Thekecritis is acceptable to me and that the generosity of the pharaoh in giving a city for her price is munificent. I have accepted your gifts. I have requited them with other gifts. Be mindful of your son-in-law, Solomon, lord and king of the Hebrews, who sends this to you by Mahir, a swift courier."

I had high hopes, not only of this Egyptian alliance but of a genuine bond between Solomon and his new bride-to-be. I was sharply disappointed. On the morning when her caravan arrived from Bubastis, winding up the steep streets toward the old palace where Solomon waited, I craned my neck over the king's shoulder to try and see Theke in her veiled palanquin. Needless to say, it was useless. But I was shocked when the bearers set it down and she stepped forth.

I had expected a woman, in body at least from the hot climate of Egypt, if not in mind. Instead she was a child—her breasts, thighs and buttocks undeveloped, her skin a rich bronze. Her most appealing characteristics were her slender hands, her long graceful neck like that of a bird, her proud carriage and her aquiline face with its sharp yet beautiful features. Her great eyes were framed in square-cut bangs of her own black hair. Her first glances toward the richly apparelled Solomon, I thought, were frightened and appealing. Yet under them was unbreakable strength, the knowledge and pride that she was one of the first daughters of Egypt.

Solomon welcomed her impassively. He personally escorted her and her eighteen women to private quarters in the harem. As he pointed out, it had been a long trip from her native country. She would need time to cleanse herself, rest, and acclimate herself to a different country. He put off until the following night the state banquet he had ordered. He showed her the greatest consideration in allowing a week before he commanded the nuptials to be performed.

Marriage, among our people, is an informal affair with rights reserved for both man and wife. Although some tribes, such as the woman-depleted Benjamites, sometimes used to make war simply to capture mothers for their sons, such was not the rule. There was a simple agreement between the two individuals—usually managed by the parents in solemn conclave—that was its basis. Its final consummation was the agreement upon the *mohar,* the bride's price. Afterward there were customary ceremonies. These included presents from relatives and friends, outfitting of the new household, wedding eve entertainments, the next-day procession (with the bride veiled and guarded) and, of course, the vows of the *beulah* toward her chosen: "I marry you as my husband" and his similar assurances of faith and love. Afterward there was a feast that might last for as much as a week for a rich man, night and day.

It was not much different with kings—except that the process was vastly richer and more ornate. Yet there were a few significant exceptions. Inasmuch as the king and his body and the fruit of his union belonged to Yahweh and the state, he was allowed to have more than one wife and as many female companions as conquest and his fancy dictated. I was always against this—as all prophets had been before me, ceaselessly pointing out that even our ancestor Noah was content with one spouse—but people such as Zadok were complaisant. And the flesh being what it is in every man, his point of view took precedence. Finally, it was important to all that high officials should see the carnal connection at first hand to make sure that the coupling had been complete. So that, if no child was forthcoming, the fault was not to be attributed to the king.

Preceding Solomon's wedding, there was one strange ceremony I must mention. Among Theke's train of attendants, slaves, and guards, there was a fantastically tall, emaciated man with a great hooked nose. He had a brooding look like that of a hawk. He called himself Petabast and was one of the priests of high rank in Egypt. I tried to exchange the civilities of our mutual profession but he was a dour, uncommunicative fellow. I soon gave up. I even got the impression—later proved to be quite wrong—that he understood very little Hebrew.

A note he presented from Shishak to Solomon indicated that, as a preliminary to the wedding, the pharaoh asked that the king have a session with this priest-diviner in order to see if omens were favorable for the marriage. I advised strongly against it. But Solomon felt intrigued by the proposition. "What possible harm can be in it?" he asked.

"I have no idea," I said darkly.

"Then why do you protest?"

"I say no more," I said with finality. "I wished to point out the dangers, that is all."

"Dangers? What are they?"

I could not answer because I did not know. To appease me, Solomon asked Petabast if I might share in the seance. The high priest unwillingly granted permission.

So it was, on a still, hot afternoon, Solomon and I found ourselves alone with him in an inner chamber of the palace. Petabast had prepared two couches—one, with a bolster for the king, the other bare, for me. He had also ready a golden bowl half full of water covered with an oily substance. It shimmered and took on glorious colorings as it swam on the surface. In a corner, an incense burner wafted sweet fumes over our heads, sprinkling us with the finest ashes as we waited.

Petabast waved his hands over the bowl, inviting Solomon to stare into it. In the waning sunlight from the high windows, he made gestures of incantation with his fingers. He crooned a soft chant of indistinguishable words into Solomon's ear. I strained to hear—but out of them all I gained only a kind of esoteric nonsense which meant nothing at all.

After a time, I began to feel sleepy. Then I saw Solomon stand up, his eyes glazed. He slowly obeyed the order of Petabast to recline on the red mat of the bed. I suspiciously assumed a reclining position on my own cot. I waited. I felt increasingly drowsy but my eyes refused to close.

Lying on his back, on the red sack of flattened feathers supported by the low rawhide bedstead (as he described it later), Solomon felt the same strange sensations as I. His body seemed detached from his senses. And his senses seemed alien to a single great realization: as if he—his inmost soul—were united to the greatest soul. He inhaled the faint sweet odor of the incense. He grew intoxicated. He gazed at the ceiling of this lower chamber and thought he was in the fabled Egyptian Labyrinth, seeing its pictures of stylized men and animals, its mysterious hieroglyphics, its colors that glowed in the half-gloom. Light surrounded the flicker of the sacrificial embers only. Then Solomon seemed to be gazing up into heaven opening. He could no longer taste the inside of his mouth; he was helpless to touch the dainty vase of clear alabaster at his side, or even his own body. Only hearing and sight remained. He felt drugged, yet free. Perhaps, he wondered, he inhabited another form with a thousand unknown points of contact with the mighty known, the true God of gods.

On the other side of the room, reclining as was Solomon, Petabast, the Egyptian high priest of all mysteries, commenced to speak in measured tones. Solomon and I understood every word, as if the syllables were formed delicately, one by one, inside our separate heads. They did not appear as words. They were instead a set of growing and vanishing pictures, like those we might have seen if we had existed in the far-off times.

The priest Petabast spoke.

"Know that you must put aside the sheath of flesh, the curtains of the mind," he intoned, "and enter another region. All that belongs to your body arises in time. Time devours what time fosters. Yet all that comes to be in the years is born in eternity and is itself eternal. We must therefore pass, hand in hand, to those regions where all is everlasting, the source and base of all that is temporal.

"There was a time when all that is now water was land and man was happy and most secure in the favor of the gods. In those days, he did not think, he did not reason. He remembered. He did not calculate as do we: he recalled similar instances of similar sums. The teaching of a child was nothing else than giving him, mind to mind, a set of such pictures that took him back to the beginning of the race. When something new occurred, our ancestors had to combine these pictures or create new ones by acting. They did not act by abstract rules. Over very long periods men did the same things in exactly the same way: the wisest men were always the oldest.

"What they used was the life-force of all things. We know that everything in the world from stones to birds has life—but in stones it is very weak while in birds it is very active. But as we draw fire from the spindle and the rubbing-board, so man in those times could draw energy from things. Think of the seed of corn, what immense energy it possesses to take earth and sun and water and produce its own image a thousand times multiplied, with stalks and leaves besides!

"Moreover, the very elements were different. Fire was less hot, though no less powerful. Water was more fluid. The air more dense. The earth lighter, more responsive. All of these were at the command of man. He could extract and concentrate their forces so as to make the best use of them in whatever he wanted."

Solomon broke into the drone of Petabast. In a dreamy voice, he said: "That was the golden age."

"Yes."

"Where was it? When was it?"

"On a great island of the sea to the west of your country, to the north of Egypt," answered Petabast. "Its date is lost in the mist."

"What happened to this land of those mighty times?"

"The wrath of envious gods, manifest in earthquake and waves, destroyed the city that was a country, built in rings with canals between, with towers of gold and domes of silver."

I closed my eyes, trying to visualize what Petabast had described. The incense in my nostrils clogged my brain. Faintly, in the distance, I heard Solomon's voice once more: "Why have you told me this, O Petabast?"

"I have summoned these images, oldest of our race," the Egyptian priest responded, "to engender in your mind a sight for myself—the sight of your own kingdom and what will happen to you and to the princess."

"Do you see?"

"The clouds are lifting," Petabast said enigmatically. His voice faded away. I knew no more until I was roused by Solomon himself energetically shaking my shoulder. In a moment I had flung off the webs of sleep. I leaped to my feet.

"Pardon, O king, pardon," I muttered thickly.

Solomon laughed. "It is no disgrace to be charmed into repose by such as the great Egyptians, learned in lore," he said.

Tantalized by what I remembered, I glanced quickly about. We were alone. Petabast had vanished. I came closer to Solomon, still feeling the effects of stale incense fumes in my head. "What did he predict?" I asked sotto.

Solomon frowned. "That all would turn out very well for his princess and myself," he told me, picking his words carefully, "but not as we expected nor in the manner apparent."

"Good, good," I murmured. "Yahweh's arms are upheld even by their own gods."

"More, he said my kingdom like that he conjured out of his ancestral memories would last until the very end of my own life."

"Marvelous!" I cried.

"But," Solomon said with an indescribable intonation, "not a week longer."

Before I could utter the questions bursting to my lips, he turned and went out.

Eighteen young Egyptian maids, ranged nine to a side, walked sedately with us, eyes cast down to the ground. Before us came the dancers, with the cymbals and the thunderous drums drowning out the pipings of the flutes. Then came Solomon in his richest robes—he was always fond of dressing up to an occasion—next to Theke. She looked dazzling in her high jeweled headdress, her wide necklace of lapis that half-covered her tiny nude breasts, her shimmering short jacket of cloth of gold and her girdle of flashing gems that weighed heavily on her young loins. Below this fell a transparent skirt of gauze, dropping nearly to the ground. Only a small apron, embroidered with the figure of protecting Isis, was between her thighs. But for all the celebration, Theke looked tired and unhappy.

After Solomon and Theke, almost treading on their heels, came the figure of Zadok in his sacerdotal robes, carrying their weight as best he could while still maintaining dignity. Then, in plain white, myself, and Benaiah with his ever-present decoration of Joab's old sword. After us came Petabast and his Egyptians and the rest of the king's household. They were followed by yelping dogs and a crush of spectators who fought each other every step of the way to gain a vantage view. On and on we went in the bright noon sunlight, moving up the hill toward the temple, past the gorgeous pile of the unfinished new palace which Theke would one day inhabit, on into the series of our sacred courtyards.

The royal pair walked slowly up the steps between the massive pylons and bronze pillars. The dancers and musical instruments ceased. On the left, the nine maidens with pomegranate-embroidered gowns commenced to sing:

Only once is spring so rare,
Putting brightness in the air—
Time it is to wed;
Time it is to bed;
Man and mistress led
To a maidenhead.
Ishtar, show this pair the way,
Yahweh, make night fair as day!

The antiphonal response of the epithalamium came as Solomon and Theke, hand in hand, entered the holy place, trailed by puffing Zadok and the gaunt old Egyptian priest—who was to remain on the porch outside. On the right the young girls chorused in their bright young voices. Their fresh mouths formed the words in unison, their blue robes flicking in the breeze:

Tybi is the month of sighs,
Suited to a swift surprise—
Dispose of every doubt;
Shut the weather out;
Turn the world about
By its waxen snout!
Ishtar, show this pair the way,
Yahweh, make night fair as day!

Scarcely had their voices died away when Solomon and Theke reappeared. Up the exultant cymbals and drums! The ceremony had been brief. It was completed in a few words, a clasp of hands, and an obeisance. The grave and colorful procession re-formed, taking substance behind the king and his bride. Now Benaiah and I took precedence over Zadok as we wended the short way toward the old palace.

Here the final part of the ceremonies was to be executed: that of bedding the queen of Solomon in style, publicly.

I may interject here that the arrangements for the marriage—all of which, despite Zadok's protests, I insisted on handling myself—were not easy to achieve. When a couple is wed under the aegis of more than one god, things become complicated; when the rites are different, things become involved; and when two different countries and royalties are to be joined, things become fantastically complex. But with due protocol, blending the respect owed to the beliefs of others, I had satisfied both Zadok and Petabast, the most nit-picking of critics.

Thus one may understand my feeling of relief when we finally filed into the sleeping chamber of Solomon. Here a wide couch, surrounded by curtains of the omnipresent purple and gold, was prepared with down pillows and coverings of splendor. The attendants of Theke moved in. As was the custom, they completely disrobed her stiff, trembling dark-young body.

At a signal from Petabast, the maidens lifted her and placed her on her back on the bed. Slowly, as if disclosing the mystery of the virgin, they drew her legs apart. I felt my loins warming. Beside me, Zadok actually began to slobber, as he fixed his eyes on the spectacle.

Solomon disrobed, a fine figure as he was of a man and a king. As everyone assembled about the couch could testify, his manhood was ready, virile for the task at hand. He sprang upon the bed. He stood straddled over Theke. Zadok sucked in his breath.

At that moment, I became aware of the piteous gaze which Theke lifted to Solomon. I swear I have never seen a more pleading look, one which begged him to spare her. My heart contracted with compassion. But Solomon, staring down at her, gave no indication that he recognized its import.

This king spares no one, I thought with indignation. But at that moment Solomon did something entirely unexpected, at odds with custom. He lifted his hand. In response, the golden cords were loosed from the heavy, gold-starred purple curtains. They fell into sleek folds, as stiff and still as if the fabric were proud of the act of marriage they guarded. Instantly the choir of maidens burst into song once more:

Marriage is the sweetest state
Man may come to contemplate—
Two made one entire;
Two that set a fire,
Kindled by desire,
By the days piled higher.
Ishtar, show this pair the way;
Yahweh, make night bright as day!

At the foot of the couch, Benaiah and I simultaneously turned our heads. We saw each other's solemn countenance at the same moment. For the first time in our acquaintance, upon this notable occasion, a bond fashioned itself between us. I made a slight nod and gave a half-smile. Benaiah returned the nod. He gave a lewd, portentous wink. Sang the choristers:

Each the other's own delight,
World created overnight—
No unhappy tears;
No inconstant fears!
Gods will keep arrears
Of the happy years!

Ishtar, show this pair the way;
Yahweh, make night bright as day!

Benaiah stifled a yawn. With duly respectful stride, he came to me and took me by the arm. He squeezed it hard enough to make me gasp.

"Come, Nathan," he said in an undertone, "we rank all others, including Zadok, in this room. Shall we lead the way out and leave our monarch to reign over his new kingdom in privacy?"

"I had no idea generals were so sensitive to true love," I said with dignity.

Benaiah bared his teeth—in mirth or resentment, I could never tell. We joined arms and turned, walking out of the chamber. After us came the maidens and Petabast, and, perforce, following them came all the rest—including the reluctant Zadok, still licking his thick lips.

PART TWO

CHAPTER ELEVEN

The Song of Solomon

"I have a gift for you, O Nathan," Solomon said to me whimsically. "It will be one of your most precious possessions."

Visions of gold and jewels, amber and crystal, whirled in my head. I bowed myself down to the ground, rubbing my forehead on the carpets of Babylon woven with strange figures. "I am overwhelmed by the generosity of the king," I said. "May I ask what it may be?"

"I shall present it to you here and now," Solomon responded. "It will be valued by you above all other things. It is a state secret."

Again I bowed. This time it was more to cover my embarrassment and confusion than to indulge in fancies of riches. "I am most grateful for the king's confidence," I said.

Solomon laughed. "Confess you are disappointed," he said. "Even though you are a prophet dedicated to Yahweh, Nathan, still your fingers clutch. You dream of earthly splendors, as well as those of heaven."

"No, no," I said hastily.

"Yes, yes," Solomon mocked me. "Do you indeed think that I am unaware of your net of spies about the court? Take only one: long ago, Benaiah got the truth out of your servant Elihaph and brought him to me. You forget I have more power to rule and more power to reward than you—and that he has been faithful to me because I have more power to punish."

I said nothing. I bowed for the third time. My heart was filled with devouring rage against both Benaiah and Elihaph. But there was nothing I could do. By his pronouncement and knowledge, Solomon had brought them at one stroke under his protection.

"That is not what I wish to discuss," Solomon said briskly. "What you have done you have done for the good of the king—I knew your heart, Nathan, and it is turned entirely toward me. That is why I wish to share this state secret with you alone."

I waited, hands folded within the wide embroidered sleeves that had become fashionable in Jerusalem. Solomon lifted his head, bidding me come closer. I approached. He bent to my ear:

"You know that the Egyptian princess Theke came to Jerusalem five years ago."

I nodded.

"You know she was frightened of the harem. That I ordered a special dwelling place for her to be built, the Millo tower."

"I know," I said.

"Do you know that she is now nearly twenty—no longer a child, but a woman—and that I have ordered her to be returned to the harem?"

"I had heard such a rumor," I said cautiously.

Solomon smiled. "Elihaph told me last night that he had informed you of it," he said. "But here is something that only thee and me will know."

My curiosity had got the better of my fury against Benaiah and Elihaph. I listened intently.

"You recall the ceremonies of our marriage five years gone, Nathan? How carefully all the elements of our joining were prepared for the satisfaction of both nations?"

I nodded.

"Well," said Solomon, coming to his grand disclosure, "that marriage was never consummated."

My jaw dropped. But I remembered how the king had ordered the curtains of the bed to be lowered just before he coupled with the child princess from Egypt. Certainly this was possible.

"But this would be an insult to Egypt!" I protested.

Solomon shook his head. "She was only a child, frightened and alone on that vast bed," he said. "To have taken her then would have been cruelty, torture. I know women, at least, Nathan: I know there was fear, not love, in her eyes as she stared up at me." The king sighed slightly. "Besides," he went on, "I am not sure that I could have performed my diplomatic office. You have no idea, Nathan, how effective our high ceremonies are in reducing the swelling of low passion!

"So Theke has been put away these five years," he said, "to grow up. And I have waited for my passion to become directed toward her, of all women. Thus she waits for me, here in the very next building, at my command and will."

I bowed. "She will be honored to receive you," I said.

Solomon did not respond. His eyes turned inward. He meditated. "I shall tell you yet another state secret," he said slowly. "I am not sure that she is a pearl unpierced, a filly unridden—in short, a virgin."

"What!" I cried, scandalized. "Who has dared to rob the king of the chiefest of his treasures?"

Solomon knuckled his finger and put the seal of his six-pointed-star ring to his lips.

"Silence," he said. "Benaiah has brought me further information. I wish to be sure of it myself. Do you come to this room, Nathan, two hours after sunset tonight."

Sitting atop the palace in the cool of the night—possibly at the same spot where David had first glimpsed Bathsheba in the court next door, I thought, with a pang for that lovely vanished figure—I could believe we were part of a dream. We sat near the edge of the roof, able to look down into the narrow starlit, slightly odorous passage below us. I was content to rest on my couch. I thought sad, unutterably pleasureable thoughts supine on the pallet, staring upward, but Solomon rose. He paced noiselessly back and forth like a caged lion.

Lion in truth was the word to describe the king in the thirty-fourth year of his age—lion not only of Judah but of Israel which had felt the weight of his displeasure. How many things had happened in those years since his first battle and Shishak's propitiatory gesture!

The temple itself had become part of our daily life. The palace beside it was more than two-thirds complete. Hiram-abi, I know, had estimated it would be finished in less than five years more—but its magnificence was already unmistakable, the sheen of white stone and blaze of gilt already making it a landmark for coastal sailors in the distant sea. Yet its construction had caused grievous wounds in the body of our country, the wounds David had worked so hard to bind up. More and more of the northern tribes were forced to contribute labor. There were more and more taxes throughout the country. The army had increased hugely under Benaiah's prodding. So had the number of arrogant overseers imported by Hiram-abi from Phoenicia.

Still, few complained. Trade had increased with Assyria and Egypt. Solomon's friendship with Hiram of Tyre, purple gifts and bets on riddles, had got stronger than ever. In spite of the burdens of conscription and contribution, the Hebrews found themselves with more money and goods than ever before. More than that, they enjoyed a sort of religious unity and national solidarity. It pleased them to their marrow. Even the follies of Solomon—which were many—excited their gossip. His elegant misdeeds filled their eyes with vicarious glory.

One, perhaps the chief, of the reasons why Solomon had not pressed his right to deflower Theke before this was that he no longer was in a hazardous position for a successor. When he was thirty-two he had elevated a girl of the slave Ammonite people, one Naamah, to the position of concubine. Unlike his other wives (including Abishag with her feverish seeking for charms that would make her fertile), this mating proved immediately sound. Thus far Solomon had fathered only daughters; a son was needed. The first child of the Ammonitess was a boy. He was an unruly, squalling infant but I saw Solomon grow tall with pride as he watched him in his mother's arms on that day.

"Are you frightened of children, Nathan?" he asked me.

"You forget, O king," I replied, "that I have had my own sons. And that I saw you in Bathsheba's arms when you were no more than this bit of flesh."

Solomon's face clouded. "You have not answered me," he said.

I sighed. "Yes," I said. "They frighten me because they remind me of a future that we shall not see."

Solomon did not appear to hear me. He contemplated his offspring and smiled. "My firstborn son," he said. "He has enlarged my family famously and that is what I shall call him in due time."

I understood and nodded approval. Rehoboam would be his name, "my family is enlarged." Solomon bent and touched his first male offspring as gingerly as if the baby were fine ivory from the south.

"Since Bathsheba died," he murmured, "despite my wives, despite everything—I have been lonely. Now I have a son. I shall see him grow and train him in the ways he must follow."

"And teach him how to rule the Hebrews when we are gone," I said.

Solomon quivered. "Enough, Nathan," he said sharply. "I do not choose to look that far into the future."

All this had come about a year before the arrival of

Theke—and at the time of her return to Solomon's harem, Rehoboam was more than six years old and the darling of Solomon's eye.

In a real sense, his male offspring filled the void that Solomon felt opening when Bathsheba died. Naamah was raised to honors almost equal to those of Abishag. The child was cosseted and spoiled in every possible way. It was a procedure I warned against but was powerless to prevent. Solomon became more carefree—though with an odd intensity and persistence about anything he did—and less inclined to follow Yahweh. He treated his women contemptuously, using them for his lusts, often degenerating into cruelty.

But, I reminded myself as I squatted by the king in the soft darkness of the rooftop, it was unfair to believe that women were his only preoccupation next to the kingship. In sober fact, he had interests that captivated him much more. Love of horses, of chariots, of speed with the wind on his forehead had become a passion with Solomon. At times I was convinced that these surpassed even his taste for women. He had learned how to be expert in choosing such beasts for his pleasure. His desire turned toward white horses. "Not only for the purity and sparkle of their hides," he told me, "but also for their wisdom which is infallibly indicated by this color."

I had not believed it—but my ignorance kept me silent. I noticed that the king, in his passionate indulgence, treated steeds as if they were guests of royalty. He built special stone stables for them at Megiddo that provided room for nearly five hundred steeds, all broken carefully to be harnessed to the chariots. Solomon also bought hundreds of chariots with light wicker bodies and large wheels suitable for one driver, decorated with rare woods. They were specially made to his order in Egypt. As charioteers, he trained a corps of two hundred young men, dressing each one in a long flowing gown of light purple and giving each a wig of long blond hair heavily dusted with gold. He loved the colors and the sight of the chariots bouncing and swaying on their desert runs but was soon forced to bar them their wild rides through the streets of Jerusalem as too much of a danger to pedestrians.

As recompense, he established prizes for adeptness at driving. Further, he set up racecourses in the flats of Jezreel—often taking part himself (and winning), the most reckless and careening of all. It was a brave sight, colored robes and long bright hair streaming behind, the drivers whipping and reining their chariots on, shouting and laughing at disaster or success. I wished Zabud were alive again: he would have enjoyed such mad things more than anyone else.

As it was, Solomon often ordered the whole court to attend the races and applaud his driving. More than once, I stood between Zadok and Benaiah, all of us at the trackside and dutifully mouthing compliments. I remember well one occasion.

"Rare, rare," muttered Zadok as he watched. The track was like a stretched skein of wool in shape, with long straightaways and tight curves at either end. The former were wet down and packed; the latter were left soft and dusty in order that the chariots might take closer turns about the stone pylons.

"If I were only young," Zadok sighed.

"The king would not have a rival," said Benaiah. "Your weight of fat would break the rawhide netting of the chariot floor."

"I was not always so," Zadok said, patting his stomach as if it belonged to someone else. "But now it would not fit the dignity of a high priest."

I pricked up my ears when Benaiah intimated that Zadok might be a rival to Solomon. I stared at the rotund high priest appraisingly. Before this, in many kingdoms, these men had seized power. "You could never hope to have the skill of a king," I said meaningfully.

Zadok shrugged and lifted his hands. He twisted them in mincing mimicry of driving. "The wrists, so," he said. "The balance maintained. Long reins for whipping, with the ends, wrapped, so, around the palms. That is all there is to it."

"Except a knife at the belt to cut yourself loose of the reins if you are dragged out of the chariot," Benaiah said.

Now I stared at him. "A knife?" I said. "Surely that is not necessary."

Zadok gave a shout. He drew back in alarm. There was a muffled thunder of hoofs. We were engulfed in a boiling cloud of dust, our eyes blinded and our throats and mouths stuffed with it.

We retreated, coughing into our hastily lifted robes, wiping our streaming eyes. I caught a glimpse of a chariot tumbling end over end in the dust. I heard a stifled cry and the savage whinny of horses. I peered into the cloud as it subsided, only to recoil in dismay. I saw Solomon's white horses plunging down the track, kicking his expensive chariot to bits as they went.

I began to cry out in fear. But the next moment I saw the

king and Benaiah coming through the dust. Benaiah sheathed his sword. Solomon unwrapped the bits of leather reins from his hands and tossed them down. He was unhurt but filthy with horse spittle and dirt. His face was frowning.

"Praise Yahweh for your safety!" I croaked. Zadok echoed my words but Solomon paid no attention to either of us.

"You did not need to cut the reins," he said coldly to Benaiah. "I was able to manage the horses."

"O king, forgive me," Benaiah said, bowing low. "I acted before I thought, out of my own craven fear for your welfare. It shall not happen again."

My ears sharpened to hear that sardonic note once more. But Solomon appeared unaware. "Very well," he responded and turned toward his nearby litter.

The races were over with the king's mishap. We stood aside and watched the young men form up behind Solomon's litter. Benaiah lifted his blade and let it chock back into its scabbard. "You must admit, Nathan," he murmured, "that the sword will cut a knot faster than it may be untied."

Solomon loved also to take his personal chariot afield to hunt. He had imported hawk-trainers from Babylon. He carried the royal goshawk on his arm to toss aloft for its waiting-on period, circling some four hundred feet above until it spotted game. Then it folded its wings, stooped in a dive that stunned the prey, and finally rolled over and bound it tight with its talons to bear back to its master.

"These birds are perfect soldiers of the air," Solomon said to me one day. "They have no fear, no love, they can endure all kinds of punishment, they are stolid and loyal—as long as they have their reward of food." Once in a while he boasted of a fox or a wolf falling to their stoop, as dazzling a blow as a stone flung from a sling.

In such cases, the victim was obviously too heavy for the bird to bring back. For such retrieves, Solomon had trained greathounds from Assyria. Speedy, seldom barking, they had long tails, square faces, arched necks, and pointed ears. They wore short shining coats of fawn and stood well above the thigh. To any not known to them, they were suspicious and, occasionally, ferocious. In time, Solomon came to use them as night guards about his palace.

As I lay in the soft darkness of the rooftop, all these thoughts came to me—and more. Solomon had not neglected his duty as a ruler. I began to concentrate on what had been done at the mines of Ezion Geber, how they had improved. I envisioned what might be done if the proposal of Solomon—that Hiram's people be employed along the gulf of Aqaba to build him a fleet to sail the southern seas—was accepted. But my meditations were rudely cut short. I roused myself from a half-doze at an unexpected signal.

Without warning, from the deserted street below, came a soft sound. It was the slightest slurring of footsteps. Solomon looked at me as the vague whisper of nothing came upward. He nodded. I rose without a sound. He put his perfumed lips to my ear.

"Listen," Solomon said softly. He held up his hand to enjoin silence. Puzzled, I tiptoed up beside him. I looked over the edge of the roof. Below us, two shadowy figures—one inside the harem rooms, the other outside at one of the harem lattices—had their heads together. I heard the unmistakable voice of Jeroboam in throaty adoration.

"Kiss me with the kisses of your mouth," he whispered, "for your love is better than wine."

"The smell of your body is like fine ointment," I heard the voice of Theke respond, "and therefore the young women love you."

"What!" I cried in amazement. Solomon closed his hand over my exclamation too late. The two conspirators beneath us had taken alarm at the slight sound. They separated instantly, gliding off in different directions.

Full of indignation, I looked at the king. To my surprise, he smiled. "I shall see Theke tomorrow," he said softly, "and you shall come with me."

"What does this mean?" I asked—too late, in a whisper.

Solomon shrugged. "Cheap poetry," he responded, "that of a wandering singer, as practiced by street singers and imitated by Theke. Do you not agree that such an infection of rhetoric deserves to be heard?"

"Yes, yes," I agreed, my head in a whirl.

The following day, I entered the harem rooms at his side. But we did not go directly into the bath of the women. Solomon paused outside. He beckoned me forward. Again I listened with him, the sounds within coming clearly through the panels of thin ivory.

"Do not disdain me, daughters of Jerusalem," Theke's voice said proudly. "Perhaps my skin is black as the tents of Kedar or the curtains of David's tabernacle, but I am beautiful. The sun has looked upon me with favor, so much so that my own mother's children were envious of me. In my own land I was queen of all the vineyards of Egypt—but I was not able to stay there."

"Tell me," came the mocking voice of Abishag, "O Theke that my soul loves, where does your heart feed? Where do your dreams rest when you sleep at noon?"

"If you do not know," came Theke's defiant reply, "come with me in my dreams and feed your own heart upon them."

Solomon pushed open the door. He approached the startled, half-naked covey of women. They parted as he advanced, chattering excitedly. Solomon confronted Theke in their midst.

I had not seen the immured Theke at all for the past few years. Now the looks of the Egyptian princess delighted my heart. She had become a woman of rare beauty, a flower in a jeweled crevice, in this room hung with lamps and silken stuffs, carpeted thickly, cushioned about an alabaster pool, with couches of juniper wood and nets of fine gauze held back by golden chains, pillared with gold and fretted with ebony and ivory work. She was high-bosomed and heavy-loined, swaying as she walked. Her black hair glowed with inner lights, her eyes seemed like great depths of darkness. Her mouth was sea-coral and pearl, her lips like Solomon's own seal in crimson. My eyes watered as if I were viewing the full moon. I sneezed twice in embarrassment.

At last Solomon spoke. I realized he was adopting the same ornamented, semipoetic diction that we had heard used the night before. "I have compared you," he said magniloquently to Theke, "to a company of horses with pharaoh's chariots. Your cheeks are beautiful with rows of jewels, your neck with chains of gold that I have placed there. Have you nothing to say to me?"

"A bundle of myrrh is my well-beloved to me," she replied defiantly. I knew her answer to be double-edged. "He shall lie all night between my breasts." Clever woman that she was, she had matched Solomon in his high style without hesitation—undoubtedly realizing the meaning of his words.

Solomon nodded, never taking his eyes from her. "Behold," he said, "you are fair, my love, you have the eyes of an innocent dove."

Theke gazed past the king. Her defiant gaze met mine and melted as she looked away at an invisible lover. "Behold," she replied, "you are fair, too, my beloved, yea, pleasant. Our bed is green, the beams of our house are cedar and the rafters of fir. I am your rose of Sharon and your lily of the valley."

"As the lily among thorns," Solomon said, looking about him meaningfully at the other women, "so is my love among the daughters of the court."

He dismissed them with a wave. They scattered like a flock of hens, bowing and curtseying. I repressed my tongue with difficulty as we made our way out. I was about to speak outside the door but Solomon put his finger to his lips. "They will chatter about our visit," he whispered imperiously. "I wish to hear."

From behind the door we heard at first only the confused murmur of the women. Then the contemptuous accents of Abishag cut through the muffled hubbub: "You have learned passion, my dear, since you have come out of Egypt to join the daughters of the Hebrews."

"As the apple tree among the trees of the woods," came the soft voice of the princess, "so is my beloved among the sons of men. I sit down under his shadow with delight, his fruit is sweet to my taste. He brings me to the banqueting house of love and places his banner over me. I need drink no wine. I need only the fruit of the tree, for I am sick with love and only love can cure me. His left hand is under my head, his right hand embraces me."

Solomon looked sideways at me with a grimace. "I charge you, O you daughters of Jerusalem," he whispered to me ironically, "by the rose and by the hinds of the field that you stir not up my love till she please."

He took my arm. We went away as quickly as possible. I said nothing. Solomon's brow was furrowed in thought. But we were no more than a few paces away from the door when we heard Theke's ecstatic voice once more:

"I hear the voice of my beloved as he comes leaping down the mountains and skipping on the hills! He is like a roe or a young hart! He stands behind our wall, he looks in at the windows and shows himself at the lattice!"

Solomon shook his head. "We shall see if he will show himself at the lattice again tonight," he said grimly.

"Rise up, my love, my fair one," said the shadow at the lattice in a low voice. "Come away with me. For lo! the winter is past and the rain is over and gone. The flowers appear on the earth. The time of the singing of birds is come and the voice of the turtle is heard in our land."

He paused and continued in a voice that, despite itself, was rising in intensity: "The fig tree puts forth her green figs and the vines with the tender grapes give a good smell. Arise, my love, my fair one, and come away with me! Let me see your face, for sweet is your voice and your face is beautiful."

Listening on the rooftop, Solomon nodded as if to himself and said almost inaudibly: "Take us the foxes, the little foxes that spoil the vines, for our vines have tender grapes." We withdrew quietly from the roof edge.

"I seem to recognize that voice," I said breathlessly.

Solomon glanced at me. "I recognized it long since," he said. "It is the voice of that young knave Jeroboam, whom I commanded Benaiah to let go unscathed."

"It was a mistake," I stammered miserably.

"You recall, Nathan," Solomon said with what seemed to be almost malice, "that four years ago—only a year after Benaiah slew his older brother—Jeroboam returned to the court as a suppliant."

"Yes," I said.

"He sought my favor. Benaiah again advised killing him but you—you counseled patience and mercy."

"Yes."

"And I followed your advice," Solomon said. "I set him to work building the walls of Jerusalem to the south."

"He did very well," I said defensively.

Solomon nodded. "So very well, you remember," he replied, "that two years later I set him over all the tribe of Joseph as the chief in authority. His, too, was the task of building Millo tower more securely."

"Yes," I replied disconsolately.

"Now you see what has come of mercy. The ungrateful fool has made the walls and tower secure—but he has come to steal what they guarded!"

"I confess my mistake," I said contritely. "Benaiah was right. The traitor should have been killed."

To my confoundment, Solomon laughed quietly. "No," he said, "this affair amuses me more than it alarms or angers me. Let us see, Nathan, what may be done."

"We shall take him and kill him," I said.

Solomon shook his head. "I have a better plan," he responded.

He gave a shout. In response, shouts came from either end of the street: sparks, the lighting of resinous torches. I saw the shadow below dart desperately about. But both exits were sealed off by what I recognized as Benaiah's palace guards. They advanced on the culprit at a half run, torches flaring and spitting above their heads. They closed upon him—weaponless as he was—and seized him after a brief struggle.

Solomon wagged his head in satisfaction. "Let us go down to the street at our leisure," he said. "The fool is taken in the trap that he baited for himself."

At the foot of the steps, he hesitated. I halted just behind him, seeing over his shoulder the pale, distorted face of Jeroboam in the grip of the soldiers. Solomon advanced to the group which parted deferentially to let him through. He gazed upon the face of Jeroboam. A soft wail came from the lattice behind. Deliberately Solomon spat in the face of the man. "That is royal spittle," he said, "and more than you deserve." He turned on his heel and spoke to the guard. "Tomorrow," he said.

Next morning, following the official business of the court, Solomon beckoned me to approach. "Now that our little fox Jeroboam," he said, "has been caught in his own snare—the snare of love—he waits our pleasure. We shall see him in the very place that he sought to defile. Do you wish to come with me? To see the rest of this business, Nathan?"

"Most certainly," I said fervently. "An insult to the king is an insult against his officers."

Actually, I was curious to see the end of the affair. Solomon knew it as well as I. I waited for the disclosure of his judgment but Solomon did not enlighten me. Instead he said: "I first became suspicious when Theke asked to live in the harem again, rather than in the tower—which, as you know, I had built for her special residence because she was so timid with the other women. But the Millo, being on the walls, is guarded twice as vigilantly as the harem here."

"You think they met while Jeroboam oversaw the building of the walls?"

"How else?"

"Perhaps it is your fault, O king," I said, greatly daring. "A lonely woman in a strange land—a youth who believes himself aggrieved. This is to thrust fire into tinder."

"Whatever is done, is done," Solomon replied, dismissing the subject. "I ordered the harem to be unguarded last night," he said offhandedly, "and the gates unbarred."

I gaped at him. "But why?"

"I am fond of experimenting, especially with women. We shall see what has happened."

At the outer door of the harem two soldiers with Benaiah beside them held Jeroboam erect. He threw back his shaggy head as we came near. I was shocked at the change in the boy I remembered. I had not seen him in his duties except occasionally at a distance during the long interval. Now, close at hand, I found him taller, thinner, his face careworn. But he had an air of pride, of hardness and endurance—qualities which I was to discover would serve him well in his reckless career.

Solomon did not look at him. He passed by disdainfully. At a gesture from Benaiah, Jeroboam was thrust after us. His guards held him beyond earshot as we approached the inner ivory door of the women's quarters. The eunuch moved aside. As before, Solomon made a sign of silence and waited. It was not long before we could distinguish voices.

"Your beauty is not what it was, my sister," I heard one of Solomon's women say—not in cruelty but compassion. "You are bruised and weary."

"It was my fault," came the tired voice of Theke. "By night on my bed I sought him whom my soul loves—but he was not there, he had not come to abide with me. I rose to go about the city in the streets by night, to seek my lover in the broad ways."

"But were the gates unlocked?"

"Yes."

"And there were no guards?"

"No."

"This is a strange thing," said the unknown sympathizer in a wondering voice.

"I did not stop to consider it," Theke said. "The watchmen that go about the city found me. I asked them if they had seen him I love. They took me for a woman of the streets and beat me. I fled from them, back to this refuge."

"And you did not find him?"

"Only in my dreams last night. I held him then and would not let him go until the dawn. Nor shall I cease to seek after him until I bring him to Egypt, to my mother's house and into the chamber of her that conceived me."

"That will be a long time," said the other dubiously.

"I dreamed that he came and knocked at the locked door. He said: 'Open to me, my sister, my love, my dove, my undefiled—for my head is filled with dew and my locks wet with the drops of night.' I dreamed that he put his hand on the latch and my soul was moved with love. I went to the door and put my hands on it, dripping with myrrh; I opened it to my beloved—but lo! he was not there! My soul sank within me. I awoke. I called his name aloud but there was no answer."

"What shall we do with you, princess of Egypt?"

"Nothing—except I charge you, daughter of Jerusalem,

that if you find my beloved, tell him that I am sick with love to hold him in my arms."

"But what is your beloved more than another beloved, fairest among women? Why should you so charge me?"

Theke's voice suddenly became strong. She commenced to speak in a tone of exaltation. "My beloved is white and ruddy," she said, "chief among ten thousand. His head is fine gold, though his locks are bushy and black as a raven. His eyes are as the eyes of doves by the rivers of water, washed with milk and fitly set. His cheeks are as a bed of spices, as sweet flowers; his lips are like lilies, dropping sweet scents. His hands are as gold rings set with beryl. His belly is as bright ivory overlaid with sapphires. His legs are pillars of marble set upon sockets of gold and his countenance is as Lebanon, as excellent as the cedars. His mouth—his mouth is most sweet." Her voice lifted. "Yes, he is altogether lovely! This is my beloved and my friend, daughters of Jerusalem!"

I glanced apprehensively over my shoulder. Theke had spoken so ringingly that it was impossible for Jeroboam not to have overheard. True enough, his head was erect, his eyes shining, a flush in his cheeks. Solomon saw it, too. His face showed impassive as he opened the door and entered, turning to command Benaiah to bring in Jeroboam as well. I wondered at this, especially when Jeroboam, no sooner inside, began what amounted to a chant of defiance of the king's authority.

"I have entered your garden," said Jeroboam to Solomon, throwing back his head defiantly. "I have made your virgin my spouse. I have gathered my myrrh with your spice; I have eaten my honeycomb with your honey. I have drunk my wine with your milk!" He swung about exultantly—but a trifle theatrically also, I thought. "I have eaten and drunk abundantly at the king's table!" he cried.

In the silence which ensued, Solomon said nothing. Instead, he eyed Jeroboam critically until the eyes of that young man fell. As if satisfied, Solomon nodded for the guards to take him off. He bowed silently to Theke and turned his back on her.

"The fellow boasts very well," he said aside to me, as we left. "We shall imitate the Egyptian sage with Susannah, who questioned the elders separately."

"Will you not slay him?" I inquired of the king.

"For his boasts?"

"But," I said in bewilderment, "you slew Adonijah in times gone by for desiring Abishag only!"

"Adonijah was of the line of David," Solomon said. "And even if his sin was great, in aspiring to the throne, my heart sinks when I recall the deed. It still lies heavy on my mind. No, the thing and the sin here are not yet fully apparent to me." He pondered a moment. "I wish you to act for me, Nathan," Solomon said finally. "Post yourself at one of the spy-holes and report to me what is said."

"Hearing is obedience," I said.

As everyone knows, each harem has a dozen or more secret niches—from which vantage points the interior may be either seen or the inmates heard. This, of course, is very necessary when dealing with women who might hatch plots against the kingdom—but it is rare that a person as high as myself in the court would be used as an eavesdropper. Nevertheless, I was glad to render the king what services I could.

Solomon's wisdom was never less apparent than on that occasion. Scarcely had I concealed myself in my nook—with my small skin of wine and loaf of bread for sustenance—than I heard the women chattering excitedly of Jeroboam's boldness, admiring him for facing the king so fearlessly.

Then the heavy ironic accents of Abishag: "Where is your beloved gone, Theke? Where, fairest among women? Where has he turned aside fom you? Tell us, we will seek him tonight with you!"

"You know well where he lies," Theke answered dully. "In dreams, even as I do, he is gone down into a garden, to the bed of spices, to feed among the lilies and to think of my love."

"All very pretty," grumbled Abishag, "but you shall find out that Solomon is not merciful with those who rob him. He is a miser at heart."

They moved off. I could hear no more. That was all I learned for my pains. Soon I extricated myself from the niche, stretched out my cramps, and went to inform Solomon. Solomon listened in silence. "Is that all?" he demanded.

"All that I could hear," I answered respectfully.

"Abishag," he said. "She has been a long time without a whipping. I shall see to it."

I made no objection: I thought it proper. Solomon went on in the tight voice of anger: "I see now that this must be fought with other weapons than spears or swords or axes. It is a quarrel with words and high-blown sentiments. I shall see." He looked at me. "At dawn tomorrow, come to the harem. Bring Jeroboam with his guards once more to the same place."

Solomon looked scornfully about him in the growing dawn-light. His audience of women, centered by Theke, stood before him. Near him was the pinioned Jeroboam. The pink flushes of sunrise suffused the room.

"If this has turned into a contest between a king and his subject, with poetry as a weapon," said Solomon flatly, "I accept the weapon and engage in the duel."

He drew himself up. "Do you dare to think that the son of David—who was the poet of the world, whose harp still sighs with the wind in my chamber—cannot better you in a battle of honeyed words? Do you believe my tongue cannot turn itself to whatever pleases me? You have plied each other with sweet stuff indeed—but I shall outdo you." He took a deep breath, closed his eyes for a moment, then stared at the pair.

He addressed Theke directly: "Behold, you are fair, my love. You are fair with your dove's eyes within your locks. Your hair is as a flock of goats that appear from Mount Gilead. Your teeth are like a flock of sheep that are even shorn and which came up from the washing whereof each one bears twins and none is barren. Your lips are like a thread of scarlet, and your speech is charming. Your temples are like pieces of a pomegranate within your hair. Your neck is like the tower of David, built for an armory wherein hang a thousand bucklers, all the shields of mighty men. Your two breasts are like two young roes that are twins, which feed among the lilies."

Solomon extended his arm toward Theke. I noticed a slight drawing back of the girl. But Solomon did not see this, carried away in his own improvisation: "Until the day break and the shadows flee away, I will get me to your mountain of myrrh and to your hills of frankincense! You are fair, my love, and there is no spot in thee!"

Solomon dropped his arm and stepped back, looking at Jeroboam. "Have no fear in speaking before the king," he said. "Do your best. See who will triumph."

To my surprise, Jeroboam accepted the challenge. Like the king, he addressed Theke directly. Her eyes beamed, and her fingers intertwined tightly as she paid attention to every syllable that fell from his lips.

"You have ravished my heart, my sister, my love! You have ravished my heart with one glance of your eye, with one chain of your neck. Your lips drop as a honeycomb and honey and milk are under your tongue. Even the smell of your garments is like the smell of the wood of Lebanon. You are a garden enclosed, my sister, my spouse. You are a spring shut up, a fountain!"

He halted, panting with emotion, almost weeping with the fullness of his heart. Solomon took advantage of the moment to nod to the guards to draw Jeroboam back.

"Let us see if the king can put aside his robes altogether and rant with the best of the street-corner chanters," Solomon murmured. He stood a moment, thinking. Then he advanced his foot and raised his arm melodramatically.

"You are beautiful, my love, Theke," he said. I was startled at the bitter sardonic tone of what he said. "Turn your eyes away from me, for they have overcome me. I have sixty queens, eighty concubines, and virgins without number in my harem. You, my undefiled dove, are but one—the only choice of your mother, the choice of him who fathered you, to wed with me."

The king gestured grandly—imitating the broad wave of Jeroboam's hands—before the rest of the intently listening women. "The daughters of Jerusalem saw you and blessed you," he said ironically to Theke, "yes, the queens and the concubines praised you—but not the virgins."

He bent his glance upon her: "Who are you that looks forth as the morning? Are you fair as the moon, clear as the sun, terrible as an army with banners?"

He looked down at her tiny feet and smiled: "How beautiful with shoes are your feet, O prince's daughter!" Solomon's glance moved darkly, slowly upward over her slim, tensed body: "The joints of your thighs are like jewels, the work of the hands of a cunning craftsman. Your navel is like a round goblet which does not want filling; your belly is like a heap of wheat surrounded by lilies. Your breasts are like twin roes, your neck is like a tower of ivory. Your eyes are like the deep fishpools of Heshbon by the gate of Bathrabbim; your nose is as the tower of Lebanon which looks toward Damascus."

Carried away by his own eloquence, Solomon spread his hands. "How fair and pleasant are you, O my love, for my delights! Your figure is like that of a slender palm tree, your breasts like clusters of grapes!"

He took a step toward Theke. She recoiled, only to be pushed forward again by the lascivious hands of Abishag. "I will go up to the palm tree," Solomon said, "and I will take hold of its bough. Your breasts shall indeed be to me like the clusters of the vine—and the smell of your nose like that of apples. I shall kiss you. The roof of your mouth shall be like the best wine for your beloved. It will go down his throat sweetly, even making the lips of those that are asleep to speak."

He folded his arms slowly. He looked at the immobile Jeroboam. He contemplated the Egyptian princess, a half-smile on his face. There was not a whisper in the room as he waited for her reply. None broke the silence. Even the voluble Jeroboam did not dare to speak.

"What have you to say?" asked Solomon at last of Theke. His voice, to my ears, held more of curiosity than of anger. The finely chiseled head and the long flawless neck of Theke rose in pride: "I am my beloved's," she said simply. "His desire is toward me and mine toward him."

Solomon raised his eyebrows delicately. "But desire fails as man nears his long home," he said meaningfully. He looked again at Jeroboam. "And you, young man," he said, "and you?" Jeroboam set his teeth in his lips. He still said nothing, sure of his fate.

"Come, my beloved," pleaded Theke with him, "the king will be merciful. He knows our love. Let us go forth to the fields, let us lodge in the villages. Let us get up early to the vineyards to see if the vines flourish, whether the tender grapes appear; to see whether the pomegranates bud forth. There I shall give you all my love."

Jeroboam looked at her longingly. Truly, I believe if his last moment had depended upon it, he could not have resisted answering in the same strain. All his braggadocio was gone. He was simple and direct. "Set me as a seal upon your heart," he said in a proud, calm voice, "and as a seal upon your arm. For our love is as strong as death."

"And jealousy is as strong as the grave," Solomon broke in, nodding his head, gently stroking his beard. "The coals thereof are as coals of fire which has a most painful flame."

"Many waters cannot quench love," flashed out Theke, turning to the king. "Neither can floods drown its fire."

Solomon kept nodding. I saw a certain excitement rising in his eyes. He waved his hand graciously.

"Take her," he commanded Jeroboam. "On condition that you never reenter the gates of Jerusalem. Take her, man!"

"Make haste, my beloved," cried Theke exultantly. "Come swiftly! Let us flee like a roe or a young hart on the mountain!"

Literally, she dragged Jeroboam from the royal presence. Jeroboam himself seemed paralyzed by his astonishment at Solomon's mercy. He permitted his unrelaxed body to be hauled backward out of Solomon's sight, his eyes wide, his face fixed at this untoward decision. No sooner had they vanished from the harem than I advanced to Solomon's side.

"What have you done, O king!" I cried, over the surprised murmurs of the women. "You have allowed the prize of your harem to escape! You have set free an enemy! He shall yet bring you sorrow and wretchedness!"

"Let them go."

"I shall send the guard after them!"

"Let them go!" Solomon repeated. "I lose a bride that never loved me, that I never loved. I keep her dowry. Besides, this romantic young girl will soon tire of sleeping in the byres and byways. She will return to her father in Egypt. There she may explain herself and her actions to the pharaoh. Shishak cannot hold me responsible in any way."

"But Jeroboam?"

"Poor idiot! He is worst of all. Can you imagine a woman like that with you night and day? Who only spouts the most romantic kind of language, with never a bit of common sense?"

"But—but—" I stammered.

He laid a kindly hand upon my arm. "Let them go, Nathan," he said for the third time. "I have something better, something they left behind."

"Something better?" I repeated stupidly, misunderstanding.

"The whole is a great poem!" Solomon exclaimed. "A love poem of pure gold, of passion and beauty! It is worth ten of the girl and Jeroboam, too, villain though he is for taking her!"

"Yes, king and lord," I managed to murmur.

Solomon thrust me toward the door. "Go, Nathan," he urged.

"To bring them back to punishment?"

"No, no! Send me your scribe, Elihaph! That he may set down the sayings of their love and mine which are flaming in my head! I shall call it—I shall call it the Song of Solomon!"

"Which is to say," I said over my shoulder, like any good courtier, "the Song of All Songs."

CHAPTER TWELVE

The Wisdom of Solomon

In all human affairs, I suppose—but especially in the business of kings, since the tree sways most at the very top—there is a peculiar gap between seeing and doing. The wisest of men may peer so far into the future. He may anticipate what is coming. But circumstances and the shackles of his own inability to act often render this knowledge useless. What makes the difference is the goad of Yahweh driving us to our destiny.

It was so with Solomon. The years that had fled past his youth like dead leaves in a gale now commenced to slow their pace to match his glory. His reputation spread over the world, as glittering as the oil of the soothsayer upon the bowl of water. His defeat of the forces of Shishak, the most powerful monarch of the nations, his marriage to Theke and his disdainful divorce of her to Jeroboam made him famous beyond measure. His prediction that the pair of lovers would take refuge in Egypt came true. So, too, did his prophecy that he would hold the city of Gezer. But the interchange of couriers between that country and the land of the Hebrews ceased. A sullen, menacing silence took the place of the former cordiality.

I remonstrated with the king about this state of things. "Shishak meditates revenge," I told Solomon. "You have insulted him doubly. You have delivered over to him your most dangerous enemy, who can raise a following in Israel at any time."

"Do you mean that the pharaoh will vent his displeasure on his son-in-law?" asked Solomon mockingly.

"Yes."

"You yourself, Nathan, pointed out that Shishak sent his lovely Theke here only to conquer by marriage."

"That is so," I conceded, "still, the manner in which you sent her away—that was the dangerous act."

Solomon shook his head. "You are wrong," he said flatly. "I was merciful and magnanimous. It is this which embarrasses Shishak. Under our laws and theirs, I might have put them to death. Instead, I set them free." He laughed. "Shishak may be a mighty man of arms but he is also stupid."

"It was the manner of it," I objected.

Solomon waved his graceful, gold-ringed hand. "You are right," he said. "Style is everything. But you and I have always disagreed about style, Nathan."

"Shishak may invade suddenly."

"No. He is very cautious. He respects the skill of Benaiah. He is, I imagine, in considerable puzzlement about myself—all because I did not do what he would have done. Besides, there is the prophecy of his own scryer—that my kingdom shall last out my life."

"Surely you do not believe this?" I cried.

Solomon frowned at me. "Surely you do not disbelieve it," he said.

I realized my error. I said hastily: "Your kingdom will last forever, O lord and king! I merely wish to point out that—"

"What?" Solomon broke in.

"That I was wrong," I said.

Solomon eyed me. "Has Yahweh appeared to you? Have you heard His voice?" he inquired.

"No," I said.

"Nor has He come to me," Solomon replied thoughtfully.

"You no longer go to Gibeon to seek solitude," I said.

"No," Solomon answered. "I do not wish to leave the palace."

His reluctance to quit that enchanted edifice was altogether understandable. It was like a city within a city—like another world in which one could not cease marveling, no matter how long one stayed within its walls. Though the temple had been finished eleven years after Solomon assumed the throne, the completion of the palace had come in the twenty-fourth year of his reign, thirty-eighth of his life.

As specified by Solomon and designed and built by Hiram-abi of Phoenicia, it was an extraordinary building. It must be admitted that to worldly eyes it was superior to the temple in everything but holiness. It took nearly twice as long to build. It was more magnificent, more expansive, higher and larger, and more to be wondered at. The only concession Solomon made to the house of Yahweh was to place his palace at a spot to the left of the temple and a little lower down, thus indicating his respect for the Lord.

Here I must say that I never approved of the palace of Solomon. The temple had been built and decorated for the glory of the living Yahweh—but the palace, richer and more ornate, had been built for the glory of Solomon. It was a compound, centered around the great hall called the House of the Forest of Lebanon, so named because it was upheld by as many squared and gilt pillars of cedar as a forest—sixty of them. Upon these were laid great beams of cedar, carved and brightly colored, mostly in Solomon's favorite hues of purple and red. All about it were three banks of windows. They filled the hall, it seemed, with triple buttresses of sunlight at all times of the day. The walls were covered with carved cedar panels. The floors were laid in polished cut stone with zigzags of black and white.

Herein Solomon set his famous throne, fashioned by Hiram-abi. It was carved from ivory and overlaid with pure gold plates. It stood upon a dais raised six steps above the floor, with a gold footstool, a rounded seat. Six images of lions upon each side symbolized the twelve tribes. Along the walls were hung the no less famous shields of Solomon—five hundred of them, beaten out of gold and engraved with heroic figures. Two hundred shields took six hundred shekels of gold apiece to make; the rest were half as large. All the drinking cups and the platters were made of gold—for in those days Solomon accounted anything less—even of silver—as an insult to his majesty. "I shall make silver of less account than the stones in the streets of Jerusalem," he told me scornfully, "the cedars of Lebanon as common as the sycamores in our valleys."

Hiram of Tyre himself contributed a special feature to the palace. His sailors had discovered a unique forest of large sandalwood trees—usually such growths are small and slender—in the far south. They had cut them down and conveyed them back to Tyre. The king of the phoenicians forwarded the logs to Solomon who had a "Porch of Wisdom" with seven huge pillars of inimitable fragrance erected outside his judgment hall. Musical instruments, such as harps and psalteries, were wrought out of the rest of this rare timber.

The other main buildings were two: Solomon's private dwelling and the house for his wives. The latter was designed much after the fashion of David's palace, rooms branching off a central court. It was luxuriously furnished. A fountain worked by slaves ornamented a central pool. As for Solomon's own retreat, it was lavishly decorated with gold and hung with purple, linens brought from Egypt, paneled with cedar throughout—it being his favorite wood with its rich brown color and crisp scent.

About these buildings—which included a small guardhouse and some guesthouses for the visits of any of the two hundred and fifty officials whom Solomon had appointed to act for him in various parts of his kingdom—Hiram-abi built a paved court of great sawed stone. He enclosed it with three tiers of hewed rock and a cedar palisade.

It was Hiram-abi's idea to add a touch which made the palace unique in the world. That craftsman secretly imported a set of clear glass blocks—then more costly than pure gold—from the Canaanite workers of Tyre and Sidon. These he set carefully, joint to joint, just before the great ivory-and-gold throne. It appeared that Solomon sat over a pool of shimmering water. "Now you can make the boast of my own master," Hiram-abi told Solomon, "that you are a god and sit in the seat of a god, among the waters. Except, of course, that you are more magical than he—since you can cause men to walk upon the waters." For this Solomon offered to reward Hiram-abi with whatever he wanted in all the kingdom of the Hebrews—but it was not until later that the skilled Phoenician architect availed himself of the king's promise.

The installation of the glass flooring was the last addition to the palace. It was done at night by chosen workmen, sworn to secrecy. In the feasting that followed, I noted, Solomon had the area carefully guarded from any visitor. It was a clever device that Hiram-abi had given the king. Solomon had the good wit to use it on at least two occasions thereafter which I shall relate.

Almost the first ceremony of importance after the week-long feasting and ceremonies that dedicated Solomon's palace was the memorable duel of wisdom. The reputation of the king for apt and witty judgments had spread over the earth. But, as is usual in such cases, there was no lack of earthy peasant visitors and scholars from other lands to test out this still-young paragon of knowledge. I trembled for fear of Solomon's being trapped by some of the cunning queries posed to him. I need not have been afraid; never did I see him embarrassed. He invariably answered in such a bland and charming way—no matter who the petitioner might be—that he sent even the most skeptical away satisfied.

His first genuine ordeal came with the arrival of Ethan the Ezrahite. Ethan was a bent, gnarled old man with sunken cheeks and a long tawny-stained beard. He spent his days meditating on the hills, living on gifts of food from shepherds and travelers. He was reputed to be very holy. He rarely traveled as far as Jerusalem—since he refused to ride an ass and insisted on walking, supported by his staff which, legend declared, was one of the offshoots from the miraculous flowering of Aaron's rod in Egypt.

He arrived unexpectedly in the city one afternoon, followed by a silent and admiring crowd. He spent the night on the temple porch and the next day demanded an audience of Solomon. It was readily granted him. As may be supposed, at the given hour the House of the Forest was crammed with a rapt mass of sweating eager listeners of every sort. Solomon waved the old man forward. Ethan, with an abrupt bow of his head, hobbled before him. He halted in sudden dismay at the edge of the glass pool.

"Pardon, great king," he mumbled, "I shall sink."

"It is not deep, O Ethan," replied Solomon.

Ethan still hesitated, like a cat afraid of getting wet. Solomon glanced briefly aside at the grinning Hiram-abi. He affably waved his hand. "If you will not wade, he said casually, "I shall use my arts to make the water solid." He lifted his arms in hieratic gestures. "Now, advance," Solomon said imperiously.

Timorously, lifting his garments like a skeptic, Ethan obeyed. A gasp went up from those packed in behind him as he found his weight supported on the surface. The coolness of the glass disconcerted him; skidding, he almost fell, even with his staff. But he regained his balance in time.

"Solomon's magic will win him a mighty reputation," whispered Hiram-abi to me. "This one will hardly be able to think of a proper question."

In that, he was wrong. Ethan set himself in the position of a man about to wrestle and said: "O king, I have heard of your wisdom. I desire to hear it from your own lips. Am I permitted to ask questions of your majesty?"

"Ask what you will," Solomon assured him, "and it shall be answered."

"Tell me then," said Ethan in his thin piping tones, "why is the acacia tree sacred to our people?"

"Because it partakes of the nature of Yahweh, blessed be He," Solomon replied promptly. "Like Him, it is unapproachable because of its thorns; it lives and flourishes without water or soil; and yet it flowers with blossoms of mercy and beauty. Too, its roots reach out and destroy all that is near it—and has not Yahweh told Moses, His servant, that He is a jealous god?"

Ethan's thin jaw dropped. I could see he had not expected such a complete answer. He nodded slowly in agreement. He regained control of himself and asked him his second question: "Three creatures are sealed to serve the needs of royalty: one is faithful, one is speedy, one is of the air. What are they and what are their duties?"

Solomon blinked, then gave a measured answer: "The first is the dog, who guards the secrets of the throne; the second is the deer, who carries and hides the secrets; the third is the plover, whose duty it is to deceive and lure away those who would seek out our secrets and is therefore deemed unclean."

Ethan seemed bewildered and, for a moment, as if he had another answer in mind. Then he nodded. The close-knit crowd behind him sighed in ecstasy at witnessing this contest of wits between the old man and his young enthroned opponent.

"What three things feed forever on man and are yet unsatisfied?" he croaked at last.

Solomon did not hesitate. "The horseleech that sucks our blood," he said, "and the woman that sucks away our youth, and the grave that swallows our life."

Ethan gazed up at the king for a breathless moment. Then, as the audience began to shuffle and murmur in applause, he slowly slid down his staff. The aged man had fainted. He died two days later—of what cause except his own years we could not determine. Solomon commanded that he be buried honorably within the walls of the city.

All the hubbub and gossip caused by this preliminary skirmish had scarcely died away in the marketplaces—sometimes grossly distorted but always repeated with relish, as if every Hebrew took personal pride in the wisdom of his king—when the most important clash of the sort came to pass. A messenger arrived from Shishak—the first in years. He asked if the wisest men in the Egyptian kingdom might test the wisdom of Solomon that was so highly touted. Shishak declared he would send the three mighty sons of the deceased sage Mahol—by name, Heman, Chalcol, and Darda.

"I suspect this mission," I said nervously to Solomon when he required my counsel. "Shishak is not your friend. Perhaps they are spies."

"We shall have them well watched," Solomon said.

"I have heard that the pharaoh believes you have cast a

spell upon him. Possibly he wishes these sages to defeat you upon your throne and thus break the charm."

Solomon laughed contemptuously. "He cannot be such a fool as to believe it," he said. "I shall receive them. Do you send a messenger to Shishak!"

Two months and a week later, the three Egyptians—from the land that had taken nine parts of wisdom and given the rest of the world one—arrived in Jerusalem. They were no starved ascetics or flagellated, shaven-headed priests. These were tall, barrel-chested men who exuded confidence.

Their lean hairless faces, squared off under their wigs of dark red wool, seemed disdainful of every sight their large dark eyes lighted upon. They wore plain but rich clothing. Each had seven servants behind, to bear them, to carry their writing materials and papyrus rolls. I was disturbed beyond measure when Solomon again decided to admit the rabble to witness the exchange of wisdom. "If you fail—" I breathed. "But I shall not fail," Solomon assured me, "and my people shall see the discomfiture of the wisest of the Egyptians."

They brought the usual gifts and made the customary compliments. Solomon received them genially. As a mark of favor, he had three gilded chairs set out for their use.

"You realize," he said, his words ringing out over the heads of the impassive visitors and through the packed hall, "that on such an occasion as this, I may ask three questions of each of you as well. But I waive that right. I shall be content to stake whatever wisdom Yahweh has given me upon my answers to you."

I bit my lip. I could see faint indications of surprise in the Egyptians' faces. I felt dismay within myself. This was surrendering an advantage that might prove to be critical—and a king could not take back his word. But I could not protest. The first of the foreign seers arose. He was the shortest—burly and uncompromising—Heman, a bull of a man.

"If it please the king," he said shortly, "I shall speak first." I did not need to translate his remarks for he spoke in fairly good Hebrew.

"It pleases the king," Solomon said tranquilly. He did not display the slightest concern. He sat back in his glittering throne as if he expected to be entertained.

"What is the name of the true god?" asked Herman. I felt some relief. It was not an unexpected query to us Hebrews. All gods had secret names which it was death for anyone but the high priests to know and utter. Ours was the object of special jealousy, so well was the mystery kept. They might have guessed that only Zadok, the high priest, knew but they had no way of proving it.

"When Yahweh judges he is named Elohim," Solomon said promptly. "When He wages war against the wicked, He is called Zebaoth. When He is merciful toward man, He is denominated El Shaddai. And when He has mercy—as He has now upon you for such an impious request—He is indeed named Tetragrammaton."

Heman flushed. He bowed low in acquiescence. If he had not been wholly answered, he had been defeated by guile. He lifted his head once more. "Tell me, O Solomon, great king," he asked softly, "what are the three great sins?"

"The sins brought by the evil with seven names," responded Solomon, "are charity, humility, and mercy."

Heman's head jerked stiffly upright in surprise. I confess that even I was taken aback. Solomon went on smoothly: "Charity is evil when the *yezer* persuades one to give to his family rather than a stranger. Humility is evil when the *yezer* persuades one that he is so unimportant as not to pay a visit of sympathy. Mercy is evil when the *yezer* tells one to do as he pleases, trusting to the ultimate forgiveness of Yahweh. These are the most subtle, the most enticing of all sins."

Slowly Heman knelt and brought his head down. He knocked it solemnly twice on the glass floor. He lifted his face for the final question.

"How can one know the true god?" he whispered.

I shifted my feet under my robe. Such a question was too easy; even I might have answered it.

"Each may know as he who plucks and tastes the fruit of a tree," Solomon replied. "If the savor of the deeds of Yahweh are as love, fear, and strength, those that enjoy His favor know him indeed." He made a slight gesture. "As Moses, blessed be he, has said, Yahweh is known by His works. This is the only contact, the only love, the only meaning we can return to Him."

Heman seemed to grow even smaller. He bowed for a long instant, then slowly retreated backward. It was the tall Chalcol who rose and advanced next, his long, sour visage solemn as a monument. He made a respectful obeisance, then folded his arms and stared hard at Solomon.

"You are wise in truth, O great King Solomon," he rumbled. "Your answers to Heman are altogether sound. We in Egypt have heard aright from afar. Our journey here is worth the pain and time of travel. But my questions are quite different from those of my brother Heman, I presume to say."

"Speak," Solomon advised him shortly.

Chalcol licked his lips. His face showed the raw sunburned flesh of a farmer, one who spent much time in the open. "This one is a riddler," said a small voice beside me. "He will not puzzle the king. But beware of Darda, the last one."

I looked down. As I might have guessed, it was the deformed scribe, my erstwhile spy, Elihaph. "Be silent," I said, putting my hand inconspicuously over his mouth. Chalcol had already launched upon his first question, a lengthy affair.

"What is the creature from before the Flood," he demanded in stentorian tones, "without flesh or bone, head or feet, vein or blood, that yet exists forever in field and forest and over the sea, as wide as the world and as narrow as a woman's cheek, not born but often dying, not seen but often felt?"

Solomon smiled for the first time since the duel began. He leaned back into the gold embrace of his throne. "You will have to provide better questions, Chalcol the Wise," he said. "This is too much like the questions that Hiram, the king of Tyre, and I have been used to exchange."

"I have not heard the answer, O king," Chalcol responded stiffly.

"The answer, of course, is the wind."

Chalcol swallowed hard. His big Adam's apple ran up and down his throat like a mouse on a red column. He nodded, indicating that Solomon was right and thrust his other foot forward.

"O Solomon," he boomed, "what writes upon the sky and what writes upon the earth?"

"That is better, much better," Solomon nodded. "But it is still not wisdom. The wings of the cranes and herons form letters as they fly in the sky; on earth, the twigs of the trees form letters as they grow. All speak in a language of their own, from the birds on high to the cedar on Lebanon that gossips to the hyssop which springs out of the wall."

Chalcol gulped again. This time his face had grown pale. His nod of admission seemed almost ungracious. He did not relish being defeated before an audience that radiated confidence and pride in their own king, silently cheering him on as they might have applauded the head-on meeting of two rams in the meadow.

"The third question," Chalcol said, more subdued than

before, "is this: Every man longs for a child but there is that which is more to be desired than a child. O king, what is it?"

Solomon hesitated, his chin upon his fist, gazing at the indomitable face of the Egyptian seer. "Children are much to be desired," he said at last. His eye had wandered into the crowd about the throne, settling on the small sturdy form of the six-year-old Rehoboam with his nurse.

"Is that your answer, O mighty Solomon?" demanded Chalcol, a note of triumph in his voice. Solomon looked at him disdainfully.

"No," he said. "Lovely and desirable as are the children of the body, there is a child of the spirit more desirable. Its name is Virtue. It is to be cherished above all else because it is immortal and known both to men and Yahweh. When it is present, men follow it; when it is absent, men desire it. It wears a crown of its own fashioning and triumphs forever as it gains the victory."

Slowly, like a tree felled, Chalcol shuddered down to his knees. He prostrated himself before Solomon. He remained there a long moment, then moved backward to join his comrades.

The crowd sighed windily. It hiccuped and coughed with enjoyment behind the motionless three. I felt the lips of Elihaph writhing under my hand. He pushed my palm away and whispered excitedly: "Next is the mightiest of all! It is Darda. He is chief of all the mysteries of his land, the writer of charms and spells and incantations! Solomon, as wise as he is, will find Darda a worthy champion!"

"I trust in Yahweh," I said.

"Better to trust in the wits of the king," said Elihaph slyly. He sprang backward, as I snatched at his impudent face, and wriggled out of sight in the crowd.

Chalcol had resumed his seat. Darda stood up smoothly. He deserved attention. He was as graceful in his movements as a serpent. He made only the slightest motions with his hands, gliding rather than walking to give obeisance to Solomon. Yet his face, I thought, contained a supernal calmness, his eyes a depth of knowledge that radiated confidence as the sun did warmth. My belly hardened under my sash. I felt for the first time uncertain about Solomon's ability to meet the wisdom of this man.

"I shall ask three questions that if correctly answered will shake the earth, O wise Solomon," said Darda in a voice like the hollow note of a drum.

"Ask them, O Darda."

Darda made a swift sign with his fingers. "Do you recognize the sign, O king?" he asked.

Solomon lifted his left hand. He turned it so that his huge signet ring glinted in the sunlight. "I know it and this is the answer," he replied.

On his knees, Darda advanced and studied the ring. I could see his face pale, his eyes widen. He bowed and retreated, head low. He remained silent for a moment but, when he lifted his gaze, he had regained his confidence. Yet ever and again his eyes roved to the mysterious symbols that glittered on Solomon's finger.

"My first question," said Darda, "concerns the nature of the gods. You say that your Yahweh is both perfect and one. What can this mean since all things are separate and different?"

Solomon thought, resting his chin on his hand. He seemed to be in a world by himself. He roused and spoke directly to Darda in a low, rapid voice.

"Yahweh is perfect in Himself and is only separated within Himself by Himself. He is throughout the most perfect," he said, "but He is also superperfect as befits His eminence over all. By Him infinity is both limited and surpassed. By none is He contained or comprehended. But He is felt by each one of us since He extends to us His unfailing graciousness and endless energy. He is called perfect, both without increase and undiminished, holding all things in Himself, overflowing and inexhaustible, the same superfull abundance in accordance with which He cherishes all perfect things and fills them with His own perfection. Yahweh is celebrated as the Ancient of Days, but He is before days, before age, and before time; He is also time and has appointed age in a sense befitting His omnipotence. He never grows old but He advances through all things from beginning to the end."

Darda stood like a statue, his face graven stone. Solomon observed him closely. "Are you satisfied?" he asked.

Darda drew a deep breath. "I am," he acknowledged. "You have opened many doors to my soul, my lord."

"What is your second question?"

"You say your Yahweh is omnipotent. Is there anything He is not able to do?"

"Yes. The Almighty Lord is not able to deny Himself."

Darda bent down. His forehead touched the crystal floor. When he raised himself up once more, his face was filled with wonder. "This is indeed wisdom," he said, "which surpasses understanding."

"Is this all you wish to know?" inquired Solomon with a tinge of condescension in his voice.

Darda shook his head. "No, great king," he said. "I wish to ask the ultimate question."

"What is that?"

"What is your Yahweh?" asked Darda steadily, with deliberate emphasis.

Again Solomon plunged into thought, but after a few moments of breathless waiting by myself and the court, his face lighted up. He sat erect. "It is not possible," he said, "to say what Yahweh is but it is possible to describe Him by saying what He is not."

Darda appeared bewildered at the answer. "Will the mighty King Solomon deign to explain?" he asked.

Solomon took a deep breath. "Yahweh is the cause of all, above all, but is without being, without life, without reason, without mind, without body. He has neither shape nor form nor quality nor quantity. Nor is He in a place nor is He seen nor has He contact with the senses nor has He disorder or confusion nor is He driven by passion. He is in need of nothing. Neither has He any change or decay, division or deprivation."

Solomon paused as if collecting himself before going on with his tremendous declamation that shook me to the soul.

"Yahweh is neither soul nor mind nor has imagination nor opinion nor reason nor conception. He is neither expressed nor conceived, is not numbered nor ordered nor has greatness or littleness. He is not equality nor inequality, not similarity nor dissimilarity. He neither stands nor moves nor is at rest. Neither has power nor is power; neither lives nor is life, neither passes through events nor eternity nor time. He has no kingdom, no wisdom, neither one nor oneness. He is not goodness nor spirit nor any of those things known to us nor to any existing being. There is no expression of Him nor name nor knowledge. He is not darkness nor light, neither error nor truth, nor is there any telling at all of what He truly is.

"What we know is that He is both above and beyond every definition, absolutely free from all and beyond the whole that we know, above every word that the tongue can utter or mind can conceive, now and forever."

As Solomon spoke, first hesitating, then increasingly strong as his thought developed and filled his breast, Darda had undergone a transformation. His face, which had been so doubting and skeptical, filled with light. His expression beamed. He stood with his head thrown back, as if receiving the rays of the midday sun. He seemed almost like a brown gleaming blossom of flesh, expanding under the light and warmth of what Solomon said. As the king ended his burst of speech, Darda swung his arms wide. He brought his palms together in a loud clap, swinging them apart again in a gesture that was at once homage and benediction and gratitude.

"Mighty king of the Hebrews," he said in a voice suffused with emotion, "you have spoken from the treasury of the ages! What you have said is from soul to soul, not mind to mind; it can only be understood with the heart. That is true wisdom, indeed! We acknowledge ourselves vanquished. We beg only to retire to our own land to consider and discuss what you have given us, the priceless gifts for which we can make no fitting return."

He waited. I watched Solomon with alarm. He, who had appeared so full of vigor and life while responding to Darda, almost incandescent with the light of inspiration, now appeared crumpled and lifeless. Some vital force had gone out of him with his answer. It had left him weak, somehow smaller and shaken, as if he had poured out his blood itself. Solomon made a weak motion of dismissal with his hands. The three Egyptian wise men bowed in unison. They stepped backward, salaaming profoundly, toward the other end of the vast room. The crowd opened like the Red Sea for their passage; panic seemed to take the auditors. There were no plaudits, no cries of approval. Suddenly fear was in the room. Those who had heard Solomon stampeded like crazed goats to get out of sight and hearing, jostling, shoving, heads over shoulders, a flood of men divided by the golden pillars of the room.

I approached the throne as the others dispersed. I felt more than a quiver of veneration for such a display of power as I had just witnessed. Solomon glanced up at me, his eyes blank as a man rousing from a dream.

"Why do they go?" he said in a muffled, uneven voice. "What have I said?"

I bowed deeply. "You have defeated the wisest men in the world," I said. "They go in disorder because they are in fear of your powers."

"My powers?" Solomon said vacantly. "Have I spoken?"

He shook his head from side to side, a man trying to collect his thoughts. "What have I said?" he asked again brokenly.

I realized that Yahweh had in truth used the king as His spokesman. Solomon had no consciousness of what he had told Darda, though he recalled very well all he had said to Heman and Chalcol. If it had not been for the busy pen of Elihaph, his words would have been lost to the world afterward. As it was, I have often pored over them since to suck out their meaning—and with me, eager to learn as I, has been Solomon.

Yet it was not only by divine inspiration that Solomon had spoken, as I discovered. What he had said to Darda could have been no other than from Yahweh but he had been both cunning and resourceful with the others. Half a month after the three visitors from the south had been dismissed with gifts, loaded with treasure, to return and report to Shishak (a report that would further fill him with doubt and dismay), I went to the king to tax him indirectly in wonder and obedience on this score—only fools will question kings directly on such matters. I was relieved to observe that Solomon was not offended.

"Come with me, O Nathan," he said. He had quite recovered from his ordeal. His old spirit of raillery and cynicism was upon him. "I shall show you something of which you have never dreamed."

Together we passed into the old palace of David, through its corridors, and into the room where I had once persuaded the king to institute a school of scribes. To my amazement, it had been more than thrice enlarged. Its arrangement had been vastly altered. Here were still the teachers and their pupils, fearful of the rod, chanting their lessons, correcting their tablets and papyri—but on every wall there were shelves of wood, crammed with scrolls and tablets of every description. With bewilderment, I passed down the shelves, handling their contents. I saw collections of Assyrian, Canaanite, Phoenician, Hittite, Babylonian, and Egyptian writings. I handled some of the curious Cretan tablets and some in the easy running script of the sea peoples—and there were many in unknown inscriptions.

"What is all this?" I asked of the king, turning with a tablet of chiseled script in my hand.

"Good Nathan," Solomon said tolerantly, "wisdom begins at home, if it has the proper foundation. These are the writings of all the wise men that I have been able to gather together. I have not spent the substance of my kingdom wholly for walls of stone or chariots and horses. What you see represents much gold, even jewels. There are a few other collections such as this—chiefly in Egypt and Babylon—but none as complete."

"You—do you read these languages, O king?"

"Many of them," responded Solomon. "It is pleasant to study here an hour or two a day. Those I do not understand I order to be read to me by slaves who comprehend—and I remember. Has not your spy Elihaph told you of this?"

"But there is much in here that must be alien to the decrees of Yahweh," I said, my brow darkening, disregarding what Solomon hinted.

"Perhaps."

"All wisdom is His. What does not have His voice is either useless or pernicious and should be destroyed in either case."

"Yahweh has given us wisdom, that is true," the king said. "But not all wisdom."

"He will depart from us if we seek to explore past His will," I said fiercely.

"The true god will never be with us," Solomon said.

"What blasphemy is this?" I whispered.

"Neither with us nor with any nation," Solomon repeated. "He will be always beyond us, beckoning us. We shall never in this life arrive in His kingdom. He is He-Who-Is-To-Come—not He-Who-Was or He-Who-Is."

"He has said, 'I am what I am'!"

Solomon sighed. "What our fathers heard Him say now has another accent for our ears," he said. "We cannot live in the past glories of David or even in the present peace of Solomon—we must live in the future of our people. Yahweh does not fulfill our destiny; He fulfills Himself through us. We were not chosen as His people for selfish reasons; we were chosen, as Noah says, as Moses affirmed, to be His messengers for all to Himself."

I could not answer. My mind felt stifled. Solomon looked at my expression with interest; a slow smile dawned upon his lips. "Is it so hard for a prophet to understand me as a prophet?" he asked. "You hail me as wise. Yet when I say that which is truly wise—not the solution of a riddle with Hiram of Tyre or the resolving of a silly dispute between harlots or a contest with alien slippery-tongues—you are amazed."

"But Yahweh has always said that He would be with us," I muttered.

Solomon made a gesture of impatience. "Of course," he agreed. "But in so doing, He has put Himself into time. If He is with us today, He will not be with us tomorrow, He will be in the past. But if He remains in the future, as I foresee, He will always be the head of the Hebrews."

"It is very hard to understand," I said slowly. "Even if it comes from your own lips, O great Solomon, I cannot believe it."

"You mean," Solomon said with a flicker of his peculiar humor, "if I were not king, I should be stoned in the streets?"

Again I was silent, almost in acquiescence to his statement. Solomon shook his head. "It is hard for you, Nathan, to understand that our faith is not altogether our religion," he said. "What we do, what we accomplish, that creates what we believe every day. It dies before our eyes when we sacrifice on our altars. We must go out every day to battle to re-create it, to win it back into our souls. Religion is what we think we are at rest; faith is what we are when we do that which we believe to be right. Perhaps too much religion kills faith—I do not know."

He looked about the busy room of scribes. "Our nation is eternal only because Yahweh is eternal," he said quietly. "When we cease to exist in His eye, in His heart, when we no longer caress Him by the beard and kiss Him on the lips—but merely adore Him, worship Him, sacrifice to Him—then we shall disappear like morning mist upon the sea. Our way can never be back to our father's. Nor can we remain where we are. We must march forward, die advancing; and our children must advance over our bodies."

"This is wisdom?" I asked hoarsely. I felt the first signs of inspiration from the Lord coming over me, tingling of the flesh, haze over my sight. My tongue was dry but my forehead started with sweat. I knew it must come to the moment when I should be forced to speak, even as Solomon had done, with the tongues of Yahweh.

"Let us return to your palace," I muttered thickly, "I beg you, O great Solomon. I have that to ask you which must be inquired of you alone."

Without a word, Solomon turned, sedately leading the way, pacing before me toward his own chambers. Not until we were within his elegantly appointed chambers, the door closed, did he face me. "What is it, Nathan?" he asked coldly.

I bowed and bowed again, trying to control my unruly tongue, that serpent in my mouth which might betray me. Still there was no surcease. I was forced to speak.

"O gracious king," I managed to say, "when Darda began to speak on that memorable day now past, he made a signal to you. In return, you showed him your ring. It seemed to satisfy him; he was able to proceed. What is this ring?"

"I have devised a ring, O Nathan, carved with sly devices. A ring of charm, of magic, engraved with mystic symbols."

"I hear but I cannot believe," I said.

"See this," Solomon said. He extended his left hand to me. On it was a ring of gold and jewels, a six-sided star, set with four jewels. "This is the ring," Solomon added, "with the gems representing the angels of the winds, the birds, earth and sea, and spirits. Read what is engraved upon them."

My skin crawled as I bent over his hand. I could read the characters clearly graven on each jewel. The first said: *To the Lord belongs majesty and might;* the second: *All created things praise Yahweh;* the third: *Heaven and earth are slave to the Lord's will;* and the fourth: *There is no god but Yahweh and Solomon is His person on earth.*

"I have dominion over all mankind," Solomon said with dignity. "Not only of men and their doings but also over birds and beasts, over wind and weather and the demons under the earth and the angels above. All this has Yahweh given me in return for my faithful worship of Him. When He speaks in the thunder, it is to me; when His glance shines in the lightning, He looks upon me and my works and He finds them good."

"O king!" I implored.

Spittle began to gather at the corners of Solomon's mouth. He gesticulated unsteadily, the muscles of his face contracting and relaxing in a manner incredible to see. His words rolled on, unhurried and paced in sonority: "I know the speech of birds and can tell the meaning of the serpent's hiss. I know the language of every living thing, yes, of trees and stones and of the sea that hides the hulk of Leviathan. I call all creatures to the worship of Yahweh and tell them how to serve Him."

I drew back. I knew what I must say. "O king," my lips uttered almost without my will, "Yahweh bids me tell you that you commit a great sin to use His name in magic, inventing ways of putting yourself about His footstool."

Solomon stared at me, his eyes piercing. "Do you dare to tell me this, prophet?"

"I dare because the truth in me must come out."

"What else does your foolishness bid you say?"

I took a deep breath and pronounced the fatal words:

"You shall not suffer a wizard to live." They were the words uttered so long ago by Moses against such an abomination.

Solomon screamed in a high-pitched voice, tilting back his head like a dog. It was so unexpected that I, who had been prepared for nothing like this, fell back a step in horror.

"Benaiah! Benaiah!" Solomon shouted. He had long ago assumed the fancy of carrying a curved cane, carved and inlaid with gold and gems, in imitation of that of the kings of Assyria. His own bore the head of the lion of Judah—the tribe that always upheld his edicts most faithfully—wrought in gold with turquoise eyes. He beat this slender emblem of his royalty furiously upon the walls, dinting the cedar. It flew into flinders. "Benaiah!"

His commander must have been waiting just outside the door. He bustled in and stopped short, seeing the purpled face of Solomon, his starting eyes and working mouth. "Yes, my lord king?" he responded.

Solomon pointed a shaking finger at me. "Take this pretended prophet, this man of foulness!" he cried. "Fling him into the caves beneath the tower Meah! Guard him and bind him so that he cannot escape!"

Benaiah touched my arm. I needed no further signal. Without a word, for the first time in my life, I turned around, showing my back to the king, and marched out. I heard Benaiah gasp as he bowed and backed out as was customary. He hurried to keep up with me outside.

"Are you mad, Nathan?" he whispered in my ear.

"No," I said wretchedly, my bones softening with grief, "but know this, Benaiah, Solomon himself is mad."

CHAPTER THIRTEEN

The Wooing of Tamar

"You were right. The king is not himself," Benaiah said thoughtfully. "If he were not ill with so much thinking, he would never have told me to imprison you. These tests of the mind with strangers are foolishness."

"You would not understand wisdom, being a military man," I said.

Benaiah grinned. "As a military man, I was bound to obey, to bring you here," he said. "I hope you understand that."

"I have been a denizen of worse quarters than the caves of Meah," I said. "Once I meditated in the cliffs of Adullam."

"Where David hid? I have been there many times, routing out robbers and desperate men. The spot controls the Valley of Elah. There is good food, good water to be had in the countryside. Here there is nothing except what I choose to give you."

I closed my lips upon my retort. It was worse than useless to bandy words with a bandy-legs, if I may use some humor.

I had been in my cave-prison below Meah for two days. My guards were of the palace, amiable, even a little awed at keeping one of my prominence in duress. The food, despite Benaiah's polite threat, had been excellent—and long ago I had got used to hard sleeping. In fact, it was nearly a relief to be out of the cursed round of duties heaped upon my shoulders at the palace. The only drawback was that Benaiah himself visited me every morning to offer his commiserations. I shuddered in the cool shadow, drawing my heavy cloak closely around me.

"You agree that Solomon must have been ill to command me to do such a thing as this," Benaiah began again. I was silent.

"Do you think he will recover?" he asked.

"I am sure of it," I said.

"Enough to remain on his throne?"

"There is nothing in a momentary fit of temper that disqualifies a man from ruling," I said. I had begun to distrust this quizzing soldier more than ever. "I shall be out of confinement in a few days," I said.

My prediction proved true, even sooner than I supposed. On the very next day, Solomon summoned me to be brought to his side. It was Benaiah himself who did the honors and, when we arrived, he was dismissed (to my secret pleasure) without ceremony. Solomon turned to me. He embraced me with his old, irresistible affability.

"I understand that in the fever of my brain," he said, "I ordered you to be imprisoned."

"Yes, O king."

"I am quite well now. Do you remember the reasons I had you flung into the caves?"

"No, O king."

"Good. No more do I remember the reasons. Let it rest there. All shall be satisfied."

I bowed deeply and prostrated myself. Solomon personally raised me up. "Frankly," he said, "the affairs of government have been in chaos, since you left so suddenly. I had not realized how much you mean to the state. You are indispensable, Nathan. You shall be rewarded."

His praise puffed me up, I admit. But I was wary enough of the whims of kings to agree, to do what I thought would serve his purposes rather than demand justice for myself. It was best to forget what had passed between us lest the mention of it inflame his passions again. There would be other, more propitious times. Solomon was aloof and regal, more than ever the oil-anointed holy king of the Hebrews.

"Your generosity overwhelms me, O great Solomon," I said. The king nodded. Whether or not he ever recalled the incident, it was never spoken of again.

Nevertheless, as I picked up the threads of my authority and disentangled them from the hands of those who had dared to assume my duties during my absence, I wondered about the end of Solomon's studies in the mysteries. I had always accused him—in my heart and sometimes openly—of neglecting the proper worship of Yahweh. But at least, before the sons of Mahol, there had been nothing else, no yearning after the forbidden. Now, it seemed to me, Solomon had plunged into the dark labyrinths of the most esoteric kind. He wrestled no longer with the problems of the state and people. Instead, he turned them over to my judgment. He became engaged in studying the most complex and difficult problems of the occult. I saw him gradually turn in this many-pathed direction—despite all my efforts—instead of following the plain straight road that led to the foot of the throne of the Lord.

My own feeling grew to be that his encounter with the three wise men out of Egypt had, to a degree, really though temporarily addled his brain. He spent more and more time in his palace and its grounds, entertaining visitors of the lowest caste, deliberately avoiding those who came on important errands of state. He entertained himself with jugglers and vulgar strollers, minstrels and magicians: soon the court of Solomon became famous in the surrounding nations as a place where the most arrant charlatan might find food and lodging, even applause, from a monarch.

Again and again I expostulated with Solomon over this

kind of a life. "It takes away from your dignity in the eyes of the world," I told him.

"You have often told me that dignity is in the heart," Solomon replied. "Do you ask me now to put on a mask, as if for a revel, for the world to see?"

I held my tongue. It was always possible for him to silence me in those days. His wit and thought were so quick that it sometimes took hours of study for me to find the appropriate quotation from the scriptures wherewith to contradict him.

"Do you know this trick?" Solomon said. He poured water into a curiously shaped jug that had cabalistic figures dug into the clay.

"What trick?"

For answer, Solomon poured out the water. He held the jug upside down so that not a drop remained. "Is it empty?" he inquired.

"Completely," I assured him.

Solomon turned the jug upright, then again upside down. Again a fresh stream of water gushed out. I started back. "Now is it empty?" asked Solomon, thumping the bottom.

"It was empty before," I said.

"You see you were wrong. But now?"

"Now, certainly!"

For the third time Solomon set the jug upright and upended it—and a third time the stream of water spurted out! I sprang to my feet. "Magic!" I shouted.

"Nonsense," Solomon said. He induced me to look inside the jug. I found two reversed sleeves of hardened clay inside that had held back much of the original water. I looked reproachfully at my king. "You have deceived me," I said.

"I told you it was a trick," Solomon said. "A special jug from Sidon."

"It is not worthy of you."

"See this," Solomon said casually. He plucked up from beside him a pair of scarves, red and yellow, knotted together at one end. He began to draw them through his lightly closed fist, left to right. I watched closely as the first scarf, that of red, passed through his fingers. But as the second came through, I sank to my knees.

"Sorcery!" I shouted. Before my very eyes, as the cloth passed through Solomon's fist, the color of the second scarf had changed from yellow to blue!

"The work of the Adversary!" I shouted.

"Hush, hush!" Solomon said quickly, throwing down the scarves. "This is merely play, juggling. See, the second scarf is, in fact, a yellow bag with a blue lining. I merely turned it inside out as I passed it through my hand. It is a juggler's deceiving, it has nothing to do with magic."

But I was not assured. He guided my own reluctant fingers and they discovered that what the king said was true. A dull resentment began to burn in my bosom. I did not relish being taken in by such child's play. "I cannot condone such—such foolishness," I said.

"Folly it is and it fooled you, Nathan, did it not?"

"There is nothing good in this."

"On the contrary, there is," Solomon replied tranquilly. "These itinerant tricksters have taught me much besides their tricks. I have learned about human nature from them."

"How?"

"The trick of ruling is the same as that of hand-juggling. To make the people look otherwhere than where you are truly performing. It is quite easy."

"I do not understand, O king," I said bluntly.

"In such things, they will only understand what you want them to understand," Solomon said. "Notice that where I look, you will look; where I point—" and he showed me how true it was "—you will look. You will turn to anything that moves, to a flash of light, a loud noise. A pretended stumble or fall, an accident—anything like this, even as it affects apes, will affect men."

"Just as you deceived me when you ordered me confined to Meah," I said. "I thought you were angry."

Solomon glanced at me briefly, red sparks deep in his eyes. "Perhaps that was a louder noise than I intended," he said. "But you must learn that your king is no wizard, Nathan, that he abhors enchantment and necromancy."

I accepted what he said as both an apology and the truth but I must admit that often afterward I had cause to wonder. Solomon spent many nights alone with jars and saucers full of strange substances that smelled vilely and burned with weird exhalations. He ordered odd-colored materials from about the Dead Sea and mixed them with still others imported from far countries. He made varicolored lights in the saucer-oil of the lamps, blue, green, red, by adding powders. He often consulted with Hiram-abi in conferences from which every other person—including myself—was banned. Midnight became his favorite hour. He set aside a special chamber for his trials with the elements. He filled huge copper cucurbits with carefully distilled messes and sealed them with wax stoppers stamped with his own seal ring, the device I shuddered to see when I looked at it.

Once he opened such a one on the rooftop of the palace in my presence. Out of it flew a stinking, thick-black cloud that rose straight upward. Then it passed off to the east, forming wings and a dreadful vaporous body as it went. But Solomon appeared pleased, not frightened, as if he controlled the demon. "It will be useful as a signal in our villages if attacked," he said obscurely.

More than this, he commenced to catalogue and put into written recipes and formulae all that he had done. He compiled parables and stories that were brought to him by travelers, being especially interested in tales that concerned trees and beasts and birds, reptiles and fish. "The world that surrounds us must be known," he said to me, "if we are to know ourselves."

"We are likely to know too much," I replied gloomily. But whatever my forebodings—which at last proved triumphant—the experiments of Solomon went on. His scribes were kept busy under the tireless direction of Elihaph, writing what he told them, and what was dictated to them by the strangers he rewarded with gold according to the excellence of their stories. Day by day the *onomastica* of the palace grew longer and longer.

Even as this happened, so the rumors and tales outside the palace mutiplied and grew enormously. They hovered darkly about the simplest acts of Solomon, as though he were a god himself. It was whispered that the trees walked out to meet him, that the stones rose up in salutation and flung themselves under his feet; that the cucurbits held demons and forces of nature; that water gushed from his fingertips and, a moment later, flames of fire. He was credited with being able to move mountains, to walk upon water (as I have written), and to transport himself in moments from one end of the world to the other on the gilded wings of the temple cherubim.

Travelers from half a dozen countries spread tales about our king. They asserted with the barefacedness of all liars that he ruled by virtue of a magic ring—the same one about which I had warned Solomon. It was claimed that at one time a demon had stolen it, while he was bathing. He ruled the Hebrews evilly for a year and a day, they said, while Solomon was a beggar. Others said it was an angel who assumed the similitude of our king and ruled divinely. I have no doubt that these foolish rumors came about because of Solomon's fits of temper. They annoyed me hugely.

"Sacrilege!" I said indignantly. "These idle tales of the people should be stopped in their mouths!"

"How do you know they are wrong?" asked Solomon idly. I gaped at him. We were in the newest of his chambers, one designed for private audiences, fitted out with a smaller throne of ivory and gold after the one in the great hall. A magnificent present from Hiram of Tyre—a rug woven in the similitude of an orchard and garden with gold and silver threads, surrounded by emerald borders of shrubs—covered the whole of the cypress flooring. "What do you say?" I asked, not believing my ears.

Solomon shrugged. "It may or may not be true," he said, "and no man can tell, except myself. It does no harm for them to believe whatever they want. It increases my influence."

"Such things should be attributed only to Yahweh!"

"He will not begrudge me the shadow of His power."

I shook my head unhappily. Solomon leaned upon his fist as he meditated on the throne that stood on its little dais before the heavy purple curtains that surrounded the whole chamber.

"Did I choose," Solomon said musingly, "I might make thought expressed in will to be the supreme power in the world. Thought does not die with the thinker; will remains stamped on the succession of lives which come after its execution. Every deed, however small, has echoes in the ear of Yahweh."

"Amen!" I said fervently. "It is not for us to question the future, however. It is for us to do the best we may with the life that is given us, to live for the glory of Yahweh."

"Not for our own?" queried Solomon.

"Never."

"You make a king worth very little."

"You must have no will for glory that is not the will of the Lord."

"Yet," Solomon said, "I have read that in the old days when demons were summoned they sometimes destroyed him who summoned—or were destroyed by the behest of another more powerful. What is this power of evil that Yahweh permits?"

"The Adversary struggles mightily," I said. "He places his wickedness in the most hidden places, in the most innocent of minds. You, O king, who have wrestled with this one in secret—do not yield but pray to Yahweh to be delivered!"

"I pray but Yahweh does not come to me."

"Pray again! And yet again!"

"The Lord holds Himself aloof from Solomon; therefore Solomon will hold himself aloof from the Lord."

The king rose and strode out of the chamber. I stood where I was, looking after him, intimidated by his more-than-mortal pride and overweening assurance.

One distraction remained to Solomon. He neglected his favorite sports in the field, but his love for chariot racing continued. It gave his high-strung temperament release in frenzied competition (his courtier competitors always allowed him to win but usually by the narrowest of margins) until that day he intiated his young son Rehoboam into the art of driving.

The child was barely eight years old at the time but robust and well formed, stubborn and courageous to the point of being foolhardy. His proud father determined he should go with him in the royal chariot. He wanted him to experience the thrills of such a ride (something that even I had never permitted myself to experience).

I remember the incident well. It was early in the morning in the first days of Abib, the first month of the year. Long lines of Hebrew villagers, dressed in their holiday clothes, toiled up the slopes toward the temple, bearing their offerings of green ears of barley to Zadok as the firstfruits. Passover would soon be here, I realized. I had left the palace for a stroll in the city—one of the most enjoyable and useful of my hobbies. I had determined that, by evening, I would stand on my rooftop to be one of the first of the trusted observers to see the rising of the moon crescent. "For He appointed the moon for seasons," I began to quote devoutly. I heard a tumult behind me. I stopped to draw aside in the narrow way. Solomon was out for his morning ride—since we had completed the business of state—and his runners came down before him.

I should say at this point that Solomon's favorite chariots had changed from the original light, wickered things of Canaan with their four-spoked wooden wheels. He had taken lessons from the Egyptians and added armor to the body. Thus it was heavier, easier to drive at top speed, the wheels strengthened with six spokes and a copper rim. Each chariot had a team of swift sleek white animals to draw it. Each had a quiver of arrows and a pair of bow cases attached for the use of the driver and the archer.

Such a chariot—enameled purple, the ever-royal color—was that which Solomon drove as fast as his picked men could run ahead. I should add that the axle was to the rear and that the shaft ran from the floor of the vehicle between the horses. Most important of all, a strong taut cord of twisted hide ran from the chariot front over the backs of the horses. It served to ensure that the horses would be retained, even if the shaft broke; it also served to keep loose reins from being entangled. This day it served a third purpose, that of Yahweh's mercy.

Solomon had set Rehoboam upon his shoulders, twining his chubby legs about his neck. The child sat there erect and excited, shrilling encouragement and beating his kingly father on the head. The people hailed the youngster as much as the monarch as they passed in a swirl of dust. But at the end of the street, the runners fell aside. Solomon whipped up his team, passing between the retainers at full speed. As he did—according to his habit—he bent low, hunching over to balance himself. But this upset the equilibrium of the child Rehoboam.

With a wild scream, clutching at his father's locks—failing to hold them because of their oiliness—the boy tumbled forward. He landed struggling, directly across the leather thong between the horses. Exactly as does an arrow shaft when dropped on the tight bowstring, the body of Rehoboam bounced upward and to the right. It flew into the air like a stone from a sling.

All this happened too quickly for anyone to act. It must have seemed to most, as it did to me, a blur of action, a cry, and the child slung into the air, about to have his brains dashed out on the cobbles. Yet there was one—no more than a girl at the tail of one group—who dashed forward. She flung back her mantle. She held out her arms. She caught the tumbling, screaming Rehoboam expertly. His weight drove her to her knees. She dropped him. He landed on his feet, poised, amazed at his deliverance. He took a tentative involuntary step. Then he turned and sprang again into the bruised arms of the still-kneeling girl. She burst into tears.

Farther down the steep street, Solomon hauled his quivering team back on their haunches. Flinging the reins to a servant, he leaped from the chariot. He raced back to where Rehoboam had fallen—only to find the young prince folded in the embrace of an unknown young woman who was weeping copiously. Even the bystanders wiped their eyes.

"What happened?" Solomon demanded, almost in tears himself at his relief. To me, hastening toward them through the surging crowd, the thing that happened next was the most surprising of all. The woman, instead of remaining on her knees before the king, stood up. She smiled unabashed at Solomon, brushing aside her tears.

"I have caught the young prince," she announced. "I shall not let him go."

Young Rehoboam held to her hand with both his fists. "She caught me," he echoed, "and I won't let her go."

Solomon drew a deep breath to calm himself. "What is your name?" he asked her unsteadily.

"Tamar," she said. "Tamar, daughter of Tamar."

Of course it was the daughter of Tamar, fruit of the rape of her mother by Amnon, the oldest son of David. It had happened twenty-eight years before. That was her age. She and her mother had lived retired since David's death outside the walls of Jerusalem.

This accident to Rehoboam had happened like the providence of Yahweh. Or had it happened by the providence of women? I had no idea but I am congenitally inclined, when in doubt on such matters, to attribute the happening to the connivings of the female. They plan and scheme and execute their plots in the most subtle ways. Still, it was difficult to see just how Tamar had been on such a spot at such a time—and now it makes little difference, as long as it happened as it did.

Tamar was not a beautiful woman. Her frank tanned countenance could not compare with the lovelier occupants that already held positions of honor in the harem of Solomon. Her form was robust and buxom rather than languorous. She had no pale lilies in her complexion but the ruddiness of bursting life. Her hair was always a tousled mass of darkness. Her eyes, far from being as enticing as poetic pools, were sparkling as the stream of Kidron itself. She cared little about dress: she had been too long a country girl. She had imitated the boys in their games and her nature was rough and boisterous. Her wit was crude. Yet her mind was cleared of foolishness and her insight into the nature of Solomon was to be little less than marvelous.

Solomon commanded her to live with him as one of his wives. She accepted. But I verily believe that had she not loved the king for himself—at the first touch of his hand when he took her personally up into his chariot—that she would have refused and suffered death. As it was, she became almost instantly queen of the seraglio simply because she was so different. Abishag, turned old and insanely jealous of each new arrival, attempted to put Tamar in her place. She not only failed to win the battle of wits (as a giggling lady of the court informed me later), she tried to attack Tamar with hair-pulling and nail-gouging. At this, naturally, she was completely overwhelmed by the younger woman. Tamar simply put her down and held her until her futile struggles and screams were exhausted. Then she turned Abishag over and spanked her before all the other women.

It was a crushing humiliation. Solomon heard of it. He laughed and had Abishag instantly isolated before her intrigues could poison the newcomer. He thoroughly approved of the downfall of Abishag. Possibly his own infatuation with Tamar came about as a result of this encounter in the harem.

I was at his side when he interviewed Tamar upon the occasion of her victory. He ordered the girl to be brought before him out of curiosity. She appeared, demurely enough, in a rich mantle from Shinar over her plain dress of blue Egyptian linen. The cloak was of wool, draped with many rams' tails, each dyed a different color. Tamar's hair was drawn back into a simple knot on her neck; her hands lay clasped meekly before her. Only her eyes, raised mischievously, and her slight smile betrayed the hoyden.

Solomon surveyed her for a long moment. His first words betrayed an unusual depth of feeling for his newest female acquisition. "Does she not appear as the rainbow does in the dawn after a night of rain?" he asked me.

"She is, ah, very acceptable," I said diplomatically.

"Does not the holy Nathan like me?" Tamar asked deceitfully. "But then he is old and you are young, great king."

Though it was true that I was ten years the elder, I hardly considered myself old. Her remark jarred me. The girl had a gift of ruffling or soothing men, just as she pleased.

"Well said, my dear, well said," Solomon chuckled.

"I was asked for an opinion, not a flattering lie," I said.

"Whatever it was," Solomon replied, "I think you are beautiful, Tamar. Which is all that is necessary."

"Then why have you brought me here?" she demanded.

Solomon glanced at me, disconcerted. "Why, to admire you," he said uncertainly.

"Not because you love me?"

"I love each of my wives," Solomon said expansively. Even I, so much less wise than my king, could have warned him against a remark like that. I can only think he was caught momentarily off guard. As it was, Tamar's face grew dark. It was a flush he imputed to modesty but that I guessed correctly to be anger.

"How is it possible to love so many women?" she asked.

To my stupefaction, Solomon kept right on blundering into the traps of words she laid for him. "Quite easy, my dear," he said amiably. "A man is a complex creature. He needs many different women to satisfy his longings."

"Do not women need the same?"

Solomon caught himself at last. "What are you speaking of?" he said with asperity. "You cannot be suggesting that women should have many husbands?"

"I do not say for myself," Tamar told him, "because I am satisfied with one. With you."

I looked up at the gaily gilded and decorated ceiling. Tiny beads of sweat formed on my forehead. I knew that the discussion was bound to come to my judgment. Already I realized what my answer must be. I dreaded the fatal moment.

"Unhappily for you," Solomon said in a kindly fashion to Tamar, "I am the king. You do not understand these things."

"Men and women are unequal in many things. That is good. But they should be equal and faithful in love. If the man may have many women, why not the women many men?"

"I have explained that to you," Solomon said. "Men are not made the same as women."

"I know. Blessed be Yahweh for that!"

"That is not what I mean!" Solomon cried in exasperation. "I mean our needs in love are different!"

"How, O my lord and king? Deign to explain to your female servant." Tamar sank gracefully to her haunches on the floor.

Solomon drew a deep breath. He turned to me. "Tell her, Nathan," he said abruptly, "and explain that what I say is true."

"I cannot," I said painfully.

"What!" exclaimed Solomon. "Speak to her! I command it!"

"All the prophets have spoken otherwise," I said, bowing deeply. "We have always held that one man must have only one wife."

Solomon's fingers commenced to intertwine. I recognized the signs of a coming fit of rage. "It has always been so," I said hastily. "I say nothing new. It is clear in the words of the holy books."

I braced myself against the storm of his wrath but there was an interruption. It came from Tamar squatting before the throne.

"You hear, O king," she said gravely, "what the man who hears the voice of Yahweh says. You do not love me. I am no more than the gold or the jewels that you bring here to count over. I am the possession of your pride. Not of your heart."

Solomon scowled. He leaned toward her, secure between the glittering arms of his throne. "What you say has brought death to others," he told her coldly. "Much less has brought whippings to many more."

"You will never dare whip me," Tamar said intrepidly.

"Will I not? Did I not execute your uncle Adonijah for nothing more when I was only a youth?"

"He was Adonijah, I am Tamar," she said. "You will never touch me!"

"Whore! Daughter of a whore!" Solomon shouted passionately.

"My king!" I implored him. I was too late.

Before either of us could move, Tamar acted. She sprang up from her haunches, lithe and graceful as a wild cat, upon the dais. Solomon rocked back upon his throne too late: she flung back her hand in a lightning gesture. She swung it hard upon his cheek. The slap echoed in the room, the sound magnified a hundred times.

My gasp died away into a sigh. Tamar, impetuous and unruly, had committed the final sin. She had struck the living embodiment of Yahweh, the anointed of the Hebrews, lord upon earth and ruler on the right hand in heaven, the appointed and chosen after David. She must die as soon as possible. Her impious deed must not be avenged upon the people by Yahweh.

She stood panting and furious before Solomon. Her flushed face was bright, even beautiful. Her hair lay tangled about her head like a net. The king recovered from his momentary stun as I withdrew my jewel-hafted knife silently from my girdle. Tamar's back was toward me. I advanced two steps. I chose my spot. I lifted my dagger high.

From his throne, Solomon gave a hoot of warning. He cried out in anger himself. Without warning, he flung his gold scepter. It whirled through the air in a brilliant arc, even as I hesitated and blinked. The king's aim was true. The handle of the wand of office struck me a numbing blow on the wrist. My knife clattered to the floor.

Tamar wheeled. She saw me stoop for it, rubbing my wrist. Involuntarily, she drew back in fear. As she did, Solomon leaped down from his throne. His brocaded arms went around her waist. His golden slippers kicked her feet out from under her.

He held her before him, writhing, scratching, biting. He disregarded her struggles. He actually smiled. "Do you know, you vixen of the woods," he demanded loudly, "that you have struck a god? Do you know that I am the representative of Yahweh? The anointed? You have committed sacrilege! Nathan knows it. You must be stabbed to death!" He threw back his head and, amazingly, began to laugh.

Tamar broke from his clasp, landing lightly on her feet. She whirled, the hundred tails of her cloak swirling about her. Her face lost its hostility. Her husky laughter joined that of the king. She pointed. "And you, Solomon," she managed to say, "carry the hidden weapon under your robes!"

Solomon looked down at his thighs. Suddenly the expression of his face changed, from amusement to the placid and predatory. "You are right, Tamar, beloved," he said softly. He lunged at her. This time she did not try to escape. As I turned to flee the royal presence, I could not help seeing that Tamar clasped him as tightly and eagerly as she had rejected him a moment before. The king crushed her down backward to the steps of the dais atop the forgotten scepter. As I rushed out of the room, her skirts were already up to her waist, above her naked brown legs.

A prophet's lot is not always a happy one. He is assured of rewards in heaven from Yahweh. He has the satisfaction of doing the will of the Lord while on earth. But his path is often filled with rocks and thorns. I discovered that, soft and delightful as they are, nothing in the world that Yahweh made can be more flinty and obdurate, more prickly and piercing than a gang of women determined to obtain power for themselves. Men are only a mask for their ambitions; children are only pawns.

In her day, Bathsheba had ruled the king's women with an iron hand. After her, Abishag had assumed the role by default. But as she grew older, she singled out favorites—and her very sex became in doubt. When Solomon removed her from power, because of her dispute with Tamar, it was generally believed that the newcomer who had taken the king's fancy would rule the harem. It was not so. There was another, Naamah, the gentle Ammonite mother of Solomon's firstborn, Rehoboam, who rose to become equal to Tamar in authority. It split the seraglio into two continually quarreling factions.

Never a whisper of this came to the royal ears. It was I they came to with their tears and reproaches. I, Nathan the prophet, forced against my will to act as an overseer of females!

Yet it was a fascinating situation, for all its intolerable aspects. I cannot relate how many times I was offered the fairest bodies in the kingdom merely to decide such things as who should be served first or who should receive a disputed jeweled girdle. Occasionally I was forced to squeeze shut my eyes, to push away the nude lasciviousness of those who were simply bored with their confined life. Now that I am old I may relate such things with propriety, without naming even the names of those of Solomon's wives who have long since perished. But I must also confess I was greatly tempted once or twice, perhaps more often.

I may affirm, however, that I never once indulged the passions of the flesh. A kiss or two, possibly, a pat here and there, a caress bestowed upon the deserving—this is as far as I wanted or dared to go. It is true the terror of discovery worked as efficaciously upon me as my own conscience. But the result was the same.

What brought the disputes in the house of women to an intolerable pitch as far as I was concerned came about on a complaint from Naamah. Ordinarily this sedate, retiring woman with the seductive brown eyes was silent, reserved. She rarely criticized anyone. Nor did she engage in the usual spats with the other women. But it was she who came to me one morning about Rehoboam.

"My son is no longer my son," she said.

"He grows up," I told her. "One must not expect a child to be always a child."

"I do not mean that," she replied with dignity. "I am happier than anyone that he is coming into manhood. What I mean is that I am no longer honored as his mother."

"You must be mistaken!"

"On the contrary, he has made it plain that he obeys and honors only Tamar, the newest wife of the king."

I sat silent. I could see there might be more than a little

truth in what she said. The child knew that his life—in all probability—had been saved by Tamar. He had inherited a strong sense of gratitude, not the least of Solomon's virtues. No doubt he exercised it toward Tamar. "Let it be known," I said to Naamah. "I will have audience today with Rehoboam and Tamar and yourself here in my dwelling at the hour after noon."

At the appointed time, they appeared. They ranged themselves before me: Naamah, silent and reserved, Tamar, smiling and confident, Rehoboam, defiant and watchful. I considered them. I hoped in my heart that I was calm and unprejudiced in my speech.

"Rehoboam," I said with deference, "prince of the Hebrews, it is said by Moses, blessed be his memory, that he who honors his father and his mother shall have long life in this our land."

"I honor my father," Rehoboam said curtly. A shadow of pain crossed Naamah's face.

"And your mother?"

Rehoboam looked down at his painted sandals. He did not answer. It was Tamar who spoke.

"Who is a child's mother—she who gives him life from her womb or she who saves his life?"

"Whatever is done for a child is a gift to Yahweh," I responded. "Who knows which He considers best?"

"Then the judgment on earth is that of the child."

"Never shall it be," I said with energy. "Tender years may not sit in the seat against the sages. But you, Tamar, have been the bed-companion of the king these two years—yet you are not with child. Does this mean that Solomon does not love you?"

Before my thrust, the eyes of Tamar fell. "I have not given him a child," she confessed in a low tone. "Perhaps it is the will of the Lord that I should be as barren as Sarah was to Abraham."

"Even were you as fruitful as an olive tree in season," I said sternly, "the word of Yahweh is clear. Even if the king hates Naamah—which has not been proved—and loves you—which has not been proved—the word is clear." I quoted sonorously: " 'If a man have two wives, one beloved and another hated, and if the firstborn son shall be hers that was hated, even the king may not make the son of the beloved firstborn before the other. He must acknowledge the son of the hated for the firstborn; he is the beginning of his strength and the right of the firstborn is his.' "

To my bafflement, it was Naamah who burst out weeping. "Solomon loves me!" she cried. "It is this witch that has enchanted him and seduced my son!"

"I said nothing of that," I protested, appalled. I saw that what I said—while overruling Tamar's pretensions—had offended Naamah. I had done no good for anyone. Rehoboam's mother rushed from my chambers still in tears.

"You cannot prevent what will come to pass," Tamar said quietly. Rehoboam went to her. Her arm encircled his waist. They left together. I remained to contemplate forlornly that I had given judgment to Naamah and she had cast it away. Tamar had taken it up to her own advantage. I shook my head. How strong, I thought, the vital blood of David still coursed in the veins even of his female descendants!

It was only a few weeks afterward when Naamah again sought me out. She had lost weight. Her face was less serene and beautiful; there were dark pockets under her eyes. "Tamar has brought into the harem another child with the permission of the king," she said.

"There is nothing wrong in this," I told her. "We should have pity upon her since she is childless."

"But this child," Naamah said quietly, "is a girl. Her name is Maachah. She is beautiful. Rehoboam, with the encouragement of Tamar, plays with her constantly."

"Well?" I demanded.

"Maachah is the granddaughter of Absalom."

I felt confused. "Why do you complain?"

"Tamar intends they should marry."

I flung out my arms, thrusting this new problem away from me. "Do not come to me, Naamah," I said. "This is not for me to pass upon, nor you, nor Tamar, nor even the great Solomon. It will be judged by Yahweh Himself in due time."

Naamah fixed her enormous-eyed gaze upon me. "The mother of that girl worships idols, not Yahweh," she said. "So does Tamar."

"Gossip, gossip!" I cried. "At any rate, I am unable to do anything about this now. Tomorrow I am to leave Jerusalem. I go to the country to visit and judge the people."

"You will do nothing?"

"Nothing!"

"Then I must look for help elsewhere." With that Naamah left me. I stared after her, wondering what she meant. I was not to know her true intentions until months later.

CHAPTER FOURTEEN

The Chastening of Zadok

My excuse—for it was no more than that—for escaping the nagging of Solomon's harem, fleeing from the questions which hung about me like dogs clinging to my skirts, was invented on the spur of the moment. What I had told Naamah was true. But my yearly tour of the provinces of the Hebrews was not due for a fortnight or more.

Nonetheless, I was committed by my words to her. I made preparations for Elihaph to assume my duties (warning Solomon to pay more attention than usual to the affairs of his kingdom, while begging his permission to depart) and went my way.

Judging was a special, almost religious, rite. Ruling and passing upon disputes were much the same function. The king himself could issue a judgment only after the decisions of a circuit judge like myself had been made. It was my task, assigned by Solomon after Samuel's absolute sway, to ameliorate the lot of the people under his rule, more by mercy than by strict justice.

In this I departed from the tradition of Samuel, greatest of all prophets. But I went to his old dwelling place of Ramah to begin my trip, a journey which took me to Bethel, Gilgal, and Mizpah, all holy cities. For my soul's recruitment, I visited Hebron, Shechem, and Gibeon. The old pool of Gibeon was still in use—a vast cool hole in the ground, thirty-six feet across and as many deep, with forty-two stone-carved steps that led down into its depths. The taste of its waters was sweet and always palatable—and the world was shut out. Shechem with its mighty grove of oaks, revered since the time of the Patriarchs, was the only other spot that could be compared to Gibeon's quiet pool or Hebron's peaceful orchards. In the latter a man rested and refreshed his spirit, seeing only shepherds or farmers, reposing in the shade of the breeze-laden groves, sipping wine, tasting the loaf fresh from the oven.

I rejoiced to find everywhere that the Hebrews worked,

every man to his task, with diligence and skill. The shield-maker stretched his leather and molded it on blocks; the chariot wheelwright carved his spokes; the bowyer wrought his quivers and checked the straightness of his shafts; the women gathered flowers, squeezing their juices into oil to let them steep for perfume attar.

On the borders of the Negeb Desert, I joined the joyful occasion of the sheep-shearing festival where the wool flew in white shreds with the wind like manna blown in from the sands. The shepherds brought their animals to the edges of the desert, to the river, and washed their fleece to cleanse it of dust. They hobbled the sheep, then threw them on their sides on the rocky ground despite their bulging eyes and bleating struggles. They upended them between their legs as they squatted and commenced to shear off the thick overcoat of wool. After the last sheep had been sheared, there was a great festival and I was glad to share in it.

In other places I watched our surly slaves, those whom we had captured in war or gained by treaty. Among these were the Canaanites, Hittites, Hivites, Perizzites, Girgashites, Ammonites, Amorites, and Jebusites. All went wearily—bearded and dusty in their loincloths and rough sandals, a few with shaven crowns, one or two with pigtails, the others with filthy hair that covered one or two precious copper earrings or amulets. Hewers of wood and drawers of water were they: the lowest forms of labor were good enough for them.

On my travels I heard incredible stories about Zadok and his minions back in Jerusalem. Like the bold priests of ancient Shiloh, he was not satisfied any longer with the peace-offering of the breast and right thigh. He demanded much more from those who came to sacrifice. Even as much as would stick to a long-tined fork, taking it even before the fat was burned to Yahweh. He also took to himself the fine-meal offerings and the drink offerings of wine. Nor was this all. I began to hear disturbing and recurring country gossip to the effect that Solomon was building shrines to foreign gods in various high places about Jerusalem. This more than scandalized the faithful. It was, of course, direct disobedience to the words of the Lord given to Moses.

I felt deeply disturbed as I turned back to our capital city. Solomon, I knew, had already violated one of the warnings of Yahweh by his many marriages to alien women: "You shall not go in to them neither shall they come in to you, for surely they will turn away your heart after their gods." This was no prohibition of having them in his seraglio—merely the forbidding of their use for sexual purposes. But there were, I realized now, not only Egyptian women but those of such alien and lesser tribes as the Moabites, Ammonites, Edomites—even of the Hittites and the Phoenicians. It would have been queer otherwise since Solomon had inherited so much of womankind from his father—but David had never yielded to their enticements on the religious side, even to those of Bathsheba. The rumors kept on, however, that Solomon had built small temples to such gods as Ammon and Milcom, the Ammonite abominations, Baalzebub, Syria's lord of the flies, Chemosh of Moab—to say nothing of allowing the rise of the old worship of the Phoenician god and goddess, Melkarth and Ashtoreth. There were, it was said, secret rites held and incense and actual idol worship. On this score—hoping that Solomon had no part or knowledge—I prayed to Yahweh. To my waiting heart came no response—a circumstance which made me thoughtful.

On my way back to Jerusalem atop my bony-backed onager, strumming his ribs absently with my bare heels, almost imperceptibly my conviction hardened. I possessed a mandate from the Lord in regard to Zadok; for the rest, I would have to bide my time. In this mood I passed through the pleasant city gate of Ephraim—near the house inhabited by Benaiah, since he was designated as governor of the Upper City by Solomon—and went toward the palace.

Back in these familiar precincts, I pondered my course of action, unwilling to be hasty or misguided.

It was a strange situation. In those days power was well balanced within the Hebrew tribes. King, prophet, priest—and over all the might of Yahweh. Zadok was the slave, I the voice, and Solomon the will of the Lord. With whom His commands lay depended upon whom He chose to visit.

In the spiritual realm, I might prophesy, recite, warn, curse, or bless as the Lord ordained. But still I could not enter the most holy place. Zadok could not see the future, or stand at the king's side, nor did he know the past—but he had a band of priests with special privileges while I stood alone. Both of us were within the hand of the king—except as Yahweh spoke to us—but Zadok might be deposed, while none but heaven might take my office from me. Solomon had the power of the army and the state behind him with all his wealth and prestige. I had the ineffable glory of Yahweh, and Zadok his petty politicking.

Yet my position always left me uneasy. It was impossible to tell the moods of the king—and the moods of the Lord were beyond all guess. Zadok I could afford to disregard unless he united himself with the king—and then I was in danger indeed. It was this that fretted me. I had no inspiration; no vision had come to me to tell me the course I must take—except that I had been told by Yahweh to rid the kingdom of Zadok's arrogant prerogatives. How and when it was to be done were not vouchsafed me.

In such a mood I waited for Zadok on the porch of the temple. It was well into the afternoon. The high priest was engaged in the last of his rites. When he emerged and greeted me, I saw a difference in him. During the past few months that I had been gone from the city, something had changed. Or perhaps I saw Zadok with fresh eyes, not staled by habit. He seemed to me, even in his sacred and gorgeous costume, as fat as the hogs we were forbidden to eat, greasy and laothsome. He squinted cheerfully at me as he waddled up, wrapping his hands in his rich sleeves.

"Welcome, Nathan," said he in his wheezing voice. "I have not had the good luck to see you lately."

"I have only just returned from walking the land," I said.

"You have been away?" he said in feigned surprise.

"You see me with the dust of my journey still upon me," I told him.

"Why do you wait?" he demanded. He waved his hand: "Go, cleanse yourself, and make ready. Soon it will be the Sabbath and you will be unable to do so." He pointed at the declining sun.

"The Lord Yahweh has ordered me to speak to you."

Zadok put his head to one side, a capon plump for the plucking. "Did He indeed?" he responded. "What did He say, according to you, Nathan?"

"Do you intimate that I lie?" I demanded hotly.

Zadok raised his hands as if to ward off the words. I could not help noticing their pink tenderness, like that of a child. It enraged me even further, conscious as he had made me of the stain and dirt of travel.

"It is well known Nathan cannot lie," Zadok said placatingly. "Say on, I shall bow my head."

"There is no need for it," I said irritably.

"The good Nathan rarely has a good word for Zadok," the high priest said with smug humility. "I cannot understand why. I have always endeavored to please him—but I accept what is."

It was this quality, I realized, which had been growing in Zadok—this sham, this hypocrisy. Perhaps it had always been latent. Possibly it had been seeded-in on the night David had elevated him above Abiathar. But however it had come, it made me grind my teeth with suppressed dislike.

"You have grown fat, Zadok."

"A little, perhaps."

"Much fatter."

"Perhaps."

"You have been living well."

"As well as one may expect in these starving days."

"Our land has never been more prosperous. And I hear that the same is said of you and your priests."

"Who has said that?"

"Everyone."

"Everyone who has a lying mind. Priests do not prosper except in holiness. The tongue is an evil rudder to steer opinion."

"It is said that the priests of Yahweh enrich themselves, instead of the altar of the Lord."

"We have our lawful perquisites, as well you know, Nathan."

"But no more!"

"What man accuses us? Let me face him."

"I accuse you! The mouth of Yahweh accuses you!"

"I see. I see, Nathan. You wish to make the priesthood a scandal and a disgrace. Very well. Let us take our quarrel before Solomon himself."

"What scheme is this? If what you do is wrong, it must be confessed, penance done and never repeated. There is no need to go to the king."

"But none admits wrongdoing. Is this not a case of the jealousy of a prophet against the estate of the high priest? How are we both to be judged except by the king?"

"And Yahweh."

"And Yahweh, of course. But the king is His agent on earth."

I restrained myself with difficulty. I felt my hands quiver. I reminded myself that I was no longer young, that I needed rest and repose. "There is no need for that, Zadok," I said. "The Lord has appeared to me. He has commanded me to tell you that it shall not happen again—and that you shall seek His forgiveness."

The rosy face of Zadok expressed nothing but surprise and meekness. "How can I confess and do penance for a sin that I have not committed?" he asked. "Surely Yahweh has given you proof?"

"You know best what you have done."

"But I have done nothing—nor have my priests!"

I saw there was no help for it. "Very well," I told him, "let us go before Solomon."

The king welcomed me back with affection. He told me that as usual the royal affairs were muddled—as ever when I was called away from the palace—but also that Elihaph had done his best. As he sat at ease on his famous golden throne in the ceremonial throne room, I could not help but admire the ability of Solomon to pervade his relationships to everyone with the aura of his personality. He was able, like the little lizards flashing in and out of the sun with their changing colors, to be what he wished, almost from moment to moment—a regal unapproachable monarch or the most amiable of human beings. I realized, after my sojourn away from the court, how much of the fate of the Hebrews depended upon this one man. David had built his power on the coalition of the tribes; Solomon had erected his own kingdom solely on the magic of his person.

Smiling, Solomon regarded the solemn jowls of Zadok. "What brings my high priest before the throne?" he inquired.

"We have a dispute, Nathan and I," Zadok said with a heavy sigh that reeked of sham. "We have come to you for its resolving."

"How is this?" Solomon said to me. "Have you visited so many cities in the robes of a judge, yet you cannot decide whatever this argument may be?"

"Its roots lie deep," I said. "They may even underlie the throne itself, O Solomon. Only a king may speak judgment here."

Solomon's face became shadowed. He turned to Zadok. "Do you speak first," he said. Zadok was prompt to reply.

"Your servant Nathan, O king, has accused me of being a thief."

"Is this true?" inquired Solomon of me.

"Not precisely," I said.

"And my helpers are called thieves, also," broke in Zadok.

"What have they done?" asked Solomon, again of me.

"I know of nothing myself. I have heard of them taking an undue proportion of sacrifice—and, it may be, other things."

"What is your proof?" asked Solomon.

"Precisely what I said," interjected Zadok.

"I have been told by scores of people who have seen the priests doing it." I strove to be calm.

"Lies!" cried Zadok. "Lies!"

"Yahweh has instructed me to say there will be no more of it!" I shouted, my patience at an end.

"Where there is no sin, there can be no repentance!" said Zadok. "I have told you that before!"

"Peace," Solomon said quietly. "Peace, both of you."

He considered Zadok. "If they are liars that tell of your thieving at the sacrifices," he said, "count me among them. I have seen you, Zadok. Do you dare say that I lie, high priest?"

Zadok's face changed. It flushed a bright red, then became pale. He prostrated himself. "O great Solomon," came his muffled voice, "it shall be so."

"There shall be no more stealing from the people," Solomon went on in an even tone, "and you shall render up an exact account of all that is in the temple to Nathan. I wish, for your sake, that nothing is missing."

Zadok beat his head against the floor. "Rise," Solomon said. "Go. See my command is obeyed."

Again Zadok prostrated himself. He moved backward to the door, his face stricken. As he vanished, I heard the low mellow sound of the ram's horn—the *shofar*—indicating that the Sabbath had begun.

"It is lucky that your chamber is in the palace precincts," said Solomon as the solemn sound drifted off. "Otherwise you would be as you are, travel-stained and weary, for the whole time. As it is, you will get no food, Nathan."

"I want nothing but sleep," I said.

"There will be little sleep for you this night," Solomon said gravely. "I have disposed of Zadok for your sake but there are other, weightier matters."

I nodded in agreement. "There are indeed, O king," I said.

Solomon regarded me with an indescribable expression. "You are a bold man," he said. "It was you, in your youth, who accused my father David to his face of adultery with my mother Bathsheba, saying 'You are the man.' "

"Age has cooled my forwardness," I said, "but I must still speak what Yahweh bids me speak."

"What are these roots that you say may underlie the throne?"

" 'You shall have no other gods before Me,' " I said.

Solomon's face did not change. "I worship only the Lord," he responded.

"I have never been satisfied with the cherubim in the

temple," I said. "They are not in accord with the words of Yahweh given Moses about graven images."

"You are wrong, Nathan," Solomon said calmly. He quoted the scripture: " 'You shall not make any likeness of anything that is in heaven above or that is in the earth beneath or that is in the water under the earth.' Nor have we done so. Hiram-abi obeyed me when he carved them. When were such things ever seen on earth, in heaven or in the sea?"

His logic was irrefutable. I could not answer. I was forced to change the subject.

"I have heard that even the children in the streets and the miners in the desert use your name as a lure," I said severely.

Solomon appeared interested. "Tell me," he said.

"When the pets of the children do not respond to their call, they make mysterious signs with their tiny fingers and say: 'If you do not come here this very moment, you shall be a rebel to King Solomon and a rebel to King Solomon is a rebel to Yahweh!' "

"And those that work in the desert?" I could see that half-smiling Solomon was fascinated by what I told him. My lips tightened.

"As they walk through the valleys, they repeat in a loud voice what they call a charm: 'Appear, O copper and iron, for it is Solomon the great who calls you to decorate his palace in Jerusalem!' They shout this. Where there is a fall of earth, they dig. I have heard they are quite successful."

Solomon leaned back, a satisfied smile on his face. "I see nothing wrong in these," he told me. "We have tried to establish a united kingdom after the model of my father David. All this is useful, in my name, to bind the kingdom together more closely."

"It would be better to use the name of Yahweh rather than the name of Solomon," I replied. "As your father David has said, the people should cast their troubles on the Lord, not upon the king."

Solomon did not respond. I tried the last arrow in my quiver of complaints. "You say you worship the Lord alone?"

"Yes."

"And your wives?" I said. "Do they worship only Yahweh?"

Solomon was silent. "What have you heard in your travels in the countryside?" he said finally.

I told him of the rumors about his women. Solomon

nodded slightly but did not interrupt my recital. "None of these things," I finished, "could have been done without the royal permission."

"I have permitted it," Solomon said candidly. "I have even commanded Hiram-abi to build the high places they request—just as he built the high place for my mother Bathsheba. Surely you remember her, Nathan?"

His ironic tone was lost on me. "Yes," I said.

"You waste your time on these things," Solomon said more strongly. "These contemptible shrines for the women are not worth your thought for a moment—much less mine. Their gods are toys for them to tease, to implore, to give them release from their female anxieties! They have no meaning beyond that." He leaned toward me. His tone became more intense. "But I have been thinking of Yahweh and what He is, more than ever. This is a true man's task, worthy of his mind, not a feeble woman's conception."

I could no longer restrain my ague. I shook violently as I nodded, helpless. Solomon waited until my fit had passed. He addressed me in a tone which was surprisingly even. What he said now seemed to me at first far removed from what we had talked of before.

"I desired you to stay when I dismissed Zadok," said Solomon, "because he has become my enemy."

My hair prickled at the nape of my neck both in pleasure and in fright. "This is not possible," I enunciated.

"Not yet openly," Solomon said somberly. "But it is coming. I foresee it as truly as I foresee tomorrow. Listen well, Nathan. Do not misunderstand me. I have been thinking long, studying deeply since the three wise men of Egypt confessed defeat."

"You showed them your boundless wisdom," I said.

Solomon made a gesture of contempt. "I thought as a child," he said. "But in reading again what Elihaph wrote of what I said—for I take oath I did not know it—I found hidden truths. Nathan, we think too little of Yahweh. He is much more than the thought of our people can encompass. Much greater, much more holy, vastly more powerful."

"Your wisdom in such matters is well known," I told him.

"If I am wise it is in small matters," Solomon said wearily. "I know enough to tell the priests that Yahweh is god not only to the Hebrews."

"Sacrilege!" I managed to sputter.

"Is it? We are not alone. We worship a god of the week and its planetary powers. A god whose powers are symbolized by the seven branches of our sacred candelabra, by the seven pillars of wisdom. But so did the Canaanites before we entered this Promised Land."

"Mad king!" I cried, not caring what I said.

"Do not the Canaanite tablets tell that 'Today and tomorrow eat and drain drink and do the same until the seventh day'?"

"That is not at all the same as keeping the seventh day holy for Yahweh!"

"Was not our world formed by a Spirit brooding over the waters—exactly like that of the Canaanites? Have we not put down Anatha, their goddess of the sacred willow here at Jerusalem and claimed her powers of rain-bringing for Yahweh? Shall we be honest with each other, Nathan? Have we not borrowed, from the beginning, many things from Babylon, from Egypt, from Phoenicia—even from those we have conquered? True, we have made them our own and conformed them to Yahweh's will. But we should remember their source—and take hope therefrom."

I attempted to speak but only strangling sounds came from my throat. Solomon waited, wryly observing me, his prophet, trying to overcome my fury and terror.

"What you say," I said at last, fighting for composure, "is that the universe is ruled by women rather than men."

"Why, of course," Solomon returned. "Have you not learned that yet? I discovered it at my mother's breast." He smiled slightly. He had taken refuge in satire, I perceived.

"Blasphemy, blasphemy!" I cried, released at last from my fear, overcome by my anger. I bounded to my feet, feeling like a man inspired. "Do you hint that Yahweh is one of these despicable eunuchs who pretend to be women?"

"My good Nathan," Solomon said, "you amaze me. This is an entirely new theory."

"No, no! That is not what I mean!"

"In Egypt we have learned almost all our lessons from their people and priests. Did you know, Nathan, they began the practice of our circumcision?"

"No," I answered sullenly.

"They began long before us to write from right to left."

"I do not believe it."

"For ages before Abraham, the pig was regarded as an unclean animal, so much so that if a man merely touched one he hurried to the nearest river and plunged in, clothes and all."

"No."

"The very tune we sing, that sad one called *linus*, which is sung in so many other lands as well—that comes from Egypt, too. Its origin is lost in antiquity."

"I wonder that you are not king of Egypt rather than king of the Hebrews," I said spitefully.

Undisturbed, Solomon looked at me benignly. "Because I am a Hebrew of Hebrews, born here, living here, to die here," he said. "Because I love the Hebrews. Because they are my people."

My eyes suffused with tears. Solomon saw my state and changed his tone.

"Do not misunderstand me, Nathan," Solomon said. "You may think I have made Yahweh less by talking thus. In reality, I have made Him much more, infinite, all-encompassing. The curtain has been torn for me, I tell you: I have seen something of His true divinity!"

"But what you say I do not understand," I wailed.

"You say He rules the Hebrews; yes, but also the world and all people by the same laws. Others have had their glimpses of His power and compassion. Noah knew this. He told it to our forefathers. Moses made it our commission to spread His word and judgments. We are the instruments of an even mightier destiny than we had guessed, Nathan!"

Overcome at last, I crouched like a beast, then slowly backed out of the throne room without another word. Solomon silently watched me go. As the curtain fell, he sighed. I heard him beat the heel of his staff three times upon a golden gong that dangled beside him. From the smaller door on his right, I knew, came the stocky figure of Benaiah.

"Yes, O king?" I heard him ask.

"Nathan. He seems to be disturbed. See that he does not do harm to himself. He may even go so far as to speak against the king—and this must not be permitted except in the most private way. Do you understand, Benaiah?"

I could envision Benaiah saluting. "To hear is to obey," he said. "I go to do the king's bidding."

"Do you understand my reasons?"

"No, O king," Benaiah said.

"Good," Solomon said. "You may go."

I waited no longer to eavesdrop. I fled. As I ran toward my house my legs gave way under me and my body felt as shuddering-cold as if I had been plunged in water. It was Benaiah's soldiers who found me and carried me into my home to put me down on my pallet. By that time I was burning-hot. Somewhere in my travels I had contracted the deadly fever of the swamps.

How many weeks I tossed in the alternating torments of chill and heat, I had no way of knowing. But I recall lucid moments and a woman changing the linen of my couch from its soaked cloths of fever to warm dry ones to comfort my chill, again and again. I knew there was little to be done about the disease. Those who underwent this ordeal from the Adversary suffered and got well or they died. All that could be done was to offer them liquid when their lips were parched and coverings when they shivered.

But when my eyes opened, I saw who had been near me during the whole time. It was poor Naamah, Solomon's own first wife, wan and haggard from sleeplessness. She greeted my return to consciousness and my beginnings of health with a tiny smile that bordered on the tears of hysteria.

"Naamah," I said weakly, "why are you here?"

"It has been a long time since you fell into the fever."

"Did Solomon order you here?"

"The king has inquired after you every day, O Nathan."

"How is the king?"

"He is well and fortunate." It was the common answer, the first direct reply she had given me. "Zadok forbade him to visit you for fear of contagion."

"Have you been my nurse all these days?"

"Someone had to take care of you."

I raised myself with some difficulty on my elbow, finding out with alarm how thin my flesh had become on my bones. "I cannot bless you, I dare not curse you," I said. "I have heard you were the first to turn to false gods. Is this true?"

Her eyes held mine. "I worship Milcom, the god of my fathers," she said.

"And the others?"

"They followed but I did not lead them—each to their own, to the god of their childhood."

"Why have you done this?" I asked her.

"No one else would help me with Rehoboam against Tamar," said Naamah. "Not even your powerful Yahweh."

"You cannot know that! Have you asked Him?"

She looked me straight in the eye. "I spoke to you and you speak with His voice," she said. "You would not aid me. What could a poor mother do?"

Stricken, I lost my ability to reply. I held my head a

moment in grief then said: "But this outrageous god called Milcom! What induced you to worship him?"

"Hush!" Naamah said fearfully, finger at her lips. "You will be punished! He is our god, the god of the Ammonites. Where else should I go? What else should I do?"

"You might have appealed to Solomon himself."

"He laughed at me."

"Your fears are groundless, Naamah." I strove to comfort her. "All will be well. You have been charitable and compassionate."

She looked at me mournfully—I still recall that look with abasement—and walked away.

She did not return for my convalescence. It was gnarled Elihaph who brought broth and wine—and once or twice, Azariah, my eldest son, who had not spoken to me since his mother's death. They both inquired, with a solicitude I knew that neither felt, after my recovery. I longed to know the news of the court but what they rattled into my ears made no sense. It did not remain in my memory.

In ten days I was able to rise; in two more, I found myself able to walk. Three more found me putting on my robe, preparing to cross the court to pay my duty call to Solomon.

My way to the palace led past the rooms for the women. As I advanced with slow care along the beamed hall, I was amazed to see Benaiah. He had his ear pressed against what I knew to be the chamber entrance of Naamah. Doors had long since replaced curtains in the palace. Evidently the Hebrew commander knew as well as I that voices carried well through the solid wood.

I called out in my rusty voice. Benaiah sprang noiselessly away. He hurried to me, seized me, and brought me back to the door. To my further amazement, he pressed me softly and silently back against the door myself so that I could not help but hear. And, after a moment, I confess with shame, I did not lift my head away. For what came to my ear from inside that room were the voices of Tamar, the king's favorite, and Solomon's son, Rehoboam.

"Listen, my darling, I have made a song to the Lord in praise of you," Tamar said. She crooned barely loud enough for us to hear:

As my soul lives, it praises the Lord.
For I have prayed for a child, a man
To stand before the Lord. He answered.
I dedicate him as a king

Over the Lord's people, therefore.
My children are enlarged by the Lord
Over my enemies; the Lord
Has raised me to the wife of a king.
He has placed in my hands those that hated me.
I have set my own among the princes.
He will sit in the throne of glory.

"Has my father heard it?" asked Rehoboam.

"Solomon is pleased with it," Tamar answered. "Will you go to war with him?"

"What war?" I demanded of Benaiah in a whisper. He shook his head to silence me, pressing me even tighter against the door.

"I do not like wars," Rehoboam said.

"Benaiah has done badly if he has not taught you to relish the blood of your enemies," said Tamar.

"These are the quarrels of my father. Not mine."

"But they shall be yours," Tamar said with sudden intensity. "You shall be king after him."

Rehoboam was silent. Tamar spoke again: "Never have I known why the blood of enemies is as sweet as sugar, sweet as honey from the honeycomb. This I learned from my own mother—who taught me that even women have ways of revenge."

"Do you revenge yourself on someone?"

"No, no, my Rehoboam! I am only talking as a lonely woman to herself. I love only you and my blessed mother, who is dead—so now it is only you!"

"I did not ask to be born the son of a king," Rehoboam said disconsolately.

"Of course not! But now that you are you must bear your high estate fittingly. I shall be by your side."

"I swear to you, I shall never kill a man!"

"Vengeance is the duty of a king. Your enemies must be slain, else there will be no law and order in the land."

"No!"

"It is the will of Yahweh, in heaven as on earth."

"Never!"

"Perhaps it is terrible the first time," Tamar's voice said soothingly, "but after that the rest are all alike."

"I cannot understand," Rehoboam said hoarsely.

"You are still young," Tamar said. "When you are a man, you will understand these things fully."

"Why do you wish to make me a murderer?"

"Do I make a mistake when I call you the son of a king?" demanded Tamar in a rising voice. "What black, foolish language you speak!"

Suddenly I felt Benaiah pull me away from the door. I resisted feebly but he half-carried me along down the corridor. "We have heard enough," he said. "She will persuade the youngster soon enough."

"She spoke of revenge," I said wildly. "What did she mean?"

"Have you not heard?" asked Benaiah. I shook my head. Thereafter he told me, to my utter horror.

Naamah was dead. Never had the words that "all will be well," spoken by a misguided, benighted, short-sighted prophet, been put to shame more swiftly. Three days before, just when I had been able to walk, Naamah had been found by the fountain in the harem. Evidently she had been trying to reach water. She had been poisoned by the same purple-spotted plant which killed our cattle and sheep—which had mysteriously killed Ithream, the son of David, so many years ago.

"Ithream," I muttered to Benaiah. "Tamar's mother, taken by Amnon, his brother, against her will."

"Who knows?" said Benaiah phlegmatically. "But Naamah had the same smell of strange garlic in her mouth, the same swellings."

I rocked myself to and fro in grief for a moment, then stopped and straightened. "She spoke of war, Benaiah," I said.

Benaiah grinned. "The king has asked to see you as soon as you are able. Are you able?"

"Yes," I said.

I managed to totter into the audience room with Benaiah; the king was there and greeted me, coming down from his throne. Seeing my condition, he graciously allowed me a chair. I slumped into it. Solomon's first words took me aback.

"What do you think of Naamah's death?" he demanded.

"I have no thoughts," I mumbled.

"Why should she kill herself?"

"She was a quiet one, too much to herself," Benaiah said smoothly.

"I never should have married her in the first place," Solomon said petulantly.

"Naamah gave you your first son," I said slowly.

Solomon dismissed the subject of Naamah with a peremptory wave. He appeared to have weightier matters on his mind.

"It is opportune that you have arrived," he said somberly. "If you had not come today, I would have sent a courier to take you up from your bed."

"What has happened?" I asked anxiously. I could not imagine an emergency so dire that such a summons would be needed.

"This talk of a woman's death is very well in its place," Solomon replied, "but it is useless prattle after all. While we split these hairs of doubt, other events, important events come to pass that must be dealt with in their place—which is to say, first of all."

"King and lord, what do you mean?"

"I mean that the Hebrews may no longer have their women—or a city or a temple—or even a king."

The weakness which I had noted in myself when I talked to Benaiah again asserted itself in my scanty flesh. I strove to keep myself calm but I found that no words were possible with which to reply.

"Benaiah tells me what his spies in Egypt tell him," Solomon said. "I have interviewed some of his men myself. They say, with one voice, that Shishak is about to put us to the test again with his army. Not alone this time but in joint action with the Philistine army from Ashkelon and Rezon of Syria."

He paused and shook his head. "Shishak is always hungry for conquest," he said, "and apparently he thinks little of the reports of my wisdom. The swords of the Philistines have always been hungry for the blood of the Hebrews."

CHAPTER FIFTEEN

The Invasion of Shishak

"It is the fault of Hadad, the Edomite," said Benaiah angrily.

"He is dead," I objected.

"Dead at the court of Shishak from grossness and overfeeding," concurred Solomon.

"But it was he who first induced Egypt to invade the ancient kingdom of his father," Benaiah replied, "and he who convinced Shishak that the land of the Hebrews should either belong to Egypt or pay it tribute!"

"Actually that is not true," Solomon said. "The ancient records of the Egyptians show that they held this land a thousand years before the Canaanites."

Benaiah pursed his lips. He looked down at his big muscular hands, flexing them again and again. We sat meditating, taking counsel from our own thoughts. It was true, by the grace of Yahweh, that the old rebel who had raided against us across the border so many times, had perished. He had been unrelenting in his vengeance against us. Rising out of Midian, crossing to Paran, he and his father after their defeat had made their way to the country of the Nile. Shortly after their arrival, the old monarch of Edom had died of chagrin—so we had heard—and the prince had assumed charge of his government-in-exile. He had prospered with his raids against our land, but at length the hand of the Lord had reached out and smote him down. He had already lived too long: the pharaoh had given him a house, appointed food to be allotted to him, and even offered him land. The rulers of Egypt were always crafty. They loved to give refuge to those who might one day be a trouble and a shaft in the side to the Hebrews.

Now Hadad's widow, sister to Tahpenes, the queen of Shishak, grew incensed against the Hebrews. She urged Shishak to take action against our country. Shishak—in view of his defeat and the wondrous reports brought back by the three wise men Solomon had defeated—was ware of our strength. Instead, he had encouraged the organizing of a league against the Hebrews (contributing veteran levies from his own army) to be headed by giant Rezon, king of Syria, and the Philistine enclaves along our coasts.

The master plan of our enemies, as it came to Benaiah—and was outlined by him to Solomon and myself in private conference—was simple, as all good battle plans are. It was merely that Rezon and the Philistine-Egyptian army should concert their movements and invade the land of the Hebrews at the same time from opposite directions.

"What can you do against it?" Solomon asked Benaiah anxiously.

"They have already defeated themselves," Benaiah growled.

"How may this be?"

Benaiah traced the kingdoms on his map-box of sand—he preferred the old way rather than the papyrus charts—and indicated with his stick. "The hordes of Syria will come from the north," he said. "They will have a long way to march in the desert before they may do much damage. On the other hand, the men of the Philistines must come from the southwest. They will broach almost immediately upon our land "

"What do you propose?" inquired Solomon.

"I propose to march against the Philistines," said Benaiah bluntly. "To destroy their army in the first days of its advance."

"You believe this will save us?"

"I shall send disguised messengers of disaster to Rezon's forces—and he will turn and flee. That is, of course, if we triumph."

"How can you be sure of this?" persisted Solomon.

"I am sure, O king."

"You have not said the reason," I broke in severely.

Benaiah gave me a black look. "Because once his ally has been defeated, Rezon would be a fool to advance," he said harshly. "And Rezon is not a fool."

In fact there was more to Benaiah's counterplan than he confessed. Six months later, having news of the mobilization of the Philistine sea peoples together with the Egyptians, he sent messengers to their joint force to warn them of defeat. They treated them with contumely, shaving off half their beards, cutting off half their garments, and stoning and hooting them out of camp, thus to bring Benaiah back his answer. It was ridicule and shame to us, to be sure, but the superstitious enemy thought it more than that. We were contemptuous of the beliefs they held; it made no difference to us that their wizards would perform enchantments over the shorn hair and severed skirts in order to bring victory to their own. "We shall see them fall on their knees on the ground," predicted Benaiah savagely. "Their children shall plead for them with their hands on their heads but we shall not listen. We shall lay them prostrate. We shall ride over them with spiked harrows, cut them with saws, bind them and throw them into fiery kilns!"

Both Solomon and I dissented from such ferocity but we said nothing to discourage his warlike mood. I myself attended the giving of the war vows by the army. Our forces gathered on the plain below Jerusalem. Seven men were chosen by reputation and prowess to participate. They gathered about a huge shield reversed, like a shallow bowl, in the midst of the hosts. A young black bull was led up to it. His throat was cut with a single sword slash. The thick jetting blood was caught in the shield. The seven men dipped their hands into the warm, sticky stuff and lifted the libation to heaven. Then they washed their faces in it and daubed their bodies, looking like tar images abuzz with flies in the midst of the soldiers. Following this, they cavorted about the shield, chanting the oath in which everyone joined: "Let our words to Yahweh be heard! We shall raze the walls of the enemy cities, we shall destroy the enemy armies! We shall win the victory! The blood of our dying enemies shall cover the ground as this bull's blood covers us!"

It was impressive. There was nothing blasphemous or evil in such a vow, and I allowed it to proceed. It seemed to be the way of soldiers to inspirit themselves before a conflict. I felt I should do nothing to damp their martial spirit.

What happened next was altogether unexpected. There was a commotion as a figure clad only in white walked through the army. It strode up to the blood-smeared seven warriors about the shield. They parted to let him through. He dipped his hands and rubbed his face. He turned, red-masked with dripping gore. With a shock, I recognized Solomon. The king had driven his chariot up behind us while we were engrossed in the ceremony.

"I shall lead the army myself," he announced solemnly to Benaiah and me as we rushed forward to escort him away. He began to lift his arms to cry out to the soldiers when Benaiah halted him. "I beg you, O Solomon, not to speak this to the troops," he said in a harsh low voice.

"Will it not inspirit them?" demanded Solomon. He looked about us at the silent waiting hordes of soldiers.

"Possibly," said Benaiah.

"What do you mean?"

"In this struggle, we shall need experienced leaders—experienced, that is, in warfare rather than statesmanship and wisdom, great king."

Solomon's eyes glittered upon the imperturbable Benaiah. "Am I not king of the Hebrews?" he enunciated distinctly.

"Without doubt or shadow of it, O great Solomon," Benaiah answered promptly.

"Can I not raise a slave from the dust to drive a chariot or to sit at my right hand?"

"Yes, O king."

"Can I not tithe the produce of the land into my treasuries and put a tax on the flocks? Can I not send whom I will to what toil I will? Are not death and life in my hands?"

"Yes, O mighty lord," Benaiah responded.

"Can I not pass even my kingdom from one man to another?" cried Solomon.

Benaiah looked at me and shrugged slightly. I knew what he meant. I moved forward. "O Solomon," I began, "none of your faithful servants wishes to influence your will. But as Benaiah has said many times before, to hazard the soul and heart of the Hebrews in battle is not the most sensible plan. If our nation loses you, what is left?"

"What indeed?" echoed Benaiah.

Before anyone could say more there was a high, breaking voice from the rear. "If you go into battle, Father," it cried, the voice of Rehoboam, "I shall ride with you in the chariot! I shall be your armorbearer, I shall hold your shield before you! I shall say as did Jonathan's servant of old: 'Do all that your mind inclines to; lo, I am with you in all. Even your mind is as my mind.'" The son of Solomon rushed to the clotted, sticky stuff in the shield, hurdling the body of the bull. He splashed it on his face. He, too, wheeled around, grinning frightfully as he did, like a youngster playing a game with his elders.

Benaiah glanced at Rehoboam, who had struck a young, heroic pose. "That is all very well," he said tauntingly, "but a javelin, a spear, or a sword or a slung stone—and, most of all, arrows—cannot tell crowded, anointed heads from the heads of the common peasant soldiers."

Solomon sat on the chair that was always behind him and cupped his chin in his palm. "You have seen many campaigns, many wars," he said. "You have taken many cities. Tell us about war, Benaiah."

"Some say war is dreadful," said Benaiah, "but such have never seen it. It is the only splendid time in life."

"Tell us."

Benaiah meditated, then spoke slowly with rising fervor. "The roaring wave like that of a great storm arising out of a camp, fronted with rearing horses, topped by dust, signals sounding from cymbals and trumpets. Rattle of bits, groans of carts and wheels, crunch and thud of stones, clang of armor and shields, creak of leather. Men with plumes overshadowing their helmets, sharp-bossed shields, armor slung about the necks, peering from behind with the right eye, right arm weaponed to throw or pierce, bells jangling."

"Bells?"

"Warriors often wear bells of copper on shield or armor to make harsh noises, discomfiting the enemy. So, too, with shouting and the terrifying pictures painted on their helmets."

"I see. Go on."

"There are three ways to break down a city wall," Benaiah said. "Breaking it with battering rams, taking it apart with picks or axes, undermining it from beneath. Some day, I think, we shall throw fireballs upon wooden walls and burn them but that is not yet."

"You paint a terrible picture," Solomon said.

"Best when storming a city," Benaiah said, his dark face lit with inner flames of ferocity. "Air fllled with spears and stones and flaming arrows, blaze and smoke from behind the wall, smearing the sky. Armed men climbing up runged poles with torches and spears, archers and slingers supporting. Siege machines hammering at crevices, being trapped by those upon the wall, towers fired with oil despite of water poured over them. Charioteers dashing up to the gates, wheeling and halting, despite a rain of death, prodding their horses to kick down the gates!"

"Enough, enough!" Solomon said.

"There is much more painted into my mind by long experience," Benaiah said maliciously.

"But the Philistines are no such warriors, are they?" inquired Solomon.

"You forget your father David organized a special band of fighters from the Philistines," Benaiah said. "There were men of the same tribes as the sea peoples, the Cherethites and Pelethites. They are professionals, they will fight anyone—even their own sons and fathers—for money and sheer love of battle. And, O king, they do not fight in internal disputes of the state—they are scrupulously neutral. Are not these the perfect fighting men?"

"I shall be first in such a battle," Solomon said decisively. Again he lifted up his arms but Benaiah forestalled him. He swung about toward the troops and shouted: "Your mighty King Solomon shall go with you into battle! I shall go with him, at his side! He will bring the favor of Yahweh and victory upon the battlefield!"

"Eeeeeyah!" shrieked the soldiers. The drums boomed, shields and spears clashed. Cymbals and trumpets made a deafening din that continued minute after minute. Solomon, even had he wished to speak, could not have been heard. He gave Benaiah a malignant stare. He signaled for his chariot. Still garbed in the horridness of the bull's blood, he and Rehoboam mounted. I saw them drive furiously out of sight over the hills toward Jerusalem and I thought sadly how well Tamar had triumphed.

"You will not be in favor on your return," I told Benaiah after the clamor had died down and the army had been ordered to disperse to their homes. I stood in the chariot beside him. He drove at a trot toward the stables of the city.

"A good soldier is always in favor in time of war," he grunted.

"But afterward?"

"Solomon will be pleased," Benaiah said. "He will participate and gain glory enough. But someone better, safer shall lead. He will be pleased if I accompany him. That will be enough to assuage his wrath."

"You risk your head spiked over the gate," I said warningly.

Benaiah laughed abruptly. "One like me risks it every day," he said. "Would you mourn for me, Nathan?"

"I would mourn for the Hebrews," I said.

Benaiah shrugged. "That is enough," he told me. "That is what I meant, of course."

"How do you propose to fight the Philistines and their Egyptian allies?" I inquired.

Benaiah grunted. "The usual way," he said shortly. "Bows and slings for approach, chariots for speed, light javelins for middle distances. Spear, sword, and mace for the close fighting—and knives, too. I may tell you that our men are shortening their spear shafts now to make them easier to handle."

"Nothing else?" I felt disappointed.

"Mighty warrior Nathan," said Benaiah sardonically, "who hates to see the blood flow except at sacrifice, you shall see something different, I assure you. Even you will be surprised."

"Surprise, you have told me, is essential to the good strategist," I said stiffly.

"But if I tell it to a talkative prophet," Benaiah returned maliciously, "it will be no surprise."

"Very well."

"Request Zadok to make ready. I need his priests and Levites to go with the army."

"Priests and Levites, fighting men!" I ejaculated in amazement.

"If you will take the message, O Nathan," Benaiah said.

"I see no purpose in it," I protested.

"You are a prophet," replied Benaiah jeeringly. "Meditate upon it."

"This is the place where I wish to get off," I said with dignity.

"Will you favor my request?" asked Benaiah ironically as he pulled up his team. "Or shall I see Zadok myself?"

I stepped down. "There is no need for anyone else to take the message," I said.

Benaiah laughed again. He whistled to his horses. They sped off, leaving me blinded by a cloud of dust. It forced me to cough for long minutes before I could proceed.

"Let the young men play," said Benaiah comfortably. "Let them be chosen by lot."

I stiffened. The captain of the Philistines nodded agreement. I knew what they meant. In such a case, twenty-one of the soldiers on either side would be selected to fight twenty-one of the foe. I had no illusions about the drawings: this was no sacred urim and thummin. I knew Benaiah would rig the lots so as to present his best-trained, disciplined, high-morale men—and I was sure that the Philistine general (a tall, angular-faced man in bronze breastplate and greaves with the usual round shield and feathered headdress) would cheat in the same manner. This was, after all, war.

We had encountered the enemy not far from Gezer, the city which Shishak had given Solomon as a wedding present with Theke—and now seemed anxious to recover. It was an old royal Canaanite place, on the border of Ephraim, near the Philistine claims. It had been allotted to the Levites long ago but they had been driven out by raiders. The place since had been rebuilt and reinforced by Benaiah. It had a strong position—that of an isolated hill commanding the western road to Jerusalem, just where the mountains of Judah began.

To my surprise, Benaiah had moved out of this impregnable fortress before dawn onto the plains below to receive the Philistines. Long before the enemy came, we had notice of him by the yellow dust-clouds blown toward us, by the wind-carried sound of their drums and clash of arms. They too undoubtedly had seen us—at any rate, we had detected their spies among the gullies in the hills.

Some time shortly after sunrise, we halted, within a hundred yards of each other. Benaiah had sent his herald, and he—this time backed by armed men—had been treated with courtesy. It was the Philistine captain who parleyed with Benaiah halfway between the two hosts. He suggested openly that the ancient mass duel be fought. "For," he said through his barbaric interpreter, "we shall need men for the harvesting. There is no use killing too many of them." Benaiah nodded—even as he plotted within his heart the sort of treachery that is always present in battle.

Three things were clear to my untutored eyes. The first was that we were, as usual, outnumbered by the invaders—but that Benaiah had reserved a rear-guarded route for a retreat to the city of Gezer. The second was that the strength of our foes seemed greater. They were superior in slingers, bowmen, and javelin throwers—and at least one of their sidearms for close fighting was different. Each man carried the *hepes,* a deadly sickle sword invented in Egypt. It was shaped like the foreleg of an ox and sharpened on the outer side of the curve. Light and keen, it had been capable of wreaking widespread slaughter. But it comforted me to know that our men now also had iron tools of battle. We no longer had to fight for our lives with weak bronze or copper. But our blades were not curved. They were straight, short, pointed, with a keen edge ground on each side.

Finally, most importantly, neither our forces nor those opposite appeared to have many chariots—possibly because of the longer journey of the Philistine-Egyptians but in our case apparently by the deliberate choice of Benaiah. And though the unarmed Levites and priests clustered behind us, Solomon was not present.

"The king is not here," I whispered to Benaiah.

"I had not noticed," he said.

"Perhaps he slept too late," I said. "I shall return to Gezer and seek him."

"You will be too late," Benaiah said. "We have already begun our fight."

The lots had been thrown, the choosing ended. The picked men stood erect, ready and expectant. Up shot the brown arm of the Philistine leader; Benaiah answered it with a like signal. The two small ranks of combatants approached each other, stiff legged, like animals. They halted almost chest to chest in the middle of the sandy space between the two armies.

They dug in their bare toes opposite each other, man to man. For a long moment they paused, each striving to strike terror into his opponent by his fierce stare.

The old formality of a duel to the death was to seize the hair with the left hand, to strike with the sword in the right. Not so had Benaiah trained his young men. In the split second before the duel, they shifted their swords to their left hands. They paid no attention to grasping the hair of their foes. Instead, enduring cuts that in some cases struck to the bone, they used their right hands to ward the other's weapon. They thrust home, left-handed, into the unprotected gut of the enemy.

A shout went up from the Philistines and Egyptians—a cry of frustrated fury and alarm. It did no good. All of their champions—except one, badly wounded—lay prostrate, dying on the sand. The last began to crawl back to his enraged spear-shaking comrades.

Over all sounded the Bashan roar of Benaiah to our army: "On them, on them! Forward! Kill and spare not! Run them down, flush them from hiding, cut off their heels! The day, the victory is ours!"

Behind us, a shocking thing happened. It came suddenly, without warning. Benaiah gave a signal with both hands upraised. All the priests put their thin brass trumpets to their mouths. With one accord, they blew a great blast. It shook the air like a curtain, subtly discordant, so piercing that the hearer could scarcely endure it, hardly fight on without clapping his hands over his ears.

As they ceased for want of breath, the Levites raised their rams' horns. All together they blew a profundo blast. It seemed to trouble the earth, to put tremors in our very bodies. Then the priests again, then the Levites; again and again and again. It was a tremendous fanfare of noise calculated to put panic into the hearts of those that opposed us. I could see shields going down, weapons slacking, mouths gaping, arms loose and nerveless. I could see some visibly wilting where they stood, helmets awry, their legs shaking.

Others saw this beside myself. There was a mighty shout, a shaking of spears, brandishing of blades. The Hebrews drove forward into the dismayed hosts of the foe. Like those who brayed down the walls of Jericho, so we struck at these walls of men and pierced them through.

There was the sudden booming of shield against shield, clash of swords, close work with maces and daggers. There were muffled cries and shouts of resistance, but as I watched, I could see the line of the Philistines—prominent in their clipped feather helmets—bending inward in the middle under the press of our attack.

Here Benaiah's genius was clearly displayed. The short-hafted spears were doing well but the thrust and slash of the straight handblades of the Hebrews, against the clumsy curved *hepes* of the others, were making the battle a slaughter.

I had no sooner observed this than the whole character of the encounter shifted. The Philistine-Egyptian line broke in the middle, men staggering back and tumbling, like the breaking of a dam weakened by a flood. The Hebrews surged through with shrieks of triumph. They circled about—evidently in a prepared maneuver—to either side. They cut off and surrounded each of the separated and weakened pair of groups that now formed the two wings of the opposing army.

In the midst of the indescribable din and confusion, the swirls of sand, the shoutings, clangings, and cries, the nameless Philistine general was everywhere. His war cries rose above the battle. Angular and thin, he swooped like a hawk. He hewed down our men with a blade that dripped like the blood masks I had seen on our men only a few days before. By his desperate, superhuman endeavors alone he was changing the fortunes of the day. His men commenced to recover their courage, to regroup and advance, to assist him in resisting the tide of the fighting.

Beside me, Benaiah gave a growl like an animal. He seized his sword. He plunged forward, head down, thrusting his way into the pack of human beings. He was intent on nothing but reaching and killing the Philistine leader who had so successfully rallied his followers.

As he did, a shout arose behind us. "The king, the king! Solomon comes!"

I glanced over my shoulder and saw a rising cloud of dust coming at breakneck speed down the road from the walls of Gezer. No one could have recognized it at that distance but I, as well as every man of the Hebrews, knew that it was Solomon racing to join the battle. Our hearts swelled and lifted. I waved my arms on high, I shrieked encouragement.

Our soldiers again pressed forward—for in that moment of announcement, the Philistine leader had faltered. A long spear thrust by the doughty Benaiah had pierced him in the armpit. He whirled about, tottered, and fell from sight in a crush of bodies.

From the spot where he had vanished went up a wail of anguish and defeat. His warriors commenced to fall back from the center of the struggle as if some quick black contagion had dropped there. I could see that the spirit was gone from the enemy, as surely as if it had been withdrawn by a mysterious god. I stared at this miraculous fashioning of victory.

"We lost two good fools in that first duel," growled Benaiah's voice in my ear. "All because they wouldn't follow my instructions. Because, they said, I was not honorable."

"Nor were you," I whispered. I fell to my knees.

"Perhaps you are the best judge of these things in the temple, Nathan," Benaiah said as softly, "but this is not holy ground."

"Indeed it is not," I said miserably. "A valiant captain has been slain."

Benaiah grinned. "He is most valiant who survives," he said. He was gone again, flinging himself recklessly into the middle of the swaying, cursing rout. I got dizzily to my feet. I recalled, as if it had been put into my mind by Yahweh, the curse of David against the house of Joab. I raised my hands and intoned:

"May this slaughter not rest on Solomon but on the head of Benaiah and all his father's house! Let there not fail from the house of Benaiah one who discharges pus, one that is a leper, one that is crippled so that he must use a staff, one that starves daily, or one that sees life as fear and falls upon his sword!"

The wheels of a chariot crackled beside me. I turned and made obeisance to Solomon and Rehoboam as they jumped down. Solomon flung the reins to a priest. "What shall I do?" cried the king. "Where is Benaiah?"

As if he had been expecting a summons, the grimy figure of Benaiah emerged from the melee that was already melting into individual flight and skirmish. Saluting Solomon with a deep bow and bloody sword, Benaiah said: "You are in time to see the utter defeat of your foes, O Solomon!"

Solomon eyed the unflinching Benaiah with a piercing gaze. The clamor died down afar. "Benaiah," he said, "I am too late for the battle."

"So it appears, O lord and king," Benaiah replied.

"But we shall speak of these things at a better moment."

"As your majesty commands."

"I shall never believe anything he says," exclaimed Rehoboam suddenly, his eyes darting hatred at Benaiah.

"Hush, my son," said Solomon, turning away. "A fool's wrath is presently known. The wise man waits his opportunity."

The homecoming into the city of Jerusalem was breathtaking. It seemed that the whole city had turned out to honor Solomon and his army. The windows were hung with colors. Banners floated over the streets. There were green arbors above the marching, waving men. Dancers and players of music were everywhere. Screaming children and barking curs burst out at every corner. With us this time, proud in their unaccustomed role—for had they not aided in victory for our people and yet not shed a drop of blood, as had happened long ago at Jericho?—were the priests and Levites.

Solomon came back from the battle as befitted a victorious king. Erect in his chariot, unsmiling, he rode slowly along the steep streets without looking aside. He was driven by the proud and excited Rehoboam, who could not resist—from time to time—waving at the young children who ran alongside. The king's vehicle was preceded by a Negro slave with a staff to clear the way through the crowds. Behind him came a tall, fully armed Hebrew soldier, solemnly beating his sword with a booming sound against his bullhide shield. On either side of the royal chariot, its sides dinted, walked other slaves with cudgels to fend off the crowds. Two captive Philistines in full regalia stumbled in chains behind Solomon.

All about us, the Hebrews rejoiced. Oddly enough, most of them were women, not men. There were as many crowds of them as flies in summertime, dancing with legs naked under transparent skirts, with ecstatic expressions and upflung arms, singing in broken choruses, thrumming lyres, beating timbrels, or merely shouting in what seemed to me to be senseless madness.

As I had feared, immediately after the triumphal procession disbanded near the palace, Solomon summoned Benaiah and myself to report to his presence. Despite the interview on the battlefield, there had been no moment at Gezer after our victory in which the king could confront Benaiah. We had left that city almost directly after returning from the field, so eager had Solomon been to return to Jerusalem. Now the reckoning could be delayed no longer.

We were ushered by the guard into the smaller audience chamber with which I was already familiar. Benaiah was on my heels, his dark dusty face unmoved, his scarred armor—I suspect he had not cleansed himself or changed his garb for a purpose—still upon him. We found Solomon refreshed and rerobed, seated on his throne. Next to him stood the young prince Rehoboam. I shot a furtive look at Benaiah. This was not unprecedented but if a rebuke were to be forthcoming it was certainly demeaning. He made no sign that he noticed Rehoboam's presence.

After the doors had closed, Solomon allowed us to wait a long moment. He swept us with his eyes as if we were common criminals. His manner was haughty, his brow forbidding. I had never seen him in this mood before. Benaiah and I waited in silence, lowering our eyes before his majesty. When Solomon spoke, I knew he addressed Benaiah.

"At last," Solomon said, "you shall render your accounts to me."

"I could wish for no better judge, O king," Benaiah returned intrepidly.

"Why was I not awakened when the troops left Gezer?"

"Such was the duty of your guard—or Nathan here."

"Not I!" I exclaimed at this unexpected malice. "I had no such duty!"

Solomon disregarded the shaft tossed in my direction. "My chamber guard was unconscious, bound and gagged," he said.

Benaiah appeared interested. "Perhaps the work of a spy of the Egyptians," he said. "They are clever at such things."

"My horses were gone! My chariot was wrecked!"

"Ah!" said Benaiah, nodding. "This was truly the work of a spy within the walls."

"Where were the other chariots?" demanded Solomon, conscious that his dignity had deserted him in his anger.

"That, at least, I can answer," Benaiah said promptly. "I sent them all out before dawn. A scouting sweep to the south. They came back too late to aid us."

"Late!" Solomon said, grinding his teeth. "The first that I could commandeer was too late to join the battle!"

Benaiah bowed. "You arrived just in time to hearten my men, to put the enemy to flight," he said. He grinned at Rehoboam. "And your noble son, as well," he added politely.

"I do not believe a word you say!" burst out Rehoboam. He edged close to his father. "Do not be deceived, my father!"

Solomon observed Benaiah mordantly. His glance shifted to me and back again. I prostrated myself. "I knew nothing of this," I said, raising my head. "Had you trusted me, O Solomon—"

"Enough," Solomon said, breaking into my plea. "Both you and Benaiah should have known it was my will to head the troops."

"If your highness had only so informed us," Benaiah murmured.

"I did not know," I said wretchedly. "How could I guess?"

"You lie!" screamed Rehoboam, pointing at us with both fists, "both of you lie!"

"Go," Solomon said, giving him a slight push. "Seek Tamar. Say I shall come to see her soon."

Reluctantly Rehoboam left the chamber, not without a malignant look backward. Benaiah braced himself casually as Solomon considered us again. His brow was black but he said nothing for a time.

"This shall never happen again," he said finally. "I will be obeyed."

We bowed in assent. Solomon went on: "I believe you had no part in it, Nathan. You stand free. As for you, Benaiah, you shall resign your office. Another shall command the king's armies."

"Whom shall I appoint to succeed me?"

"You shall wait my command," Solomon snapped.

"A thousand submissions," Benaiah said. "The campaign is not yet over. Who shall lead the Hebrews against Rezon from Syria in the north?"

It was too much for me. I could not restrain myself. "The king has made an altogether righteous judgment," I said, stepping forward. "There was no need for the brutality and slaughter of the battle past. Even in its midst, I invoked the wrath of Yahweh upon Benaiah for his bloodthirstiness. I approve heartily of selecting another leader!"

Both Benaiah and Solomon looked at me as if I were a curious insect brought to their attention. "I do not need your advice upon military matters, Nathan," Solomon said coldly.

"But the hosts of the Lord are—are the hosts of the Lord," I protested.

"The hosts of the Lord are the hosts of Solomon," the king said.

Then Benaiah made his most telling point with Solomon, one that the king's vainness could not resist. "The king knows well," said this subtle chief, "that only through conquest can fame and glory be won. That battle is the only path to conquest. Every other king in the world knows it."

"But wisdom, glory for knowledge, peace and multiplying fruitfulness and worshipping Yahweh!" I said wildly. "Are not these things fame? Have they not brought Solomon all that you have or will have?"

I was unfortunate in my choice of phrases. I had seen Benaiah on the brink of disgrace and dismissal. Now, unaided, I brought him back into the royal favor. My mention of credit to others than Solomon had been my downfall. I had forgotten that flattery must ever remain the most potent weapon of a court.

"Yahweh has truly been good to the Hebrews," Solomon said icily, "but I have been His agent on earth. He has allowed me to make His decisions here."

"What else but your wisdom has led the Hebrews to the heights they now enjoy, where all the world hears their name and fears their king?" asked Benaiah.

"But we are surrounded by enemies!" I cried.

"Idolaters of abominations, not knowing the Lord," Solomon said sharply. "How could they be our friends?"

"But Yahweh made Adam, He made all men in His image and we destroy that image when we kill!"

"The Lord has commanded us to destroy such images," Benaiah said. Solomon sat on his throne like a statue. The commander, believing he might have made an error, hastened to retrieve it. He spoke to me in a mild tone, like a friend.

"Your compassion does you credit," Benaiah said, "but not with Yahweh."

"How?" asked Solomon sharply. "How is that?"

"Have you forgotten," said Benaiah composedly, "the laws of war which the Lord laid down to Moses? They are recorded for all to read. The men who have new houses, new vineyards, new wives—even as those that are fainthearted—are not to fight or go with the army. When the army is assembled and captains chosen, they shall advance with the Lord. If against cities, they shall call the peaceful surrender. If this is denied, they shall besiege it, capture it, and put every male to the sword. The cattle, women, and children shall be saved alive. But the cities of those who are our sworn enemies—we are ordered by the Lord to leave in them nothing alive that breathes."

I swallowed hard. Benaiah had indeed read the words of Moses aright. He had crammed them back down my throat. "Those were other days," I said feebly, "and today we are victorious and need no such measures."

"It is just such measures that have made us victorious," Benaiah said politely. "It is for this reason that I have rejoiced that the king has been delivered to us. For though he has new houses, new wives, new vineyards, he has something more important, a new nation planted by his father to be kept for the future. Therefore it is good that his person and kingdom be not endangered by misplaced pity."

Solomon spoke, interrupting our colloquy. "Benaiah," he said in measured terms, "since there is no other captain of your prowess and knowledge in these things, you shall have temporary command of my army still."

"All honor and obedience to Solomon," Benaiah returned, bowing deeply.

He lifted his hand and looked at me triumphantly. I averted my eyes from his as if they might infect me. We turned to Solomon for our permission to leave.

The king's eyes were far away, no doubt hearing the cries and acclaim of multitudes unknown. His hand raised itself in dismissal.

"Fame and glory!" cried Benaiah, drawing his sword and raising it to his lips. Solomon smiled slightly.

"Vanity of vanities, all is vanity," I murmured to myself. I hooded my head in my robe and left to pray.

CHAPTER SIXTEEN

The Visit of Sheba

"B'hemah, b'hemah!" cried one watcher over the top of the gate. He was a huge man with a bristling shock of tangled flame-hair. In his alarm and excitement, he waved his arms wildly. He sprang upward again and again—as if he could not do enough with his twisting body to express his emotions: "The Beast! The Beast!"

"What is it?" I demanded of Elihaph. We hurried to the walls of Jerusalem—anxious as all Hebrews always are to view something new and different (the very invalids will rise from their pallets and walk to gawk at a street seller's spectacle).

Elihaph cocked his head up at me as he labored to keep pace. "I don't know," he panted, "but I have heard that the scouts of Benaiah in the south have come in, by foot or astride, to report the advance of some rich caravan headed by some monstrosity that they have never seen before. They call it The Beast."

"How is it that I have not heard of this before?" I demanded.

"It has been current in the marketplaces for days," Elihaph responded cunningly. "Perhaps you have been thinking upon other, more important things."

"Does it come in war or peace?"

"Peace, peace," said Elihaph. "Else Benaiah would have sent his slingers and archers south long before this."

"Surely the king knows this thing."

"I have no doubt," Elihaph said, managing a shrug even at our rapid gait with our skirts tucked up. "But there is a secret about this caravan."

"What is that?"

"It comes in peace from the south. It makes gestures of conciliation. But no man of its company will speak as much as a word. It is the richest and most magnificent company ever to enter the gates of the city of David." His breath was gone. He could say no more.

By this time we had climbed the inner steps of the wall. We stood over the Old Gate with its winding road below that clung to the side of the rocks. Beside me and about me, like snails in their perches, were hundreds of the city's inhabitants. All were delirious with enthusiasm and wonder, cheering and screaming as if to break their lungs—and abruptly I understood why.

A dozen yards beneath me, no more than a long bowshot away, I saw the strangest and most terrifying creature that had ever come into the sight of my eyes. It walked on four legs like pillars, swaying with full confidence in its strength as it came. It hulked a dozen feet into the air (half as high as the walls), with ears like enormous palm fans sticking out on either side. Two five-foot fangs gleamed white, protruding under its tiny red eyes. Between them writhed a long nose like a snake, two tiny fingers at the end of it probing the air as it moved. All of this monster was covered with some half-hairy gray hide that shambled as it moved, like an ill-fitted garment.

As I watched, fascinated, it lifted its snakelike nose in a curl and screamed. I stopped my ears and reeled back. I saw a score of my countrymen flung from their coigns by the very impact of the blast and beast spittle.

" 'His strength is in his loins,' " I quoted in awe, " 'and his force is in his navel; he moves his tail like a cedar, his bones are strong pieces of brass, like bars of iron.' "

"What is it?" breathed Elihaph next to me.

"Surely," I said solemnly, "it is the behemoth that is spoken of in holy writ."

Even as I said it, I stared again. On the back of this beast, swaying with him, stood a little house with a pointed roof, all done in red and gold, shining in the sunlight. Inside, her face like finely cut ebony, sat the most beautiful woman—saving only Bathsheba—that I had ever seen.

Without knowing it I had taken my first glimpse of the unveiled queen of distant and romantic Sheba.

It was natural that the victory of Solomon over the combined forces of the Egyptians and the sea peoples—and the subsequent retreat of Rezon back into the safety of his own Syria—should have vastly increased the renown of the Hebrews and their king in the ears of the world.

Once the Philistines had been broken on the field, the issue had been decided. In all likelihood, when Benaiah had brazened out his position before Solomon, he already knew that the war was over. He had sent swift riders, as it came out, to the north disguised as friendly tribesmen. They gabbled to Rezon of the disaster to his allies. Rezon had verified the news in his own fashion, rewarded the couriers, and promptly retired to his homeland with oaths of vengeance to await the next opportunity of invading our frontiers.

In one sense, of course, Benaiah had deceived his king to avoid punishment for himself. But in another, more vital way he had been perfectly right in his calculations. By this second triumph, this time over a coalition of enemies—in addition to his already established reputation for wisdom and wealth—Solomon had triumphed immeasurably. Not only his glory and fame resounded within the four seas, his own confidence in himself and his kingship became assured—to the point that he dared for the first time to take a long trip out of Jerusalem.

In those days, as today, it was hazardous for a monarch to issue forth from the heart of his web of power, especially in the precariously welded union of the Hebrews. Sitting as it did at the crossroads of the world, our land was always the prey of others. It was vulnerable to raids from without or intrigue from within. Solomon's own time was one of thrones toppling everywhere about us under the levers of ambitious priests or orgulous generals. Now, however, after thirty years of ruling his turbulent people, the king felt secure enough to visit the south—especially the establishment of Ezion Geber and the port that opened onto the gulf that led into the Red Sea made famous by Moses. Here was Solomon's latest present from Hiram of Tyre. It was a fleet of Phoenician ships.

All this I learned too late to advise the king against acceptance. I had no love for the sea, the element of all-destroying Leviathan. I judged it enough for us to till and mine the ground, to trade with our neighbors for what else we needed. I deemed that all sailors were madmen—and that the Phoenicians, in their yearnings for further lands in the west, were the worst.

Possibly it was this which caused Solomon to make me vice-regent in Jerusalem during the time he was away. Or perhaps he did not trust anyone else to rule in his absence. Whatever it was, he took his royal train and departed one fine day, with courtiers and soldiers, to the south, for an express but hidden purpose. I do not doubt he received a privy message from Hiram which did not pass through my hands, advising him of the arrival of the ships. I ruled the Hebrews for more than a month in his place, doing justice and right as I was guided by Yahweh, until Solomon returned home.

He arrived, of course, amid rejoicing. Yet the joy of his people was nevertheless much diminished from the days of his accession. The tribes—though prosperous and peaceful as never before under his aegis—had suffered under taxes and forced labor in the mountains of Lebanon. Many of the inhabitants of Jerusalem had shared in this tithe of tasking for the king. Thus there was as much grumbling, as many black looks as there were hosannas and prayers for the king's health on his return. But Solomon noted little of this. He strode into his chambers as if he had left them only the day before, not even pausing to visit his wives. He was eager to take his vacant throne above my own seat once more. I blessed his return, praised his appearance, and inquired after his journey.

"Most successful," the king returned complacently. "There are many curious things to be discovered outside Jerusalem, Nathan. We Hebrews live in too narrow a world."

"Were there dangers along the way?"

"No more than crossing the courts of the temple. Shall I tell you what I found waiting in the bay of Elath, Nathan?"

I bowed my head. "If it pleases the mighty Solomon," I said.

"I am well pleased to tell you. I found the greatest present of all from my friend, Hiram of Tyre—a fleet of seagoing vessels, Nathan!"

"It—it sounds altogether glorious," I stammered in surprise.

"They are magnificent ships!" Solomon cried enthusiastically. "I have seen others at the port of Joppa and they cannot compare. Each is in the shape of gigantic fishes, both their heads and tails upraised. In the middle is a mast, a basket at the top for lookouts or for fire cressets to warn other travelers by sea at night. Ten oars to a side, thrust through holes in the hull, secured by ropes, with slaves rowing from benches, three to an oar. The sail is orange and may be seen a great way off: oblong, with a single spar at the top."

"Altogether a marvel," I agreed weakly.

"Steered by huge oars at the rear that take five men to work in a storm! Upright tips at each end painted yellow, the broad-bottomed hull pitched, painted green! The anchors are baskets of rope filled with rock, Nathan. There is a sandpit for fire for cooking and smoke-signaling, even colored banners for messages from ship to ship!"

"How many of these wonderful vessels did Hiram of Tyre send you?" I inquired slowly.

"Six," Solomon said, with more hesitation than he had evinced previously.

"As a free gift?"

"Virtually so," Solomon said defiantly.

"Not entirely so?" I pressed him.

The king rounded on me. "Nathan," he said imperiously, "I tell you all this because it is my will. Not because you are like one of my wives, forever nagging and reproachful if I do not repeat some gossip or other. You may as well know that these ships were handsomely paid for."

"I hope not too handsomely," I said in some anxiety. "The saying is that the Phoenicians are the closest traders on the Great Sea. The Phoenician boast is that they will outdo a Hebrew every time."

"I gave Hiram a kingly gift in return," Solomon responded flatly.

"What gift?"

"I have given him twenty cities in Galilee, with all their territory."

I reeled back, striking my forehead thrice with my fist. I could barely speak. "Twenty cities!" I ejaculated. "Twenty cities! Twenty cities gone from the patrimony created by your father David! Twenty cities vanished from the Hebrew fold!"

Solomon regarded me with a frown. "You seem to disapprove, Nathan," he remarked ironically.

"Disapprove! I abhor it! David in his grave might rise up and demand of his son by Bathsheba the right to censure him!"

"This is not your accustomed way of speaking, Nathan," Solomon said easily. "More often you speak upon either side, balancing your arguments. As carefully as the women balance their water jars upon their heads when they climb the steps up into the city."

"This allows of no other point of view," I said bluntly.

"What you complain of is that your king did what he did without consulting you."

"It is not usual," I said sulkily. Thereupon Solomon took it upon himself to tutor me like a backward child.

"We have not been living an inexpensive life in Jerusalem," he said. "Nathan, you know that our tribute to Tyre—for the cedar, fir, and gold and other things, whatever they may be—amounts to two hundred thousand bushels of wheat a year and nearly two thousand gallons of oil. Hiram has also sent us sandalwood trees, gold from Ophir, precious stones."

"All for your further glory," I retorted.

"Who shall say that such glory is dear?" Solomon replied sharply. "It is not my fame but that of the Hebrews that shall ring down the ages. For a prophet, Nathan, you read the future poorly."

"Common sense, not prophecy, is needed," I said.

"We owe much to Hiram that has not been paid."

I remained mute. Solomon resumed his enumeration. "All this I was reminded of courteously by Hiram's emissary on the shores of the gulf," he said, turning bitter. "It is not pleasant, however politely, for a king to hear such things. It seems I am in the hands of bloodsuckers and moneylenders such as the world has never seen, in the debt of the Phoenicians."

"Very possibly."

"Then, too, I have spent much to build the city of Tadmor in the wilderness. I have built Beth-horon with walls, gates, and bars in the lower city and the noble upper city. I have built the cities of storage such as Baalath and Hamath. No one thinks of these deeds."

"You have also," I said slyly, "built Megiddo with its four thousand stalls for horses and quarters for twelve thousand horsemen—and there are other such cities."

"Benaiah urged me to it."

"O king," I added maliciously, "every three years ships of Hiram come in from Tarshish with gold and silver, ivory, apes, and peacocks for your delectation. And Hiram-abi has been here lo! these many years working for the wages you pay his master. There are presents given of fine vessels and clothing, harness, spices, and—"

"Nathan, I forbid you!"

"Fine linen yarn out of Egypt, horses at one hundred fifty shekels apiece, shining chariots for six hundred shekels each!"

"Nathan!"

"Goods from Syria and the Hittites yearly!"

"I shall lose my patience!"

"As the good King Hiram wrote to you," I said solemnly, " 'Blessed be your Lord that He has given David a wise son to rule over his people!' "

Solomon did not respond to my daring remark like an angry king. My voice had rung through the audience hall but he had not noticed it. He was considering his inner thoughts. At length he spoke.

"Nathan," he said to me, slowly and gently, "we have been extravagant, it is true. None knows it better than you, who keep accounts. None better than Adoniram who is the most hated man in the kingdom for collecting my tribute. But there is more to the business than the mere commerce. The name of Solomon and the Hebrews goes to the corners of the earth. With these ships and our own seamen, we shall be able to sail ourselves to Ophir and gather gold—without paying Hiram for transporting it."

"That is something," I admitted grudgingly.

"More," Solomon said. "These cities of which you complain are in the mountains opposite Tyre. They might be captured in a moment if the Phoenicians became our enemies. They are not cities at all—but villages, as you know, and our people really hold but few of them. Then, too, at the southeastern end, there are only bare hills and stinking marshes, feared by men for their noxious smells and lights at night. I have seen such by the sea at Elath myself. They are terrible at night and with unknown insects and weird sounds."

"It represents a diminution of our territory," I argued.

"We shall conquer more."

I shook my head in despair. Still Solomon would not let me go. "Nathan," he said with that eagerness that always was part of him, "I saw a strange tree. Its branches drop roots which grow upward, into the air, tree by tree, until a single growth is a whole forest—and it cannot live except in salt water!"

I could not reply for I could not believe it. I contented myself with an obeisance. I drew a deep breath and determined to ask the king concerning another matter—since he had just returned from that part of our land. But to my astonishment his next words anticipated what I wanted to say—though in quite different spirit.

"Have you heard of the massive furnaces of Ezion Geber?" Solomon asked me eagerly.

"Yes, O Solomon."

"How they are built of stone, stoked with wood, how they are constructed so that the wind from the north drives through their flues, more heated than the fires of the Valley of Hinnom?"

"Yes, my lord."

"How earth is dug from the sides of the Valley of Arabah to be melted into copper, sometimes into iron, poured into ingots? All this I have seen myself. But you have only heard, not seen, Nathan."

"Has the great king," I asked humbly, "seen of what I have heard? That the children of the Hebrews are, together with our slaves, penned within stone walls there? That they labor until death in your mines?"

Solomon's brow grew black as thunder. "I have seen this," he said, holding his voice in trembling check. "All this is for their own good. They work for the greater glory of their country. They are fed well and housed well. They do their duty as I do mine."

"I have heard that Hebrews are fed and housed and worked like the slave Edomites, my king. Is this right for a free people?"

"These mines, these furnaces," Solomon said, his words trembling with passion, "are the chief wealth of my kingdom. You have listened to false tongues, O Nathan! Go, go!"

Summarily was I dismissed from Solomon's presence. I went forlornly—because I had spoken not to offend him but to plead the cause of my countrymen. I comforted myself that the mines and furnaces had been established by David, not Solomon; but then, I knew, David had them worked only by the alien peoples he had captured, not by Hebrews. In his days the production had been small, the people taking pride in the name of Qenites, smiths and forgers. It had been Solomon's insatiate pride and his need to sustain an ever greater glory that had brought about so many Hebrews reputedly in chains at the furnaces.

So it was that I did not enter the presence of the king again for nearly two weeks. It was at that time I heard the summons of the watchers from the gate towers. I hurried to see what outlandish beings might be approaching.

Solomon was kind. He allowed me to kiss his hand. He raised me up himself and told me the news. "If you had not been so intemperate in your remarks, Nathan," he said, "I would have told you weeks ago of what the glory of the Hebrews means and how far it has spread. When I was at the seaport of Elath, I returned as quickly as I could when I heard."

"Heard, O Solomon?"

"That the queen of far-off Sheba, the mystic kingdom in the south, had taken a caravan and was on her way to visit me in Jerusalem."

"How might I have heard?"

Solomon sighed. "Like so many others," he told me, "you think all wisdom lies in scrolls or in visions, Nathan. Such are useful and necessary, certainly. But tell me, while I was in the south, did you summon my women?"

I felt humiliated. "Never!" I protested. I knew what Solomon meant. Each night he viewed the women of his seraglio, each one clad in exactly the same costume—a diaphanous flowing gown—with her hair arranged to suit herself. He spoke to each, of news and gossip, of events of the town and harem—but never of love. Afterward he sent his famous ring to one of them. He had her bathed, dressed richly, and perfumed, to spend the night with him.

"One learns much from women," Solomon smiled. "Their bodies may be the same, varying little in delight to delight, but their minds are strangely different."

"Such as that of Tamar?" I hazarded.

"Wildly different," Solomon said, smiling even more broadly. He added: "Did you never speak to the merchants in the city?"

"Never," I said submissively. I knew that Solomon was in the habit of calling before him all the travelers who had come into Jerusalem the day before. After he had disposed of affairs of state, he inquired keenly of what they had seen and the news they bore—but never of merchandise.

"Merchants, women," Solomon said. "One may learn everything from these—if one adds observations of the world of animals and earth, sky and plants."

"And prophetic visions?" I said anxiously. Solomon gave me a quizzical glance. "Perhaps," he said. He waved his hand. "Tonight we shall prepare a banquet for the queen of

Sheba," he said. "See to it that you dazzle not only her eyes but my own."

I bowed as the king left. The task he had assigned to me was not too difficult. The three parties he always traveled with—one to occupy a town before his arrival, one that stayed with him, and one which searched the town afterward—had already come back to Jerusalem. Among them would be the cooks and provisioners and inventors of delights for the king's pleasure.

In the press of the royal command, I did not see Solomon greet our royal visitor. But the news was brought to me that she had retired to her apartments to rest, to compose herself for the coming feast—always the most arduous ordeal for visiting royalty and the chief reason, I imagine, that kings do not often venture outside their countries. I heard also that the queen, on coming to Solomon on his throne, had spied his famous pool of petrified water. She had lifted her skirts high—thus betraying a charming pair of legs. It was a good joke and we enjoyed it.

The feast was to be held in the state dining hall, just off the hall of the Forest of Lebanon. Here a great set of a dozen polished ebony slabs had been set in the earth, joined with gold. About them had been dug long mains, lined with lapis lazuli and having seats of gold-encrusted wood. The guests—there was room for nearly two hundred—might sit and dangle their feet in the coolness of the ground, yet have all the comfort of seats. At the head was a raised throne of gold for Solomon. Lesser seats at his right and left were reserved for honored guests.

The list of things to eat was endless. Roast meat and boiled, birds and lamb stuffed with rice and spices, fish boiled in milk (but never that most succulent dish, kid seethed in its mother's milk, forbidden by Moses as an old pagan sacrifice), puddings of flesh and grain, white milk and thick yellow milk sweetened with honey, with the wines of Egypt, the best to be had, even foaming beer and plump raisins (my favorite delicacy), figs, and all kinds of fruits. There was to be music, of course: lyres, harps, drum tambourines, sistra, pipes, flutes, horns, cymbals, and the like. There would also be dancers and jugglers and magicians (which always pleased the king) but no women could be allowed to attend except the guest of honor. Feasts such as this were for men alone. I was pleased and excited; I arranged it carefully so that the lovely queen of Sheba would sit between Solomon and myself.

At length I surveyed the hall with its green chaplets and clumps of flowers after the whirlwind of servants had passed through, and felt satisfied. I turned to Zadok—whose responsibility, too, this was, as high priest and expert in ceremonies—and said: "All seems in order. I shall command the thousand lamps to be lit."

"Light the lamps," said Zadok maliciously. "But there is one thing missing."

"Missing? What is it?"

"A jester, Nathan. You may remedy that yourself."

Before I could find a suitable response, he had slipped away. He was agile as an eel for all his fatness.

It was night. The music wailed and sobbed, jangled and shrilled from the brilliant hall. I had had barely time enough to change my gown into the proper high costume when it was the hour for the feast to begin. The procession had already formed. I rushed up to the very head of it. I took my proper place, relaxing my expression from wrinkles of care into the smooth mask of calm.

We approached the feasting hall through a wide aisle of maidens dressed in white, each either holding a torch—soaked in aromatic oils—or waving a broad palm fan to ward off the night gnats which would collect to the odor of roast meat. We proceeded very slowly to the entrance, as fitted the state of Solomon and his greatness. This was so that the people who clung to the top of the walls might cheer with one breath and sigh in ecstasy with the next. Music—strings, cymbals, pipes—resounded everywhere. It took its tempo from the tread of the king's feet. Light sparkled in every corner, reflected by the torches from the jewels and polished gold of the ornaments of dress into multicolored fragments of light. As we entered, the gilded roof over us seemed itself to reflect Solomon's glory.

Solomon wore his usual dress of purple wool that he reserved for the occasions of greatest ceremony. Over it he had cast a tunic of woven gold thread. This one was embroidered in intricate designs, with jewels that flashed all colors. The white sash of fine linen about his head bore his six-pointed star outlined in rubies. His sandals were of gold. He reeked of the most aromatic perfumes.

As for the queen of Sheba, she moved proudly—but with a certain demureness—at the king's side. Wrapped spirally about her slender figure, she wore a fringed robe of rich linen worked with gold and silver, so thin that through it the movement of her brown limbs might be seen. She had about her neck heavy collars of gold and jewels and a scarf of purple and red that was as fine as a spider's web. I wondered if it had been one of Solomon's gifts. On the head of Itamara was a long-curled yellow wig braided in blue, contrasting oddly with her sharp-set, beautiful little dark face.

I have thought many times since of the queen of Sheba as she was that night. With her long graceful neck, wide, heavily lashed eyes, taut cheeks, and air of delight, she reminded me irresistibly of a wild deer surprised at dawn on the hills. So did she look around her at the resplendent scene; so did she move that she seemed to swim along the polished floor. Every movement of her body adorned her more than her dress, and her expression of curiosity and pleasure went to my heart.

We entered the hall in perfect state, going each to his place in the blaze of the thousand oil lamps that burned within. Solomon, with the queen—her expression a mixture of wonder and delight—made his way to the head of the table on the raised dais. Here only he and the lovely visitor from Sheba were ensconced. He did her the great honor of seating her first at his right hand, then stood before his own throne.

At the other side of Solomon, naturally, sat Rehoboam, as the favorite son of the king. But next to him was a figure everyone abhorred. According to the Egyptian custom, Solomon had propped up a small coffin which contained a gruesomely carved skeleton of wood. It was not to restrain the merriment of the feast. Rather the opposite, for it bore a notice: "Look here and drink and be gay; for remember that when you die, such as this you will be." I must add that as the feast grew more boisterous, this remembrance was passed from hand to hand and finally its wooden bones were strewn in jest about the hall.

Solomon clapped his hands. As a mark of honor, he rose and ordered the steaming right leg and tail of lamb placed before her. He sank upon his own seat. The rest of the hundreds of distinguished guests sat with him.

Instantly each person was served with food and wine. A half dozen specially trained slaves were designated for each individual, to see that none of the courses should fail, that the golden plates should never be empty, that the golden, gemmed goblets should always be brimming. Seated as I was at the feet of Solomon, first to dangle my legs to sit at the low table, I could hear the murmurs of conversation between my king and his favored visitor.

"Your kingdom seems built of gold," Itamara ventured.

"We have been fortunate in trade," Solomon admitted, "but I hear that Sheba has much more that is precious."

"We owe it to the ants of India," explained the queen of Sheba. Curious, I strained to listen.

"The ants?" Solomon's eyes, between their lines of blue kohl, widened. "What have they to do with your gold?"

"They hold all such metal as their own," explained Itamara artlessly. "The ants live in the great deserts of India, less in size than dogs but larger than foxes. They have seven legs and four wings. They dig huge burrows underground and the earth they throw up is full of gold. The ants do not value it as gold but they are jealous of their work and protect it."

"How is the gold gathered?" asked the fascinated Solomon.

"The Indians who seek the gold take swift camels and approach the burrows of the ants at midday—when the ants are sleeping in their burrows. They hastily fill their saddlebags with sand and ride away as fast as they can."

"To escape the revenge of the ants?"

"Assuredly," Itamara said. "The ants are always roused by the vibrations of their footsteps, however light. They pour forth in pursuit. They run faster than camels for a short time—and therefore those that seek the gold always have a few beasts that are slower than the rest. These they turn loose in mid-flight. The ants stop and devour them."

Solomon stroked his beard thoughtfully. He glanced at me. "I see you are listening to everything, Nathan," he said. "Do you believe this story?"

"Do you allow your servants to listen to a queen?" demanded Itamara, her eyes sparkling with anger.

"Great queen," I said humbly, "I mean no harm. Your voice charmed me first, then your fascinating story enslaved me. I could listen forever—but I shall close my ears unless I have your gracious permission."

"Nathan is an old courtier," remarked Solomon, "and it is too late to change his habits. Once he was a prophet—but of late the Lord has not spoken to him," he finished sardonically.

"I did not realize your station was so exalted," Itamara said in a subdued tone to me. I felt a flush of pride in her commendation. "Certainly you are forgiven." She looked up smilingly at Solomon again. "But that story about gold is nothing compared to that of spices. The sailors come to my court, you understand, and I question them as you do me. It is thus they respond."

"Spices?" queried Solomon.

"There is frankincense which comes from a gum that we burn to make the spice. The trees that ooze with this substance are guarded by winged serpents—small in size and varied in color but deadly to the spice-seekers. Only the smoke of the burning gum drives them away."

"What of fragrant cinnamon?" Solomon was covertly amused but the queen of Sheba did not notice. She prattled on.

"Cinnamon comes from a far country where great birds gather the sticks to make their nests. They fasten them with mud to the faces of cliffs where none is able to climb. So our men cut oxen and asses into four quarters for bait. The birds carry these to their nests. The weight breaks them down, and we collect the cinnamon. But the worst of all is cassia."

"Tell me, my dear, about cassia."

"It grows in a shallow lake only. About the lake live numbers of winged animals resembling huge bats. They screech horribly and are very fierce, always trying to put out the eyes of a stranger with their beaks. The cassia seekers must disguise themselves under the hides of oxen. They use cudgels to beat them off with one hand while they pluck the cassia with the other."

"And what of ladanum, that sweet stuff which we use for incense?" Solomon inquired in a stifled voice. He placed his hand over his mouth.

"That is strangest of all," Itamara said, unnoticing. "It is gathered from the beards of he-goats who browse it off the bushes where it grows."

Unable to restrain himself any longer, the king burst into a loud guffaw. The queen of Sheba looked up at him in surprise. Her expression changed into indignation. With a lithe spring, she stood upright, tears gathering in her eyes. "I did not journey all this way into the north to be made a fool!" she exclaimed, her voice cutting through the din of the other feasters.

It was a tense moment. All the other diners, myself included, had seen the queen rise. Out of rigid court ceremony, we too had risen. Solomon alone remained seated. Controlling his mirth, he reached out. He took Itamara by her small, soft, trembling hand.

"Come, my dear," he said soothingly. He exerted all the

pleasing arts that he knew so well how to exercise over women. "Sit down. Accept the greatest gift that I can give you: the apology of a king in his own house. I did not laugh at you nor your marvelous stories, Itamara."

"Then at what?" she demanded, eyes angrily averted from his wooing.

Solomon chuckled again. "I have met many he-goats," he said, "but none whose beards smelled as sweet as ladanum." He raised her hand to his lips and kissed it. "See," he declared, "my own beard is fragrant with the same scent."

Itamara could not resist his overtures. The smile began in her eyes, struggled through her cheeks, and bloomed on her lips. Solomon tugged gently at her hand. She sat down beside him again. With her subsided the rest of the revelers.

"Now I have a gift to soothe your humor," Solomon said. He signaled for silence. The hall grew quiet. From the recesses of his robe he took a slender phial of alabaster, as thin as shell, carved with delicate figures and containing some dark substance. He raised it above the queen of Sheba's head.

"As aromatic oil was poured over the foundation stone of the temple," Solomon said loudly, "and as such oil was poured upon me by the servants of Yahweh, so do I give the contents of this costly vase to you, O queen. Not for your peculiar holiness but for peculiar honor." So saying, he broke the phial on the back of her head. Almost instantly, heavenly fumes filled the warm room from end to end. Itamara smiled up at him.

I was somehow shocked but there was nothing really impious in what Solomon had done. He had simply bestowed upon her an honor which none of the Hebrews had ever seen before, one that had previously been reserved for the rituals devoted to Yahweh. I lowered my head. I paid full attention to my platter of gold.

"Gold is not found as you have been told, cherished Itamara," Solomon said. "It is found in lumps and nuggets in the rock, in the earth. If you wish more gold, then the female and the male gold must be distinguished—for the gold resembles men in this wise—and buried close to each other. They will then produce children which resemble themselves."

I nodded in approval. Solomon was correct. We had been told this many times by the most expert miners of gold. It had been found to be true in the hills where gold was found. Solomon caught my expression of approval and was pleased. He bent closer to the upturned face of Itamara. "Such is true of precious stones, as well," he told her. "Even the most rare gems obey these laws of reproduction."

"When I return to my kingdom," the queen of Sheba said, not without some vagueness, "I shall have the heads of those who have told me lies."

"Be not severe with them," Solomon said, fondly gazing upon her. "Prospectors and sailors lead lonely lives. They tell such tales to while away the time."

"Nevertheless," Itamara said—and stopped. Solomon bent over her. "Kings, too, are lonely in their work," he said.

Itamara looked away from him, her eyes suffused and beautiful. "All things work alike to the glory of the gods," she said softly.

"To one god. To Yahweh."

She smiled deliciously. By accident, it appeared, she touched the king on his beringed hand. "On such a night as this," she murmured, "I shall not argue like a priest."

"Nor I," Solomon whispered ardently. I engaged my neighbor, some drunken ambassador from Assyria who was beating on the table with his golden spoon to demand more wine, in hasty, overloud conversation.

As the feast continued the hall grew perceptibly warmer. The hordes of black slaves, rushing back and forth with their platters of meat and jugs of wine, increased. From the ceiling golden nets suspended, filled with many-colored flower petals, were shaken by other slaves. A delicious rain descended upon the guests. The tumult grew louder.

Solomon put a finger in his goblet. He drew out a petal. "This," he said, "is like your cheeks, Itamara."

She smiled and looked away, her eyes humid from wine. I myself thought it was rather an insipid compliment but I realized that the wits of even the wisest king might become befuddled on such an occasion as this.

Other slaves passed behind each guest. On their heads they broke eggshells filled with perfume. Almost immediately the hall became filled with intoxicating odors. More and more it appeared to me that our guests—in spite of a few who had gone outside to vomit and return—were pushing aside food for wine. The feast was becoming abandoned.

"I have never experienced such a glorious hour," murmured the queen of Sheba to Solomon.

"You will see a thousand more of them," Solomon said drunkenly.

He raised his braceleted arm in a signal. Almost immediately the doors were opened. The throng of court women poured in, as was the custom at the end of every state banquet. Naturally, the wives and concubines of Solomon were forbidden at any feast—except alone with their master—inasmuch as this would be the same as throwing open the treasures of his kingdom.

With little shrieks of pleasure and excitement, the mass of females separated. They broke like a warm wave of flesh upon the diners. They were clad in every costume to entrance the eye, to take the lustful imagination. Forbidden until this moment, they surrounded the guests with soft enticements. Most of them were instantly pulled down beside the banqueters. Bodies became inextricably tangled. Cheeks, bare shoulders, breasts, were the object of the greedy lips of the men.

I could stand it no longer. I rose to my feet. What disgusted me most was the sight of Zadok, high priest of Yahweh, rolling about the floor in unrestrained passion with one of the king's handmaidens.

I was not alone. Solomon and Itamara rose with me. He assisted her with his arm. "You were right," Solomon said to me. "Love is better in private."

It must have been the din of the feast and the wine in my had that deadened my perceptions, Before I realized it, a figure rushed upon the royal pair. I recognized her at the last moment: it was Tamar. I was too late to stop her. It was Solomon himself who fended off her rush at Itamara, placing himself between them.

"Will you go back to Sheba, whining bitch of bitches?" screamed Tamar. But Itamara did not retreat. In the gleam of the lamps her white teeth shone in a half-smile. Her expression was feral.

"You shall not touch me," she said softly. "I am a queen."

"What am I?" exclaimed Tamar. Itamara did not answer her but inclined her head slowly to one side in a motion that was more contemptuous than any words.

I stared dully at them all, appalled but unable to act. Solomon, half-sobered by this untoward happening, pulled his wits together. "This is no place for you, Tamar," he said severely. "The women of the king are forbidden these feasts. You expose to the vulgar the jewels of my kingdom."

Tamar paid no attention to his words. She strained like a wild beast at the queen of Sheba. I felt the dull thudding of alarm in my heart.

"I shall kill you!" Tamar hissed. Her eyes glinted in the room, her skin glistened in the exudations of rage.

"Does the beloved one of Solomon kill her own kin?" asked Itamara disdainfully.

"What do you say?"

"Has not Solomon told you?"

"Told me? Speak quickly!"

"Of what I shall carry in my belly," Itamara replied.

Tamara glared at the impassive king. She spoke to Itamara while watching Solomon. "He has told me nothing," she grated.

"Tell her then, my dear," Itamara said to Solomon.

"Do you dare tell me," demanded Tamar of him at the same moment, "that she will carry your child?"

"Yes," Solomon said flatly. His tone was so unmoved that I felt it to be a deliberate provocation to Tamar.

If so, it had its calculated result. Tamar gave a passionate cry—one of desolation and grief, of rage and frustration. She lashed out at Itamara heavily. Solomon intercepted her hand. Her ringed knuckles scored a weal across his bronze arm. "See the royal whore!" shrieked Tamar.

The soft sound of the gong beside Solomon paralyzed her, stopped her voice. In response to the signal, the royal guard of the door stepped next to the king and saluted.

"Take that woman and bind her," Solomon said, pointing to Tamar. "She has violated the king's commands, and shall be punished." He had got control of himself. His tone was deliberate.

For a moment, everything held still in tableau. Into my mind flashed the disapproving thought that, although it was not unusual for a king and queen to cement friendship between their countries by the union of their bodies and offspring—still it should have been done with ceremony and dignity. I blamed Tamar for this unseemly revelation.

Tamar made an involuntary, furious movement toward him. But the stalwart soldier seized her. He held her, despite her struggles. Both Itamara—still unmoving as a statue—and Solomon watched the wrestling, disheveled woman with a curiosity that was almost inhuman. Solomon's voice cut coldly through her muffled cries.

"Yes," he said. "Itamara and I shall make love. It is on such a night as this—warm, fragrant, a moon like a blaze in the sky, with music, and perfume and silken coverings in my chamber. She is willing. I shall take the offering of her body—and she will give me back a child. What have you given me, Tamar?"

"She may carry a child but it will not be yours," panted Tamar.

"We shall have a child," said Itamara, so softly that only I heard. "His name shall be Menelik, He Who Is Weighed and Chosen—for you and I, Solomon, do tonight only what we wish."

Solomon made no answer. His eyes shone moist, dreamy with desire. He raised her in his arms and she looked up at him like one in a radiant dream. No one else, it seemed, out of all the drunken and riotous feast saw them go—except the anguished Tamar, still the prisoner of the guard in the corner. In one mighty, desperate effort, she broke loose from his hold. But she made no attempt to follow the king and his lovely visitor. Instead, with a strangled cry of agony, she plunged out of the door into the darkness.

"Itamara should not have told Tamar that she was about to be kin," I remarked to no one in particular, "because the line of Jesse and David has a long record of killing its own." I hiccuped pleasantly and felt relieved.

My attention was solicited by a tapping on my elbow. I turned about with dignity, since I was the ranking worthy at the feast after the departure of Solomon. To my surprise, it was Elihaph. I blinked owlishly at him, not sure there was one or two of the scribe before me.

"Yes?" I inquired. "Yes?"

Elihaph crept near me. His lips writhed in a whisper.

"Did you see the prince Rehoboam arrive at the feast?" he murmured.

"Yes," I said. I looked across the ebony table but the place of Rehoboam was empty. I bent a frown upon Elihaph.

"He came, he was here, he was drunk," said the scribe softly. "He is gone outside. It is a rich and dazzling night. Only this last moment did he go."

"Very well," I said.

"The prince is enjoying himself. Very much. The prince, good Nathan, is a man. Especially with one of the women who entered the hall. With Maachah, the granddaughter of Absalom."

CHAPTER SEVENTEEN

The Sickness of Solomon

Two days after the feast of the queen of Sheba, Solomon fell sick. It happened altogether unexpectedly. His fit came during the early hours of the morning, when we were about to conclude the routine business of the kingdom. He had just dismissed a messenger from the Syrian kingdom, disdainfully ordering his hair to be shorn and the clippings stuffed in his mouth as an answer to the threats from the north.

Abruptly he seemed to stiffen on the throne. I stared up at him. Luckily, we were alone. I had only a few of the usual documents ready for his six-pointed seal. Solomon did not move. His face turned pale, his shaking hands gripped the arms of his golden throne. I was alarmed. "What is the matter, great king?" I asked.

Solomon gave me a high look, one full of hauteur and resentment. His head cocked queerly to one side. He stared at me with glassy eyes. "The king must be obeyed," he said in a shrill voice. "The king will be obeyed."

"Submission and obedience, O Lord," I said, bowing in fear.

As I rose from my kneeling position, Solomon glared at me in a way that was even more peculiar. He seemed to twist on the throne. "The king must be obeyed," he repeated faintly. I caught him as he fell, straight forward into my arms. His body felt ten times heated. His face flushed, his tongue was scarlet. I cried out for the guard. I ordered him to be carried to his sleeping chamber immediately.

Posthaste, I sent a messenger to summon Zadok, the high priest, and those of his assistants who knew about such matters as these. I stood by in the room while they inspected the inert body of the king—not touching him, of course—and put their heads together in consultation.

"What is it?" I asked Zadok.

The fat little man shook his head ominously. "I have never seen this before," he said. "It is like one of the plagues Moses sent upon the Egyptians."

"Is it a plague from Yahweh?" I asked fearfully. "Is that what you say?"

Zadok raised his brows expressively. He said nothing, but I knew his thoughts. As a matter of fact, I shared them: that the Lord had brought His vengeance upon Solomon for his misdeeds.

In the midst of our anguished silence, there was a stir at the door. I looked over my shoulder to see who dared enter the room at such a moment. I saw, to my surprise, that it was Itamara herself. The queen of Sheba had come alone and unannounced. She moved toward the couch. Zadok and the priests fell back as she advanced. We stood on either side of the king, who moaned slightly, and looked at each other without speaking.

The queen stooped. She drew her fingers across the hot, dry forehead of Solomon. She glanced up at me. "He is very ill," she said.

"I know," I replied. "No one has any thought of what it is. What may be done?"

Itamara shook her head. "I have seen this before," she said, "in my own country. It is a killing fever brought by the tiny insects that buzz and bite at night. In my land, as in Egypt, it is well known. We are very careful about such things. Clouds of these insects gather where there is no wind but they do not rise above a certain height. So we build towers for sleeping in those places where it is windless. But if we are forced to sleep on the ground, we kindle fires with much smoke to drive them away, or sleep under linen netting."

"If you are so well acquainted with this disease, O queen," I said, "then surely the wise men of your country must have found a way to save the lives of those afflicted." I felt a quick rise of hope.

"It is very difficult," the queen of Sheba murmured. "Much of it lies with the gods whether such afflicted die or become well."

"Is there any wise man in your train who knows the cure?"

The queen shook her head. "I brought no such men with me," she said.

I wrung my hands. "Then Solomon will die," I said despairingly.

Itamara gazed calmly at me with her huge black eyes. "I know something of the lore of healing," she admitted. "Such as was taught me as a girl by my mother. But what I know is very ancient. It may not be successful."

"Great queen!" I cried, falling to my knees. "Solomon must be saved! His life must not be surrendered to the demons!"

The queen of Sheba looked away from me, her expression full of doubt. "I do not know if I may cure him," she said nervously. "I only know that with others I have had healing powers for such a sickness, this wasting that makes the body seem as if cinders had fallen on it. In my land, it attacks those who live near the swamps or the rivers. They are seized, as is Solomon, by stiffness, then by a trembling which shakes them so that they cannot walk. If such a one lies down, he is attacked by cold. Fever comes again, then chills, then heat once again until the sick man lies as the king does now. Moaning, as you see, out of his mind with fever and fear."

"The king must be made well," I said fervently.

"Perhaps this is not the same disease. How can it be? You have no swamps near Jerusalem. The city itself is on a high place."

I thought rapidly. "Just before your arrival," I said, "King Solomon returned from a visit to the south—to the city of Ezion Geber, on the gulf of Elath. Perhaps there are swamps in that region."

Itamara nodded. "I have seen them," she said.

"Then it must be the same. I beg you to try what you know to save his life!"

"Possibly the remedy I know works only with our own people—or in our own country."

"Gracious Itamara, it must be tried! The king lies near death!"

"But what I shall do may be thought indecent and sacrilegious in your land," the queen of Sheba said. "I am in the jaws of the lion. My people, who would understand and defend me, are far away."

"You will do what you do at my request," I said boldly. "The responsibility shall be mine."

"And if the king dies? Dies, in spite of all? Shall I not be accused of having used witchcraft and charmed him out of life?"

"I am the prophet of the Lord," I said proudly. "What I do, I do in His name."

Itamara looked at me skeptically. "What of the priests?"

she asked. She inclined her head toward the corner where Zadok and the others mumbled among themselves.

For a moment I could find nothing to say. Then the needed words came to me by inspiration. "Great queen," I said solemnly, "I can only beg your assistance. Not for the kingdom of the Hebrews, not for the power and glory of Solomon, but for Solomon himself. You and he have been lovers. Perhaps there will be a child, your child. Could you tell this child that you refused to save the life of his father?"

The queen of Sheba stared at me imperiously for a long moment. "You must clear the room," she said.

This I hastened to do, in spite of the protests of Zadok and his crew. I turned to her for further instructions.

"Bring cloths soaked in perfume," she said. "Strip the body of the king naked. Place it on the floor."

"Nothing else?" I asked.

"Nothing. Except a jar of stone or clay. You must bar the door and admit no one but us two to his chambers for the next three days."

Wondering—and not a little in doubt—I did as she required, bringing her a jar of carved, transparent alabaster lipped with gold. As I turned back to her after barring the door, I saw that she had already stripped the body of Solomon herself. I helped her lay him on the cypress floor. Then I watched in fascination. Itamara commenced to divest her own clothing, until she was almost as naked before me as Solomon.

She stood over the stark, unconscious body of the king, clad only in the filmiest of skirts. She knelt beside Solomon. Lovingly, she pressed a kiss upon his fevered forehead. Her slender fingers caressed the marks upon his body, red spots that seemed as if he had been beneath a fall of fire-cinders. She tucked the perfumed cloths about his neck, being careful to let his mouth and nose—with their stertorous breathing—free of all impediment.

Then Itamara stood erect. She took the jar and straddled it, setting wide her graceful legs. She looked upward to heaven. Her graceful arms made a gesture of entreaty. "Grant that this fire of the flesh may be quenched," she said in a prayer so soft that I barely heard it. "Give me the power of the goddess Isis who saved Horus in just such a way. Let the healing flood of waters that I have between my thighs pour over the body of this man, to wash him clean of this fire."

She gestured to me. "Give me drink, of water only," she

said. I hastened to bring her a bedside gourd. She drank deeply. She looked upward again. '*Edera'edesane 'ederagaga 'edesana matmu edesana!*" Itamara cried. It was a language I did not understand and have never heard before or since. She gestured again for drink. I brought it. She said reverently: "Water in my mouth, the Nile between my legs."

She filled her mouth and cast the gourd away. She straddled wider and squatted. To my stupefaction, torrents of her urine poured out into the jar. She moved aside and, cupping her hands, poured the warm stinking fluid over the king, massaging every corner of his body furiously. I did not know what to do: whether to rage or to weep at this desecration of a king by a woman even though she were a queen.

Next instant, she bounded from him. She took me by the arm as I stood paralyzed. "I shall eat nothing today, tomorrow, the next day, but leeks, radishes, garlic, onions," she said rapidly. "I shall drink nothing but clear water."

Before I knew, she had left me alone in the chamber with Solomon, the king of glory who had fallen so low in his sickness as to be treated thus. I had no idea whether I had done wrong or right. I only knew that the illness of Solomon—if some remedy was not effective—would be his death.

Therefore, I ordered his bedchamber—as Itamara had ordered—to be closely guarded at all times. No one was admitted except myself and the queen of Sheba. Twice more she performed this outrageous rite of healing on the king and her hands massaged him from head to foot with the waters from between her legs. She demanded that he remain in his befouled condition for at least two hours after every treatment. Only then was I able to cleanse his body and bear him to another chamber.

At the end of the third day, I was aware of a growing change in the nature of Solomon's illness. He could drink only cool water and light broth yet it was apparent he was slowly recovering. But he was still too weak to talk, to do more than make feeble signals with his fingers.

"He is still a sick man," Itamara told me. "And he must rest. I shall return to my own country."

"But you must stay until the king recovers!" I protested.

Itamara smiled. Her clear childish face with its expressive eyes, the proud head set on a swan's neck, entranced me. She touched me gently on the cheek. "I have seen the wisdom of Solomon in the house that he has built," she said. "I have eaten the meat of his table and I have seen the sitting of his servants and the attendants of his court and their apparel. I have seen his cupbearers and the ascent by which he goes up into the house of the Lord. I came here as a proud woman and a queen—but I go away humbly."

"You have not heard the wisdom of Solomon," I objected. "That is our true treasure."

"I came to Jerusalem with a great company, with spices and much gold, with precious stones. I thought these were more than wisdom. But in the night your king and I spent together we communed with each other concerning all that was in our hearts. My questions were answered, my treasures put to shame. There is nothing hid from your king."

"Happy are the subjects of Itamara," I told her, bowing deeply.

"No," she said. "Happy are the servants of Solomon who stand continually before him and that hear his wisdom. Your god Yahweh must delight in the throne of the Hebrews."

"Will you not stay until the king recovers?" I implored her.

Her hands passed over her body in a strange stroking movement, as a miser might caress his treasure. "King Solomon has given the queen of Sheba all her desire," she said.

Despite all I could say she dismissed me. She ordered her servants to make ready for the return to Sheba. But first she deposited in the royal treasury one hundred and twenty talents of gold and a great abundance of spices.

Four days later, the day before that which was decreed by the queen of Sheba that she would leave Jerusalem, I came up the hill toward the palace. As I walked through the dusk, I could see the camels, which had formed the long train of the queen, being loaded with their burdens and gifts from Solomon in return.

A little farther apart, tethered to a stake in the ground, leather strap about his great hoof, was the behemoth. His gray skin crawled and jerked under the sun, as he swayed in his place. He flapped his huge ears continually against the flies. Now and again he would throw back his strange nose and utter a trumpeting sound. But the children of Jerusalem had learned that this monster with his tiny twinkling eyes and good nature was nothing to frighten them. They clapped their hands, they teased him with switches, and fed him bits of food.

I stopped to watch them at their play. As I did I felt a touch on my arm. I turned to confront Benaiah.

"An excellent animal for war," he remarked, watching the

behemoth. "Properly trained, such creatures might crush a whole army of men."

"He is too gentle," I said. "He eats grass like the ox and loves to lie under the shady trees and in the reeds. He is too lazy to be fierce."

"Still," said Benaiah, "if we had our stables full of such animals, trained to war, we might conquer the world."

As he spoke, the behemoth sucked dry a large jar full of water. It sprayed the delighted, screaming children who scrambled to get away. Benaiah grunted. He strode stiffly off.

I continued on my way to the palace. There I found Solomon still feeble but able to speak his farewell to the queen of Sheba. What transpired between them during those last moments, no one knows. No one was with him in his private rooms just before the queen set out for Sheba in the cool of the evening. But I have heard since that she asked him many questions—and that Solomon gave her the single answer that always satisfies a woman.

The problem which now lay before me after her departure was the stewardship of Solomon's kingdom. Rehoboam was too young to take his father's place. It was clearly my responsibility. I acted in it as best I knew, with the hand of the Lord extended to me in many prayers and meditations. But I still believed that the best act of my short administrative reign was the one which Solomon later denounced most savagely.

I must say how it came about. It was on a twilight evening, when I ascended to the roof of the palace to escape from the stifling air of the rooms below. To my surprise, in the dim golden light, I saw another figure squatted near the edge of the roof. I recognized who it was by the hunched shoulders, gnarled muscles, and close-cut hair. It was Hiram-abi, no more than a few days returned from his duties of construction in Solomon's network of Hebrew strongholds.

Hiram-abi had finished designing fifteen chariot stables for Solomon, long structures divided into three aisles by square stone pillars, each stall having a stone manger and a hole in the corner for tethering horses. At Megiddo, one of fifteen such stables, he had made provisions for one hundred and fifty chariots—or four hundred and fifty horses.

In addition Hiram-abi had planned a series of border fortresses, especially along the Egyptian frontier. These could be entered on foot only by a small gate. This could be approached in turn only by a steep winding path in full view of the guards. There were great cisterns for water, huge buried jars of wine and corn.

The plan for the chariot gates of these cities was unique and wonderful. Strangers were forced to drive along a narrow one-chariot road to a battlemented gate, square towers on either side. This led into a courtyard surrounded by other square towers—all occupied by sentinels and guards. Turning left, the visitor was faced with a second, stronger gate, armored and towered like the first. This led into a stone-roofed passage more than sixty feet long, lined with loopholes and guardrooms where any passerby might be inspected again and again.

Now, knowing Hiram-abi's extraordinary energy, I wondered at his stillness. As the light thickened on the roof, minute after minute, Hiram-abi made no move. He might have been a graven image, perched where he was to protect the palace. At last my curiosity overcame my scruples. I rose and approached him.

"You sit here a long time, Hiram-abi," I said.

"Yes," he said.

He squatted where he was, looking westward. The slatting of the palms Solomon had planted, the ripple of the fountain, the distant fading cries of the vendors in the streets and marketplaces of Jerusalem came up to us like strange incantations. I had noticed the grizzled Phoenician artificer at this perch early in the morning. Now it was late afternoon and he had not stirred. Idle designs were traced in the dirt at his feet by his fingers.

"Are you not lonely?" I asked curiously.

"Yes."

"You choose loneliness?"

"My work is over," Hiram-abi said. "The stables at Megiddo, the gates of Hazor are finished. All that is left to me is to watch the sky and the hills, to see the blink of the sea in the distance."

I shaded my eyes against the glare of the setting sun and stared out in the blue direction that Hiram watched. "There is nothing to be seen there," I said. "Are you sick for your home in Tyre?"

"No," Hiram-abi said.

I grew impatient. "There is no need for the man who is most honored by Solomon of any to sit in this eyrie all day like a black crow," I told him.

Hiram-abi raised lackluster eyes to mine. "You, too, tell me my color?" he asked.

"Nothing of the kind," I said, astounded. "What do you mean? This is another kind of illness."

"Perhaps," he said.

Careless of my fine white robe, I squatted down beside the little artist in metals and stone. "The sky is empty except for hawks," I said, "and the hills are empty except for lions, and the sea is empty except for fish. Why do you sit here, you, the man of mighty craft?"

"I wait."

"One must wait for something."

"I wait to die," Hiram-abi said lugubriously.

I drew back. I commenced to laugh. "Here is the true sickness," I said, "that of love. You are in love, confess it!"

"I confess it," Hiram-abi said in a low tone.

"Who is the woman?"

Hiram-abi said nothing. I repeated my question and added: "Does she love another?"

"Tamar loves me," said Hiram-abi. "But she belongs to Solomon."

I stood up slowly, feeling my face grow cold, despite the afternoon heat. I could find no words.

"I wait to gain the courage to dash myself from this rooftop," Hiram-abi murmured.

"That is not the wish of a man," I said sharply. "You are honored of kings as I wish I might be, here and in your own land."

Hiram-abi nodded. "But I am not you, I am not the king of Tyre though I was named for him, nor am I King Solomon. I am merely myself, who loves Tamar."

"Each man is himself, certainly—but it is evil and foolish to talk of taking life for love."

Hiram-abi sighed deeply. I decided to test him.

"He who is higher than you, more favored than you, does he love Tamar?"

"I do not know."

"Would she not tell you?"

"She tells me nothing. She teases me, laughs at me, but tells me nothing."

"Would she scorn you if you had godlike ancestors, a great name, and mighty deeds?"

"Is not love more than all those?" demanded Hiram-abi, turning his monkey face and longing eyes up to me.

I sighed in turn. "I say they are much more but you who are smitten will not believe me. Fortunate is the man who escapes in time, like the fowl from the limed net, from love."

Hiram-abi rose. With a swift movement, he sprang to the side of the roof. He hesitated, then launched himself headfirst over. I sprang upon him just in time, bearing him down half upon the edge. He did not struggle; I dragged him back.

"You are a madman," I said with conviction, looking down at him.

"There will come a time, Nathan, when you will not be here," he said dully.

"You cannot disgrace yourself and our king," I said, panting angrily at him. "If Solomon did not send you safely home, Hiram might declare war against the Hebrews."

"What does it matter?"

"A woman is a matter of indifference. A man like yourself can have many women."

"Indifferent to you, perhaps, as a holy man—and I want only one."

Shaking my head as I gazed at this lovesick artisan, I was struck by a sudden thought. "Tamar, you say, favors you?" I demanded.

"You are trying to trick me."

"I swear that I ask only for your good," I exclaimed.

Hiram-abi looked up at me suspiciously. "We have met," he said.

"Does she return your love?"

"Yes!" he shouted, leaping to his feet.

I was forced to put my hands on his shoulders to still his quivering. At last he had thrown away all restraint.

"Very well," I said soothingly. "Very well. There is no need to announce your love to all Jerusalem. I have a suggestion." Hiram-abi glared at me as I went on. "I suggest," I said, "that you take your beloved Tamar and leave Jerusalem. That both of you return to Tyre."

Hiram-abi fell back, flabbergasted. "But—but—the king!" he stammered.

"Your work for him is done," I said. "And for many more days he will lie ill in his chamber."

"But so many difficulties!"

"I will overcome them."

"But Solomon!"

"I will persuade him."

"But my own king!" said Hiram-abi despairingly. "What will he say when I return with one of the harem of Solomon?"

"He will say nothing," I assured him. "Is there another craftsman in the world who is your equal?"

"Not one," replied Hiram-abi pridefully.

"A man like yourself is worth a hundred women, as I said, even those of a king."

Hiram-abi's face fell. He shook his head. "Impossible," he said. "Tamar is the chief jewel among Solomon's women. If he were to discover that she was gone into Tyre, there would be war between him and my king. I cannot do this."

I considered him thoughtfully. "You have forgotten that our king promised you anything you desired in his kingdom," I said. Hiram-abi's face lost some of its lugubrious expression.

"That is true," he said. "And I have asked nothing."

I pressed him further. "How did you come to know Tamar, Hiram-abi?" I asked him. "The harem is not an easy place to enter."

Hiram-abi's face began to assume the ghost of the ironic smile I knew so well. "There are rooftops, even as the one from which David first saw Bathsheba. Guards may be bribed and windows opened. And do not forget, Nathan, it was I who designed the quarters of the women for Solomon."

"But these are small meetings on which to build your great passion," I said.

"There is something more," replied Hiram-abi. "I knew Tamar long before she was taken by Solomon."

I became thoughtful. This was an opportunity not to be lost. If I could spirit Tamar out of the kingdom of the Hebrews, she would no longer be able to influence Rehoboam. I might still be able to prevent the young prince's marriage to Maachah, the seed of Absalom, the alliance that the scheming Tamar desired to consummate.

"Are you sure Tamar will go with you?"

Hiram-abi nodded. "She has been confined by the king ever since the arrival of the queen of Sheba," he said. "Her love for Solomon has turned to gall."

"Very well," I said slowly. "I shall help you to take her away."

Hiram-abi regarded me suspiciously. "How can I be sure," he said, "that you do not lead me into a trap with such words?"

"What I do, I do for the sake of the kingdom," I said loftily. "It is to the best interest of the king and his children that Tamar leave Jerusalem." With that I proceeded to explain to Hiram-abi how desirable it was that the progeny of rebellious Absalom be prevented from occupying the throne. Hiram-abi nodded again and again as he listened. Finally, he seemed convinced that I spoke in good faith. I went on rapidly to give him my instructions. He pledged that he would follow them.

The next night, before moonrise, it was done. From an outside window of the harem building—next to the city wall—a rope tied to a large reed basket was lowered to the precipitous path below. The basket contained Tamar and a small bundle of her jewels and clothing. Waiting for her, with two onagers, was Hiram-abi.

They stole away in the dark and I had no doubt that their trip to Tyre would be successful. What was left, of course, was to explain it to the king. What I did not anticipate was that I would also have to explain it to the young prince, Rehoboam.

Not that he had seen Tamar depart. But I was a fool not to have realized that she would not have gone without bidding her adopted favorite a long farewell.

"He should be impaled upon the city walls, as the Assyrians punish!" cried Rehoboam. He pointed at me, his accusing finger seeming a cubit long.

Solomon looked wanly at me. "You are accused of robbing the king of the Hebrews, Nathan," he said. "You are said to have stolen one of the king's chiefest jewels among women and of having encouraged her to escape with my servant Hiram-abi."

"All this I have done," I said boldly, lifting myself from my obeisance.

"Benaiah tells me that Tamar was freed on your request," Solomon went on in a weak, relentless voice.

"That is true," I said. "I have only one request to make of mighty Solomon."

"I will hear it."

"That I might speak to the king alone."

Solomon lifted his arm and made a languid signal. Rehoboam squared about and marched out. Behind him followed the guards, who closed the doors of the chamber. Solomon gazed at me with somber, dark-ringed eyes. His health was returning but slowly; he still was unable to rise. I had watched his face while Rehoboam had denounced me and I was surprised to see that the king's features remained calm, without visible emotion.

"Why have you abused your powers?" he asked. "What have you to confess?"

"What I have done," I said, "I freely admit. I blame no one else. But I say to you, O Solomon, that I was justified."

"Explain this mystery to me, Nathan," Solomon said slowly. "It will be more amusing than the riddles of Hiram himself."

I set myself to my task. "Great Solomon," I said, "the jewel of your harem was already fouled. Haram-abi had lain with Tamar—he confessed as much to me."

Solomon roused himself. "How was this possible?" he demanded.

"You will recall, O my lord, that it was Hiram-abi who designed and built the quarters for the women. There were entrances and hiding places of which no one else knew. And Hiram-abi knew her before you deigned to accept her."

Solomon looked darkly up at me. "If this is so," he said, "why did you not order them both to be executed?"

"The woman meant nothing," I said. "Since you and Itamara were lovers, Tamar has been filled with hate and bitterness against you. But Hiram-abi—that was a different matter. He was most skilled among all the workers of Tyre, sent to you by his master as a special favor. If he were slain—for whatever reason—there would be war between the kingdom of Tyre and the kingdom of the Hebrews."

"Why did you not keep them prisoners?" Solomon asked. "In such a case, I would have judged them myself at a later time."

I drew a deep breath. What I said was to be a monstrous lie but it was one which I could not escape. "I had a vision from Yahweh," I said steadily. "He commanded me that the twain should be set free and given help on the road to Tyre."

Solomon was silent for a time. His sunken eyes watched me. After awhile I could not endure this mordant gaze. "Besides," I said desperately, "I had such another example before me, that of a king who set free an Egyptian princess to return to her own land with a Hebrew subject."

"That was a matter of state," Solomon said slowly.

"This was no less, O king," I replied.

Solomon turned his face away from me, toward the wall. I saw him shudder along his length on the couch. When he looked at me again, I found to my alarm that his face was wet with tears. He must have seen the fright in my countenance for he managed a sigh and a twisted smile.

"They have told me that Itamara is gone back to her own country," Solomon said.

"She could not wait, O king."

"I have had many women," Solomon said, "and I have been envied of men. But none of them has been true to me for love's sake." He sat upright on his couch, a tremulous angry man. "What reason had you to let Tamar depart?" he cried. "She was not beautiful but she was an enchantress."

"Remember, O king," I said deliberately, "that she stole the affection of Rehoboam and cunningly coupled him with the girl Maachah."

"Is that what you complain of?"

"That was the vision," I said. "It was a scheme to set another line than yours upon the throne. For you know that this girl with whom Rehoboam is infatuated is of the tainted blood of Absalom, the rebel against David, your old rival. His kin still plot against you."

Solomon did not seem to hear me. "And Tamar?" he asked. "Did she leave willingly? I cannot believe that."

"Very willingly."

"She was not forced?"

"Perhaps she was frightened by your wrath at the feast," I said.

"But she is gone?"

"Yes."

"I cannot, I will not believe that she did not adore me," Solomon said, bewildered. "I cannot think she would prefer an artisan to a king."

"Women cannot be trusted," I replied.

Solomon sank back among the exotic furs and pillows of his bed. He stared upward for a long moment. Then, without looking at me, he said quietly: "Send me Rehoboam. Do you remain, too, Nathan."

I hastened to obey. Rehoboam swaggered in, stalwart in his young manhood, and halted by the couch. "You have commanded me to come, my father," he said with a scowling glance toward me.

"Help me," Solomon said to me. I assisted him to sit upright, propping him with cushions and bolsters. At last he was comfortable. He waved me away.

"I wish to speak to you, not as a father to his son but as a counselor," he said firmly, drawing energy from some unknown source. His glance became piercing as he bent it on the prince.

"I listen and heed," Rehoboam said, bending his head.

"My son," Solomon said, "you will remember these, my commandments. Keep my words in your heart."

"My father Solomon," said Rehoboam, "I will."

"Say to wisdom, you are my sister, and make understanding your kinswoman. These will keep you from strange women who flatter with words."

"I understand, my father," said Rehoboam.

"I have sat at the window of the palace," continued Solomon, "and looked through the lattice. I saw among the sons of simplicity a young man without understanding passing through the street on his way to the house of a woman in the evening of the day."

Solomon stopped. He kept his eyes on his son. Rehoboam stood silent.

"Behold!" Solomon said. "A woman in the dress of a whore and subtle of heart caught him and kissed him. She said impudently, 'I have peace offering with me, and this day I have paid my vows. Therefore I came to meet you and I have found you.' She took the young man into a chamber whose walls were covered with tapestry and striped cloths of the fine linen of Egypt. I knew her bed was perfumed. With myrrh, aloes, and cinnamon, was it not? Do you know, Rehoboam, the young man of whom I speak?"

Rehoboam stood stiffly before his father, his face brick-red either from anger or shame. His lips did not move. His fists were clenched.

"Such a woman would say," said Solomon, " 'let us take our fill of love till the morning, let us comfort ourselves for the king is ill. With fair speech and the flattery of her lips she causes him to yield. He goes after her as an ox to the slaughter, or a bird to the snare. And he knows not that his life and a kingdom are at stake."

The effect of so much speaking had exhausted Solomon. He leaned back, limp on the couch. He closed his eyes and spoke again, "Listen to me then, O my son," he said. "Do not let your heart follow her ways and lead you astray. Such a one has slain many strong men. Her couch is the way to the grave. It goes down to the chambers of death."

I could see Rehoboam—always haughty and high of temper—begin to shake where he stood. But he could not move. Solomon had not given him permission to go.

"Between her legs," Solomon said distinctly, "are the gates of hell. You have heard my parable and its warning. You will seek wisdom in the schools, you will curb your desires. You will remember that you are my son and that women are nothing. You may go."

Stiff-legged as an animal ready to fight, Rehoboam turned. He went out for the second time, his head high and muscles tense. He would have slammed the tall door of the room except that the guard on duty outside caught it and latched it softly.

Left with Solomon, I found his attention had turned to me once more. The king was weak—but not too weak to let his will be known.

"This is not the last of this," he murmured through his pale lips. "You have done great wrong, Nathan. It must be set right. I shall recover from this sickness. When I am strong enough, I shall go to Tyre myself and demand Tamar of Hiram, the king. It is not a matter of intrigue but one of justice. You shall go with me, Nathan, to confess your part in the whole." Solomon shook his head helplessly. "It is unnatural, out of the order of things," he said.

CHAPTER EIGHTEEN

The Visit to Hiram

Six weeks later Solomon was on his feet, using his ceremonial scepter privately as a cane. He was still weak but his determination was firm. He was restless—eager, for the first time in his life—to visit another kingdom. He had not forgotten what had been his chief spur back to health, the desire to see his onetime friend, Hiram of Tyre, face to face and demand his own. His growing convalescence sealed his mood. He shut himself up for days on end, seeing no one. Later I discovered that he had spent his time writing bitter parables and proverbs, mostly against womankind—hundreds of them. He had in addition, like his father David, composed many melancholy songs in his solitude. But David had celebrated such primitive emotions as joy, grief, repentance, and faith. Solomon had on the contrary mused on the changeableness and vanity of all existence in a much more sophisticated mood.

His feelings toward me were mixed, I knew. Solomon believed what I had claimed was the will of Yahweh but he heartily disliked it and was therefore inclined to be suspicious of my advice. I was hardly on the best of terms with my king—and the pangs of my own conscience were torment in my soul. It was true that I had sent Tamar and Hiram-abi away for reasons which I still considered were the best for the well-being of the king and the state. But I could not close my mind to the fact that I had concocted a vision from the Lord. "It was for the best, and surely the Most High will forgive me," I said to myself again and again but I gained no peace. I spent much time in fear and prayer, in meditation and silence, waiting for what I hoped would be my justification from heaven. What I wished for did not come. All was silent in my heart. I was left alone with the weight of my decision. I felt lonely, cut off from communication with Yahweh, but my own stubborn will persisted. Obstinately, I felt I could have done nothing else. Increasingly I believed that the revelation of the matter did not lie in Jerusalem but in Tyre. I actually began to long for the promised journey to the north as much as the king.

Thus I was relieved when Solomon gave commands for us to proceed. He ordered that the pomp and ceremony of his progress, such as that to Ezion Geber, be sharply curtailed. We were to travel with a half dozen soldiers only, as a protection against the hazards of the road. I protested this but Solomon said coldly: "I wish to see the king of Tyre as a friend. I do not want him to believe that I come with an army."

"Perhaps his men will seize you as a hostage," I said.

"Benaiah," Solomon said to his general who stood spraddle-legged by the throne, "I shall be gone for a month. If I have not returned by that time, you know what measures to take. Does that satisfy you, Nathan?" he asked me.

"But we pass through the northern tribes of Israel as we go," I said. "Does not my master wish more protection?"

"If they do not respect Solomon," Solomon said grimly, "they still revere the son of David."

"The king's opinion is also mine," Benaiah said. His face was impassive but his eyes flickered. "You will be safe enough, Nathan. You will not have to be brave."

His sneer annoyed me yet I did not reply. That was an end of the affair. I had failed again, as events were to prove.

The land of Phoenicia was a near neighbor, no more than two days of leisurely travel to the northwest. Before we set out, Solomon ordered that a swift courier be sent ahead of our litters to announce our coming. I saw to it that the affairs of the kingdom were in proper order and endeavored to give both Rehoboam—who would be regent—and Benaiah—who would be his right arm—some advice. Both listened coldly. I perceived I was wasting my time and gave up the effort.

Our trip was without incident—except that when we crossed the border, an escort of forty Tyrians met us. They were heavily armed troops, bearing swords and spears, round shields and body armor, but their captain was extremely polite. He told us that he had been sent as a guard of honor through to the coast. There a special galley awaited to transport us from the mainland to the famous island city.

This escort slowed our progress to the extent that it was the evening of the third day before we arrived. The sun set directly before us, throwing this city in the sea into sharp, rosy-dark relief. It was so magnificent that I sucked in my breath at the sight.

Tyre arose before us like a dream. Built on two chains of rocks, with two fine harbors—one to the north, the other southeast—it was surrounded with anchored biremes in great numbers, all gaudily painted. The city itself was an amazing structure, like one huge building, its walls higher than our temple pylons, windows and ramparts still at this hour black with its citizens scurrying about like ants. Its works extended fearlessly into the sea. There was a mole a half mile long and twenty-five feet wide with a fortified entrance. The harbors were complete with quays, breakwaters, loading sheds and every device known to facilitate trade. Behind us was Palaityros, another city spreading eight miles along the coast, surrounded by green fields burdened with grain, fruit, and vegetables to be used for the inhabitants of Tyre. The captain of Hiram's escort had told us that there was no water, however, except for an everflowing spring some five miles south of Tyre. Here the Tyrians had constructed canals to lead this flow northward for irrigating their crops. They also set up a daily ferry service to transport the water to the island city.

"Thirst would make you surrender to an enemy," I said to the captain.

He grinned and ducked his head. "We have cisterns deep in the rocks," he replied. "So huge that it would take a dozen years for any foe to dislodge us. Besides, of course, there are the jars of wine."

I could not believe this, especially when he told us that more than twenty-five thousand citizens swarmed within the dawn-pink walls before us. But I held my tongue.

An ornately decorated galley—painted and gilded—upped its gleaming oar blades and glided to the side of the pier where we waited. "This is the king's own ship," said the captain to me in a low, respectful voice. I heaved a sigh of relief. This seemed far from a hostile gesture from Hiram. As we embarked, the clouded light from behind the city brightened. It was a good omen. I felt better. But the stern expression of Solomon's face did not change.

"Welcome to King Solomon of the Hebrews!" cried the usher.

"Welcome to King Solomon of the Hebrews!" cried the chamberlain.

Hiram put down his golden, gem-studded cup. He raised his green-crowned head. "Welcome," he said in a thin, mild voice that carried clearly to our ears despite the noise of the court. "Welcome nine times to my old friend, King Solomon of the Hebrews."

I struck the gleaming stone floor thrice with the heel of my staff. I bowed deeply. "Greetings!" I cried. "Greetings to the king of Tyre from Solomon, great David's son, king of Jerusalem, king of the lands of Israel and Judah, king of Ammon, ruler of the provinces of Aram and Edom, lord of the kingdom of Moab! Hail to Hiram, king of Tyre!"

Hiram smiled thinly. He was a little, bald man with a wizened face, creased by wrinkles of humor. On either side of his dais stood two slender pillars, one of gold, the other inlaid with what seemed to be chips of emerald. He sat upon a throne upheld by half a dozen gilt sphinxes, ornamented with jewels. His feet rested upon a golden stool. He held a scepter of gilded wood with a lotus-blossom head in his left hand. As Hiram put down his cup beside him, he picked up a flyswatter of rich design with his left hand, waving it about him negligently. Seven retainers waved palm-frond fans about him in attitudes of deep respect, clad in gold-embroidered robes, but Hiram's dress was of fine, plain undyed Egyptian linen. Above the dais of the throne I saw carved the motto of which Hiram-abi had told me. I understood the simple Phoenician characters very well: "I Am a God, I Sit in the Seat of a God, in the Midst of the Waters of the Great Sea."

Hiram rose. He indicated a seat for Solomon, no less enriched with gold and precious stones, at his right. He gestured to the steps of the dais for myself. Slowly, with immense dignity, Solomon advanced to his place. I gathered my garments about me and squatted where the king of Tyre had pointed.

Hiram and Solomon sat down at the same time. The little

king turned to my master and said lightly: "That was quite a list of titles that your servant recited to me."

"It was Nathan's own idea," Solomon returned equably. "He insists upon such things."

"I have no titles to compare with yours," Hiram replied. "I am simply king of Tyre." He put down the flyswatter and sipped at his cup. "I am happy that you have come at last to my kingdom," he said. "We have been friends for a long time and friends grow better with age. Have you brought me some fresh riddles?"

Solomon smiled faintly for the first time. "We may exchange a few," he admitted. He indicated the cup. "You drink early in the evening, noble Hiram," he said.

"We celebrate today the birth of holy Melkarth," Hiram responded. "And wine, I find, is good at any hour." He gestured again. An attendant promptly gave Solomon a full goblet and respectfully crowned him with a green-leaved chaplet. Hiram signaled once more and one of his servants led into the hall a tall harper in a red robe. His eyes were white and sightless. He sank to the floor and thumbed his nine-stringed lyre. Satisfied with its tuning, he drew his fingers across it, thrumming while he sang.

"Men pass away," he chanted in a deep rich voice, "and though their sons remain, time does away with them all. Even the gods rest—and beneath the gods in their tombs sleep the noble and the great. We remember them, we sing of them; we see their monuments and their houses that last forever, their treasures and their garments—but what has happened to them in the darkness? None comes back from thence to tell us how they fare, whether well or ill. None comes back to tell us what they need or if they are happy and well served. None comes back to set our hearts at rest. We shall know nothing of our friends again until we ourselves depart to that far land where they are gone and where we may again greet them, feast and drink with them."

As the blind harper gave his sonorous recitative, I observed covertly, with much interest, the palace of Hiram about us. From without, it had been unimpressive, crowded as it was among other buildings. But within, it rivaled our own royal dwellings in lavish decoration and expert building. There were vessels carved from alabaster and ebony, cressets inlaid with every device, covered with motifs of chainwork, lotus buds, fish scales, and sails. There were chairs of carved stone, stools of ivory and engraved horn. Woven linen tapestries fluttered on the walls.

Back of the throne of Hiram hung grinning vacant-eyed masks of precious metal. Pillars topped with bull heads stood ranked along each side. Niches held strangely shaped figures of what I could only surmise were gods and goddesses, judging from the everburning lamps before them. I glanced down at the floor and was amused to see its polished stones cut deeply with patterns borrowed from Egyptian work. Above me, the heavy wooden ceiling of the king's hall was carved in the same fashion.

The harper ended his threnody. He drew his fingers across the strings in one muted cry of sorrow and was silent. Solomon glanced at Hiram. "This is a sad song with which to greet us," he said.

"Yet it is true," Hiram replied gravely. "We who live beside the sea, with the melancholy moaning of the waves forever in our ears—who have storms and shipwrecks—have learned to live with what must come. Joy is always keener after sorrow. But there are other songs as well."

He raised his hand. The harper's attendant touched him on the shoulder. Instantly the harper struck up a livelier, sweeter strain and began to sing a second tune, his voice sliding from note to note in a fashion I had never heard before. As he began, two dancers appeared, women with slim white bodies, shining with oil, passing again and again before our eyes. Their bare feet pattered on the mosaic floor, their perfume filled our nostrils. Their flying dark hair and dreamy eyes were part of an enchantment woven by their movements. So dextrous were they in their dance I thought to myself that their bones must be as flexible as reeds in the wind. The harper cocked his ear to the beat of their feet and sang:

Sweet and ready for love are the daughters,
Yea, the daughters of the moon!
Black are their tresses, black as starless night,
Black as ripe grapes are the clusters of their hair.
Yet their skin is white as moonlight, their eyes as sparkling as stars;
Their movements are those of the lion stalking on the hill.
The hearts of men turn toward them with delight;
They cannot turn away from gazing until the dancers depart—
Such is their incomparable beauty.

He ceased. The dancers swirled in a series of final giddy movements and sank before the throne. Hiram nodded them off and looked at Solomon. "Did that please you better, noble king?"

"You speak in Hebrew," Solomon said slowly.

"I have studied many languages," Hiram replied.

"But the harper also sang in our language."

"He is dutiful toward his king's desires," Hiram said. "He is an artist beyond compare, do you not agree?"

"I agree."

"I have heard that you have heavenly sounds of your own—that the harp of great David sounds at midnight and plays without a harper."

"I have heard it myself," Solomon said. "But it is only because it stands in a corner of my chamber where the wind blows. The fingers of the breeze play upon it."

Hiram smiled his wry grimace. "That is an answer worthy of Solomon," he said. "But are you sure that you are that same great king of the Hebrews? I have heard it whispered that you were deposed by an angel who took your form and ruled in your place."

"Only," Solomon answered, "if my prophet Nathan here is an angel."

Hiram laughed until he choked. "I have nothing more to say," he managed to sputter. "We have our own prophets and not one of them is an angel!" I smiled and bobbed my head as best I could at this unseemly humor.

"At this moment," Solomon said meditatively, "I wish I were Abner, the man of heroic strength in my father's time. He once said that if he could get his arms around the whole earth he could shake it like a dog with a rabbit."

Hiram eyed him keenly. "Do you wish to tear down the moon and stars?" he queried. "Are you unhappy?"

"Great King Hiram," Solomon responded, "I shall put what I feel into my first riddle. You may guess the answer. There was a king who had concealed a treasure and the servant of his friend stole it away. What is the answer?"

Hiram chuckled. "Is this for a wager?" he asked.

"If you wish."

Hiram shook his head. "I know the answer only too well," he said. "I have guessed the reason for your visit. I am sad that you did not come only to meet me. But kings, like all men, are driven under the lash of love. I shall not solve your riddle, I shall let your own wisdom be the answer. Is that enough?"

For the first time, Solomon's expression relaxed. "It is

enough," he said. His eyes glistened with tears. Hiram tapped him gently, familiarly on the shoulder with his gilded lotus bud. "But in due time," he added. "You have not seen my domain. And you must first sleep and rest after your journey."

Indeed the sight of the city of Tyre and its bustling, bargaining inhabitants the next morning was a wonder. Hiram himself came with us as a guide in a carved litter with Solomon in another next to him, curtains raised. I rode in another, less regal conveyance behind them. I stretched my ears to hear every word they spoke.

There were crowds in all of the streets, celebrating the second day of their heathen god festival, casks of wine at every corner, green wreaths for everyone, music and dancers, jugglers and tricksters. We made our way with difficulty, even with an escort from Hiram's palace guard. The noise was such that the king of Tyre had to speak almost in a shout. He seemed a popular monarch with his subjects. More than once the women who leaned out of the casements in the tall buildings that shadowed the streets of the city showered him with flower petals.

As we swayed along, blinking and sweating in the bright sunlight, I wondered if Hiram would keep his promise to allow Solomon himself to answer his riddle. Solomon had insisted on seeing the king of Tyre immediately the evening before. As soon as we had got off the galley which took us to the island, Solomon had become so impatient that he could hardly wait to bathe, refresh himself, and put on a new robe before being taken to Hiram's presence. But this, it seemed, had flattered rather than angered the little king. His answer had been mild, and Solomon had slackened his desire.

I was surprised at the fashion in which Hiram boasted of his people. His voice drifted back to me as he lectured Solomon through the cool of the teeming streets.

"Five thousand years ago," he said, "my forebears came to this place. The people here did not live in houses of brick, lifted up into the warming sun but in caves like animals. They lived on fish and mussels, enduring what came and cursing their lot. We showed them how to anticipate the seasons by the rising and setting of stars, to plant the fertile seacoast, and to use the waters of the springs. We created the harbors. We traded with all men, hating none."

"These are wonderful achievements," Solomon said.

"We discovered that there was only one star in the sky

that kept its place. We navigated solely by its light, and today all seafaring people call it the Phoenician Star."

"Excellent," Solomon said.

"Our great ancestor Cadmus invented numbers for the merchant. We taught our scribes how to join letters into words to send messages and record the past. We were first in all these things."

Hiram paused and looked at Solomon questioningly, as if he expected his guest's praise but the king of the Hebrews maintained his sober expression. He looked straight ahead. I smiled to myself. Solomon was becoming bored—as I had become some moments before—with the boasting of the king of Tyre.

"I have been told," Solomon said carelessly, "that others—the Egyptians chiefly—had long ago done all these deeds you speak of."

"We were the first," Hiram said condescendingly. "The records in our temples prove it. I do not say the Egyptians lie, for we are friends; I simply say they are mistaken. We taught them how to sacrifice, to tell from the color and shape of the entrails what is the will of the gods."

"You will forgive me as a friend," Solomon said, "if I say that there is only one God. Yahweh Himself appeared to Moses and showed him how to worship."

Hiram shrugged, his face screwed up. "There may be, as you say, one god or many gods. Or one god with many faces. I have found it convenient and useful to worship them all, Melkarth and Ashtoreth above the rest." He looked slyly at Solomon. "I have heard that your mother did the same."

"Women, such as they are," Solomon replied, "are free to indulge in their fancies. Their minds are weak, their actions ignoble." As he spoke, he lifted his head and wrinkled his nose in disgust. "What is that odor, good Hiram?" he asked.

We had passed from the rich buildings of the city of Tyre into another district where the people were even more numerous. But they were poorly dressed and their houses less solid and decorated. Here the passersby crowded up and stared at us. It took all the wit and strength of the soldiers who escorted us to keep them from accidentally overturning our litters.

I could smell the stink myself, something like rotten fish mixed with garlic. I covered my nose with the skirt of my robe lest I should inhale sickness. Just before me, Hiram gave a hoarse chuckle. "If it were not for that smell, O Solomon," he said, "you would not have your garments dyed your favorite color."

The odor, he said, came from the vats of purple maintained by the dyers of his city. "We catch the snails from the sea," he explained. "They are crushed and allowed to stand in a kettle of salt water for three days until they begin to rot. After that we boil the remains, strain the liquor, and dye our fabrics, spreading them in the sunlight to fix the color."

Hiram shouted commands to the bearers and our escort. The litters were lowered from their shoulders before what appeared to be a mansion of stone, towering almost three stories upward in this disreputable quarter. Puzzled, Solomon turned questioningly to Hiram. The king of Tyre grinned and rubbed his hands. "So I have baffled the wisdom of Solomon," he said. "This is the house of one who is the friend of two kings—and of many more people besides. Will you enter as honored guests?"

There was nothing for us to do but assent. We gathered our garments about us so they would not be stained by the filth of the street and approached the pillared doorway. A soldier before us cried our coming. We followed him through double bronze doors flanked by pilasters. On either side of the large interior were small square windows; light was given from a square opening overhead, reflected by a pink floor set with cubes of marble. The little sunlit inner courtyard beyond was gay with flowers. A fountain played idly in the midst of it, pumped by a slave hunched near the wall.

"Rest if you will," said Hiram, indicating a stone bench. Reluctantly, Solomon sank to a seat. I squatted at his feet, my eyes roving resentfully about the room with its painted patterns of blue sea and orange boats. I felt trapped and angry. "I shall send the mistress of the house to you," Hiram said. With no more than that, he vanished into the further shadows at the far side of the courtyard.

"This is a trick of the worst kind," I muttered. "He has done this to humiliate the king of the Hebrews."

Solomon shook his head. "I do not think so," he said. "At any rate, we shall remain to see what will happen."

He had no sooner spoken than he rose abruptly with a stifled cry. A woman came running into the courtyard, almost into his arms. I recognized Tamar.

"Solomon! King!" Tamar curtsied deeply but rose almost instantly, her cheeks glowing. Solomon regarded her impassively. He said nothing.

"Are you well?" demanded Tamar. I had never seen her look so handsome.

"I am well."

Tamar took both his hands. "That makes me very happy," she exclaimed. Solomon looked round about him meaningfully. "Are you happy, Tamar?" he asked. "Here?"

"I have never been so happy," she replied instantly. She motioned proudly around her. "In all this, I am queen. You will understand that, Solomon."

"I understand only that my wife left me," Solomon said.

Tamar's eyes glinted mischievously. "One of your wives left you," she replied. "That is different."

"You were a king's consort."

"One of them."

Suddenly Solomon's voice became pleading. "Were you unhappy with me, Tamar? In Jerusalem?"

She shook her head slowly, almost uncomprehendingly. "When I was with you, when you loved me," she said deliberately, "I was very happy. But were you often with me? Apart, I longed for you—but you could not be close to me. You were with Benaiah, with Nathan here, with Zadok—with the merchants or the visitors. And I could give you no children."

"That made no difference to me," Solomon said strongly.

"It made all the difference," Tamar said in a low voice. "I needed a child if I was to endure you so far away from me. That was why I took Rehoboam for solace. I am a jealous, wicked woman, O, I confess it! But it is what I am."

"You should repent, you should change," I said.

Tamar laughed, a merry laugh like a bird chirping in a tree. "You prophets!" she said. "How little you know about women! You think that a prayer and a sacrifice will change a woman's nature. Nathan, not even a new way of doing the hair, not even a new gown will do that!"

I felt shocked. I turned to Solomon for corroboration but I saw he was smiling—always the sign of leniency with him. I was inexpressibly depressed.

Hiram the king appeared out of the far shadows, bouncing toward us with his energetic, excited walk. A most informal king, I thought with some contempt, one who too lightly dispenses with attendants and formalities which alone shield royalty from the common touch. Solomon saw him and hesitated in his reply to Tamar. Hiram waved and smiled.

"Here is your woman," he said happily. "I should have brought my servant with her but he is just pouring a sand casting in his foundry. You know the kind of work he does, great Solomon—a delicate business. It is hard to interrupt art."

I could not endure to be silent longer. "Tamar indeed is here," I said to Hiram, "and I thank you, noble king, for my master."

"But you wish to know for what purpose?" asked Hiram, his face bland. He ignored me, speaking directly to Solomon. "I give her back to you, to take with you to Jerusalem, to do with as you wish."

It was this intolerable offhand renunciation that decided me to turn in my course and contradict all I had said weeks before to Hiram-abi. I had been the instrument of Tamar's escape with him, I had encouraged him to steal her. I had sinned against Yahweh and lied to my king. I was ready to confess this on the spot, to take my punishment. Before I could speak, Solomon addressed me in a tone so soft it was almost confidential.

"What do you advise, Nathan?" he asked.

My tongue failed in my mouth. I had meant to stammer out my guilt. Somehow I could not do it. Instead, I said: "Let us take our own, lord, let no more be said."

"But you said it was the will of Yahweh," Solomon replied.

"Even so," I cried in desperation, "this woman is your property. She has been granted to you by even the king of Tyre. It has always been your right to seize her, to take her back to Jerusalem! Myself, I now strongly advise it."

It was Tamar who looked at me pityingly. She shook her head. Her stained hair and smeared cheeks somehow made her even more attractive. "How many years have you been counselor to the king, Nathan?" she asked.

I felt impelled to reply. "Nearly forty years, woman," I said disdainfully.

"And in all those years you have not come to know your master. It is a very hard thing to understand."

I swung about to Solomon again. "Shall we endure this insolence from a woman?" I demanded.

Solomon's smile broadened. "Yes," he said. "You shall endure it because it is not insolence but the truth."

"That I do not understand you?"

Solomon brushed me away with a gesture. "That I never understood Tamar," he said. "That is what she means." He addressed her again. "If you come back," he said, "I shall make you truly happy. He whom they call the wisest man in the world has become immeasurably wiser in this moment. Will you come, Tamar?"

"You plead with her?" I felt astounded.

Tamar advanced. She placed both her dirty hands in his. I noticed Solomon gripping them convulsively. Slowly she shook her head once more.

"You believe that now," she said, "but it would be different in Jerusalem. I mean, it would be the same—as it has always been. You could not help it. Your life would not allow you to change. Your love is your people, not your wife. That is the duty of a king and I cannot change it, you cannot change it." Her voice was full of sadness.

I felt I could crush her. "Then why have you come so willingly to meet the king here?" I challenged her.

She spoke like a little girl. "Because Solomon, I knew, would be no longer passionate and willful. He would be wise and pitying."

"Do you believe this nonsense?" I stormed at the king.

Solomon raised his hand. "It is so," he said quietly. "Be still, Nathan. To you, Tamar, I say that my desire—purified by what you have told me—still yearns for you."

Tamar looked steadily into the eyes of Solomon. Verily, I think that at that moment she wavered in her resolution. She turned away and a movement in the distance caught her eye. "Here!" she cried. "Here comes Hiram-abi!"

It was he, swathed in a smutched leather apron from head to below his knees, grinning like an idiot, happier than I had ever seen him before. He advanced toward us. A few yards off, he louted on one knee, doffing his cindered cap. "Greetings and health, O lord and king of the Hebrews," he said respectfully.

"Rise, Hiram-abi," Solomon said to the artisan, as if he were noble.

Before he could continue, Hiram—who indeed resembled his subject in his sly, humorous face—broke in. "Hiram-abi," he said severely, "you have stolen from a king!"

Hiram-abi glanced up at his master. Then he peeped furtively at Solomon and, last of all, at me. He bowed his head. "I plead for mercy," he said humbly. "I am at fault, great lords."

Hiram nodded. He turned to Solomon. "This is a matter which might easily turn into war and break many friendships," he said. "But we of Tyre are not fond of fighting—only if we must, and then at sea, not upon the land. We have learned that every man in this world, even kings, has a price for what he wants. Very well: I want the skills of Hiram-abi here in Tyre. I am willing to pay for them. What is your price, king of the Hebrews?"

"You speak of things of the heart like a common merchant," Solomon said.

Hiram shrugged. "Such things, if not ruled by the head, become expensive," he returned. "And I have heard that my own servant was not altogether to blame." He looked at me as he spoke. I flushed.

"This is not a matter of tribute or ransom," Solomon said slowly.

"I know that," Hiram said easily. "A matter of property."

Solomon seemed to increase in stature. "No," he said with scarcely disguised contempt. "It is a matter of choice. That does not lie with either of us. Nor with Hiram-abi."

He turned toward Tamar. Before he could speak, Hiram-abi hastily reached beneath his leather apron. He brought out a shining little statue: a grinning grotesque of gold. He proffered it to Tamar. "I have made this for you," he said in a low voice.

Tamar's dark, tormented face lighted up, as if her spirit had flared up. She took the image tenderly. She looked long at it, then pressed it to her lips. Last of all, she gazed at Solomon.

"You see," she said softly, "that here I am loved. In Jerusalem, I loved. There is a great difference, my lord."

"What more could I have done to keep you contented?" asked Solomon. "There were other duties I had to perform as king. I could not be near you every hour."

"No," Tamar admitted. "And there were other women to keep contented—and state visitors such as Itamara to make happy. All this I was resigned to—until Hiram-abi brought me here. He showed me that I was the only woman in his existence." Her voice strengthened. "I came away with him because I hated you," she said boldly. "I shall remain here because I love him."

"With my permission, if I grant it," Hiram put in.

Tamar bowed in obeisance. Solomon's face twitched as if in pain. "A continual dropping in a very rainy day," he said bitterly, "and a contentious woman are the same." He turned away, his shattered pride evident in his shaking voice. He started toward the door.

"We have not agreed on a price!" cried King Hiram after him. Solomon halted.

"I give Tamar to you as a free gift," he said over his

shoulder. "But to you only, friend Hiram, to dispose of as you wish."

Hiram raised both palms upward in recognition of this generosity. "I accept, most wise of all monarchs," he said. His face broke into a thousand wrinkles, changing its whole expression into one of sly rejoicing.

"A gift from one king must be equaled by a gift from another," the ruler of Tyre said. He spread his hands. "Therefore, I shall give back to you, Solomon, the twenty cities that you gave me for my ships," he said, "in return for Hiram-abi and his maid Tamar. Is that sufficient?"

"A kingly present!" I cried, carried out of decorum by the unexpectedness of such munificence.

Solomon frowned at me. "Surely you will not refuse," I said faintly.

"Of course he will accept, prophet Nathan," returned Hiram blandly. "The righteous Solomon knows those twenty cities are villages. He knows as well as I that the land is barren hills or marshy worthless valleys. He recognizes as well as I that it will take more time and goods and money to rule the worthless rebels that dwell there than the whole of that country is worth." His tone sharpened at the end, despite himself.

"I shall find other means of repaying Tyre," Solomon said stiffly.

Hiram, victorious, waved his hand casually. "I shall take it out of Hiram-abi's hide," he said. "He is tough enough."

It was the last that Solomon and I saw of Tamar and Hiram-abi. Nor did Solomon mention her name again, except once at the very end of his life. My own sin and the elopement of that pair slid into the past. Solomon had been defeated by Tamar and her boldness as Theke had defeated him by her meekness and womanly resignation—nor did the king accept another wife as long as he lived. He granted all sorts of freedom to his wives thereafter, not caring what they did or how they fared. I remonstrated with him for this in those short-lived days, as a neglect of some of his chiefest treasures. He made only a single reply: "It is better to dwell in the wilderness than with contentious and angry women."

"But all women are not like Tamar," I objected.

Solomon laughed grimly. "When the scorner is punished, he is made wise," he replied. "When the wise is instructed, he calls it knowledge. When the knower finds the truth, he becomes a scorner. It is an old circle, Nathan, trod by the feet of many men before me. Let us say that I have learned. I shall endure the lesson of the Lord."

In the days that followed in Tyre, King Hiram could not do enough for us. His minions swarmed about to perform our slightest wish. Solomon was the chief guest at high feasts and low revels. As a special mark of honor, he was even taken for a cruise along the coast in the king's own bireme one sparkling-bright day, when the sea was lapis and the crests diamonded. This last favor, however, became tainted by the fact that he turned deathly green-sick aboard. Solomon recovered as soon as he landed but he renounced the sea forevermore.

Meanwhile, I was free to roam the streets of Tyre. I discovered to my satisfaction that the Phoenicians were a nation of hucksters, not of sages or of great men in war and peace. They manufactured an endless supply of cheap wares to be sold in their chaffering protracted fashion, clasping hands upon the bargain, swearing oaths by their fantastic multitude of gods. All the art that they had, despite Hiram's boastings, was borrowed, designs I had seen before in Egyptian and Assyrian work. Yet there were also wonderful skills at woodcarving, brasswork, and bronze tempering. Their ships were a never-ending source of wonder to me, though I steadfastly refused to put a foot aboard them after Solomon's cruise.

Despite all this, no one in the great city of Tyre seemed contented. They envied one another. They exchanged unceasing gossip about the sorrows and trials of their crowded lives. They seemed to live in the covered marketplaces at the street corners, drinking their dark sour beer, arguing day and night.

The third afternoon, I found the city filled with wailing mourners—men and women, beating their breasts, with disheveled hair and painted faces—but all was sham. It was actually a religious ceremony. It confounded me, the celebration of the death and resurrection of Adonis. Images of that handsome god, made of black wax and red clay, were passed about like sacred dolls. They were oiled and scented by everyone, wept over, their little costumes rearranged and decorated. Dancers in shimmering costumes of shell pranced, clattered, and chanted to the sound of the flutelike *giggras*. Under arbors of green boughs lay even larger statues, on silver beds, in golden robes. About these handsome replicas of ivory and cedar were vases of perfumes, fruits, honey, and cakes. Baskets contained tiny gardens of Adonis—especially lettuce, dedicated and holy as the bed on which Ashtoreth had first conceived her son.

I squatted by a beer shop, next to its sour-smelling marble counter. Another customer, dressed in the coned hat, fringed tunic of all colors, and high laced boots of a soldier discussed his career loudly. "A soldier has the worst fate of any," he proclaimed. "He is shut up in his barracks day after day like a wicked child. He must march every day, clean his weapons and exercise every day with them."

The man squatting next to him, a dour older man with the red, seamed neck of a man who works in the sun, disagreed. "You get your pay and your food and bed," be declared. "The farmer finds that mice eat half his corn, that beasts of the field devour the rest. The locust descends to devour whatever is green, the sparrows steal seed from the furrows."

"We are bruised with flogging," objected the soldier, glaring at the farmer, "for the slightest disobedience, even if we did not hear the order. When we march, it is always uphill. We are forced to carry our own bread and wine on our backs, bowing our joints like an ass."

"What makes you think a farmer lives a better life?" demanded the other heavily. "When the scribe of the city comes to register our harvest, he demands corn from us. When we say the truth—that there is none—he stretches us out and beats us with sticks. And if we give further offense, we are tied hand and foot and thrown from a cliff into the sea. That very thing happened to a poor neighbor of mine. His wife was bound and carried off. I last saw his children chained together to be sold as slaves."

I pretended not to listen. Squatting at the corner of the street, my jug of beer at my side, I drew aimless patterns in the dust at my feet. But my ears were strained to hear what I might of this shrewd people. When the argument between the soldier and the farmer languished, I did not lift up my head and betray myself. But a sweet odor came to me, piercing through the stinks of dyeing, of fish, and stale grease that cut the air of Tyre as if they had been so many knifeblades. Then I dared to look. I saw a stranger had arrived—a youth, perfumed and well dressed, short-shirted and tassel-girdled with a shoulder cape and high sandals, a scarlet band about his forehead. He took his drink at the marble counter in silence. He put down the empty jug and a coin haughtily, wiped his lips with his scarf, and departed without a word.

"Mad youngster!" muttered the soldier. "Spoiled as meat in

the sun ten days old, without work or purpose. I say put all such in the army! We would soon change their habits!"

"Has he no work to do?" inquired the farmer.

"His father is rich, why should he work? He drives a chariot where he pleases—and nothing pleases him as much as a good race. He comes through the streets every morning, scattering the citizens like fowl, bouncing behind his new horses. I have seen him many times. He has been punished only once."

"How was that?"

The soldier chuckled with relish. "He was racing near the border of our land where it joins the Hebrew kingdom. He went off the road into a thorn thicket. His fine horses were snared, ripped unmercifully—and so was he. He had to walk back with slashed legs and torn sandals, his tunic pierced, bleeding in a dozen places. But his chariot was wrecked. His father knew it cost seven shekels, that the pole alone cost three. The fool got beaten soundly."

The farmer grunted skeptically. "How do you know all this?" he demanded.

The soldier put his finger alongside his nose. He winked. "I did not see the accident," he said, "but I was on border patrol. I escorted the young fellow home. I heard and saw—and listened to him scream under the rod. He was not punished enough for my taste—he had brought back a sop of news from his racing in the Hebrews' land."

"What was that?"

"That Solomon's son, the prince Rehoboam, one of his friends—he says—is going to be married to some girl or other."

"Maachah!" I cried, springing to my feet. My beer jug overturned and broke into shards. The farmer and the soldier gaped at me.

"True," said the slack-jawed soldier, staring up. "But how did you know, stranger?"

CHAPTER NINETEEN

The Plans of Benaiah

Coming back across our border from Tyre, I noticed it was spring in the land. Everything reminded me of it. The winds had changed. Their caresses were softer against our faces. Field flowers were beginning to blossom. The stars rose in their old, assigned places above the horizon. I thought nostalgically of my own small garden plot outside the city walls. There were swallows to be seen, sure sign that I should prune my vines. But I had not yet had time to do so. It was time to sow and plow, as indicated by the cries of the migrating cranes signing the sky above our heads. But there were no snails on the plants I observed along the roadside so that there was clearly time left in which to begin cultivation.

Obviously I should not have had time to observe these things if we had been skeltering toward Jerusalem at the pace I had expected. Solomon, who always surprised me, did not press our journey. He rode on almost sedately, deep in thought. None of us dared to break his silence, even if we fretted that it might take as long as four days before we arrived.

Two incidents out of the ordinary served to put us on our guard. I shall relate them as they happened. We had, as I said, crossed over the Phoenician border into our own land but were still traveling in the north. It was that part of the Hebrew nation which not even David had entirely subdued and which had always been sullen about what they thought was Solomon's preference for Judah in the south.

Early one morning on the second day, as we went warily along with our escort, on our left—by a field just turning green with newly planted grain—I saw a curiously ludicrous figure in the evening twilight. I pointed it out to Solomon. We laughed together at the sight. The king pulled back on his reins to enjoy it. We halted with him, of course.

At first the object seemed a solitary scarecrow, bareheaded in the heat of the sun that wavered up already off the land. It was ragged and tattered, but it was alive. It moved in a shambling dance, careless of the furrows or the grain that it crushed under its bare feet. I wondered why the farmer did not drive the thing out of his fields—but we soon discovered why. In one of its gyrations it came reeling close to our road. I recognized the man: it was Ahijah, the prophet who had allied himself with Jeroboam so long ago. He had grown ancient, thinner, wasting almost to bones. But the light in his eyes was no less fanatic. He ceased his fantastic dancing when he saw our little cavalcade. He crossed directly to us over the rain-soft field. He put his hand fearlessly on the king's bridle. Nor did anyone move to prevent him. This was obviously a holy man, strong in the righteousness of his convictions, possibly given visions of portent from the Lord.

"I had not seen you dance before, Ahijah," I said.

"You have turned from the ways of Yahweh to the ways of Solomon," he replied to me in his shrill voice. "You are of no more account than one of the apes at his court."

"Why do you delay us?" asked Solomon. "Have you a message from the king?"

Ahijah flung back his filthy mat of long, tangled gray hair. The bones of his cheeks distended the tight sunblack skin of his face until it seemed they would crack through. His mouth stretched in a malicious grin of stained teeth.

"I have this to say to a king who has followed other gods and whored after strange women," Ahijah fearlessly pronounced. "You have wandered far from the covenant of the Lord and the ways of David. Yet there is time given. Will you repent, Solomon, son of David? Will you get down from that litter of shame, kneel in the dust, and abase yourself to me, Ahijah, the servant of the Lord?"

"I have not done this for kings from the ends of the earth," Solomon replied. "Yahweh has not told me of such sins nor has Nathan."

"Nathan! Pah!" Ahijah spat contemptuously into the road. "His ears are filled with everything, with every noise, except the still voice of the Lord. He squinted keenly up at Solomon. "But has the Lord not put His hand upon you before this in a fever? And have you not avoided His just punishment by the witch-arts of a woman from a foreign land? Tell me, O king!"

Solomon made no reply. He twitched his bridle from the grasp of Ahijah. He kicked his steed ahead. We followed him. As we did, one of the soldiers whacked the old prophet soundly on the side of his head with his scabbarded sword, trotting on.

I had not thought the king noticed. But just afterward, he beckoned me to his side. "Take note of the soldier who struck Ahijah," he said. "Have him given fifty stripes with scabbards when we return to Jerusalem."

"But," I protested, "the soldier only showed his loyalty to you by what he did!"

"I must protect my prophets," Solomon murmured. "I have too few to let them be so roundly abused." He glanced sidewise at me. "Or do you think that prophets are only to be honored if they are in a king's service?"

"No," I said.

"They think themselves so privileged of Yahweh that they are able to lie to their kings about their dreams. Is this not so, Nathan?"

I commenced to tremble. I had no doubt that Solomon had penetrated my soul. I was sure he knew my lie about having instructions from Yahweh concerning Tamar. I began to stammer. Solomon held up his hand with absolute calm.

"I have heard of a demon," he said slowly, "that the people believe in—but I have always scoffed at demons, Nathan."

"That is quite right," I said, shaking until the reins rettled in my hands.

"Now I more than half believe in this one," continued Solomon, almost whimsically, "because his name is Asmodi. The tale-tellers say that once he drove me from the throne and ruled in my stead. Perhaps that is a criticism of you, Nathan, ruling in my stead. Or is it merely popular nonsense?"

"I have nothing to do with demons," I said hastily.

"Asmodi is the peculiar demon, assigned by the Adversary as the enemy of marriage," Solomon said. "He is spoken of as the evil one who killed the seven husbands of Sarah. I have had as little luck as any with my wives and those I loved. Whom else should I blame but a demon?"

Again I felt the daggers of conscience in my breast. Panting, I began once more to stammer out my guilt. But Solomon would have none of it. He silenced me with a gesture. I realized that he was punishing me with my own lash. I groaned like a flagellant. But I resolved to endure it.

The twilight deepened from green to purple shades behind us. First casting the long shadows of animals and men ahead of us, stretching them out further and further as the hours went on, it gradually devoured them in darkness. We journeyed in silence. Silence that brought a measure of peace to my breast. I looked up at the stars and guessed we would arrive at Jerusalem before the dawn.

Slowly, imperceptibly the night changed. No more did the dew fall on our heads like a blessing. The air became dry and tight around us, charged with mysterious forces. My hair lifted in a sort of horripilation. The stars, one by one, were obscured by thick clouds. No longer did I feel the peace I had felt before—and I saw that Solomon and our guards were as nerved up as I. The very animals beneath us quickened their pace toward Jerusalem.

Without warning the sky lit up. From almost directly over us, the heavens split. Lightning, a silent, deadly river of light, poured beamingly down. The whole of the landscape about us lay revealed in lavender. The air retched of sulfur from under, the shadows lay monstrous and quivering with threat. I cowered in my place. Instantly afterward there came the most terrific clap of thunder that I have ever heard, directly over our heads. But not a drop of rain fell.

Next moment, the lightning again shot from the sky. It struck a dead tree beside the road a hundred yards ahead. The tree flared up like tinder. We drew rein with shaking hands. The air filled with musty smells unknown to me before. Stiff with fear at this sign from heaven, we remained where we were, holding tight to our beasts lest they stampede, watching the tree burn itself out like a torch flung by the way. Again the thunder, crashing in our ears, dying away, grumbling to itself, moving in the direction of Jerusalem.

In the glimmer of that pale glow I had seen the faces of our escort become drawn and white. Their eyes rolled in their sockets; one of them half drew his sword then put it by. Solomon himself, rigid and staring, did not move for a moment. He gazed ahead as we did but I had caught no more than an expression of intense curiosity on his face. I made a swift series of signs in the air about us to protect us from the wandering fiends of darkness.

"This comes of speaking lightly of demons," I muttered.

"Is it not rather the signal of Yahweh?" Solomon said coolly. "What other could it be, Nathan?"

"A warning, a summons," I managed to say. "Such are not seen except when plague and death are abroad."

"It is a warning?"

"Yes. For good or evil, I cannot tell."

"For me? For you, for others?"

"For everyone," I said loudly. I beat my breast once with

my fist. "It calls to repentance, to sacrifice, to prayer and worship."

Solomon smiled in his fashion, more in contemplation than belief. "I have long ago paid what I owed to Yahweh," he said lightly. "I am not in debt to the Lord. See to yourself, Nathan. Remember what you said to me back in the city of Tyre days ago."

I had gone directly from the street corner in Tyre to Solomon's presence. I told him, out of breath as I was from running, the news I had heard about Rehoboam. When I was through, the king shrugged.

"Why is this so urgent?" he asked.

"I have explained it before, O king," I said. "I am sure there must be a plot afoot to seize your throne."

Solomon eyed me. "What makes you sure of this?" he inquired.

"The prince would not have done this without encouragement. I know he would act only under the guidance of others. Your land is already torn in its allegiance. When the true king is away, others aspire."

Solomon raised his brows. "What do you suggest?" he asked.

"We must return at once."

"Had we not planned to spend a month in Tyre? It has been very pleasant during the week since we settled our business about women. Hiram and I are engaged in drinking and feasting—and once more in riddling."

"This is true riddle indeed," I said piteously, "but its solution lies only in your return to Jerusalem."

Solomon nodded. "We shall leave," he said. I must have showed my astonishment at his ready agreement. He laughed. "The truth is that Hiram and I are getting old," he said. "Our wittiness is only nastiness, our wisdom has soured into malice. He is a trickster and I am a conniver. We set traps for each other constantly. This is boring, Nathan. You are right. I did but test you. We shall leave."

"We shall save the throne," I said, devoutly rejoicing.

"I do not hear plots in every whisper," Solomon replied. "My throne is as solid as the rocks beneath Jerusalem. But I am sick for the sight of our land, my scented pillars and throne of gold. I shall never go away from Jerusalem again, Nathan."

I was struck, long after, by what he said then. It seemed that never had Solomon been so prescient. But I regarded it little at the time. Despite the complaints and objections of Hiram, we set out the very next morning with our little troop. The soldiers of Hiram accompanied us to the frontier, halting there and saluting us goodbye. We had left our litters behind. We rode astride—for Solomon had the whim to discard all trappings and to travel as a man, not a king. Incognito we were and I felt in my bones that this was unwise—and my bones made me suffer more even than my bruised flesh before we were halfway to our destination.

It was the encounter with Ahijah and the melting starkness of the dry thunder in the sky, the tongues of flame, that convinced me my fears were right. Such manifestations must have impressed Solomon more than he admitted. He ordered us to press on with more speed, especially during the last part of the ominous night. We swung sharply down from the north and, at length, came in sight of Jerusalem and its dark massed buildings atop the mountain in the early warmth of the morning hours.

Climbing up to the Water Gate by night after crossing the lively stream of the Kidron was not a new experience for me. But even with Solomon and our guards, it was frightening. I recalled only too well the night of feasting years before when I had interrupted the celebration of Joab and was forced to run for my life up the steep angles of the cliffs. Since then the path had changed little—except to be widened for caravans. The trees and green scrubs had perished. But the ominous shadows still persisted. The bulging walls of Jerusalem overhung our way like great clenched fists in the darkness.

All the long day and night during our hasty return from Tyre, Solomon had spoken little. His only words had been to urge our tired mounts on and on, post after post, as if some horrendous urgency beckoned him in the blue distances. As we came closer to Jerusalem, his fretting spirit seemed appeased. He actually slowed our pace. He became pensive and melancholy, altogether unlike a monarch returning to his kingdom.

Thus we arrived at the gate only in the blood-thickened hours of the early morning. Though we might have been recognized by the richness of our attire (over which the dust was an effective disguise), we wrapped our mantles about our faces as we ambled our way up to the portals. I myself pounded on the wooden gates. Usually such pilgrims as ourselves, for fear they might be spies or fugitives, were forced to spend the night outside the walls in the small square prepared for their use—I picked my way carefully through the malodorous recumbent bodies of the latecomers to reach the gate. But even the sleepy sentinels—after a moment of anger at having been roused—recognized my face by thrusting a torch almost into my eyes. We were admitted with some delay (not without grumbling on the part of those who still had to sleep without), and I restrained the watch with difficulty from rousing out the whole guard to welcome back the king.

"There is no sign of disaffection here," muttered Solomon as we passed in.

"No," I said. "There would be none at the gate. Any conspirators would prefer us to enter farther into the jaws of their trap." All the same, I too breathed easier.

As we made our way up through the streets of Jerusalem, those black odorous troughs of shadow, my spirits lightened. I felt the augmented anxieties of Solomon beside me ease also in the midst of these sleeping peaceful people. We heard again the meetings of the watch that saluted each other with their high, clear cries from the walls. The occasional fowl or cur started up from under the feet of our onagers to chutter fright or snarl curses at us. We smiled at the taste of the air, the familiar heavy warmth of a city at night, like a woman taking her rest. This was Jerusalem, this was home: I looked about me fondly at the shadows graying with the coming dawn. I blessed it from my heart with a thousand benedictions.

There was a moment of hesitation at the palace entrance. The guard greeted our party with a challenge. He recognized us as we uncovered. Solomon commanded him to stand aside. We entered the familiar precincts, dismissed our escort, and looked at each other. Solomon paced slowly before me. He spoke over his shoulder as we neared his apartments.

"We have come so far successfully."

"Agreed, great king."

Solomon for the first time showed annoyance. "Nathan," he said, "in a moment like this, true or false, I am a man speaking to another man. A friend to a friend. I am taking counsel, not issuing commands. Let us both be naked before Yahweh and see what will be the outcome."

I bowed my head. Solomon continued, as if he rendered the texture of his thoughts into words. "So many hints and omens," he said pensively. I was silent.

"What you have guessed in Tyre may be true. Or it may

be imagination. But what purpose would such portents serve?"

"None."

"How can they be true? My people love me. They would not rebel against my rule."

"Love is a strange thing," I said. Solomon paid no heed but hurried on with his thoughts. We approached the inner chamber.

"Malcontents there will always be," he said, "but never enough to threaten the throne. There must be one leader."

"Always. But there may be another who thinks of himself as a leader."

"One who will put into words and slogans the secret longings of those who hate, those who want power for themselves."

"True."

"Who might this be?" asked Solomon of the air. I was surprised when he glanced at me. I shook my head hurriedly. Solomon seated himself absently. I stood before him.

"I do not blame you, Nathan," he said. "Nor do I suspect you, inasmuch as you were with me in Tyre."

"My most humble thanks," I said, as caustically as I dared. But again Solomon did not notice.

"The late rebellions in Egypt," he said pensively, "prove that the leaders come from only three classes—those counselors like yourself, the priests, or the generals. No one else has the ambition or dares to think of himself as able to rise so high."

My thoughts whirled. "Do you mean Zadok?" I cried.

"Bring him to me," Solomon said crisply. He had assumed his kingship once more, erect on his throne.

"Yes, it must be Zadok and his priests!" I exclaimed, transported. "That oily hypocrite, that pretender to power, that—"

"I know you dislike him," Solomon said drily, "but restrain your invective, Nathan."

"It is dictated by my loyalty to you, mighty Solomon," I said.

"Bring him."

"At this hour? How may it be done? He will suspect something out of the ordinary and perhaps refuse."

Solomon's face flushed. "Refuse a command of his sovereign?"

"If he is the guilty one," I pointed out, "he has already done much more."

Solomon tapped the arms of his throne with his nails and nodded slowly. "Yes," he said. He meditated once more.

"I may tell you now," Solomon said at last, "that I did not accede to your pleas to return here on your suspicions alone, Nathan."

"I bow to your wisdom," I said.

Solomon made an impatient movement. "Nor was it rumor or anything of the sort," he returned. "Rather it was a courtier of Hiram, one Audemon, who gets much credit for helping the king of Tyre solve the riddles I send him. An unassuming man, certainly, but also one who whispered a riddle to his master who propounded it to me. A curious thing."

"May I ask, O Solomon—"

"Hiram asked me: 'When is a throne not a throne?' I thought he spoke in jest but I pretended to believe it was not a riddle. The king of Tyre answered it himself. 'You have seen Ithobaal, my high priest,' he said. Do you recall him, Nathan?"

I did indeed. A tall man, with a thin, commanding face and sharply hooked nose, with enormous black brows that jutted out below his forehead, a man of silent arrogance. I nodded.

"Know," Solomon resumed, "that Hiram said to me in a whisper: 'The answer is, When a priest sits upon it—then is a throne not a throne.' He said no more but looked briefly toward Ithobaal. I pondered upon what he said and came to take what may have been no more than a hint to himself for a warning given to me."

"You mean Zadok?" I asked in dim astonishment.

"Bring him here," Solomon said.

"It is a delight to see you have returned, O king and lord!"

"Did you expect to see me?"

Zadok looked confounded. His sweating face shone in the light of the golden lamps. "There was no welcome," he muttered, "no ceremonies. It is not fitting for the king of the Hebrews."

"I desired it to be this way," Solomon said.

Zadok glanced at me, a look of pure malevolence. "Nathan advises you badly," he said. "You are more than a king, you are the chosen of Yahweh. You are the shining light of our people who has rescued us from the darkness. You should not enter your city like a thief in the night, O great Solomon."

"I have heard there may be other thieves in the city," Solomon said, his voice like the slash of a whip. Zadok cringed before his tone.

"I have done nothing, my priests have done nothing," he said rapidly. He licked the perspiration from his upper lip. "None of us has taken anything but what is allotted to us by the laws of Moses. Your words to me once have been before my mind ever since."

"The king does not speak of golden vessels or jewels or bits of the sacrifice," I said.

"Every one of the temple furnishings, every coin and gem in the treasury is in its place!" said Zadok. His anger was righteous enough it seemed to me. It dried his flesh and made his wavering belly stiff. He actually seemed to turn into a man in his indignation. "I have appointed special priests to tally, to keep guard, and I myself have an accounting every month."

"Nathan is right," Solomon replied dryly. "We do not speak of these things but of someone who has plotted to steal something much more."

"What of more value could there be?" wondered Zadok.

"The kingdom of the Hebrews itself!"

Zadok quivered like jelly. His face, though incredulous, still remained blank of comprehension.

"The throne of David, the throne of Solomon!" Solomon said sharply. "This was what they would steal!"

Zadok put his palm to his forehead, took it away and regarded its wetness. He raised his small puffed eyes toward the king helplessly. I cannot understand," he said vaguely.

Solomon stared hard at him for long seconds. Then abruptly he made up his mind. He waved his hand contemptuously.

"This is not the one," he said to me. "Have him taken away. Imprison him."

"Me?" Zadok's voice rose ridiculously high. "Imprison Zadok, the high priest of the nation?"

"For your own safety," Solomon said.

"I cannot understand," Zadok repeated dismally.

"It is not necessary," Solomon told him. I summoned the guards and gave them their instructions. Zadok resisted feebly, moaning of sacrilege. He stumbled out between his custodians, a melting lump of obscene fat, his wails fading down the corridor outside.

I turned back to Solomon. The king regarded me unwinkingly. "There is only one other," he said at last. I nodded.

"What shall we do?" I said in despair.

"I was foolish to think that such a one as Zadok would have the courage to do such a thing," Solomon murmured reflectively.

"Perhaps the rumor itself is untrue, the gossip of women, the idle tales of the marketplace," I said hopefully.

"Go," Solomon said.

"Alone?"

"Alone."

"What has made you honor my house on this dark morning?" asked Benaiah. He ushered me into his governor's house in the new city and stood waiting for my reply.

"I come at the order of the king."

"Solomon? You mock me. Solomon is in Tyre."

"Was I not with him?"

Benaiah regarded me with a face that became suddenly haggard. He seemed, for the first time in all the years I had known him, to be without words to speak. He shook his shaggy head from side to side. His eyes filmed. "Then," he said at last, "Solomon is truly here, in Jerusalem?"

"Yes," I said.

"In his palace?"

"He is dusty and weary—and sore—from his long ride. He is bathing, being massaged and anointed."

"But he was to be in Tyre for nearly a month to come!"

I shrugged. It gave me a feeling of enormous pleasure to have the upper hand of Benaiah. "You know how the whims of kings are," I told him. "None better than you, Benaiah. They determine in a moment what they will do and it must be done the next moment."

Benaiah nodded. His face hardened and cleared. It was apparent he had regained his shaken wits. "So the king has returned," he said almost lightly. "He has sent you to me?"

"With a message."

"You were always a messenger," Benaiah said. "What is this message, this time?"

"He desires to see you immediately in his private audience room."

Benaiah pursed his lips. "Suppose," he said deliberately, "that I refuse to come?"

I thought he must be laughing at me, having his sinister joke. But there was nothing but grim seriousness in his face, in his tone. "It—to say—it is impossible," I stammered, "that you would refuse to obey a command of the king!"

Benaiah did not reply immediately. Leisurely, as if thinking, he paced across the floor. Too late, I noted that he had moved between me and the door. "There are many roads when one is young, Nathan," he said. "But when we are old—as you and I are old, my friend—all the paths in the world narrow down to one. They lead there, they entice us, they snare us into this one way. That is why I believe in fate, as does any soldier."

"I believe in Yahweh's will," I said, moving to one side. Benaiah kept himself between me and the door by a leisurely step or two. I felt like a trapped animal.

"That is a stout and foolish answer," Benaiah said. "But it fits a prophet of the Lord. What if one does not believe in your Yahweh? What then, Nathan?"

"Do you believe in other gods, Benaiah?"

Benaiah gestured aimlessly. "Bathsheba taught me much," he said. "Much more I learned by living. What if I told you that there are no gods at all, Nathan?"

It was fruitless to talk to such a man. "Solomon has summoned you," I said. "Shall we go?"

"I shall not go," Benaiah said, smiling faintly.

"Shall I bring the king such an answer from his captain?"

"You will not bring him any answer at all."

"What do you say?" In spite of myself, my courage wavered. My voice broke as I said the words.

"Not unless you tell me the reason for this command in the night. Is Jerusalem threatened? Is the life of the king threatened?"

It was the moment I had hoped for, for which I had steeled myself. My courage was equal to it. I drew myself up opposite this man of war, scarred with many battles, lion-fighter, defier of kings. I wished to show him my spirit. Then I felt my courage drain. I looked helplessly around me.

"You encouraged Rehoboam and Maachah."

"What Tamar left undone, I tried to finish. My last chance. Rehoboam is an arrogant, short-tempered youngster. He would have lost the throne in weeks and I should have been there to retrieve it—but that opportunity, too, is gone."

I felt smothered. "You have tried to turn everything to your own account, it seems," I managed to say.

"An account long overdue. It is not easy, Nathan, to defy the Lord's anointed. I have been of two minds for so long, deamons on both shoulders whispering to me. Often I have protected Solomon, often I have saved his life, as you know.

But as his confidence in me rose, I withdrew my faith in him. He is so weak! So feeble!"

"He is king," I said. "You think of strength only as a soldier."

Benaiah shrugged. "I think of him as David did," he said.

"How do you know what David thought?" I demanded, startled.

"Bathsheba," Benaiah replied simply. "David was right, that the throne needed a strong man. But I wavered, I was irresolute so many times. It was only after years, when the thought had rooted itself in my mind and slowly grew, that I came to my decision."

"That you must be king?" I asked ironically.

Benaiah nodded. "For the good of the Hebrew nation," he said. "Who else is better fitted?"

I could not help being impressed by the sincerity of his madness. Benaiah had forced himself through the years to believe that his own vanity was the salvation of the kingdom.

"You might have joined me years ago," Benaiah said.

"I?"

"Do you remember, Nathan, when I said that some had urged me to become king of the Hebrews instead of Solomon?"

"That was very long ago," I said.

"When I said there were others," Benaiah said, "I meant that I had spoken to myself and gotten approval. You were the first I wanted to be with me—you, who had dared to reprove David to his face about Bathsheba. I needed men of strength and courage like that."

"I remember," I said.

"But it was plain that you did not approve, that you were seduced by Bathsheba."

"Never!"

Benaiah shrugged. "Faithful to Solomon, then," he said carelessly. "It was the same thing. It sealed my lips for a long time, your disapproval. I saw clearly then that I would have to wait until my own strength had overtopped yours, until I could speak out without fearing the consequences."

He stopped and looked at me. "The time had almost come of its own right," he said. "Even now, it may not be too late."

"You have been thinking of this so long, Benaiah?"

"Of nothing else. I have played the double game—deceiving you and Solomon, yes, nursing his life in these hands so that the people could not say I had spilled the blood of their former king. You can witness to the success I have had—up until this very moment."

I turned away, seeking to divert his attention in order that I might escape from this terrible moment and save the throne for Solomon. In the corner I saw a pair of small, curiously shaped altars, an incense stand, bowls, lamps, goblets—and my heart suddenly crumbled in my breast. "What is this?" I asked unsteadily, moving away from Benaiah.

"For the ancient rituals," responded Benaiah.

"Rituals? Yahweh is not worshipped here—but in His temple."

"No, O Nathan, stupid to the end! These are the fittings of the shrine to Ashtoreth of heaven! This is the place where Bathsheba and I often worshipped, sacrificing after we made love, which was proper."

I drew back, as if I had seen a viper slip through a crack in the wall. "Worship?" I stammered. "Making love?"

Benaiah's voice sounded both disgusted and contemptuous. "Did you never know? Or suspect? I would think that Solomon, even as a boy, suspected and that for a long time he has known. Why do you think I killed her so quickly before him? Because it was not only she and Zabud, blessings on his long-gone memory, who bore out the ark, stealing it under the nose of Yahweh that night—it was I, also! But had I confessed or had she implicated me—my life must have been forfeit at that moment. Yet—yet I hated to do it, Nathan. Truly, I loved her—but she was only a woman."

"Only a woman!"

"What? What tone is that?" Benaiah sounded genuinely surprised. He nodded. "I confess that I am the stupid one. So you—you, too, Nathan—you loved Bathsheba!" He commenced to laugh—at first a gasping sound, followed by a shaking silence that was as much pain as humor. He recovered in a moment: "And I was deceived by you all the time! Perhaps you were lovers!" His tone shifted into fierceness.

"No," I said slowly, and not through fear, but thinking back with longing. "No, we were never lovers—though I much desired her."

"You knew that I was Bathsheba's lover?"

"No."

"You did not suspect it at all?"

"No."

"Then if you had no hint of that, when it was so clear—yes, even to Solomon—you didn't suspect anything else. Like my killing Merib-baal."

My wits began to return. Obviously the early return of Solomon had shaken Benaiah. Perhaps I should be able to force him to reveal more of the mysteries that lay behind him.

"I thought," I said, as casually as I could, "that his death, years ago, was strange."

"I had prepared for him, the descendant of the true line of kings, to head up the rebellion."

"You encouraged him?"

"Yes."

"You would have supported him against Solomon?"

Benaiah's glance was lowering. "I would have disposed of him. But he mistrusted me and lost his nerve at the last minute. I had to kill him when he tried to confess to you."

"Did Bathsheba know this?" I demanded. Benaiah was silent.

"You always wanted Solomon out of the way?" I persisted.

"Of course. What right had he to the throne except his mother's wheedling? David had succeeded because he was the best man, even better than Saul. I was better than Solomon—I had fought a lion, mind, alone—but I never had a chance."

"But you dissuaded Solomon from fighting the Egyptians," I said slowly.

"My plans for myself were not ready," Benaiah replied with perfect simplicity. "I did not want a figurehead or some child between me and the crown. If he had been killed in battle then, not I but his young son or another of his family would have succeeded him."

I took a deep breath. "Then it was necessary to use every measure to keep him alive," I said.

Benaiah nodded. "Now it is no longer needful. Enough of the northern tribes of Israel will crown me king and anoint me, even as they anointed David!"

"But Judah," I said fearfully, "Judah will not yield."

"Then we shall have a bath of blood," Benaiah said. His face stood stark and strong. "I have allies even with the Philistines and the Egyptians, yea, even with those of Babylon, six days' march from Tadmor."

"Michal, all the others, they were part of the plot?"

"Certainly," Benaiah said impatiently. He gnawed his lip, still caught in some hidden snare of doubts.

"A very long plot," I said. "A plot of many years."

"Almost as long as my life. I have no idea why I hesitated so often. Hadad's raids, deeds like that—they were all part of it." He leaned toward me. "Stealing the ark—that was what I enjoyed most, cutting real power out from under Solomon. Bathsheba never believed in the ark, she taught me that it was all nonsense. Hittite to the core, you see."

"You know where the ark is hidden!"

"Of course."

"Tell me, tell me!" I flung myself at his feet and embraced them. I would have done anything, sacrificed anything, to have had such a secret. I felt Benaiah stepping back with disgust. I clutched his legs closer. He bent over and peeled off my finger-grip, flinging me back.

"You cannot refuse to tell me!" I panted.

"Can I not?" His tone was sardonic, almost amused, even at such a sacred topic. "Have I kept silence all these years and you think I am unable to keep silence longer?"

"You shall tell me!"

"Nathan." A peculiar quality in Benaiah's voice stopped my insane babbling. I looked up at him and then rose from the floor. "If, as you pretend," Benaiah said coldly, "the whereabouts of the ark is a mystery so precious to you—there is one thing yet more precious."

"I do not understand," I said helplessly. "How might such a thing be?"

"Listen to me! Three people stole the ark—one drunk, the other two contemptuous of the god it pretended to represent. He was profane—but Bathsheba and I were simply throwing away trash."

"Yahweh will strike you down!"

"If He can, if He can, let Him strike. But listen, Nathan! Zabud is dead by his own hand. I myself killed Bathsheba. Does not this knowledge put some light into your fuddled brain?"

I breathed slowly, deeply. "Then you, Benaiah," I said "are the only man alive who knows where the ark is."

"The dead cannot speak," Benaiah said. "Only I can tell you. Therefore, remember, O Nathan, my life is sacred unto you."

He stared at me intently. "What am I to do?" I moaned. Benaiah's face changed subtly. He seemed to withdraw into slyness.

"If all else fails, I shall not have to stay in this land," Benaiah said, his eyes lambent in the hollows of his face. I knew what he meant. If he had managed to escape to any one of the six Levite cities—Kedesh, Shechem, or Hebron west of the Jordan, Bezer, Ramoth, or Golan to the east of that stream—he would have been safe, in sanctuary, anywhere within their walls. As it was, the altar was his only refuge in Jerusalem.

"Do not look for sanctuary," I said. "Even in the holy place. Solomon, when young, was not disposed to spare Joab. In his old age, he will hardly be more merciful."

Benaiah shook his head. "Know that I shall not clasp the horns of any altar," he said. "But the Egyptians or the Sea Peoples or the Assyrians will be glad to have a captain of my reputation."

"You would not!" I exclaimed. "Not against your own!"

"Did not David fight with the Philistines?"

"But he had fled for his life!"

"So may I be fleeing," Benaiah said, inclining his head. He beckoned me to a corner dimly lit by the flickering lamp. There I saw a clay coffin lying on the ground. Benaiah bent and took off the mannikin cover of clay. He lifted the lamp so that the shadow of the saucer fell away. It showed me what was inside—a dusty bare-boned skeleton, a feather-banded headdress. I shuddered. "What is this?" I demanded.

"The remains of a Philistine warrior that I killed as a boy," Benaiah returned. "He died many years ago but his bones are still defiant."

"You keep this in your house?"

"I keep it to remind me of my own fate, Nathan."

"I shall tell Solomon all this," I said, drawing on my last reserve of defiance. "You shall be taken and tortured, the secret of the ark squeezed from your lips."

"You are of a sudden so bloody," mocked Benaiah, "you who posed so well as tenderhearted and compassionate, even to the enemies of the Hebrews." He dropped his mocking tone. "Do you not know, Nathan, that it is a soldier's business to resist torture? Do you think for a moment you can rack my limbs, burn me, tear me apart—and thereby force me to speak if I do not wish to? No, no: disabuse your mind. I shall be steadfast. Only by my own will shall I tell you."

It sounded like an echo of Solomon—but I knew that Benaiah was telling the truth. He was iron, granite, bronze—inhuman, above pain and torture. "What can I offer you for such a secret?" I said painfully, myself in torture.

"Be kind to an old soldier," Benaiah said sardonically. "Seat me on Solomon's throne, raise your voice in my behalf—and we shall see."

"No!" I screamed. I flung myself forward at him, determined to force him in some unknown way to tell me about the ark. But with his left hand he brushed me off. With his right, he dealt me a blow with his forearm that half-stunned me.

"Fool!" he said, bending over me, his eyes blazing. "Fool! Tonight all shall be changed! I shall sit on Solomon's throne! I alone shall bring back the ark!"

I blinked upward at him in my daze. "You have been deceived yourself," I mumbled, my old chops aching from his blow. "The army is true to the king. Get yourself out of Jerusalem, Benaiah; there is no hope for you here."

I saw Benaiah's face change above me. An expression flitted across his stony features: cunning, wariness, a fleeting furtive shift I could not describe.

"I am leaving Jerusalem," Benaiah said thickly. "I shall be of value to other kings in other lands. Shishak of Egypt sheltered Hadad and raised his children to power; how much more will he appreciate me than Solomon! Or even Rezon in Syria, who fears me. Think of his welcome for the general of the Hebrew armies who knows all strategies, who is master of all tactics! Do you not believe that I shall be rewarded as no man ever has been before?"

"You will be a traitor!" I exclaimed weakly.

Benaiah shook his head. "Maybe it is the will of Yahweh—though you would know more about that than I."

"Traitor, blasphemer," I said even more weakly. Benaiah was no older than I in many ways but he was by far the more powerful in personality and strength.

"We have talked enough," Benaiah said, his beard bristling, his eyes gleaming. "When the time comes, I give you my farewell to Solomon: farewell to him, wretched king and coward, in search of glory and fame and riches but not the welfare of his people, who does not know how to value his servants at their worth! Think of me, Benaiah, when next your army faces the enemy—think of me as leading them and directing them! Farewell!"

He lifted up his head. "Yes," he said hoarsely. "I shall leave Jerusalem—to come back with an army and take the city for my own. That will be best."

His fist rose and descended upon my head. My senses swam. I lapsed into darkness and pain.

CHAPTER TWENTY

The Humbling of Solomon

When I recovered consciousness—no more than a few minutes later, it proved—I could not at first understand my position. I seemed to have become an ape. I was fixed in the similitude of an animal climbing a tree. I thought for a fearful moment that I had been transformed. I cried out in a terrified, half-animal croak. But when my head cleared a little more, I discovered that what I had imagined was not so. Instead, Benaiah had fastened me, hands and feet, to a post in the middle of the room. My lashings made me cling to it like a monkey.

Regaining my sense, I shouted as loud as I could. The walls gave me back deep, sullen echoes. I knew then that noise was useless. Too thick, too thick, these chambers like stone crypts! I held my nerves steady. I disciplined my mind against my sash-tied wrists and ankles. I strove for calm. I commenced to think as clearly as I could about the situation, what might be done in such a desperate case as mine.

I had to get free as soon as possible. The alarm must be raised. The fleeing Benaiah must be captured and swiftly brought to justice. At liberty he would prove more of a danger to the Hebrews than he had formerly been a bulwark. But how was it to be done?

I tested my bonds. Both hands and feet were painfully, securely tied about the post. Beyond the writhing of my body, I could not move. I twisted my head. I tried to see all the contents of the room: nothing was within reach—except the brazen stool of Bathsheba that Benaiah had carelessly pushed near me, with its burning lamp atop.

I stared longingly at this, just out of my reach. I wondered if I could use hip or shoulder to shove it nearer. I tried. It was impossible. Every effort I made thrust the stool a little farther off. I desisted, panting. I commenced to force myself to think more keenly. Little by little, an idea formed in my burning brain.

Sliding down the post, to a squatting position which was

not too uncomfortable, I bowed my body backward. I stretched my head as far as I could toward the lamp. It was a shallow red-clay saucer, the lip pinched in on one side for a wick-holder. After some struggle, I found my neck and head arched nearly over the lamp. I turned my spine, wrenching it in the process. But my heart bounded. My object had been achieved. My gray beard dipped into the open oil of the lamp.

I tucked my head about the post. I dripped what I could and wiped the rest of the oil upon the gaudy sash which tied my hands. I took a deep breath. I stretched backward to my former position. This time, straining to the utmost, bobbing my chin upward, I managed to pass the tip of my beard through the tall light of the wick.

Almost immediately, my beard flamed up. Smoke and soot rose into my eyes and nose. I gagged and spat. I snapped my head back to my bindings. As carefully as I could, tears streaming, I applied the fire to them. They flared and began to burn. I instantly crushed my half-consumed beard against the post to extinguish it. Coughing, blinded, half-strangled, I remained so until I felt the flame eating intolerably into my flesh. I shrieked. At the same time I pulled with all my strength at my bonds. The bits of charred and burning cloth fell away. My hands dropped free. They felt like dead things attached to my body, so long had blood been kept from them. Conscious of the need for haste, I massaged them vigorously against my body. As soon as I felt the tingle that announced the return of life, I commenced clumsily to untie the lashings of my feet.

It took longer than I believed. And, when it was accomplished, for long minutes I was unable to stand erect. I was forced to stay in the smoke-lowering room, full of the noxious smells of the burned wool of Benaiah's sashes and my own charred beard. I lay back on the floor, laboriously sucking in air. At last I felt my feet could bear me. I crossed my legs to get erect, feeling the strain upon every sinew. My flesh cried out in pain. I staggered to the door. I was intent upon one thing only: I must get to the palace. I must tell Solomon what had happened before it was too late.

"Benaiah must not escape!" I shouted. I was surprised to hear the ferocity in my shaking tones.

The way from the upper city to the palace was ten times as far as it had ever seemed before. I muffled my face because my beard was so unseemly. But I ran until my heart threatened to break out of the cage of my ribs. Again and again I was forced to lean against a building or squat by the wayside to regain my breath. I was challenged twice by the street watch but immediately allowed to pass, as they recognized me. I kicked sleeping dogs out of the way in the dark, struggled over other unnameable beasts, spattered through puddles of ordure, and at last managed to get up the hill, to climb up the steps into the palace.

I showed my smutted face and my burned beard to the amazement of the guards and rushed past them, not without—I noted—curious looks exchanged between them. I scrambled as fast as I could for Solomon's private chambers in the rear, bursting past the last sentinel without ceremony. The king sat there, in his favorite chair, calmly reading a roll of papyrus.

"Benaiah!" I gasped.

Solomon looked up at me, unmoved. "What about our brave general?" he inquired. He clapped the columned sheet of papyrus together.

"He has fled the city! We shall never know his plots, how many, who were involved! He must be seized!" I wheezed like a goat on the heights, snuffling as I sank exhausted to the floor.

Solomon raised one hand. "Do not be alarmed, Nathan," he said quietly. "I expected Benaiah would flee."

I gazed up at him, round-eyed. "You ex—expected it?" I stammered.

Solomon smiled. "He can only go across our borders to another nation," he said. "I have made my arrangements with Shishak and the others as to his reception. It will be more inhospitable than he expects. They wish to remain friends with Solomon, with the Hebrews."

I goggled even more. "When was this concluded?" I cried. "I knew nothing of it!"

"Your face is your misfortune in court," Solomon said, not unkindly. "It is impossible for your expression to keep a secret. I have an understanding with our neighbors—with each of them, long ago concluded—that we shall return to each other those traitors who flee from their native land."

He appeared to see my condition for the first time. "What has happened to you, Nathan?" he demanded.

I shook my head. "Little of consequence," I replied, brave with the pain of my burns.

Solomon smiled even more widely. "You have had an adventure. With Benaiah, no doubt. You shall tell me of it this night," he said. "I am in no mood for sleep."

My skin felt looser, more comfortable on my bones. I composed myself. For a long minute, neither of us spoke. Then, in a changed tone, I said: "O wise Solomon, what of the army? Who shall lead, now that Benaiah is as a dead man?"

Solomon shrugged and rose lazily. "This is not the place to discuss such matters," he said. "But I agree that it is the time. Let us go to my audience room, Nathan. There the lists of the descendants of the Mighty Thirty of David's time are kept. There you may tell your tale."

I nodded respectfully and rose to follow him from the room. We proceeded down the hall, turned right, and halted before the chamber that contained the elegant Phoenician gold-and-silver carpet wrought by Canaanite skill. Solomon stopped. He looked at the door, running his fingers lightly over its carved surfaces. He loved all beautiful things, almost too well, I fear.

"It is good to be back in Jerusalem," Solomon said. "To be at home. A beautiful door," he said in the accents he always reserved for that which struck his fancy. It was a rarity, a high paneled wooden door made for him in Babylon. Wrought in flowers, gourds, checkerwork, and scales, it was colored black at the bottom, ascending to yellow at the top. It had attached a new device—one of those gadgets which continually delighted Solomon—a bronze bar grooved into the wood. Sliding across, worked by metal pins that were a wonder of art, it could be infallibly operated by a key from within or without.

"Bar the door," Solomon instructed me as we entered. "I wish to talk to you alone, Nathan. There must be no interruptions." I bowed and turned the key on the inside behind us.

As I did, the curtains at the left of the double door flared out. The wild face of Benaiah appeared, his beard bristling. He snatched the key from my hand. He thrust me reeling to one side. He turned to face the king.

"It is the only entrance," he said in satisfaction. "You shall talk to me instead of Nathan."

"You are not at your governor's post, Benaiah," Solomon said sternly.

Benaiah grinned, rictus without mirth. "No," he responded, "but you shall be soon, Solomon! At your post in sheol!"

"It is true that we shall talk," Solomon said, strangely unruffled.

"Only to say this," Benaiah returned, "that the Hebrews

can have but one king. That will be he who goes from this room tonight."

"Would you sin against Yahweh? Would you raise your hand against His anointed king?" I demanded in horror.

"Not my hand," Benaiah said significantly. He drew his sword.

Solomon paled at the dull glitter of the weapon, at the too-evident intent of Benaiah. "We shall talk," he repeated, as if it were a formula to ward off death.

"You shall not!" I cried. I tried to restrain Benaiah. I grappled with him but he brushed me back. "Dotard," he snarled, "barely able to stand on your own legs, will you prevent me?"

"Yahweh shall prevent you!" I gasped. "I shall curse you and your blood to the uttermost!" But I never felt more helpless than I did at the moment, sitting sprawled on that richly carpeted floor, too weak to rise.

Benaiah advanced toward Solomon. The king remained unmoving in front of his throne. I never admired him as much as I did at that moment. I tried to cry for help. My dry throat choked. Solomon did not utter a word. Benaiah poised his short blade a yard from the royal breast of purple and gold. He turned his head slightly, to keep his eye cocked at Solomon. He wanted to speak to me, to gloat at the last.

"Have you ever fought a lion, Nathan?"

"No," I said faintly.

"You may have to fight one in your times. All lions are not dead. Let me, Benaiah, tell you how it is done. You must be prepared to sacrifice your left arm to save your life."

"What are you saying?"

"Face the lion with the sword in your right hand, held low. The lion will roar. His spittle will nearly blind you. He will rise up on his hind legs to seize your throat, to claw your guts. As he opens his jaws, you must thrust in your left forearm—and at the same moment, thrust forward hard with the sword, until it sinks up to the hilt. He will open his mouth in pain. Take back your left arm, rip the sword upward—and spring back to watch him die.

"Do you understand, Nathan? This is what I do to Solomon, the Lion of Judah!"

Benaiah lunged. His sword seemed to smoke in the air. It moved faster than my eye from the floor could see it.

But not faster than Solomon. As if he had been used to sword-play all his life, the king dropped his eyes from Benaiah's glare the instant before the lunge. He saw the thrust. He made a single swaying movement toward his left. It was so close that (as he told me after) the fist gripping the hilt struck his right side. He felt the cold flat of the iron against his skin as it cut through his robe.

Benaiah, not finding the resistance of flesh he expected, stumbled forward. Solomon hoped to snatch the blade from his grasp by entangling it further. He sprang another pace to the side of the dais. This time Benaiah was quicker. He managed to withdraw the short sharp blade of his weapon from the tangled cloth of the robe.

Solomon was not paralyzed. He half turned. With the edge of his hand, he cut down on the side of Benaiah's brawny neck as he stood half-stooped like a hissing goose, neck outstretched. It had no effect. It was a tricky blow, one that had been shown him by visiting jugglers who assured him it was sure death. Benaiah did not seem to feel it at all.

As he wheeled again upon the king, Solomon drew back in the last extremity. He saw his end. He himself became entangled in his robes of state. He tripped. He fell backward, supine and staring upward at the fearsome Benaiah. Benaiah sprang upon him, vaulting his body. He spanned it with his trunks of legs—even as Solomon had once spanned (and spared) the helpless body of the Egyptian princess Theke. Perhaps it was a remembrance such as this that made Benaiah pause. Next instant he lifted his blade high in both hands, ready to drive it down, home into the helpless monarch's breast.

I had not been idle. Both Benaiah and Solomon had forgotten about me in the intensity of their struggle, mind and body. Perhaps Benaiah disregarded me as an old dodderer. But I knew I could show him I still had strength left. I scrabbled my way across the soundless magnificence of the carpet toward the king's own weapon-stand in the corner. It held a richly worked sword, two gold-shafted javelins. I seized one from out its rack. I rose to my knees, drawing back my arm. I aimed the dart at the broad back of Benaiah, only a few feet from me. I could not miss! A child could not miss! Now was the moment to deliver Solomon from his clutches.

My muscles shrank within my arm. The javelin wavered, drooped. I knew, in that frightful instant, that I could not throw it. I could not kill Benaiah—though I hated and feared him, though I knew he was a black menace to all the hopes of our state. He carried with him alone the irrevocable secret of the hiding-place of the ark—worth more than a hundred kings, worth more than any gifts or gold, the heritage of the Hebrews from their very beginning, the holy spot of Yahweh Himself!

I dropped the javelin. Benaiah must have heard its thud on the carpet. He turned and grinned momentarily at me. He snapped his attention back to the prostrate form of Solomon beneath him.

Then he paused. He half straightened. He looked helplessly about him. From my position on the floor, crawling as I was to do what I could for my king, I saw his face suffuse with dark blood. Then Benaiah's swarthy face changed color. It seemed to turn green as an unripe olive. Abruptly, the tide of blood washed back into it, visibly surging up his bearded cheeks. His skin turned the color of red clay for the pot. His eyes, so fierce an instant before, became suffused, dim as those of a man about to drown. He swayed in his place. His eyes rolled upward. A look of bewilderment passed over his features. They lost their wild wrath, their rejoicing in blood. They became bland and relaxed. His form shuddered. His hands slacked their grip on the sword. His knees locked inward by reflex to support himself but still his thick body bent in the middle.

Through all these strange happenings—that descended upon Solomon's captain like a thunderstroke, in less than seconds—Benaiah managed to cling to his sword. Crooked about the hilt, his fingers refused to release it—just as his muscles refused equally to drive it downward. To the last, Benaiah tried to carry out the fell purpose of his heart. He was not able to do it. A gasp came from his lungs; he panted wildly a moment. I believe he died by the judgment of Yahweh that flung the blood into his head and burst his veins at that very moment. Yahweh's own Hand had stricken him.

As he fell upon the shrinking form of the king between his legs, toppling like a mass of masonry, Benaiah dropped his sword, point downward. Solomon saw it fall. He shrieked, a dreadful sound in the room that pierced my hearing. He writhed to escape the sharp blade.

He had little time to move his body. Yet he did manage to twist between the palings of Benaiah's legs. Not enough to avoid the sword entirely, but enough to save his life. The heavy blade sliced through the right side of his gown. It stuck in the floor. At first I uttered a cry of gratitude for I thought it had not touched him.

Next moment I knew I was wrong. The edge had cut the

side of Solomon, close to his stomach. The blood widened out in a slow, growing pool.

The dead weight, the body of Benaiah crashed down upon the king in a slow, deliberate fall. Solomon put up his arms. He wrenched his whole form, enough to deflect the toppling corpse. It struck his other side, thumped on the floor. It rolled over once and was still. The eyes of the dead man stared madly up at the ceiling. His lips were drawn back in his last snarl. His arms lay still crooked in the contraction of his final spasm.

On my hands and knees, I crawled to the side of Solomon. I plucked the sword from where it stood in the cypress floor. I flung it away. I sobbed aloud at the sight of his bleeding. I tore my own garments to stanch it. Solomon—his face white, his lips ringed with bile—gestured toward his golden gong. I understood. I flung his wand at it, hearing its signal of sound reverberate.

It was over. Benaiah was dead. Yahweh had spoken in His own fashion. Not anyone but He had taken the life of Solomon's commander. And in doing so, He had pronounced sentence upon the whole of the Hebrew nation. He had spoken: Never again would we see the holy ark! It had vanished from us forever. Yahweh had hidden His face behind His wrath. Woe, woe to Solomon and his people!

I bent my head over the body of Benaiah and wept. The tears scalded my eyes. I felt a rough plucking at my shoulder and turned my wet face. I stared down into the pale countenance of Solomon.

"What is this?" he demanded weakly, in a voice of feeble rage. "You weep for this assassin, this triple traitor, this—"

For the only time in my life, I interrupted the king. "No," I said. I stood up with a jerk. "No," I said again, "I do not weep for him. I weep for your people, O Solomon!"

The king's jaw went slack. He stared up at me, totally at a loss for the only time perhaps in his life. He found no words in which to reply to me. Beneath me, the form of Solomon seemed to recede and grow small in an immeasurable distance. My eyes became clouded with the message of the Lord. I spoke unknown sorrows in ecstasy.

"Take me to my couch," Solomon said faintly.

I came again to realize that I was within the chamber. I looked down at my feet in astonishment.

Solomon, mighty king and ruler of the Hebrews, lay fainted before me.

Solomon opened his enormous dark eyes—the eyes of Bathsheba. He stared up at me. He tried to gather his thoughts, to separate them from dreams.

"It is you, Nathan," he said in a whisper.

"Yes, O lord and king," I murmured.

"It was Benaiah who was my fate, was it not?"

"Yes, O king."

"I dreamed I felt his sword in my side. Is it true?"

"Yes, O Solomon," I managed to say. "He was a traitor dog. Yahweh struck him down at the instant he was about to slay his master."

"Let us praise Yahweh. Was it a deep cut, one that bled much?"

"Yes," I said, wondering.

"Does the blood stop?" asked Solomon feebly.

I swallowed with effort. "Not yet," I told the king, "but soon. I shall call Zadok. He swears he knows secret remedies of spiders' webs, of lint and oil, of—"

"Spare me," Solomon said with a glimmer of grim humor. "It may cease flowing, it may never cease. I found this out when I was a child with a cut, Nathan. Bathsheba told me the truth. My blood does not heal or thicken. You and Benaiah knew I was frightened of swords, timid in battle, afraid of the slightest injury that would make my blood come from my skin. Even a bruise, as you may have seen, lasts for a year or more—and oozings are persistent. My joints ache. My blood is different from others. It is king's blood, royal blood."

Already on my knees, I fell forward to his couch, fumbling for his weak white hand. "It shall be cured!" I vowed. "It shall be made right! There are herbs, unguents, the secret recipes of Egypt, of the old wisdom of the Canaanites! All, all shall be tried!"

"Tried in vain," Solomon murmured. "I have heard of kings such as I before. Never have they been cured. Always they have died."

"No one dies unless Yahweh wills it!" I said passionately. Suddenly I was closer to him than his own father. I understood in a flash why Bathsheba had coddled him so, protected him. I comprehended his own reluctance for the normal hazards of life. I shared the ultimate secret of his mother and himself at this moment, the guilty knowledge that had never come to me before.

Solomon, watching my face, understood as well the revelation in my brain. He smiled faintly at me. "Faithful Nathan," he whispered. Never had I loved him and understood him, his noble courage and his despair, as much as at that moment.

As it turned out, the judgment of Yahweh upon the impious Benaiah was hardly necessary. There had been little support even in the army for his bid for kingship. His brusque ways and harsh discipline (though it had brought victories) had not endeared Benaiah to his soldiers. The army, as Solomon had foreseen, was far from revolt. The palace guards, of course, had been infected by bribery—I had the pair outside Solomon's chamber executed without further ado.

But the real bulwark against any succession by Benaiah—even had he been in league with Zadok for his coronation, something I was never able to confirm—was Rehoboam. It must be recalled that this youngster had grown into a sturdy young man of twenty-one at the time of the attempted coup. He had more than an inkling of it. He had gathered around him a coterie of fearless young men, both as bodyguards and as a set of councilors. Benaiah had made no attempt to breach this human wall protecting the young prince. Perhaps he thought to overawe them, once upon the throne of David.

Myself, I believe that Benaiah, as was his habit, again had made league with a woman—this time, Tamar with her remarkable influence over Rehoboam. Possibly he had agreed with her that she was to persuade Rehoboam to journey with her to a remote part of the kingdom, to return only when all was secured. But this was disposed of by the Lord when He set infatuation between Hiram-abi and the king's wife and they fled together back to Tyre. After that, there was nothing left but the essay of despair I have described. It was a lost endeavor to gain what was shielded by invisible powers. Indeed, it seemed all the forces that guarded the Hebrews combined to fulfill the prophecies of the wise men that Solomon should have his throne until the end of his life. I suppose this may have accounted for the king's almost supernal confidence and calm on his arrival in Jerusalem.

Whatever the hidden story behind it all, Benaiah's aborted coup served two purposes. The first was that Rehoboam became more firmly seated in power and in succession to the throne than any other son of the line of David. He also afterward evinced a growing dislike for advice from his elders. He turned to the young men who had surrounded him in the hours of his danger. He listened to their words, rather than to those of myself and the other old advisers of Solomon.

Thus he opened the gate for Jeroboam to split the kingdom of the Hebrews in twain, an event which had been but dimly predicted until that time. Jeroboam in Egypt, hearing that Rehoboam was about to become king, dared to rouse himself to intrigue with the northern tribes of Israel. They called upon him to return. He came. He confronted Rehoboam in a great meeting among the oaks of Hebron. I was there and the rebel challenge the young king.

"Your father made our yoke heavy!" he shouted so that all the people of the surrounding tribes might hear him. "Now therefore do you make our service to you easier and lighten this heavy yoke! If you do, we shall faithfully serve you!"

Cunningly, Jeroboam omitted to say what would happen if Rehoboam did not accede to such demands. But everyone knew that he spoke of the forced labor of the Hebrews in the Lebanon mountains, of the chains beside the forges and furnaces of Ezion Geber.

Rehoboam did wisely at first. He addressed the gathering of the tribes. He asked them to return to their tents and gather once more, in three days, for their answer. This they did, peaceably enough. They expected no doubt he would give them a reasonable answer.

"How do you advise me," Rehoboam asked me later in the council-room of the palace, "you that have advised my father Solomon for so long? Should I give to this insolent Jeroboam what he has demanded of me?"

I thought of the mistakes of his father and had no hesitation in my reply. I phrased it, as I thought, carefully enough to allow the new king enough way to say what he wanted to.

"Kings were set up to serve their people," I said firmly. "If you take advantage of this opportunity, if you speak mildly in response to their demands, they will be your faithful subjects forever."

Rehoboam frowned. He had not expected this. His glance swept the serried ranks of his young men on either side of the throne. Their grim faces and set jaws reflected his own expression.

"Do you advise, O Nathan," he demanded harshly, "that I yield to this usurper Jeroboam?"

"No, O prince," I said. "The throne will be yours. But many of the northern tribes support this man and his words. It is best to speak fair words to them until such time as he may be disposed of."

What did he reply—the future of the Hebrews as a united nation hanging upon his words?

I go too fast, too far. The story must unwind itself, like the wool from the turning distaff. For this was only the first day of respite given Rehoboam. It was the day upon which Solomon recovered from his wound enough to reassume the throne—which already, in his sickness, was shared by Rehoboam, anointed by Zadok.

Contrary to his dread, Solomon's wound had healed over the long months that followed that terrible night. But he had lost much of his blood. His convalescence was slow. I must say that even Zadok lost pounds of his sleek fat in his assiduous attendance upon the king and his grievous hurt. I shall ever give praise to Yahweh for the day when we saw that the red gaping lips of the cut had come together and commenced to join into healthy flesh.

Nevertheless, the spirit of Solomon did not mend. His pride returned as he was able to walk. He assumed, as I have said, once again the leadership of his kingdom that had been assigned to Rehoboam when he believed he was dying. But his air was gloomy and austere. That first day he spent much time with manuscripts, less with people. He talked to me a long while about taking up the life of a hermit, relinquishing the rule to his son forever.

I took these for maunderings. I placed no faith in anything except the recovery of Solomon—then approaching his fifty-fourth year—and the resumption of his rule. Not until the next day, when the vision from Yahweh seized upon me, did I think differently. Then all became clear to me.

I went to Solomon privately. I told him with awe of what had appeared to me. He listened intently. Only at the end of my recital did he take a deep breath. His pale face pulsed.

"There is no other way?" he asked.

"None," I said.

"Twice I have left Jerusalem. Each time disaster has come."

"It is the will of the Lord."

"I will not give up the kingship of the Hebrews," he said.

"You must!" I replied, courageous in my soul.

Solomon rose. He commenced to pace back and forth, slowly, because the wound still pained him and he feared it would reopen. At length he stopped and faced me.

"There is no mistake?" he asked.

"None."

Solomon looked at me with entreaty. I shook my head. "What am I to do?" he mumbled.

"The Lord commands that we go to the desert of Judah," I said sternly. "There we shall meet those chosen to meet us."

The eastern slopes of the mountains of Judah are rounded hills of chalk. They front on the desolation of water that is the Dead Sea where grow the bright desert apples which vanish in smoke and dust when one squeezes them in the palm. In the cliffs facing east, there are many caves, deep and dry. Here for untold centuries, have gathered men of Yahweh, flyers from the law, hermits and rebels. There are paths for sheep and goats. For none else. There are potholes to hold the rain but plants and living green things shun the area. There, nonetheless, went Solomon and I—alone except for the bearers of our litters, and those that carried our food and drink.

I did not know what to expect of Yahweh's instructions. He had told me no more than I had told my king. But I had no fear but that the moment would come in those burning-white wastes when we would be instructed upon what would be our destiny. Solomon rode grimly beside me. He had recovered most of his defiance during the night. We advanced slowly, smelling dry dust in our noses, our skins flaking from the heat, our bodies oozing slow sweat where we reclined. Yet we saw no living things in all that pale ocean of wave after wave of hills.

At last, rounding one of the escarpments by the sea, I spied movement in the shadow. I directed our bearers to it. They quickened their pace, glad for the promise of rest. Some slight smoke rose from the midst of the small strange band of men there, as we halted. The palanquin was lowered. Solomon and I stepped out, looked, and were silent in amazement. I looked at my king.

Solomon stood by his litter, fists on his hips, his head thrown back. His rich gown glittered in the full rays of the sun, a magnificent sight. He looked at the dusty crew before him with disdain, as they huddled around their tiny fire. He looked up at the blank unthreatening holes in the limestone cliff, then at the holes in the ground about this tribe. They watched him, not suspicious as dogs might have been but wondering, as conies who see a vision from afar.

"What kind of men are you?" demanded Solomon, his voice thick with contempt. I knew the strength of royalty in him was altogether restored. The group looked from one to another. At last the oldest among them—shabby, dirty, long-bearded, half-naked—arose with a vast dignity. "We are," he said, "as you see us."

"You are miserable and vain," said Solomon angrily. He turned to me. "I have come this long way only to see a band of beggars?" he queried. I bowed my head and folded my hands: I said nothing. Solomon glanced again at their leader. "What are these holes in the ground hereabout?" he demanded.

"These are our graves," said the old man simply. "That which is nearest you is mine." Solomon dropped his miniatory hand. He shied backward like a frightened horse. "We dig them deeper every day as penance," said the old man.

"Is it so?" said Solomon in a shaken voice. "What do you expect from such work?"

"We desire to own none of the things of this world. The pegs of our lives are embedded in the bosom of one god, we hang by his mercy. We keep our graves clean and deep. We say our prayers over them and long to be gone from this earth."

"Why is this?"

"Because," said the old man seriously, "in the skies, hidden from our eyes, are all good things. There is nothing here that is good except death."

"Why do you not kill yourselves, then?" asked Solomon.

"Because it is forbidden for men to traffic in killing, even themselves. That is reserved for the one god."

"How do you eat, then?"

"We eat only grass and those fruits that grow from the ground."

Solomon frowned. "Are you all so?" he queried.

"Even so," said the old man.

"Who is chief among you?" Solomon asked.

"None is more than another," replied the old man. "But since I was born first, I am oldest and shall by the grace of heaven die first. They trust me to speak for all."

"You amuse me," Solomon said roughly.

The old man bowed in humility. "If it is so, it is so," he said.

"You may see by my face and by my clothes that I am a king," Solomon added.

"We have nothing to do with kings and they have nothing to do with us," answered the old man, still with the utmost respect.

Solomon flushed as he always did when he considered

himself contradicted. "Do you dare to speak so to the mightiest man on earth?" he demanded.

"Even if you are so," said the old man calmly, "we have no need of you."

"If you say so, you may have need of your heads," Solomon said slowly.

With almost regal dignity, the old man in rags pointed to what he had said was his grave, the gaping hole next to him. "If this is so, we shall all take the shortest way to the last of our homes," he said.

Solomon swung away from them. "You have seen what I have brought you to see, O great king," I said softly to him. "We need not stay."

Solomon paid no heed to what I said. He accosted the old man again. "I find you gathered here about a dying fire," he said in a more gentle tone. "You are hermits, dusty and starving, living alone. You have neither gold nor silver nor any of the useful things of the world. Think how much they might do for your condition—and that I might give them to you. Would you not have your fill of such things?"

"No one," said the old man, "has his fill of such. Instead, they have their fill of him."

"Why do you live amidst your graves?" asked Solomon after a pause. He could not repress a shudder.

"We need to keep them in our eyes for we have temptations as do all men. We look and renew our talk of death and the world to come where all magnificence shall be less than ashes here."

"Why such morbid talk?"

"So as to banish the image of the things such men as you love and better serve our god."

"Yet you eat grass," Solomon said in the tone that I recognized as the one he used when he commenced an intricate argument. "Is this sensible?"

"It tells our bellies that they are not the tombs of living things," responded the old man. "And even as our clothes and talk and poverty tell us that we are not supreme, the grass tells us that the pleasure of the gullet passes."

"Is not grass living?"

For the first time, the old man regarded Solomon severely. He drew himself up from his hunched position and revealed himself as an extraordinarily tall man. He spoke firmly though without a touch of malice. "You say you are a king," he replied, "but you are a splitter of hairs. We are engaged with truth, not with argument."

"A word from me," cried Solomon, "and your skulls shall be split!"

The old man stooped. He took up from the ground a yellow, gaping skull—one of a half dozen that lay about his feet. He brushed the dust from it delicately, tenderly. "O mighty king," he said quietly, holding out the ghastly relic, from which Solomon drew back, "do you know who once owned this skull?"

"Not I," Solomon managed to say.

"It was a chief, perhaps as great as you, one who dealt as a tyrant with his people, one who wronged the weak and heaped up the rubbish of this world. Death took him and left this behind."

Sweat gleamed on Solomon's forehead. "The will of Yahweh be done," he muttered.

The old man bent once again and brought up a second skull. "Do you know whose skull this was?" he inquired mildly.

"No!"

"This was that of another ruler, perhaps greater than yourself, who dealt justly by his people, humbled himself in prayer, renounced the possessions of this life, tended to all his duties as a chief of men—and death took him and left this behind."

"Then there is no difference," Solomon said.

"Only the difference," said the old man calmly, "that one is a sad souvenir and the other is a holy relic."

With a quick gesture, the king of rags clapped the two skulls together before Solomon's face. The king, whose face had become ashen, sprang back. "Do you threaten me?" he exclaimed.

"Never," said the old man, still holding the skulls before the king's face. "I do this only to compare these with your face. King as you say you are, I wish I knew which of these two skulls you are!"

To my stupefaction, Solomon began to tremble. Slowly, as if forced down by an invisible hand above, thrust upon his shoulders, he sank to his knees before this disreputable old man with the pair of skulls. I felt petrified. My tongue stuck to my jaws.

"Would that I knew!" murmured Solomon in despair. "Would that I knew, too! King of the dust and the graves, let you and your companions come with me back to my palace in Jerusalem! You shall share my kingdom with me. We shall live in true humility and wisdom the rest of our days and we shall truly know each other!"

The old man sucked in a deep breath. He slowly put back his shoulders and looked up at the sky above him. I saw without surprise that this man had the carriage of a warrior, the air of a leader of men. His abasement fell from him like an outworn garment. For a moment, I was filled with fear.

"Away!" he said hoarsely. "Away, away! I have no desire for the things of this world! I have no wish to listen to the tempter!"

Solomon rose to his feet to confront him, his knees still stained by the dust of the ground, his splendid gown in disarray. "It would be great power," he said lamely, almost apologetically.

But the other had control of himself once again. He gradually resumed his posture of stooping humility. Gently he bent and replaced the two skulls on the ground as if they were the most precious jewels.

"All men," he said gently, pityingly to Solomon, "are your enemies because of your wealth and power, because they fear your wisdom and envy and hate your glory. None regard us, none fear us. All men are our friends because of the poverty that brings us happiness and the dust that brings us content."

"Count me a friend, with the rest," said Solomon in a low, pleading tone. He put out his hand to me like a blind man. I took it and guided him toward his litter.

"Go in peace," said the chief of the hermits after us, "for you deserve pity from man and mercy from heaven."

No sooner had we gained the interior of the double litter and felt the swaying rhythm of its being lifted to the chorus of grunts and the cracking of the overseer's whip, than Solomon turned to me. His face was as yellow as old linen.

"Nathan," he managed to whisper. He lost his senses in a sigh.

Alarmed, I examined his wound. It was not bleeding. It had a wholly healthy aspect. I decided to go at speed back to Jerusalem, without halt. The unconscious head of the great king lolled on my shoulder, rolling loosely. I took the same care of him that I might have given to a child.

In those moments I discovered that I loved Solomon. Not only because Yahweh commanded me to do so as my liege, but because he was a man, human, and in distress.

Two days before, Jeroboam had arrived from Egypt by ship. Now on the final third day, he summoned the tribes again to the groves of Hebron. There Rehoboam spoke for Solomon on the day we arrived back in Jerusalem.

CHAPTER TWENTY-ONE

The Threnody of Nathan

To my left lies a pile of *gillayon* covered with columns of characters. To my right remain only a few blank sheets. I return slowly—even wearily—to my task. This is the last of the Acts of Solomon that I shall write. As I dip the worn point of the *et* into the cracked *deyo* well of my scribe's kit and commence once more to remember, I pray to Yahweh for guidance.

I do not wish to do Solomon, my onetime master and king, injustice. But even more than that I want to be just to all in this human record of the works of Yahweh. What the Lord has done, He has done for the good of the Hebrews, Judah and Israel alike. Whatever punishment He visits upon us has been like the chastisement of the child by the rod—so that henceforth we may follow the path of His ways.

The answer that Rehoboam gave to Israel, to the tribes of the north assembled, in the absence of Solomon, was this:

"My father may have made your yoke heavy. I shall make it heavier. My father may have chastised you with whips but I shall chastise you with scorpions! I tell you, my little finger shall be thicker in power than my father's loins!"

There was a moment of dumbfoundment, a moment of confusion. Then the old cry was raised: "What part or duty have we to the children of David? We have no inheritance in the son of Jesse! To your tents, O Israel! Each man shall see to his own house!" And the most stentorian voice of all was that of Jeroboam.

There are two kings in the land this day, Rehoboam and Jeroboam. They have split the tribes into warring factions. Each man follows as he wills. The kingdom that Saul and David built and Solomon enjoyed is now utterly rent like an old cloak. Ahijah, the lank and gloomy prophet of these days, stalks the ravaged land. I recall the story told of what he did when Jeroboam, his favorite, had been called a "mighty man of valor" by Solomon and put in charge of all the tribe of Joseph to shore up the walls of Jerusalem. Jeroboam had bought himself a new robe to celebrate his promotion. He was met in the field by the Shilonite prophet in those days long ago, possibly by accident. Ahijah snatched the garment from him. He tore it into a dozen pieces with hands that were as gaunt and strong as the talons of a hawk. He gave the astonished Jeroboam back ten of the bits.

"Take these," he said, "for the Lord says, Behold I will rend the kingdom out of the hand of Solomon and shall give ten tribes to you. But he shall have two tribes for the sake of My servant David."

The reason, Ahijah told him (so the story went), was that Solomon had worshipped strange gods and had forsaken Yahweh—a conclusion I cannot disagree with. Still, it is strange that the Lord sent the vision to this disagreeable man and not to me. Well, we cannot judge the ways of Yahweh. They are impossible to find out.

It may have been as a result of this or it may have been for love of Theke that Jeroboam did as he did in defying Solomon and fleeing to Egypt. The tale goes on to say he stayed under the protection of Shishak as long as he did because Ahijah warned him: "The Lord will make Solomon prince of the kingdom all the days of his life." This accorded with what the Egyptian priest had told Solomon. So it was to be.

Though Solomon recovered his senses long before we arrived at the gates of David's city, he did not speak. Nor did his pallor change. In the days that followed, he took to his bed and refused to leave it. Rehoboam was king in fact. It appeared that if the encounter with Benaiah had shaken Solomon irrevocably, the quiet words of the king of the outcasts had totally unmanned him.

I squatted by his side one dawning in the cool darkness of his magnificent chamber—the windows curtained close against the rising sun, the scents of sandalwood and cedar strong in the room—and spoke to him of dangers.

"I fear the days to come," I said.

"You were always a fearful man," Solomon said. He lay on his back in the gloom and stared upward. "Yahweh will do as He wills."

"But He commands us to act for Him," I said, scandalized.

Solomon lay motionless, only his lips moving. "Whom do you fear?" he said.

"I fear Shishak," I said somberly. "You must remember, O

Solomon, that he is now a mature man, scarcely a year younger than yourself. He still meditates revenge for that defeat, so long ago, by Benaiah. He has forgotten nothing. The years have only increased his power. He has consolidated his armies; his captains are veterans and his weapons are steel, not bronze any longer. I fear him more now that Benaiah is with his fathers and Rehoboam has torn our kingdom by dissension. I seem to see Shishak coming again with a mighty army against a weak Hebrew nation. Remember, O king, Shishak has always boasted that he waited only for our land to grow fat and rich. Then he would come and pounce upon it like a hawk, he has said, to take back from your son what he calls his own treasure."

Solomon groaned and turned his face to the wall. "This is not my trouble," he said in a stifled voice. "Its time is not mine. I leave it to you, O Nathan, and to my son Rehoboam."

"But Rehoboam is young, scarcely past his twentieth year," I expostulated. "It will be Jeroboam, a man in the prime of life, who will sever the hamstrings of our land, to make it the prey of Shishak."

"Whoever is strong enough to take and hold, let him take and hold," Solomon muttered.

"You dare not say such things!" I cried.

"I dare," Solomon replied grimly. "If you dare not listen to them, Nathan, leave me to my thoughts."

"If you grant me permission," I said, hesitating, humble, "I shall stay at your side and silently beseech the Lord to enlighten the mind of my king."

"As long as it is silently," Solomon said. He seemed glad to have my company.

I said no more. But as I watched the king, I became conscious of what he must have been thinking—of the store of memories, the sweep of the past that rode over his mind. As I did, suddenly my own recollection became overwhelmed with visions of what had been. I shook my thoughts free of them, as dust from sandals after a long journey, and set my mind toward Yahweh and Solomon.

Lying on his back on his sumptuous couch, Solomon must have seen with extraordinary clearness the painted figures on the ceiling, the figures of mystery—lapwing, wild dog, antelope—that eternally urged him to close his lips over his secrets. This was his last secret to keep: he was dying.

He could have felt no pain. Though his body was numb, his brain was lively. Perhaps his sight pierced through the roof of timber and clay into the blue arch of the sky that he knew to be the throne of Yahweh. He thought of Him as the bright mist which had filled the temple; as the invisible Presence riding the wings of the gilded cherubim; as hovering in anger, speaking in thunder, appearing in lightning. Solomon sighed. All wisdom had been his, but this, the lotus seed and the very heart of knowledge, had been rebuffed.

"Even though He slay me, yet will I trust in Him," his lips said almost soundlessly.

Nor did he change much in the days that came afterward. He seemed to be always waking, always aware of what was going on about him but unwilling to take any part in it. He had retreated to some spot remote from life. Yet he observed and commented, as he had done for so many years. It was a strange sickness, one which removed him from the world while it still left him in it. Rehoboam came often to visit him. I was constantly by his side. He recognized us each time but I cannot say it gave Solomon pleasure or displeasure: we were simply there. He knew it. Sometimes he talked to us in the husky whisper of the voice which was left to him. But what he said was commonplace and soon forgotten.

His condition puzzled all those who saw him. Outwardly, the king was in perfect health. His responses were good. He ate well—not as much as usual but enough—and he seemed interested in life. What appeared to be missing was only the will to live and rule. That seemed entirely gone. The only occasions on which he indicated emotion came when we tried to have him rise or move him: then he exhibited a terrible, consuming anger. Even when he had to relieve himself, he merely turned on his side when he pleased, his attendants hurrying to serve him.

He did not refuse treatment, however. In some obscure way, it appeared to amuse him to follow the directions of the learned men who came from all parts of the world—I spent the gold of the treasury lavishly—to see this curious sickness, to try to earn the enormous rewards I offered for the king's cure.

All that could be done for Solomon was done. The learned doctors brought from Egypt and Phoenicia consulted again and again, their heads together most of the day, buzzing and talking, waving and shaking heads solemnly. They starved the king and fed him. They filled him with sugar and sour, with decoctions of herbs and even potions of shaved gold and powdered gems. They cosseted him with incense of aloes and ambergris, they wrote secret spells and put them under his pillow. Day and night they fussed and watched over him, never leaving his side for an instant until they departed in despair, shaking their heads.

Above them all, as David himself had seen the angel Azrael, harbinger of death, above the threshing floor of Araunah, I saw dark hovering wings. Spite of man, spite of medicine and magic, spite of glory and wealth, Solomon the king lay dying.

It was at this time, in the fifty-fourth year of his age and the fortieth of his reign, that the last vision vouchsafed the king by Yahweh came to pass. Nor was it his alone. In some mysterious manner, though I was awake in his chamber—I had slept with the king for many months, both as his companion and protector, since the death of Benaiah—I shared in his dream. I was neither able to speak nor participate. It seemed that I was held there as a witness to what had happened—as one who would bear testimony to future generations of the end of Solomon the Great.

Since Solomon had never returned to sit and meditate by the pleasant pool of Gibeon where Yahweh had twice appeared to him, the Lord vouchsafed His mercy by coming to him at the palace. It was past midnight by the dripping click of the water clock in the corner of his chamber. I felt myself awake. Yet my eyes did not open. Before my inner sight, as if it were carved upon the flesh of my eyelids, appeared a monstrous figure that seemed to be wrought of gloom and despair. It grew in my eyes until it horrified me. I attempted to drive it away by waking and unsealing my lids. It proved impossible. I was forced to lie supine on my couch and see what happened. My hand shakes to write about it to this hour.

It was a shaggy thing, darkness personified. Yet it was not a cloud, rather it was a moving shadow. In length and darkness it was kin to what one sees in one's own shadow at sunset, stretching out toward the ultimate poles of the east. Yet it had depth and substance, with none of the clean-cut lines of such a shadow. It was jagged and furious, prickle-haired, as if it were the angry hackles of shade incarnate.

My eyes blurred. The shadow remained but now I seemed to hover in air, high above the temple. It was ablaze with sunset below me, the most holy place shining with the *shekinah*, the shadow alongside it. I saw Solomon far under me. He stood erect upon the left pylon, rigid and unknowing. The shadow I so feared was streaming from his form, caused by him, indivisible from his figure! And I heard this monstrous shadow speak, first in a whisper, then in growing tones that were both brokenhearted and contemptuous.

"You think it an easy matter to make your peace with God," said the apparition severely.

"Never!" cried the tiny figure of Solomon beneath. "I would not sin and then repent at the last merely to enter Your dwelling place. I must go in glory, as fits a king of Your people."

"Between us, the Adversary and Myself, We strive for your soul. Not because your deeds are evil or good—for who can tell what your acts may have done or not done for the children of the Hebrews to come? No, but because you are Solomon himself, a treasure to us both."

Solomon pondered. "Forgive me these transgressions," he said penitently. "They shall be my last. I shall put away my riches and my women, I shall cease false worship, I shall utterly cut off those who have tempted me and led me away from You. Forgive, O Lord, and make Your servant pleasing in Your sight again."

The gloomy visitant shook its shaggy shadow-head. "What will you do with your riches?"

"I shall give them to the poor."

"And what with your women?"

"I shall share them out among the young men of the tribes," Solomon responded reluctantly.

"And the strange altars and temples you have built?"

"I shall cast them down utterly."

The vision lifted a warning hand. "What of your pride, O Solomon?" it whispered. "What will you do with that?"

Sweat started out on the king's forehead. He stretched out his hands to the impalpable and unrelenting Spirit. "I shall bring it down to the dust and trample upon it!" he cried.

Mournfully the Other shook its head. "I tell you now," it said, "You will keep your gold, your harem, your alien altars—and your pride. I say that you will do nothing differently."

Solomon must have felt his kingly dignity aroused. He lifted his miniature head. "Very well," he said. "If I am to be damned in Your eyes, then know that I do it unwillingly. What You decree, must be. But I have no part in it. If I am evil, I love good—and You forbid me to continue that part of me that wishes to be good. The blame is Yours. I shall do what I may, according to my word."

Again the Spirit shook its head. "I have been with you all

your life, invisible but no less present through all your years—from the side of your cradle to this very moment. I have observed your acts. When you were a youth, you were wise and dutiful in the ways of the Lord. But as you became older you dabbled in forbidden things. Tempted by Hiram, the heathen, you made him your best friend and followed his teachings. You took unto yourself the customs of Egypt and idolators. For many years your path has led downward; do you now tell me that you can struggle upward?"

"I have done evil," said Solomon with difficulty, "but so has every man under the sun. We do not ask to live but we are turned out from our mother's womb. Living is not as easy an exercise as You may believe it to be. To some degree I have yielded to temptation but I have repented to You. May man do more?"

"Is there any one deed in the past years that you have done which was to the glory of Yahweh and not yourself?"

Solomon considered. "Not one," he murmured inarticulately in a tear-laden voice.

"Then content yourself with yourself. What you are, you will remain."

The words were spoken in a tone no louder than before but they seemed to reverberate like thunder in my ears.

"What will you have of me, O Yahweh?" asked the trembling lips of the king.

"You know your sins now," came the great voice, echoing in the halls of his soul. "Confess them!"

"I have loved strange women."

"Confess!"

"I have turned toward other gods."

"Confess!"

"I have heaped up treasure for my own."

"Confess!"

"I have been proud of my wisdom and worldly glory."

"You have done evil. You have not kept the covenant that your father David made with heaven. Your feet have not come after Me. You heart has not been Mine nor your thoughts."

"Mercy, Lord!" cried the soul of Solomon.

"Not mercy but justice," went on the dispassionate arraignment. "Mercy and justice for the sake of your father who sought after Me despite his sins; justice alone for you."

"I repent, O Yahweh!"

"Because of your deeds, I will most surely take the kingdom of the Hebrews from your children. Not from you in your lifetime but I will rend it from the hands of your son. So much is justice. Yet out of the remembrance of David, which is dear to Me, I shall keep one tribe—that of Judah—for your son and for the sake of Jerusalem, that a Light may be kept alive in the temple."

The voice had grown louder and louder. It had become deafening. Solomon and I clapped our hands to our heads to drown out the sound. As we did, the Figure before us commenced to waver. Its stern outlines became dimmer, less strong and visible. As if some sponge were passed over a slate, the figure of our dream began to vanish. I leaped up from my bed.

"Wake! Wake!" I cried, my mouth near the ear of the writhing, weeping Solomon. I dared not touch his majesty. As I drew back, his eyes slowly opened and rolled in his head. He saw again the familiar gilded outlines of his sleeping chamber. The color came back into his pale face. He heaved a long sigh. He flung his arms upward and let them fall listlessly at his side.

"Who am I?" he said in a voice so thick and strange that at first I thought he had a ghost in his gullet.

"Solomon, king of the Hebrews, lord of the earth, the visible will of Yahweh," I said, trembling.

"Who among all the worlds of men that haven been before me and that will come after me, will be like me?"

"None," I said. "None at all."

His eyes turned upon me. They sharpened into a gaze. "It is you, faithful Nathan," he said faintly. "I have had a dream and in it, my shadow spoke to me. I thought I stood upon the highest pylon of the temple toward the west and toward the east my shadow lengthened until it streamed away in darkness across the world."

"Yes, my king."

"Who is chief among the troops and peoples, foremost among the kings of the world?"

"You, O Solomon," I said humbly.

He sat upright on his couch. "Such an answer my shadow did not give me from its blackness," he said harshly.

The sun struck through the lattices of his window. The dawn poured newly minted gold across the room. Solomon's mind, I saw, little by little, was comforted. He sank back to rest once more, to rid his thoughts of his nightmare, sure that the gauze of the apparition had vanished from the crannies of his brain.

"I am myself again," he said. But the sweat squeezed out

of his pores, drenching him. "What did I say, O Nathan, close to my heart?"

"Nothing, great Solomon."

His bloodshot eyes swiveled to catch mine. "Even if I said nothing, I seem to recall your face in the dream," Solomon said. "You will not betray what was said there?"

"No," I said passionately, "not a word from my lips!"

"Then you were there."

"Yes," I said humbly.

A slight tremulous smile appeared on the lips of Solomon. "Nathan, Nathan," he said, "you have always been a poor liar. But keep your guilty knowledge that the king of the Hebrews is a sinner and will remain a sinner in the sight of Yahweh. For me, I have done what I could—what I was fated to do." He considered. "Fate and accident," he said at last, "sit on either side of the Lord to do His bidding in this world."

For all that monstrous dream, Solomon, in the days after, seemed to recover. His wound healed. He showed no fear of sleeping again, though I found myself afraid to close my eyes. Yet when I did doze, it was dreamless. Bit by bit we both returned to normal life.

But still Solomon refused to sit up. His food was of the lightest and he drank no wine, but much water. His speech was intelligible and his mind clear: his memory, enormous. He talked little about the present but much about the past.

It was perhaps two weeks later when he commanded me to usher in all his sons—forty-three, all told—and that he would speak to them. I did as he said that very afternoon. They clustered around the royal bed at a discreet distance—except for Rehoboam who stood aggressively forward. Excluded too from the chambers—for it was none of women's business—were the king's eldest two daughters, Taphath and Basmath.

Solomon signaled to me to prop up his head with a cushion. I did as he said, and he surveyed the throng, fruit of his loins.

Solomon closed his eyes. The veined darkness took him for, it seemed, no more than an instant. When he opened his eyes again, his bed was still surrounded by the crowding faces of his sun-swarthy sons, each anxiously peering at him. Solomon roused himself, gestured under the gold-heavy covering. They understood. With me they brought more cushions of down and propped him up so that he could speak.

"Sons of my blood," he said hoarsely, finding the words strange to his tongue, "what is gone will not come back.

Glory and health and youth, the wind of the pounding chariot, the taste of the sea, the coolness of evening, the heat of the day. I have done with all of them. Who is your mother, there? I know your faces but I know not the flesh from whence you sprang. So much flesh has been mine and my own flesh lies heavy on my bones like a lover to death. Who are you, eh?"

"You know me," said Rehoboam, arrogance struggling with fear upon his face. "I am your son, co-regent on your throne, Rehoboam."

"And the rest?"

Solomon must have heard a confused babble that came to his ears like the distant murmur of waters. It appeared to make no sense to him. He lifted his hand that was as heavy as if gloved in lead. "Enough," he said. The room hushed.

"As I lie here," he murmured, "dying day by day, my body stays here. But my heart floats about, above my people, seeing little of the present and nothing of the future—for I was never a seer. It lingers on the past. What I am, I was; what I will be is in the hands of the Lord. A fearful thing, to be in His hands, balanced on a finger of the everliving Yahweh!"

No one made a movement in the stillness of the room. Not a sound came from any, not even a breath: it was as if they waited for some portent to come about. It was the brashness of Rehoboam that again broke the silence.

"It is nothing to die when one is old," he said. "It is terrible to die when one is young."

"Wretch!" I exclaimed. "King that you are, shame on you! Did not Moses, blessed be he, say to honor your father and your mother?"

"So that my days may be long?" replied Rehoboam intrepidly, while the others shrank back to hear him. "No, Nathan; I wish to die, that is all."

Solomon raised his palsied hand once more. "Let the others go," he said to me. "I shall speak to Rehoboam alone."

I scarcely needed to turn before his order was obeyed. The crew of youths, which had crowded the bedroom a moment before, vanished. The older ones retreated in awe, the younger ones—their fingers wet from sucking—shooed out by their quaking mothers. Only Rehoboam and I remained.

"Do you think so little of death, my son?" asked Solomon. His voice had a ghost of his old wry humor in it.

"Death is nothing," Rehoboam said sullenly.

"Azrael is nothing as he hovers?"

"Azrael is a blessing!" shouted Rehoboam almost angrily.

The echo died against the gay drapes. Solomon looked at me. He nodded ever so slightly. He managed to turn his head and give Rehoboam a long look.

"My dear son, you are in love," Solomon said.

"Not at all," Rehoboam said indignantly. "Once I was in love. No longer, no longer."

Solomon raised his brows. "Yield to me on this," he said. "A woman has created your despair."

"You think yourself an expert," Rehoboam replied sullenly.

"I do, I am. It is as clear as the sun rising out of mist. Your melancholy is no more than love. The world is not about to come to an end; for you, it has already come to an end."

Rehoboam took a deep breath. "I am not emotional about such things," he said unsteadily. "I look at them as if I were merely a spectator."

"Of your love?"

"Of the end."

"Both are exactly the same," Solomon said. "There is not a fly-speck of difference."

"The death of my love," Rehoboam said in a melancholy tone, "is a personal fact. The death of the world is a cosmic fact."

"You are being unnecessarily modest," Solomon said.

Rehoboam began to pace about the room. "There are so many ways to wipe out the world," he said dreamily. "Fire from beneath our feet or from heaven. Thunder and earthquakes. A star may fall. There are plagues, wars to the last man."

"Cease, cease," Solomon said.

"I have not yet told you of eleven other ways."

"You crush me completely by your convictions," Solomon said ironically. "You have dashed out the light of my hopes for the future of the Hebrews. You are right: the world is coming to an end."

"I am glad you agree."

"But it can be saved," Solomon said.

"Saved!" Rehoboam said in accents of surprise.

"Yes."

"By Yahweh, I suppose?" Rehoboam was sardonic in his turn.

"No," Solomon replied calmly. "It is my thought that Yahweh is too busy to bother with us. No."

"Then?"

"It can only be saved by you, by my son Rehoboam," Solomon said.

"Me?" Rehoboam demanded in amazement.

"By your falling in love again. Then the stars will swim into their eternal positions again, the world will stop its dizzy reeling, the sun will uncover its countenance."

"You try to make a fool of me," Rehoboam said thickly.

"On the contrary. I try to make you a wise man."

"I cannot understand ou."

"Let us see," Solomon said, stretching his arms out slowly in a gesture of inclusiveness. "A collision of heavenly bodies: that is love. An internal explosion: that is love. A plague: that is love."

Rehoboam smacked his fists together angrily. "I thought of you as a friend, not as a father!" he exclaimed. "I came to you to pour out my heart, to have it filled again with healing sympathy! But it makes you happy to ridicule me!"

"No," Solomon said. "I say that your love for a woman is part of the love of all men for all women. That this love is part of the love of this world and the stars that the Chaldeans and Egyptians examine so anxiously. Who can tell? Yours may be the single drop of bliss that will overflow the great cup of love and put out all the black fires burning."

"I am no longer in love," said Rehoboam plaintively.

"Be," Solomon said. "You will be."

Restlessly Rhoboam turned away. "You have not helped me," he said indistinctly.

"I think I have. You came in to me thinking that the world would end in a moment."

"I go out the same way."

"No. Now you feel it may be several minutes."

Rehoboam wheeled. "Your guess that I hate her is all wrong."

"Of course. What is her name?"

"Did I tell you?"

"No."

Rehoboam started toward the door. Solomon raised his voice. "Are you going?" he asked.

Rehoboam halted. He turned to face his father. "I shall never fall in love again," he said with conviction. "Women are—well, they are women."

"I agree with all my heart."

"I wish I could sit and laugh at the spectacle of the world as you do," Rehoboam said fiercely. "Is this your famous wisdom?"

"I wish I could fall in love again, Rehoboam," Solomon said. His words were oddly sincere. He whispered to himself in barely audible tones like a litany: "Thckc, Tamar." Then, after a long pause, the single name: "Bathsheba." I felt startled. Moreover, he did not address Rehoboam again. He made a motion of dismissal and the youth recognized it. Silently, he bowed and backed from the room.

"Whom does the boy long for?" Solomon asked me. His voice was much weaker than it had been when he talked to Rehoboam.

"She is a damsel named Maachah, daughter of Uriel of Gibeah," I said.

Solomon nodded on his pillows. "A good family," he muttered. "Have you seen her, Nathan? Is she comely?"

"Yes," I said. "To these old eyes, she is beautiful."

"You were ever an expert in choosing women but you never dared choose the one you wanted," Solomon said. "Do you think I have forgotten your eyes when you watched Bathsheba, my mother? You were always a coward, Nathan."

I bowed submissively, answering nothing. "I wish Rehoboam to be king after me," Solomon went on. "But he must name his first child Abijah for a warning and you, of all people, know why."

I bowed again. Abijah was the second son of the prophet Samuel. His misdoings and evil deeds had made the Hebrews clamor for their first king.

Solomon looked up at me with a weak, unblinking stare. His eyes seemed luminous, as though his thought lighted them from within. His lips began to phrase a whisper. I recognized it as an old Egyptian poem.

Death is welcome to me today,
Like the healing of a sick man—
Like entering into a garden after sickness.
Death is welcome to me today,
Like the sweetness of myrrh—
Like sitting under the shade on a windy day.
Death is welcome to me today,
Like the course of the spring-flow—
Like the return of a man from war to his home.
Death is welcome to me today,

As a man longs to see his house
After spending long years in captivity.

Then there was silence. In a few moments—I could not see the king for my bowed head and scalding tears—I heard him whisper: "I should have liked to ride upon the behemoth," like a child's sigh. His head fell to one side. He seemed to sleep. I tiptoed away.

That night a dreadful storm swept out of the west from the sea. It drove across the top of Mount Zion, attacking with wind and thunder, lightning and rain. It beat insistently, like some gigantic invisible visitor against the temple and the palace gates. It blanketed the land, a black wet curtain embroidered with the pale lavender flashes that indicated the presence of Yahweh Himself. It shook with the thunder that was His unintelligible voice. The trees bowed down, then slowly uprooted themselves from the sodden soil. The altars streamed water, the brazen sea brimmed over. Floods ran through the streets. Houses melted inward upon their occupants, who took terrified refuge in the open fields. The brawling ravines gouged out new channels. The tempest crackled and howled over it all as if the sky itself were on fire and in pain.

I spent those dark hours in the temple, bowing before the most holy place in the flickering light of the *menorah*. Here all was peace. The storm outside might vent its fury anywhere else, but here, within these thick walls where the Lord protected His own, the uproar was no more than a murmur. I knelt alone. Not even Zadok was in the temple during those hours.

With the dawn, the storm, by the mercy of Yahweh, lessened. I came out of the door to find the cedar palisades cast down and the porch of sandalwood pillars awry. All was dripping with rain. It still drenched the earth with a gentle fall, with mist that enclosed all like a shroud. I made my way to the rooms of Solomon, past the guard. I entered where he slept. To my astonishment, to my real alarm, he was not there.

"Where is the king?" I demanded furiously of the trembling guard. In a shaking voice he said that Solomon had left hours before, commanding him to say nothing, feeling his way along the corridor to the door that would let him into the entrails of the raging storm the night before. I thrust the guard aside. I hurried out again: I had a premonition of where I might find him. I was right.

The figure, the facsimile of the great King Solomon was once more upon his throne.

He sat, bones and skin, perched upon ivory and gold. He was a shrunken mummy such as the priest from Egypt had once exhibited to me, clad in golden and purple garments that were still soaked—and wildly ripped, it appeared, by his own hands, whether by mistake or for penance, I could not know.

Huddled on his famous throne, shivering within the soaked rags of gold, scarcely a man: melted into wrinkles, into angled bones, into flesh as yellow and sweat-shining as the baubles and metal he had coveted for so long, Solomon raised his feeble arms against me and death. He mumbled charms, he made vague gestures, twinkling his fingers—but to no avail.

Then, as if animated by a force outside himself, the old king stood erect, unfolding himself like a new building from ancient ruins. Despite his shaking form, his gray beard, his wild eyes, he had something of the similitude of the magnificence and dignity of the young Solomon I had known so many years ago.

On my knees, I stared upward at him. I, with my own white beard and bald poll, with my own ague and disillusionments. I saw still in Solomon (as he must have seen himself in that moment) his visions of the glorious kingdom of the Hebrews revived and all the splendor of the country of eternal bliss that Yahweh had promised, revealed.

"Yahweh has come to me," he whispered shakily, "and in the night. He has bidden me to forgive."

He stretched out his stick-thin arms. "I forgive all beings, created and uncreated! I forgive Benaiah for trying to take my life, I forgive all the women who have tempted me into the ways of the lost! I forgive you, Nathan, for your stupidity! I forgive poor forgotten Zabud, your son!" His voice softened immeasurably. "I forgive David, my father, for the sin that formed me. And I forgive Bathsheba, my mother, for my life." He peered down at me though I knew he could no longer see. "I am wise, wise to the end, eh, Nathan?" he said very slowly and clearly. I waited, holding my breath.

"But though all hope of the kingdom of the Hebrews vanishes with me," Solomon said slowly, "as has been prophesied and as I believe, all hope of its renewing is not lost. There is an ancient tale of the Egyptians themselves, a story of two brothers, in which the younger says to the older—as I now say to you, my elder—something true." He wavered, considered for a moment, as if trying to remember what had been told him. Then he said in the soft, measured tones of memory:

"I shall enchant my heart and I shall hide it upon the top of a cedar of Lebanon. Now after my day the cedar shall be cut down and my heart will tumble to the ground and be hidden. Others shall come seeking it, even passing seven times seven lifetimes, but it shall be found. And when one like yourself, Nathan, has found it, if it is put into the vase of his own heart, then in truth I shall live again." I did not know what the mysterious words meant at that moment nor can I interpret their symbols now. But I record them as the last that the king spoke in this life.

Solomon took one firm step forward. He stood poised, then began to fall. I sprang up. I caught the thin light body in my arms. I lowered it to the earth. As I did, it seemed as if the throne and the city of David shook as did the old king, as if they too were dissolving in the moment of death.

The great crash of the empire of the Hebrews shook soundlessly in my ears. I caught a glimpse in my mind of the staring, rigid face of Rehoboam, I thought of Jeroboam. Solomon gazed sightlessly up into my face. He sighed. His flesh relaxed, becoming soft and shapeless, falling back from his skull in the winning lines of his youth. That moment as I looked down at the king, my wildly beating old heart seemed to stop. I saw the fingers of death molding his face—from his middle age back to his youth, to his childhood and, suddenly, before my eyes, I saw again the beloved outlines of the face of Bathsheba herself. That was all: no word, no gesture, no signal that the black wings of Azrael had closed about him, that his spirit had left his pallid, gaping lips.

His face became ghastly. His fingers crooked. He strove to clutch, to gain and hold—what? Life or wealth or passion or glory? An expression of terrible pain, of agony and despair passed over his flesh, engraving upon it the last emotion, as if the senses still remained. His lips shook and grinned uselessly. His body convulsed.

I held all that remained mortal of Solomon. The dust had returned to earth as it had been. His spirit had flown to Yahweh.

Thus died Solomon, son of David and king of the Hebrews. Thus died the glorious and the mighty, the master of that which was above and upon and within the earth, the servant (so far as his human vessel was able) of Yahweh and His will, the emblem of the powerful and the great of all the earth. With him perished the dreams of the Hebrews for all time.

Upon Solomon's death, much happened. We were never closely united until David's reign. We sprang from different ancestors and there were ancient jealousies and rivalries. Judah on the hilltops grew strong but stayed without the world and honored the promise of Yahweh that the house of David would be established forever. Israel, on the plains, had become enamored of the world and its wiles. Solomon, who had lost the northern part of David's empire to Syria and Carchemish to the Hittites and had offered twenty Israelite cities to Hiram, also lost the love of the north.

For three years Rehoboam tried to continue in the wise ways of Solomon and David—but finally he sent old Adoniram, the venerable tax-collector, into the north to receive new imposts and levies. To the amazement of all Judah, the old man was received everywhere with curses and stones. At length he was beaten down, out of his chariot, and killed with his guard and retainers. Rehoboam heard of it in one of the cities of Israel where he was visiting. He fled for his own life back to Jerusalem.

Since that time a sword has lain between the two parts of the Hebrew nation. Nor has anyone come to beat it into a plowshare—though two years later Shishak made his long-promised invasion even as far as the gates of Jerusalem. He spared that city of David only when the repentant Rehoboam himself ravished it of all its treasure, even to sending Solomon's famous gold shields to the conqueror. He replaced them with brass but the glory departed with them.

I have heard that jovial Hiram, king of Tyre, has died—and that his suspicions came true. Ithobaal, the thick-browed priest of Ashtoreth, bided his moment. When the son of Hiram, young Phales, went to the altar of Ashtoreth to celebrate succeeding his father, Ithobaal sank the sacrificial knife into his back. He has become king of the Tyrians—since with the death of Phales the royal line of Hiram was extinguished. He has been anxious to keep relations between our two kingdoms cordial, however: Ithobaal has a young daughter named Jezebel and it is rumored that he intends to try to marry her to some prince either of Israel or Judah.

As if rived by some invisible force, the kingdom which David had created and Solomon's own magnificence and majesty had held together for so long, fell apart. As for Jerusalem, the blessed city, its streets became silent and echoing as the people departed in haste—one to one side, another to another, as if it were another sea of bloody feud dividing in the midst. The viper and the scorpion writhed their way through the dust unheeded and unmolested. The birds of prey swooped over valleys and hills, closer, ever closer to the abandoned dwellings. The sounds of rejoicing were stilled: the golden bowl was broken, the silver cord was loosed, the pitcher in shards at the fountain and the wheel upturned at the cistern. Those keepers of the houses who remained went about their business silently, their side muscles trembling with the unaccustomed loneliness. The men of strength, the ancient descendants of David and his chosen band of thirty, disappeared. The windows one by one were shuttered. No one leaned upon the sills and looked down with pleasure and cries of recognition or invitation to the throngs below. The sound of talk and singing, the playing of instruments vanished. Even the cries of the vendors and the rhythms of the grinders who sharpened the knives of the householders and soldiers alike were no more. The doors were shut, the daughters of music no longer sang or played. At morning we woke only to the sober twittering of the birds in the sky passing over. At night we laid ourselves down to the vigil of the raven and owl.

We bowed ourselves under the knowledge that Yahweh had deserted us. We were afraid of that which was high. Our lives were filled with fear of that which was to come, which indeed already dwelt in the land. The almond tree grew from the walls of the houses unmolested. Grass flourished in the streets. Grasshoppers, signal of the dry season, were everywhere. The chirring of their wings seemed deafening in the somber city. Mourners went hooded about the streets. More and more pilgrims for distant places went out of the high gates, never to return to Jerusalem.

At last, I joined them. I could not remain in a place where my heart had died. I was old. I knew no other refuge than the woods of Ephraim where, long ago in the flush of youth (when I believed I should never have need of it) I had prepared a little hut for refuge. Now I was glad of it, of its buried, hidden jars of wine and meal and oil. There I went gladly. There I found my peace of soul again.

What I have written, I have written. Those who have known me or have known Solomon and his court, realize that all I have set down is true. Those who will come after, perhaps in the long march of the ages, will find something in this dusty recital to feed their mind. They may not accept what I have written but this is a fate to which all scribes are subject.

What shall be said as the final word on Solomon? Only this: that in his life, if he exalted himself, he also exalted the Hebrews, his people, for all time. Much less than this has many a mighty king achieved. No more than this has any done.

So much for these things. The events I have set down according to my ability without ever (or so I believe) consciously either keeping unjust silence or writing a lie. What comes after may be written by more able men, who are stronger in skill and learning. But none will ever write with more good will and sorrow than I.

AUTHOR'S NOTE

Like much else about King Solomon of the Hebrews (the term Jews came into use only after his reign, when the kingdom split between Judah and rebellious Israel), his dates are uncertain. One may choose any pair from 972-932 B.C. to 962-922 B.C. for his time on the throne. As for his birth, anywhere from 992 to 986 B.C. will do.

In any case, the exact year is not important. It is significant enough that he lived nearly a thousand years before Christ, at a time when the world was fairly new.

He succeeded a great father. Like many sons overshadowed by a sire, he did not do as well. Still, if his works did not, his fame came to exceed that of David. Solomon is supposed to have ruled his people for a halcyon period of forty years—a figure open to suspicion only because it so exactly duplicates the length of David's rule and the period of Hebrew wandering in the wilderness.

Despite the extraordinary amount of space given to Solomon in the Old Testament, his real character remains as shadowy as that of a figure behind some ancient golden mask. What is known about him is a mixture of some acceptable historical fact, much questionable legend, inferences from archaeological artifacts, and plain fairy tales. Most of what may be taken as true comes from the books of Samuel, Kings, Chronicles, Proverbs, Ecclesiastes, and the Song of Solomon—though the latter three are open to question. Additional material which needs critical sifting exists in the Midrash, Haggadah, and the various Targumin, as well as in the rabbinic tales in the Babylonian and Palestinian Talmuds. There are, of course, further references to Solomon in such works as the Apocrypha, the Koran, and medieval literature, but virtually all of them are incredible.

What else may have been on record of Solomon's reign has vanished. Something is known of what was lost. Chronicles II points out that the acts of Solomon, from first to last, are duly "written in the book of Nathan the prophet and in the prophecy of Ahijah the Shilonite and in the visions of Iddo the seer against Jeroboam the son of Nebat." Nathan may be the same as he who abetted Bathsheba but his identity has perished with his story.

What gives Solomon body in all ages is that he is eternally modern. His piety and his sins, his flauntings and his flourishings, his transgressions and triumphs, all have a taste that stays savory. His follies fit the flesh. Where Abraham and Moses and even David are too heroic for emulation, Solomon is one of the first famous men suited for imitation by his all-too-human life.

It must be kept in mind that the Solomonic glory rose in an era whose history—slim and unreliable, contradictory as it may be—represents some of the earliest chronicling of the human race. Only the Sumerian-Akkadian notes and the Egyptian continuity are earlier—and they present nothing like the richly worked tale of this minor Semitic king.

It is necessary to make disclaimers of error because of the paucity of details. It is no wonder that myths have accreted upon the facts. When one considers that the stories about Solomon had been current for five hundred years when Plato was a boy, the difficulty of separating the chaff of non-sense from actual history may be seen. It may be even clearer if one knows that the best friend of Solomon, on a regal level, was Hiram of Tyre, king of the Phoenicians—once a world-wide race, now utterly vanished.

But the story of Solomon (within certain limits) may be deduced fairly enough. It is part of the endless serialized story of his people through the ages. Others have undoubtedly had as vital and dramatic incidents in their national history—but none has told them so well, so often, and so convincingly. Nor has any had such a high percentile persistence of survival.

As preface, a brief summary may be useful. The nomadic Hebrews—the distinctive name appears as early as 2000 B.C.—were a proud, high-tempered dozen of tribes, interrelated by marriage and custom but not, at first, by religion. They seemingly wandered west from the overcrowded Euphrates River Valley into the rich Nile Delta. Here they were impressed into slavery by the Egyptians about 1300 B.C.

A hundred years later, with the good riddance of Pharaoh Merneptah and under the leadership of Moses (Sigmund

Freud guessed that he was a renegade Egyptian general who had adopted monotheism from the heresy of Akhnaton, generations before), the Hebrews fled east into the Sinai Desert. Here they wandered for a generation, accepted the Sinai god Yahweh, he of lightning and thunder, and bound themselves into a national pact sealed by suffering. After the death of Moses, they moved north. They invaded the rich land of Palestine-Canaan with a view to making it their home.

This small, well-to-do spot was staked out almost exactly at the crossroads of the world of that day. It was green, fertile, and cultured. It was inhabited by possibly the most sophisticated people of the times: the Canaanites, who lived luxuriously in fortified cities, and the Phoenicians, who sailed the seas of the known world and flung out networks of colonies. Ugarit and Byblos, two of their respective cities, have revealed proof of unusually advanced civilizations.

At this point the archaeological traces may be supplemented by the full-bodied (and surprisingly reliable) accounts of the Old Testament. But these need to be critically examined for propaganda. The book of Joshua—who succeeded Moses as the Hebrew leader—gives an impression of unity, purpose, and enthusiasm. This is probably incorrect. The succeeding book of Judges tells more convincingly of the twelve tribes still herding and tent-dwelling, separated and quarreling. They had chosen a land dotted with the strongholds of the Canaanites—at least one of which, Beth-Shan, survived defiantly well into the rule of David—and harassed by bands of rovers. It was a place suited to be the strategic prey of every nation in the neighborhood.

It was true that Egypt, which had controlled the area for more than a thousand years by over a score of military expeditions, had lifted its iron hand because of troubles at home. But the Amalekites from the south and the barbarian Hittites from the north invaded at their pleasure—often catching the Hebrews between the hammer of their advance and the anvil of the Canaanite cities. Nor was that all: there were the Moabites and Ammonites, the Syrians, the Edomites, and a mixture of tribes including such as the Jebusites who held Jerusalem. In addition, an alien group from Mycenae, the Sea People or the Philistines, set up an enclave along the seacoast below Phoenicia and proceeded to advance inland.

Under such desperate circumstances, it was natural that the Hebrews should reunite in order to revolt against their many masters: "Now there was no smith found throughout all the land of Israel: for the Philistines said, Lest the Hebrews make them swords or spears: but all the Israelites went down to the Philistines, to sharpen every man his share, and his coulter, and his axe, and his mattock." It is instructive to note that the Romans, a millennium later, tried the same restrictive measures and met with identical failure.

Here the story of Solomon begins to take recognizable shape. The Hebrew renaissance of power began with Samuel, prophet and kingmaker. He called the people back to Yahweh, the one God, away from the Canaanitish multiple deities that had supposedly given their enemies victory. As the self-proclaimed ordainer and explicator of Yahweh's will, Samuel dispensed the stern Mosaic commands impartially. On one occasion, Samuel personally hewed in pieces one Agag, king of the Amalekites, as an example.

Saul, first king of the Hebrews, was Samuel's own creation. A big dour man from the smallest tribe, he was given to fits of introspection followed by insane action. He was a single-minded, wholehearted leader, conscious of his mission. Once he became so exalted by his cause that he was willing to slay his own son, Jonathan, for a minute infraction of his rules.

The contribution of Saul to Hebrew unity is hard to overestimate. He brought a recalcitrant people to heel, restored their pride and hope, and gave them victories. But he quarreled with Samuel: "Then came the word of the Lord unto Samuel, saying: It repenteth me that I have set up Saul to be king."

Such a contretemps is fatal to any ruler in a theocratic state. Saul was denounced by Samuel alive and, when dead, by his ghost. The original Hebrew king sank into despair. He committed suicide after his defeat at Mount Gilboa about 1050 B.C. by the Philistines. He was replaced by another choice of Samuel: David, a member of the court, whom Saul had sometimes adored and sometimes tried to murder, a former shepherd, son of Jesse.

It may be useful to understand that the Hebrew heritage of religion—always essential to the comprehension of that people—exists on four great plateaus. Rightly known, it is neither as exclusive as has been believed by its adherents nor as narrow as has been conceived by its enemies.

The first level, possibly the most important, was the pact of God with Noah after the flood: "The everlasting covenant between God and every living creature of all flesh that is upon the earth." This universal pledge included seven general ties of God to all humanity. Second to this comes the special warranty given by God to Moses in the Ten Commandments. It set the Hebrews apart and also made them the direct instrumentality of God's will: "I will take you to Me for a people and I will be to you a God." The third was the covenant with Abraham: "I will bless thee . . . and in thy seed shall all the nations of the earth be blessed," assurance that the Hebrews were chosen for the extraordinary mission of world salvation. Fourth was the Davidic-Solomonic religious hegemony: "I have hallowed this house, which thou hast built, to put My name there for ever; and Mine eyes and Mine heart shall be there perpetually. And if thou wilt walk before Me, as David thy father walked, in integrity of heart, and in uprightness, to do according to all that I have commanded thee, and wilt keep My statutes and My judgments: then I will establish the throne of thy kingdom upon Israel for ever. . . ."

Ever since the first of these covenants, the Hebrew religion has been in a state of evolution. It had taught much less than it had learned in its wanderings with the ark. But rules laid out with remarkable specificity had been slowly collected—both as a matter of practical use and ideal practice. They covered all sorts of moral and ethical dilemmas, under all conceivable conditions. They were painstakingly put down, chiefly in the books of Deuteronomy and Leviticus.

Now, though the Hebrews had semi-settled in Palestine-Canaan, they had not yet got out of their nomadic ways. There were no proper resting place for the ark, no center for worship, no coherent body of worshippers, no needful symbols. It was toward establishing these vital elements that David labored all his life.

But before he could plan his centralization of religious practice (which, like Moses and the Promised Land, he was destined to design but not to see), David was forced to live an erratic and hazardous existence. He had been chosen by Samuel shortly after Saul's disgrace, and crowned on the spot: "He was ruddy, and withal of a beautiful countenance, and goodly to look to. And the Lord said, Arise, anoint him: for this is he." Young, brave, chivalrous, generous, and brutal when necessary, David's chief recommendation was as an expert fighter of bears and lions in defense of his flock and as a "cunning player on the harp." He was called to Saul to offer musical therapy to that monarch. He formed a love-covenant with Saul's son, Jonathan. He became at last the object of Saul's insensate rage and jealousy.

From that time on, Saul sought out David and his growing band of adherents, as well as his country's enemies. David sometimes resisted, more often fled to Saul's enemies for temporary refuge (even to the Philistines, who awarded him a city). When Samuel died, the fact of his crowning David—of immense importance later to Solomon—became widely known. It is hardly pertinent to follow David's early career further in detail except to say that when he succeeded to the throne he found his people sharply divided.

The strongest tribe was Judah in the south, having absorbed the members of Simeon and Caleb. In central Palestine, the influential tribes of Joseph and Benjamin—Saul's tribe—could find no peace between them. In the north, Issachar, Naphtali, Asher, Zebulon, and Dan were feuding. In the east, past the Jordan River, the tribes of Reuben and Gilead were being steadily decimated by their foes. In the end, of course, only Judah was to be left by the invading Assyrians in 721 B.C. And shortly after the beginning of the sixth century before Christ, the Jews as a political unit were wholly displaced by foreign invaders. Only their religion was to remain until it was shattered by the Romans seven hundred years later and rebuilt upon a different pattern.

In that cruel and barbarous age, David must have appeared rather finicky to his followers. He was an excellent leader, a passable fighter (it is probable that Elkanah really killed Goliath), a superb strategist, but hardly a doughty general. He naturally inclined to mercy and music, though ruling with a shrewd commonsensical eye to the realities of his realm. His chief aide, who did most of the distasteful chores of battle, was a vicious, cunning general named Joab. Son of David's sister, Joab was hated and feared by his king.

Nevertheless, Joab never betrayed David, though he either plotted against or assassinated almost every other figure of power in the kingdom. While David sat at home and strummed his lyre in Hebron, it was Joab who led his army in the forcible welding-by-blood of the tribal recalcitrants. He overcame the sizable territories of Edom, Syria, Moab, and Ammon to the east—though Philistia resisted until early in Solomon's reign. His triumphs were largely due to his tactics of guerrilla hill warfare—negating the use of chariots by the foe—and ambuscades which lessened the disadvantages of using bronze swords against the iron ones from the north, plus timely plagues from heaven.

Thanks to Joab and "David's mighty men," the kingdom of the Hebrews at length extended from the Euphrates in the north, south to the Red Sea; west, from the Mediterranean to Arabia in the east. David's claim to the throne was not entirely by force of arms nor altogether because of his anointing by Samuel. It derived more practically from his marriage to Michal, the second daughter of Saul. She had fallen madly in love with him early in his career but she gave him no children.

David had other issue. He had at least six recognized, legitimate sons, each by a different wife. Of three—Chileab, Shephatiah, and Ithream—nothing is heard afterward. Amnon raped his half-sister, Tamar, for which he was killed two years later by her brother, black-scowling Absalom. It was Absalom who made an abortive attempt to seize the throne by force—for which he was killed by Joab.

It would seem that David had decided to pass his crown on to his eldest son, Amnon. Next, he favored Absalom but that hope is remembered only in his lament, "O Absalom, my son, my son!" It is possible that Joab embraced the chance to slay Absalom as the result of a palace intrigue with the sixth son, Adonijah. David's later hatred of his commander may have resulted from his knowledge of this.

However that may be, David's fear for the ambition of his sons subsided. His eye turned elsewhere for a successor. And his own choice, he thought, was Solomon.

Three factors decided the handing-down of the scepter of the Hebrew kingdom. There was the precedent set by Samuel in breaking the legitimate line of descent from Saul by denying the crown to his sons (early kingships were decided strictly by male primogeniture), a walk by David on the roof of his Jerusalem palace in the cool of evening, and the unquestioning obedience of Joab.

The twilight stroll resulted in David peeping over into the next courtyard. He saw a beautiful woman taking a cold sponge bath. He inquired after her and found she was Bathsheba, daughter of the Hittite Ammiel, wife to Uriah, a Hittite officer in his army. David summoned Bathsheba and seduced her.

Three months later, she complained to him that she was pregnant. David called Uriah back from the battlefront. To cover his sin, he ordered his officer to sleep with Bathsheba. Instead the noble Uriah slept outside David's door. He declared he could not visit his wife while his comrades slept alone in the field. Thereupon David gave him a message and sent him back to Joab. His note commanded his general to put Uriah in such a post as to make sure he would be killed. Joab obeyed. David took to himself Bathsheba, the widow.

By virtue of the double crime, Bathsheba became the dominant female influence in the palace. She inveigled the repentant David into an oath that their offspring would sit upon the throne after him. Their firstborn died as a baby—some say sacrificed by Bathsheba to Molech in the valley of Hinnom—but their second (or their fourth), originally christened Jedediah, was Solomon. Prophetically enough, Shelomoth means "man of peace."

David's conscience bothered him the rest of his life. He did all sorts of penance, turning to religion and meditation. Most prominent among these was his repeated confession of guilt in the Psalms and his building of the temple by proxy: "God said unto me, Thou shalt not build an house for My name because thou hast been a man of war and hast shed blood"—a saying which Solomon used thereafter as an excuse for his reluctance in battle.

It was David who selected (in accordance with a vision) the spot on Mount Moriah that has ever since remained the holiest on earth—a huge rock used as a threshing floor by a friend, traditionally the place where Abraham had nearly sacrificed his son Isaac. He bought it for fifty shekels.

Up until this time the ark had moved with the people, from one home to another, from city to city—even being captured at one time by the Philistines. Now the people would come to the ark. Sacrifices could be ritualized. The office of priesthood concentrated in chosen families such as Abiathar for David and Zadok for Solomon. The whole fabric of Hebrew worship became as stiff as the jewel-embroidered robes. In the time of Solomon, at least, it was the most magnificent ceremony possible.

David did not renege on his promise to Bathsheba. He bypassed his legitimate issue in favor of his concubine's child. He elevated him to the throne in a secret emergency coronation to prevent a palace coup. On his deathbed, he admonished Solomon privately to do two things: (1) to build the temple as soon as possible as a mark of his father's contrition; and (2) to kill Joab as soon as Solomon could find a plausible excuse. "I go the way of all the earth," said David. "Be thou strong therefore and show thyself a man."

Solomon kept his last promise first. Joab was no match for the "young and tender" king who thought of himself as "but a little child." He had assumed his power at an age of anywhere from twelve to twenty—but he acted, probably with Bathsheba's connivance, like a master schemer. Solomon had Joab arrested on a trumped-up charge amounting to treason. He had him beheaded, even as Joab took refuge at the sanctuary of the altar. For good measure, he executed Adonijah, the last of the ambitious children of David, at Bathsheba's behest. He exiled some of David's relatives and Abiathar, the high priest, as well.

As for Solomon's second promise to his dying father, the building of the temple was put off for four years until Solomon felt himself seated firmly enough to begin such an enterprise. David had given him exact blueprints—ostensibly direct from God but more probably from Phoenicia—and a vast amount of treasure in beams, stones, bronze, iron, silver, gold, and precious stones. When he did commence building, he taxed his people heavily and actually enslaved a portion of them. He cannily combined the temple and his royal residential compound: the former took seven years to erect, the latter took thirteen.

Despite rumblings from the northern tribes, Solomon continued the unification of the Hebrews and the consolidation of their spiritual attitudes for most of his reign. Under his forty-year rule, his people enjoyed their only peaceful period in their ages-long history. The worship Solomon set up was to last for just about a thousand years, the most long-lived religious structure of any nation. After the destruction of the second temple (built by Zerubbabel, reconstructed by Herod) by Rome in 70 A.D., its foundation remained the same. But its exercise tended once more toward the migrant pattern in the Diaspora rabbinate.

The portion of Solomon from his natural father was more than power and wealth. He inherited his common sense. He added to it his own virtuosity of judgment, which was called wisdom. He continued the real gift of David in writing poetry and music, enriching it considerably with themes outside the Hebrew tradition. He did not share David's pride in simplicity—one suspects Bathsheba's blood in this—nor his reputation as a leader; Solomon was always more of a diplomat than a direct force. But he was cursed with the same characteristic that had made David commit his grievous sin, what the anonymous chroniclers of the Old Testament describe as "lust for women."

That Solomon's court was basically oriental need not be seriously doubted. It is true that his prophets enjoined monogamy; it is equally true that the king had a retinue fancifully numbered at seven hundred wives and three hundred concubines. Scaling this down in the customary reduction of one to ten, Solomon probably had about seventy wives and thirty concubines. It is likely that this community of women was the real force behind his throne: a matriarchy expressed through a harem.

Such collections of females were not merely the concupiscence of a king. Women of those times were prestige property, to be bought or sold, used or ignored, discarded or destroyed or bartered. Ownership of their bodies (which might or might not be used sexually) was simply an indication of wealth. It was also a practical measure to preserve property and inheritance rights. Such nations as the Assyrians, Persians, and Scythians took the vanquished king's wives, concubines, and daughters into the harem as a matter of course. Absalom's revolt had been signaled by his going in to David's women. Adonijah had been trapped in just such a way by Bathsheba. He had asked Solomon for one of his father David's favorite concubines. It was rightly interpreted as a bid for supreme power.

It takes a strong character to resist the multitudinous wiles of so many women, and Solomon was never noted for his strength of will. Bathsheba, as the king's mother, was the leader, disciplinarian, and administrator of the harem. Nor did the king choose his consorts. They were customarily offered him as gifts, most often chosen by his mother. And with soft feminine persistence, they worshipped other gods: Moabite, Egyptian, Ammonite, Edomite, Sidonian, Hittite.

It was Solomon's love of luxury and pomp and idolatry that finally broke up the kingdom so sorely cemented by blood and glory. Solomon loved horses, racing, money, and luxurious living; pomp, circumstance, and lavish building. In modern jargon, he might have considered himself on an all-expense account from Yahweh. As a sensual monarch par excellence Solomon encountered the admonitions and warnings of the prophets. He did not heed them. His son Rehoboam lost ten of the twelve tribes when the northern groups broke away as "Israel" against Judah in the south: "Forasmuch as ... thou hast not kept My covenant and My statutes, ... I will surely rend the kingdom from thee, and will ... give one tribe to thy son for David My servant's sake. . . ."

An informed guess might give Solomon a lifespan of about fifty-four years. He was still king when the time came for him to sleep with his fathers in the city of David. He had indulged himself in a rule which had been either too long or not long enough. He had given Jerusalem, the temple, and his people, worldwide notoriety. But he had also given away large portions of his country (twenty cities to Hiram of Tyre alone). The revolts and disaffections that followed his death had continued, as it is said, "unto this very day."

Altogether, despite his glittering repute, Solomon was not a good king. He rested largely on his father's reputation. According to one authority (quoted by Roy B. Chamberlin and Herman Feldman in their annotation of the text of Kings), he "proved one of the most foolish rulers that ever sat on the throne of Israel." His kind of regal *chutzpah* that gutted a kingdom may be regretted. But there was a fascination in it that has survived the centuries and fed the imagination of civilization. In Asia, in Africa, in Arabia, in Europe—in literature, liturgy, legend, and thaumaturgy—the story of Solomon has lived on.

It becomes increasingly apparent that the range of the fame of Solomon was far wider than previously believed. He was only the king of a petty domain—so unimportant that it is rarely mentioned in the records of the day—but his name penetrated to all the known regions of earth: England and Spain in the west, the Cape of Good Hope in the south, India and China in the east. Malay fishermen still use the name of Solomon as a charm to lure fish into their nets: "Come into King Solomon's ivory tower, let me slip King Solomon's necklace around your neck!"

The historian is justified in reducing the splendor of Solomon to a narrow cell of space and time but this is not to say that his glory is less than scripture makes it. Solomon's forte was neither bigness nor might. He did not try to rival the temple of Karnak in size but to surpass it in the elegance of his temple. It was as a connoisseur of the world's goods, as a fastidious enjoyer of life that he was distinguished. It was his discriminating hedonism which made him the envy of his contemporaries. And when, after his death, the temple was looted by Pharaoh Shishak of Egypt and the city of David was ravished, something excellent went out of the world.

Fitting authentic accounts of this faraway period into credible fiction has not been altogether easy. Not because of the lack of facts—which proleptic imagination might deduce—

but the psychological offset of thought three millennia ago. The ritual precision, the casual brutality, the sophisticated pomp, mingled with primitive slyness—these are difficult to interpret in modern terms. Not that we do not have our similar obsessions—preoccupation with sex and devotion to statistics, to mention a couple that have enlarged their scope since Solomon—but the rust of ages has simply broken down communications.

The multiplicity and jumbling of various accounts into the books of the early history of the Hebrews is well known. At least two, those of Chronicles, as pointed out by Wellhausen, are simply gilded repetitions of others. Most confusing of all are the motives for many of the actions embodied in these stories as well as the chronology. These have been hopefully untangled in the preceding narrative, as seems fair to the author—but some liberties have been taken, needless to say, for dramatic emphasis.

Lest anyone question the somewhat unorthodox methods used by the Queen of Sheba to cure Solomon, let him be reassured by the authority of the experts. Helmuth Bottscher details just such remedies in his book *Wunderdrogen*. Similar medications, however incredible today, have been verified by long research in ancient records.

It is very difficult, for example, to account for Adonijah's action vis-à-vis Solomon without restructuring the whole event. The bare account seems "hardly credible" to some editors, such as Chamberlin and Feldman. Another seemingly irreconcilable characteristic of Solomon was his reputation for thaumaturgy and necromancy. This is embalmed largely in Arabic legend—obviously apocryphal—but it is also supported in great degree in rabbinic tradition. It is not easy to explain this away. It has absolutely no support in scripture—except, perhaps, for the "wisdom" often spoken of. But certainly it must have existed in some way to justify its persistence. The most modest interpretation would be that Solomon united a high level of intelligence with trappings of mystery and adroit public relations—and possibly some primitive knowledge of science.

There are, of course, singular difficulties in reconciling the facts in Old Testament accounts. The Solomon narratives of Kings are especially perplexing. As an example of placing relationships accurately, the problem of the ages of the participants—always psychologically important—may be mentioned.

A typical difficulty lies in the given age—forty-one—of

Rehoboam, Solomon's son. This would put his birth a year before his father came to the throne. It is extremely unlikely if the traditional rabbinic age of Solomon (twelve) is true. Moreover, the fact that the mother was a Hittite increases the difficulty. So do Rehoboam's actions after his assumption of power, that is, his total dependence upon his younger courtiers, which caused Israel's defection.

The following arbitrary table, relating to key dates in Solomon's life and using as a base the known age of David at his death (seventy), has been projected:

	at birth	*crowned*	*died*
Solomon	0–1	14	54
Bathsheba	19	33	x
David	56	70	70
Nathan	22	36	81
Joab	46	60	60
Benaiah	x	20	60
Hiram	4	18	x
Sheba	x	16	x

Such an assessment of ages may be criticized on numerous grounds but it is chronologically possible.

Once all this has been understood, it is useful to declare further that other specifics still remain a mystery—the design of the urim and thummin, the description of the temple—despite the most laborious efforts to clarify them. Here the mixture of myth and theocratic symbols make the narrative an exercise in cipher.

A single instance of a fictional assumption may be given. The stealing of the ark by Bathsheba and Zabud is, of course, an imaginary blasphemy. No one knows what really became of the original ark. But the incident is built on the curious fact (or coincidence) that both the ark and the name of Bathsheba vanish from Hebrew history at about the same time. The connection between the two is very tenuous. It may be apocryphal, and probably is. But it offers the imagination an opportunity for dramatic confrontations.

What is presented is reconstruction, based on the information available. It is an effort to restore the unique picture of what the kingdom of Solomon must have looked like in the green and lovely days of its prime, when it was the jewel set in the navel of the world. Despite gaps of psychology and fact, it is possible to surround Solomon with reasonable facsimiles of the habits and manners in which he lived. But the haunts of his heyday are other, more difficult questions.

Many of the name places associated with Solomon may be identified with assurance—due largely to the excellent topographical orientation of the old scribes. There are obvious sites, such as Tyre, but others are more mysterious. The three most debated are Tarshish, Ophir, and Sheba with its romantic queen.

Modern archaeology has tentatively identified Tarshish with an immensely rich, powerful, now-vanished city called Taressus on the west coast of Spain, fronting the Atlantic Ocean in the Bay of Cadiz, at the mouth of the Guadalquivir River.

The problem of locating Ophir has been more troublesome. It has been spotted in the Indus, Peru, India, and of late at Zimbabwe in southeast Africa. The most likely place appears to be one of the earliest guesses: on the southwest coast of Arabia, in Yemen. This is based on the Chronicles account that says David gave Solomon "even three thousand talents of gold, of the gold of Ophir." David knew Hiram, king of Tyre—in II Samuel it describes how he "sent messengers to David, and cedar trees, and carpenters, and masons: and they built David an house." But their friendship was hardly long enough to amass such wealth, even had Hiram sent his heralds immediately upon his accession in 969 B.C. David was about sixty-eight at the time. He died in 972 B.C.

It would mean, then, that David had already opened an overland caravan route with Ophir (lacking Hiram's ships), had set up thriving mines in the metal-rich valley of nearby Arabah and was probably the founder of the great smelting ovens at Ezion Geber at the head of the gulf of Aqaba leading into the Red Sea. This would be essential for creating trading goods for the gold. The route to Ophir probably ran down the coast—beyond Egyptian interference—to the gold-rich kingdom of Saba (Yemen). The gold of Ophir was probably collected from a number of sources by the merchants of Saba. In view of the Hiram-Solomon argosies taking voyages of three years (half the time spent by the sailors ashore, planting, nurturing, and harvesting their supply crops), the precious metal of Saba probably came chiefly from India and southern Africa—where Solomon sent his traders to eliminate the middlemen.

Here the third unknown seems ready to be explained. The ancient Sabaean culture was widely known for its gold. Even ordinary citizens offered their gods small gold statuettes against sickness, one for each member of the family. They imported incense and jewels from India. Ethiopic-Semitic, they had colonies in southern Africa and Abyssinia. It was an ancient trading point, famous for perfumes, ivory, ebony, and costly garments, as well as jewels and precious metals. It is mentioned in Genesis and other Old Testament accounts. Very probably the queen of Sheba was the queen of Saba.

All this may mean that David is entitled to more credit on the commercial side. It is impossible that he built up the wealth he accumulated for the temple without trading. Possibly the closeness of Solomon to David came about by the former being his assistant in these operations. Solomon's contributions may well have been not much more than enlarging and expanding the trade by sea and going directly to India.

If national characteristics mean anything, the Hebrews under Solomon showed strength of will, great industry, both pity and brutality, a love of tradition, pride of race and background, hatred for aliens, outward submission to and inward contempt for those who conquered them. They also had an inextinguishable genius for discord among themselves. What had united them, if only for two generations, was the temple and its ceremonies. They had loved its magnificence; the chants and music of the Levites, the sacrifices and the blood, the lavish feasts, the glamorous robes of the priests, the sweet smells and glitter of sanctity made visible.

Under Solomon for the first time the ordainings of God were made human and manifest. All his people shared the glory—as they later suffered for the shortcomings. The masterpiece of himself and David lives in racial memory more splendidly than it could ever have been in actuality. The writings attributed to Solomon—Ecclesiastes, Proverbs, the Song of Solomon, possibly the most poetical and practical in all literature—attest to his talents. The tales of his marvels (including the ability to talk to birds and command the demons of the elements) underlie most of the ancient systems of magic like the debased Kabbalah: "And God gave Solomon wisdom and understanding exceeding much, and largeness of heart, even as the sand that is on the sea shore. And Solomon's wisdom excelled the wisdom of all the children of the east country, and all the wisdom of Egypt. For he was wiser than all men; . . . and his fame was in all nations round about."

What David achieved, what Solomon enhanced, is best

symbolized by a series of concentric circles. The holy of holies was the center of the temple; the temple was the center of Jerusalem; the city of Jerusalem was the heart of Hebrewdom; and they centered the world. The two generations of greatness that David and Solomon enshrined on this spot left an indelible impression on the Jewish mind.

But after all is said, these achievements are not what tend to make Solomon understandable to the ages. Moses thunders from his mountain and generates awe; David shoots upward and flares like a star: but Solomon is human. Like every man under the sun, Solomon had trouble with women. His mother, beautiful Bathsheba; the "black but comely" Queen of Sheba (by whom, tradition insists, he had a son named Menelik); and his seraglio of a thousand. Disillusionment with the sex—which still enchants him—is explicit in every word that is credited to Solomon. In the end, all his high-flown life is covered over by the words: "Vanity, vanity, all is vanity!"—and love itself is seen to be the vanity of vanities.

Of all his marriages of convenience, one of his earliest was the most politic. Solomon wedded a daughter of a minor pharaoh at a time when Egypt was divided among warlords and ambitious priests. This was the only known instance of one of the Egyptian rulers allowing a princess of the blood royal to marry outside her native land (though they themselves often imported mates). It was a singular compliment to Solomon—but it also probably indicated the intent of the pharaoh to extend his dominions first by marriage and later, possibly, by conquest. Her father gave the bride a royal dowry—the newly captured city of Gezer. Solomon built her a special home in the Millo tower on the edge of Jerusalem. It may be assumed that his sons spread his seed broadcast among the noble families around the Mediterranean—since he and Hiram were the small but mighty monarchs of the period just before the Assyrian emergence—at a time when people like the Greeks were still barbarians cavorting in their feuds.

The snug living of Jerusalem in those years was the envy of other nations. The dismemberment of the Jews after Solomon may be safely laid to this economic grudge. The income of the king alone in one year was enormous: "Now the weight of gold that came to Solomon in one year was six hundred threescore and six talents of gold"—or the equivalent of about $60,000,000 in a time when the poor lived on pennies a day. He received 12 talents of gold as a present from the Queen of Sheba alone. And, it may be added, "beside that he had [income] of the merchantmen, and of the traffic of the spice merchants, and of all the kings of Arabia, and of the governors of the country." He buried much treasure in the tomb with his father, David. Thousands of talents were reportedly extracted long afterward by sacrilegious spoilers. (According to Josephus, Hyrcanus, the high priest, took out 3,000 talents in 135-134 B.C.; Herod extracted another large sum many years later.)

That all of his unique civilization has vanished, that barely a stone upon a stone has been left of his temple, would be no surprise to Solomon himself. Indeed, he predicted its demise again and again: "He spake three thousand proverbs; and his songs were a thousand and five." His words have been a text for cynics through the centuries ever since.

There is little in Solomon, despite his early piety, that is truly spiritual. Examine him as one will, turn him about, he remains of earth earthy. He disdains to be anything else. His worship of his God is in fact perfunctory, eventually a kind of sophistical insurance shared among many deities. His hope of the future goes no further than his own temporal existence. This blind alley drives him into black moods of depression. He may have longed for immortality but a belief in a future state was simply not a part of the Hebrew religious equipment at the time. What Solomon is finally forced to come to terms with consists of his senses alone. His cold comfort is in nihilism. "Remember now thy Creator," he may say but he appears quite sure that his Creator will not remember him. It is a far cry from the quiet piety of his father who went down into the valley of the shadow of death as if it were green pastures.

Altogether it must be confessed that David was by far the more admirable figure but Solomon remains the more attractive—the illegitimate but direct ancestor of Christ, twenty-six times removed. Jesus always spoke of his remote ancestor in laudatory terms, paying him the ultimate compliment of comparing Solomon to himself: "Behold, a greater than Solomon is here."

It was Solomon's reign which most firmly implanted in later Jewish religious belief an obsession with the coming of the final messiah—and the glittering possibility of his success. If Solomon had reigned for forty years, certainly a greater than he might reign forever.

The charisma of this sophist king of the Hebrews has

maintained itself for a very long while. It is doubtful if it will ever fade.

Some arbitrary choices—always necessary in the modernization that historical narrative entails—have been made. In spite of incongruity, measurements in feet and miles instead of such popularly unintelligible units as cubits have been used. To avoid confusion in references to the supreme Deity of the Hebrews, the Name has been confined to two designations, Yahweh and the Lord, rather than complicating matters by God and such euphemisms as Elohim.

The list of those consulted in writing this story of Solomon has been long. A partial list—not necessarily in order of importance—must begin with the Old Testament itself, Herodotus, Josephus, Strabo Ammianus Marcellinus, Pausanias, and other ancient authorities. More modern writers have been Donald Harden, Ivan Lissner, Ovid Sellers, Richard F. Burton, Sigmund Freud, W. F. Albright, Sir James Frazer, G. Ernest Wright, John Bright, Robert Graves, H. L. Ginsberg, Gus Van Beek, Yigael Yadin, Max L. Margolis and Alexander Marx, Nelson Glueck, George M. Landes, Abraham Malamat, Roy B. Chamberlin and Herman Feldman, Frank Cross, Jr., David Noel Freedman, Cyrus Gordon, and Benjamin Mazar. Also Leonard Woolley, W. Ewing, A. G. K. Hayter, Reuben Levy, Ian Colvin, Lewis Spence, A. H. Layard, James H. Breasted, and others.

Giacomo Casanova used to say that he "corrected the mistakes of fortune" at gaming tables—that is, he cheated. So, too, here the story has sometimes corrected fact with fancy. Therefore nothing herein is to be blamed upon the eminent company above except those oases of learning that I have attempted to adapt to the broad expanse of drama.

—R. G. H.

Ojai, California
1968

ABOUT THE AUTHOR

Columnist, reviewer, foreign correspondent, publisher, teacher and writer, RICHARD G. HUBLER is a former editor of NEWSWEEK and the author of numerous works of fiction and nonfiction. He lives in California, where he writes, teaches, and serves as an associate book reviewer for the Los Angeles TIMES.